Aged to Perfection

Samantha Kane
KyAnn Waters
Katie Blu
Regina Carlysle
Alice Gaines

ELLORA'S CAVE
ROMANTICA PUBLISHING

What the critics are saying...

ഔ

4 Stars "This is one of the most erotic books I have ever read. […] I enjoyed the honesty and sincerity the main characters displayed towards each other. Of course I will warn you, the perspective reader that you might have to stop reading often, in order to fan yourselves, as I found myself doing. If you are looking for a good read this is your book."

~ *Sensual EcataRomance*

5 Pixies "If you want a smoking hot read that will hold your attention to the very end, grab *Impulsive Pleasures* by Kyann Waters. Ms. Waters' has written an erotic story with engaging characters full of witty humor and a past that will come back to hurt one of them. […] I would recommend this book to all my friends. It is a great way to spend the afternoon." ~ *Dark Angel Reviews*

4 Stars "Katie Blu has definitely succeeded in writing a short, passionate love story. As an avid reader I can not wait for more from this amazing author. Her story was absolutely breathtaking. I can not wait for the next story from this truly inspirational writer. Whatever she has in store for us should be absoultely amazing." ~ *Sensual EcataRomance*

4 1/2 Hearts "Ms. Carlysle enchants the reader as well with the well rounded plot that comes full circle. At every changing event, the author spends time detailing each new scene making it very easy for the reader to imagine watching the story play out in front of their eyes, much like a television movie. The dialogue enriches the story and seems to compliment it." ~ *The Romance Studio*

4 Nymphs "Hot, Hot, Hot! I loved this story. It was great to read about a woman that had normal hang-ups about sex and her body. Ms. Gaines made these characters real and likeable. The emotions were what one would expect. [...] In addition to great characters, the sex was incredibly well written and was what I am sure every woman wants. These characters had sensible, realistic problems and solutions. I would recommend Dr. Feelgood to other readers. Great Job!"
~*Literary Nymphs Reviews Only*

An Ellora's Cave Romantica Publication

www.ellorascave.com

Aged to Perfection

ISBN 9781419959615
ALL RIGHTS RESERVED.
A Lady in Waiting Copyright © 2008 Samantha Kane
Impulsive Pleasures Copyright © 2008 KyAnn Waters
Surprised by Desire Copyright © 2008 Katie Blu
Tempting Tess Copyright © 2008 Regina Carlysle
Dr. Feelgood Copyright © 2008 Alice Gaines
Edited by Raelene Gorlinsky, Helen Woodall, Shannon Combs.
Photography and cover art by Les Byerley, Syneca.

This book printed in the U.S.A. by Jasmine-Jade Enterprises, LLC.

Trade paperback Publication July 2009

AGED TO PERFECTION

ɞ

A LADY IN WAITING

Samantha Kane

ဆာ

Chapter One

ॐ

Sylvie, the Dowager Marchioness of Bartlebyrne, was tired. She hadn't slept a full night since she'd done *it*. She couldn't even bring herself to put a name to it she was so horrified and ashamed of her behavior. She rubbed a finger over the furrow between her eyes. The last few weeks she'd grown old beyond her thirty-nine years, watching the lines form on her face where once the skin had remained smooth and youthful. Gray hair now infused her light blonde locks. Apparently all the gossip and dire warnings were correct — illicit sex was not good for women of good breeding.

She sighed and sipped her tea, looking out over the veranda and down to the exquisite gardens of The Byrne, the beautiful family estate in Kent. It wasn't as large as the main family seat in Northumberland, where the marquis traditionally resided. Her son Geoffrey would take up residence there when he finished his studies in a year or two. He had told Sylvie she should consider The Byrne her home until she wished otherwise. All major decisions concerning the estate were hers to make. It was the greatest gift she'd ever been given besides her son himself.

She fidgeted, waiting impatiently for her guest to arrive. As she had taken great pains dressing this morning in anticipation of his visit she'd realized with mortification that she was infatuated with him, with the new vicar Mr. Edmund James. She'd almost removed the new raspberry pink gown she was wearing. It was too young, and made her feel like an old woman trying to recapture her youth and doing nothing but embarrassing herself over a younger man. Lord knows she'd seen it often enough. And therein lay the seeds of her discontent. Not only had she had sex with a younger man

11

three weeks ago, a younger man for whom she had no feelings whatsoever, a younger man who was in her employ, but she was now infatuated with a different younger man completely beyond her reach. And she felt like sex with her coachman John had been a betrayal of her feelings for Edmund.

Mr. James, she meant Mr. James. Her head fell into her hand as she rested her elbow on the table, uncaring of the impolite nature of the gesture. Working so closely with him the last few weeks on establishing his new living here and her work for the parish charity house had not helped the situation.

When her husband's old friend Mr. Horton James had contacted her about the possibility of his son Edmund taking the available living in the village of Byrnham, Sylvie had been more than happy to offer it to him. According to Mr. James, his son had gotten in with the wrong crowd during his school years and as he'd gotten older his antics had taken a decidedly rakish turn. Mr. James hoped that removing him from London and giving him the responsibility of a parish would cure that problem and bring out the sensible, noble side of his nature that his family had always recognized. Being the mother of a rather precocious son herself, she was willing to give Edmund James a chance.

Then he had walked into her drawing room and her entire world had tilted dangerously on its already precarious perch. He was one of the most beautiful men she'd ever seen. The spark in his midnight blue eyes made it easy to see why so many women had fallen prey to his charms. Dark blond unruly curls far too long for fashion surrounded a face of male perfection, with fine cheekbones, a long, aquiline nose, and a large, expressive mouth. He was taller than any gentleman Sylvie had ever met, taller even than John the coachman. She hadn't realized she liked tall men until recently. Tall and muscular, if the form outlined by his tight breeches could be believed, and Sylvie believed it, fervently.

She thumped her head on her palm several times in disgust at her wayward thoughts.

"If you have the headache, my dear, I can return later. Although I don't think hitting yourself in the head will help."

Sylvie jerked her head up, startled. It turned to embarrassment when she saw Edmund, Mr. James, damn it, looking at her with a small lopsided smile and quirked brow. Just the sight of him made her nipples peak and her pussy clench as she felt her sex grow wet. Why oh why did it have to be him? Why couldn't she have an appropriate infatuation on one of the older, eligible gentlemen in the region? Why this young man, a young man dependent on her, a rake trying to reform, a man who looked at her as if he wanted to devour her inch by slow, excruciatingly pleasurable inch?

Edmund watched Sylvie with hungry eyes. Christ, he wanted her so much he was nearly panting for it. His gaze traveled over her blonde hair, the color of ripe wheat stalks, then into her lovely, round, soft blue eyes. He trailed his eyes down her short little nose, turned up at the end, to focus on her small, rosebud mouth. He couldn't resist looking at the low neckline of her pink gown, her décolletage deliciously framed. And then lower, to the sharp points of her aroused nipples thrusting against the thin silk of her gown. He felt his cock jerk. He was already half hard when he walked in the door at just the thought of seeing her this morning. The sight of her obvious excitement at seeing him made the process complete. He deliberately looked down at the bulge that was almost obscenely obvious in his tight breeches. Sylvie's eyes followed and it felt like someone had touched a velvet hot tongue to his cock when her eyes caressed him. Even as she watched it jerked again in approval and he heard Sylvie gasp. Her eyes flew to his and then skittered away, her cheeks as pink as her gown with embarrassment.

He walked delicately over to the table to sit down across from her. When he sat he made a show of arranging his breeches over the bulge, not hiding his discomfort at sitting with a cock this hard. Sylvie bit her lip and looked at her teacup, now held in a death grip. And so it was every time they met. He'd let her know in so many ways how much he wanted her, and she pretended not to notice things like a cock so hard it was nearly poking out the top of his pants. He'd enjoyed their little dance for weeks, but had almost reached his limit. If he didn't taste her soon, fuck her, he was going to go mad. Then where would he be? The family wouldn't even be able to banish him to another godforsaken living far from the life he'd known and enjoyed in London.

"Tea?" Sylvie choked out, and Edmund sighed.

"Yes, please, Lady Bartlebyrne." Calling her that made his skin crawl. He didn't like to think of her as someone else's wife, even if that someone was dead. He didn't know why it bothered him. God knew he'd had enough widows in his time to fill the Tower. But Sylvie was different. He could tell she'd had no lovers since her husband's death. She seemed almost pure, untouched. And he longed to be the man to dirty her up a bit.

These morning meetings with Sylvie had become the one thing that made this new life tolerable. She'd been a great help in establishing him here and helping him to figure out what the hell a vicar even did. He'd had only a vague idea gleaned from his studies at Cambridge and regular churchgoing as a child and student, before he'd been forced by his father and older brothers to accept the living. It was either Vicar of Byrnham or being cut off and transported for failure to pay his debts. So they'd found a willing bishop, pushed him through a ridiculously simple examination that consisted mostly of questions about his family and acquaintance, and he'd been ordained. And so Edmund James, a Devil, was now a man of the church. It was ludicrous. Hil, Hilary St. John, the leader of his band of hedonistic friends from school dubbed the Saint's Devils by the ton, had been the only one who hadn't laughed. He'd told Edmund that he thought he'd make a very good vicar. Coming from a man who'd taught him not only how to suck a cock properly, but how to fuck a woman with another man made Hil's pronouncement suspect. His one piece of advice was cryptic, and definitely not what Edmund wanted to hear. He'd said, *Don't imagine that a new living will remake your life. You will still be who you are, no matter what you are.* Accepting himself as he was, according to Hil, would be the first step to accepting who he could be. Now what the hell did that mean?

Sylvie had nothing but praise for the job he was doing in the parish. He'd always had a flair for oratory, so he wasn't surprised the sermon part of his job had been the least of his problems. Of course, his sermons were definitely not what the parishioners were used to, seeing as how he didn't preach against vice or extol the virtues. He frequently talked to them about forgiveness and acceptance. It was something he was all too familiar with, since his family knew very little of either. As to his charitable work in the parish, what else could he do? He'd had no idea there were so many people who needed help, many through no fault of their own. He'd always assumed widows and orphans had various family members or even government remedies to choose from. He knew now he'd been a naïve fool. His work with the poor and disenfranchised would be something he would take with him when he left Byrnham, as he knew he would eventually. He was not cut out to be a vicar. His completely inappropriate lust for his benefactress was proof of that. Very few vicars masturbated at night to thoughts of tying up a widow and spanking her ass before fucking it, he was sure.

"Ed—Mr. James," Sylvie began, her voice catching on the misstep.

"Edmund, call me Edmund," he asked quietly for the hundredth time. "And I will call you Sylvie."

She shook her head. "It isn't appropriate," she murmured.

"Nothing I want to do with you is appropriate, Sylvie." There, he'd broken their unspoken agreement not to talk about the attraction between them. He watched her closely to gauge her reaction.

She looked away, blushing again. "You mustn't say such things, Mr. James," she whispered.

"I want you, Sylvie." The desire in his voice made it almost a growl, but he couldn't, wouldn't, control it today. This had gone on long enough. "I want to be in your bed. Take me, Sylvie."

Her eyes flew to his, wide with shock. Surely she knew that was how he felt? She was breathing heavily. Her breasts, barely contained by the dress already, tested the limits of the low neckline. Edmund groaned and lowered his head for a moment, clasping his hands between his spread knees. "Sylvie," he groaned, "can't you see what you're doing to me? You're killing me with this waiting."

"Lady Bartlebyrne," she whispered automatically.

"Sylvie," he said firmly. She was shaking her head again. "Yes, Sylvie. You are Sylvie in my thoughts, my dreams, my fantasies. It is 'Sylvie' I cry out at night."

Her hand flew to her mouth to smother her cry. Her head began to shake more frantically.

"I must speak, Sylvie," he said quietly but urgently. "I can't keep my feelings inside anymore. I want you so badly I ache night and day. My own hand is no comfort when what I want is to be buried inside you. For God's sake! Take me, use me, I'm offering myself to you. I'm begging you to end my suffering." Edmund ran a hand through his hair in frustration. "What must I do to convince you? I will make it good for you, Sylvie. I know how to please a woman, and I *will* please you."

She covered her face in her hands, and Edmund was stricken to see her so upset. "Sylvie, don't cry," he murmured, moving to the chair next to hers. He touched her arm and she turned away from him. He felt the cut like a knife to his chest.

"We can't," she whispered brokenly. "Don't you think I want to, Edmund?" She still wouldn't look at him. "This is the only time I will speak about this." Her head lowered and he could see over her shoulder that she was wringing her hands in her lap. "I am far too old for you, Edmund. My son is only a few years younger than you."

"Sylvie, you can't be more than thirty-five. That is not old." He hadn't even foreseen this argument. She was young, too young to be a widow and the mother of a grown son.

"I am thirty-nine, Edmund, soon to be forty. I am not a young girl anymore." Her voice was sad, and Edmund reached out to touch her shoulder in comfort.

"That is only thirteen years between us, Sylvie. It is nothing."

She threw herself out of the chair and spun to face him. "It is everything! People are very cruel, Edmund. They will say I am robbing the schoolroom. I have heard it before, about others." She leaned back against the railing, dejected.

Edmund stood and walked slowly over to stand in front of her. "Why must other people know? We can keep our affair secret, Sylvie. I don't care about your age, or mine. All I know is that I want you."

Sylvie looked at him with stricken eyes. "I cannot, Edmund. I cannot keep it a secret. I am not good at this..." her hand fluttered before her in consternation, "this type of thing. I am a wreck just knowing that I have feelings like that for you. I fear every day that someone will suspect. If we were to..." She fluttered her hand again, unable to say the word, and Edmund couldn't conceal a smile at her bashfulness. She glared at him. "If we were to...to have sex," she choked out the word, "people would know. One look at me and they would know."

Edmund sighed and caught her flailing hands. "No, Sylvie. They would suspect, but only we would know. They would never accuse you, Sylvie. To the people here, Lady Bartlebyrne is an angel who walks the earth, their very own saint. They would never say a word against you."

Her hands gripped his. "Edmund, I am your benefactress. Your living is dependent on me. I can't. It would be a monumental breach of trust between us."

Edmund couldn't stop his bark of laughter. "Breach of trust for whom? Believe me, Sylvie, making love will not destroy my trust in you."

"How can you say that?" she asked fervently. "I will feel as if I am forcing you into an illicit affair out of gratitude or...or fear."

"I tell you now that I feel no obligation to give in to your insatiable lust out of gratitude, or worry that you will take away my living." Edmund's smile was gentle.

Sylvie's face blanched. "Is that how you see me?" she whispered. "As some lusty old widow who desires young men?" She spun away. "It is truer than you think."

Suddenly she turned and raced down the steps to the garden, nearly tripping over the hem of her gown. She took off running across the green, heading for the woods. "Go, Mr. James," she called back. "These meetings are at an end."

"Sylvie!" Edmund's cry spurred her on, her feet in their thin slippers stumbling on the small rocks of the path. Her chest felt tight—fear, anger, desolation and an aching loneliness nearly driving her to her knees. She stumbled into a tree, scratching her arm, and then righted herself and kept going. Ahead she could see the almost indiscernible path that led to a small folly by the secluded pond. She ducked down the path, fleeing Edmund and the temptation he presented. She could hear his feet pounding on the path behind her and wanted nothing more than to fling herself into his arms. But she couldn't. She couldn't see him again.

When she reached the little folly she ran up the steps and inside and stopped, spinning around in indecision. What should she do now? Her predicament so closely resembled her life at the moment she collapsed onto the bench by the near wall in turmoil. She lay with her cheek on the cool marble of the bench, her sides heaving from her frantic flight. She had arrived at her destination, just as she had arrived at her age of thirty-nine. And there was nothing here. No rescue, no relief — nothing but silence, and the unrelieved white of the marble walls and floor and ceiling. No color, no desire, no friend to ease her loneliness. She would be locked in this colorless, empty world forever, locked in her life as she knew it.

She heard him before he entered — heard his booted feet crunch through the fallen twigs outside on the little-used path. His feet hit the stairs, sounding like a death knell to all she knew — the life she bemoaned. But it was a safe life, a secure life. She remembered the sex with her coachman three weeks ago. It had been a furtive swive in a dark coach on a lonely stretch of road. Over in but minutes, leaving her ashamed and unfulfilled. It, too, had changed her life, but not for the better. Would Edmund be the same? The same shame and disappointment? She didn't want that for them. She didn't want that kind of memory to blacken the sweet feelings she harbored for him.

When he entered the folly she rose wearily, dragging herself from where she lay. She wasn't prepared for the anger on his face.

"You little fool," he snarled, stalking over and grabbing her arm. "You could have hurt yourself. What were you thinking to run from me like that? And what did you mean it is truer than I think? Who else, Sylvie? Who else do you desire?"

Chapter Two

ഗ

Edmund was so outraged at her duplicity he was shaking with it. He feared what he might do to her. How dare she pretend a bashful innocence she had no right to claim? Who had she been fucking, damn it, who? He wanted to howl in frustration that someone had been there before him. The feeling was primeval and beastly and he'd never felt it before, but he embraced it. His possessiveness should have given him pause but he was beyond rational thought now. "Who, Sylvie? Who have you been fucking behind my back?"

Her eyes were wide with fear, and something else. Something that made the animal in him stretch and dig its claws into his cock, making him grit his teeth against the need to sheathe it in her to soothe the ache.

"Is this what it takes, Sylvie? Do I have to be rough with you? Is that what you like, what you desire?" He shoved her back against the cool marble wall, spinning her around. Her hands flew up to brace herself as her front pressed into the marble. He heard her gasp, felt her struggle and his vision dimmed for a moment he was so aroused by it all—aroused by the chase, the capture, her struggles and the knowledge that she would surrender to him. He would take her here and she would not deny him again. He would mark her as his, and his mark would supersede all previous claims.

He yanked her skirts up, heedless of the ripping sound something made as he tore at them. Sylvie whimpered and Edmund pressed up against her, nothing between his cock and her ass but his tight breeches and her thin drawers. The contact made him shudder and Sylvie reacted as well, with a moan and a shiver—of desire, not fear. He took a moment to calm down. He was out of control, wild, more wild than he'd ever been before. What did she do to him? He became aware of his ragged breathing and rapid pulse. He felt like an animal. He was acting like one.

He forced his hands to gentle, to caress and ask rather than grasp and take. He ran them down her hips, his thumbs gliding over the tense muscles of her perfectly round ass. He wanted to see it, to touch it, lick it, fuck it. Christ! He needed to get more control. His hands trembled with the effort, but he made them move down until they lightly held her thighs, his thumbs tucked into the warm, damp crease between ass and thighs. "Let me touch you, Sylvie," he murmured into her hair. She turned her head so that his lips grazed her temple and she sighed at the contact. "Let me touch you, love you. I only want to love you, Sylvie."

She sobbed. "Edmund," she cried softly, "Edmund." But he knew what she meant by it. He knew it was yes, yes to all that they desired. Here, in this little marble fortress, far away from tea and cakes and gossip, she would give them both what they wanted.

Sylvie couldn't speak for the lust choking her. It had her by the throat and she couldn't breathe much less talk. His hands on her, rough and arousing at first, were now gentle and oh so much more devastating. She could feel his erection pressing against her bottom, and the contact made her tense until she was so sensitive she could feel the air move against her skin like a caress. The cool marble against her breasts soothed her while his hands, so hot, gently removed her drawers. He did it slowly, reaching around her to untie them. When they were loose, he slipped his hands inside, onto her hips, and pushed them down. His palms ran down her hips to her thighs as the garment slid down her legs.

"Step out of them, Sylvie," he ordered, his voice soft but insistent. She obeyed, and he kicked them away.

He stepped back, keeping his hands on her hips. She felt his gaze on her naked backside like a brand. This wasn't like the other times, not at all. He was going so slow, looking at her, touching her. She'd never had a man do this. Her husband had been thirty-six years older than she. He had come to her at night, apologized, and then fucked her quickly and neatly, before thanking her and going to his bed. When she'd actually initiated sex it had been in code. She would ask him to stop by her room for a glass of port before retiring. She'd taken to wearing a wine red negligee, but Bartlebyrne hadn't gotten the joke. There was no passion, no love between them, only a gentle friendship, and an almost paternal protectiveness on his part. With her young coachman, it had been dark, and he'd been very rough. He'd thrown her skirts up, yanked her drawers down and shoved his cock in her. After a few thrusts she'd come—it had been so long, and she was so lonely. But he hadn't cared. He hadn't even slowed, just kept going until he grunted and slammed painfully into her. She'd frantically tried to remove him, not wanting him to come inside her. For a week she'd been insane with worry that she might be pregnant. When her courses came she swore she wouldn't do it again. And now here she was.

She was about to stop him when he touched her. His fingers traveled lightly over the cheek on her buttocks, and then one followed the center line there down to her wet, throbbing entrance. Her words were stolen from her.

"So wet, Sylvie," he murmured, almost to himself. "For me. Is this for me? Have you been this wet for weeks, darling, just as I've been so hard? If I'd known how much you wanted it, I would have acted sooner." His finger slowly breached her, pushing insistently inside and Sylvie cried out at the sheer bliss of his entrance, at the rough pad of his finger rubbing along the sensitive walls of her vagina. "Yes, yes, cry for it, darling, tell me how good it feels. God, I can't wait to fuck you, Sylvie. Can't wait for you to swallow my cock here. And here." At his last words, the thumb of his hand rubbed over the tight entrance on her bottom, and Sylvie moaned.

"No, Edmund," her voice was trembling, conquered. She didn't know that voice, had never heard it. It sounded as if she waited on the brink for something, something only he could give her, and she wanted to beg for it. That voice was made to beg. Edmund's arm came around her waist, pushing her dress higher, and he pulled her tight against him. She could once again feel his hard cock pressed to her buttocks, as his hand covered her breast and squeezed. His finger pulled out and thrust into her, and Sylvie writhed against the wall. It was all so good, it felt so good. The empty aching loneliness inside her felt full at last, and she wanted to cry at the unfairness of it, because she had to stop him.

"No, no, Edmund," she sobbed. "We can't, I can't." He froze, his finger buried inside her, his hand on her breast, his thumb in the middle of flicking her hard nipple.

"How can you say that, Sylvie?" His voice was pained as he spoke softly in her ear. "You want me, I know you do. This doesn't lie." He rubbed his hand over her wet sex, his finger moving deliciously inside her. She shivered and he growled as he bit her earlobe.

"No, not fuck," she panted, "I can't risk it, Edmund. I can't let you fuck me."

"Sylvie," he groaned, his voice a plea and an angry purr at the same time.

"Edmund, please!" She cried out even as she thrust against his hand, unable to stop herself. Sylvie had to get his promise, or this would stop, she had to stop it.

"God! Sylvie," he groaned. She started to pull away, and he grabbed her tighter. "Yes! Damn you, yes, all right. I won't fuck you today, Sylvie." She breathed easier for a moment until she felt his finger pull out of her and ram back inside roughly. She gasped and pushed back against his hand, driving it in farther, her head thrown back in ecstasy. "But I will satisfy you, Sylvie. I will see you writhing beneath me, taking all I'm allowed to give you, coming for me. You will come for me, Sylvie."

His fingers pinched her nipple and Sylvie bit her lip, enjoying the pain, the sting, the soothing way his palm rubbed over it afterward. "Yes," she panted. "Yes, Edmund, I will come for you."

He pulled away and turned her, his hand wet with her juices trailing over her hip as she turned. It was the most erotic thing Sylvie had ever felt. Her skirts were still up and she watched as he stared at her naked sex, at his hands on her. As soon as her back was against the wall he ran his wet hand over her stomach, and it quivered. His hand stopped for a moment and he looked up at her face. His eyes caught hers, and she couldn't escape from the burning intensity in their depths. He held her gaze while his hand began to move again, running down into her pubic hair, his finger grazing her hard clitoris, making her shiver, before once again sliding slowly into her slick passage.

"Christ, Sylvie," he whispered as her eyes fluttered. "You want this so badly, you need it so badly."

"Yes, yes," was all she could say as he fucked her with his hand.

"Shall I make you come now, darling?" he purred. "And then keep going? Keep fucking you even after you climax? I love how wet an orgasm makes a woman's pussy, how hot and swollen you get after you come. Will you let me play in your cream, Sylvie? Will you let me taste it and rub it on my cock? Will you?" His voice didn't match his words. He wasn't asking. He was telling her what he was going to do.

"Oh God," Sylvie moaned, feeling the muscles in her vagina clenching on his finger as he built her pleasure to unbearable heights with just that one touch.

Edmund laughed, the sound seductive. "I can make you come with just a finger, Sylvie. Christ, you are amazing." His other hand came up and pulled her dress down. He pulled hard enough to force it over her breasts, until it cut into her upper arms and pushed her breasts up. "But I want more. If I can't fuck you, then I'll do everything else." He bent down and sucked her nipple into his mouth, voraciously pulling on the hard peak as Sylvie's back bowed against the wall, driving her hip into his hard cock. He pulled back swearing.

"Be careful, darling. You don't want to set me off too soon. We'll both be sorry if I can't come down your delectable throat." He head swooped down and he kissed her throat just as she swallowed hard at the image he conjured with his words. He felt the movement and laughed against her neck. Then he moved his mouth back down to her breast and kissed the slope on the inner side. "Thank God you're not wearing a corset," he murmured. Without warning he sucked hard on the spot he'd just kissed, and Sylvie cried out, her hands coming up to fist his hair. She didn't want to pull him off. Instead, she held his head there as he sucked so hard she fought not to cry out in pain. He pulled away with a gasp, his hips thrusting against hers. Sylvie looked down and saw a dark, angry bruise forming on her breast, and felt her pussy gush with wetness at the sight. He'd marked her. She was his.

Edmund felt the beast stir again when he saw his mark on her breast. He looked at her face, and lust slammed through him at the sight of her desire, the satisfaction and surrender in her gaze as she looked at the mark. She was his, in every way. The thought was thrilling and right and the beast roared his approval.

He thrust another finger into her and she cried out. Sylvie was not a quiet, passive lover. She moaned and cried out and writhed and twisted in her passion. He adored it. Now that he'd heard her cry out in desire, he knew he would never hear her speak again without remembering it. She was tight, too tight for a woman who'd had frequent lovers. He was calmer now, and realized that even if she'd had one or two, she'd been a widow for a very long time. She was probably almost as innocent as he'd first thought her. The idea of that innocence waiting to be plundered excited the hell out of him.

"I've got two fingers in you, Sylvie, and you're so tight, so incredibly, wonderfully tight. My cock is aching at the thought of how tight you would be around it. And so wet. I've never known a woman to get so wet without my mouth on her, licking and sucking." At his words she moaned and twisted against the wall, and her felt her sex strangle his fingers. Oh, she wanted it, she was desperate for it. She just wasn't ready for it, yet. Suddenly her hands, still thrust into his hair, tightened and pulled his face down to hers.

"Kiss me, Edmund, please," she begged so sweetly, so full of passion and surrender that kissing her became the most important thing in the world. He leaned down and the heat of her breath against his lips sent a shock through his system, lodging, as these things often did, in his cock. She smelled of tea and cookies with jam and the disparity of her scent with her hot breath and open, carnal mouth fanned the flames of Edmund's desire. He'd meant the kiss to be as sweet as her plea, but the hunger burned out of control and he fell on her mouth, devouring her.

She tasted as sweet as she smelled, but her kiss more than lived up to the carnal invitation she presented. She took his mouth, his thrusting tongue and biting teeth, and gave them back to him, as rough and desperate as he was. He heard himself moan against her lips as she sucked his upper lip into her mouth and bit it, just shy of drawing blood. He slid his fingers deep into her pussy as her reward and she sobbed, letting go of his lip and her inhibitions.

"Yes, Edmund, God, fuck me darling, deep like that," Sylvie begged in a husky voice, not caring if she sounded wanton and desperate. She was both those things. She'd dreamed of him like this for weeks, and to finally have him touching her was heaven. She fucked down on his fingers, loving the feel of them inside her, loving her breasts bare to the open air in the folly, her nipples rubbing on the rough superfine of his jacket. She loved her skirts tossed up so he could watch his fingers fuck her, loved the wet sound of each thrust of those fingers inside her. Loved especially the enthralled look on his face as he watched her pleasure spiral out of control.

"Sylvie, come for me. I want to see you fly apart on my hand, feel your cunt clench my fingers. Do it, Sylvie. Come for me." Edmund's demands were spoken harshly, in a voice ragged with desire and she could do nothing but obey him. Her head fell back hard against the marble, but the pain did nothing to lessen the pleasure as she climaxed for him, loud and long. Her sobs filled the folly, his name falling from her lips again and again as he curled his fingers inside her and rubbed the walls of her vagina roughly, deliciously so. After her peak he continued to fuck her, her pussy so wet she could feel his hand drenched in her juice as it rubbed between her thighs. His thumb replaced his palm against her clitoris and began circling, making Sylvie cry out at the extreme sensitivity there. It felt so good it almost hurt. She shuddered, the pleasure one long, endless thrill.

"Edmund," she cried weakly, holding onto his shoulders, thrusting and writhing against his hand, unable to stop as the pleasure went on and on.

"God, Sylvie, God," he rasped as she continued to shudder and fuck his hand desperately. "You're still so damn aroused, even after that climax."

Sylvie just nodded jerkily, biting her lip, trying to control her reaction to what he was doing and failing miserably. "Oh Edmund!" she cried out, unable to think of anything else to say, unable to put into words what he was doing to her. She never wanted him to stop, never. Suddenly Edmund pulled his hand away, the desertion sudden and unbelievably desolating. "No!" Sylvie screamed, grabbing his arm and trying to shove his hand back between her legs.

Edmund laughed softly and pulled his arm away. "Is this the woman who told me no just a short while ago?" Sylvie couldn't even make herself feel shame at his teasing. The shame would come later, she knew. Right now she just needed to be filled. Filled by Edmund, only Edmund. She reached for him again and his voice and hands were tender as he stopped her. "I just need to undo my breeches, Sylvie. I'm going to come, god damn it, I can't wait. You are so fucking desirable. Watching you, dying of pleasure on my hand, begging me for more, I've dreamed of it, Sylvie, but it can't compare—nothing can compare. God!" He ripped open the last few buttons on his trousers and shoved them down enough for his cock to spring free.

It was beautiful. He was beautiful. His cock was long to her untrained eye, and strong looking, with veins running down its length, the head a dark red, plump plum. It rose from a nest of curls curiously darker than the hair on his head. Beneath she could see a large sac, heavy and full. The whole sight made her mouth water. She wanted to kiss it, to taste the drop of moisture on its tip. Before she could say anything Edmund grabbed her hand and placed it around the shaft of his cock. The feel of it was shockingly soft, like the smooth skin of a baby's bottom over a hard, strong column of wood. She loved the feel of it, loved his groan of pleasure at her touch. "Pump your hand along it, Sylvie," he gasped after she stood there just holding it for several seconds. "Like this," and he wrapped his hand, still wet with her juices, over hers and showed her, moving it up and down his shaft with a firm grip that pulled that soft skin roughly, and pushed her fist into the base of his plump head. He groaned again and let go so she could explore and find her own rhythm. He placed both hands on the wall beside her and hung his head, his eyes closed while she touched and learned his cock.

He was shaking when he finally leaned in close, laying a forearm along the wall. He reached one hand down and Sylvie gasped as his fingers penetrated her again. She bit her lip and her grip on his cock unconsciously tightened.

"God, yes, Sylvie," he groaned, burying his face in her disheveled hair. He fucked her in the same rhythm she'd been using on his cock, and she shivered as she resumed her pumping. "Harder," he growled, "faster." She changed her rhythm to match his pace inside her, a pace that was bringing her close to climax again.

"Edmund," she said in a shaky voice, "I'm going to come again. I'm sorry! I...I can't help it." She had so wanted to please him this time, but her own orgasm was pushing at her, refusing to be brushed aside.

"Sylvie," he groaned into her hair. "Come again, and again, and again—as many times as you can, my love. It's the next best thing to actually fucking you." He pulled his fingers back until they pumped into her shallowly, curved into that sensitive spot, and his thumb circled her clitoris again. It was enough to shatter her. As she came she felt Edmund shove her hand down over the end of his cock, cupping it. He cried out her name hoarsely and she felt a hot, wet spurt in her cupped hand, then another and another. He was coming, he was coming with her, and the feel of it sent her careening into another orgasm.

Chapter Three

ᔓ

"Fuck." Edmund felt like a foolish schoolboy. He'd lost control. He'd wanted to do so much more to her, to draw out their pleasure, and instead he'd come like a lad with his first girl.

"Edmund?" Sylvie's voice was sweet, and tired and worried. He'd worried her.

"It's all right, Sylvie." He dredged up a laugh as he leaned away from her slightly so he could see her face. She was flushed and drowsy, satiated. "I'd meant to make that last a little longer."

"It was wonderful, Edmund." Sylvie pressed her palm to his cheek and rose to her tiptoes to tenderly kiss his lips.

He didn't want tender. It smacked too much of pity. He bit her lip and she tried to pull away with a startled cry. When he licked the spot he'd bitten, it turned to a moan. "There's only one way to make sure that climax didn't go to waste," he whispered against her lips. When he pulled back she looked at him curiously. He answered with a wicked grin and raised her hand from his cock, covered in his cum. "Lick it off, Sylvie," he told her roughly. "I didn't get to come down your throat, so lick it off."

Sylvie's eyes went wide with shock, but he could see excitement and curiosity in their depths. "It tastes good, Sylvie," he encouraged in the same wicked tone, "I know."

Her eyes got bigger. Edmund laughed. "Yes, that means exactly what you think it does. I've tasted it. Mine..." he paused for effect, "and others."

Sylvie choked, which made Edmund laugh again. "I know you've heard the rumors, Sylvie. I'm very wild, I like just about everything in the bedroom, and out of it come to think of it." He looked around the marble folly in amusement. When he looked back at Sylvie her eyes had gone hot and her nostrils flared with desire. Edmund's heart, which had just begun to slow its racing beat, pounded out of control again. Most women were intrigued by his lack of inhibitions when it came to sex. But to see that look on Sylvie's face, beautiful, innocent Sylvie…unbelievably Edmund's cock stirred anew at her obvious excitement. He leaned in and licked the soft fleshy part of her hand just below her thumb. The taste of his own salty cum mixed with the sweet, sugary taste of Sylvie made his groin tighten in arousal. "Mmmm," he rumbled. "That tastes good on you."

Sylvie gasped, and Edmund took advantage of her parted lips to gently push the tip of one cum-coated finger inside her mouth. Instinctively her lips closed on it, and Sylvie moaned as her eyes closed.

"Good, yes?" Edmund whispered, and he pushed the finger a little deeper into her mouth. It was all the encouragement she needed. Sylvie sucked the cum from her finger, and then pulled it out slowly, a look of rapture on her face. She opened her eyes, and looked at Edmund adoringly, her innocent enjoyment of the taste of his seed lascivious in the extreme. The incongruity wasn't lost on Edmund. Sylvie had the gift of looking innocent at the same time she was doing something so decadent as licking a man's cum from her hand. Edmund groaned. She stuck her tongue out and ran the flat of it over her palm, licking up the still warm cum she'd caught there. Edmund couldn't resist, his tongue joined hers as they licked her hand clean together. Their tongues touched, tangled, the smell and taste of his ejaculate all around them, and Edmund was lost. Sylvie was his, as no one else had ever been. The salacious act became a communion for him, and if he hadn't been so bloody aroused he would have laughed at the irony of the vicar turning such an erotic, illicit act into a religious experience.

Sylvie pulled away, breathing heavily as Edmund licked between her fingers, his taste still lingering there, merged with the marvelous taste that was Sylvie. "Now mine," she whispered. He stared at her blankly for a moment, until she reached for the hand he'd fucked her with. She took one of the fingers he'd had buried inside her and gently took it in her mouth, sucking softly and Edmund cursed at the flash fire of desire that raced through his veins.

"Damn it, Sylvie," he rasped. "Damn. You were made for me, Sylvie, made to be loved." He crushed her to him and pressed his lips to her cheek, watching as he pulled his finger from her mouth and ran the tip wet with her saliva over the plump, swollen pink flesh of her lips. Sylvie panted, her dark pupils eating up the blue of her eyes as her desire flared into full-blown arousal again. He pulled his hand away and kissed her, his tongue dipping into her mouth to taste her, to taste himself there, the heady combination of the two of them and the sex they'd shared mixed and warmed in the heat of her mouth. More, he wanted more.

Sylvie made no protest as he led her to the bench. Her eyes flashed with disappointment as he pushed her down to sit on it. "I thought…I mean are we done?" She was so delightfully upset at the thought Edmund's nascent erection grew to fully aroused proportions. "No, darling, we're just getting started."

Sylvie looked up at him in gratitude. "Oh, thank God."

It was wrong, wrong, wrong, Sylvie chanted in her head even as she let Edmund lean over her and undo the tapes on her dress. She ran her hands over his hips, left exposed by his sagging trousers which he hadn't bothered to put right. She mentally slapped a hand over the mouth of her conscience as some devil inside her made her run her hands back to his spectacularly tight, muscular ass. Oh God, it was as wonderful as she knew it would be. She'd watched it surreptitiously for weeks, walking around, taunting her in its tight breeches. And now it was hers to do with as she liked. She rubbed her hands over its rough, warm surface and then trailed the fingers of one hand down the crease between the round, delicious globes there. She ran them back up the crease to the deep dimple at the top, and rubbed her fingertip there. Edmund had frozen at her back, her dress gaping in the front now.

"Sylvie," he choked, "God, that feels good. I like that, love it actually. I love it when someone plays with my ass." He spread his legs and Sylvie's fingers teased down again, farther this time, until she lightly scratched at the furry sac between his legs. He groaned and stood up, pulling her hands out of his pants. "Enough," he panted, "enough." He looked at her hotly, and Sylvie shivered. "Time for that later," he promised. He ran his fingers over her shoulders and down to her breasts, lightly caressing the mounds with his fingertips. She shivered again. Then he plucked her nipples sharply and she gasped.

"Do you like that, Sylvie? You must tell me, you know, what you like, what you want, what pleases you and what doesn't. We will learn all there is to know about each other's bodies, darling, until we can play them like finely tuned instruments." He plucked her nipples again and Sylvie's breathing grew ragged.

"Am I a harp then," Sylvie said breathlessly, "that you should pluck my strings?"

Edmund laughed at her teasing. She liked to make him laugh. She'd never made anyone laugh before. She had not been encouraged to display her wit by her family or her elderly husband. "Yes, a harp if you like." He pulled the legs of his breeches up and then knelt before her. "Or a mouth instrument instead, if you would prefer."

Oh, Sylvie preferred. The thought of his mouth on her breasts again made her nipples peak and ache and burn for the wet of his tongue. "Yes, please," she asked meekly, and Edmund grinned rakishly up at her.

"So polite," he murmured as he leaned toward her breast. "You must say please all the time now, Sylvie. I quite like it.

Polite begging, yes, I like it." The last was said with his lips rubbing on her nipple, and Sylvie thrust her hands into his hair and pulled him closer. With a deep chuckle he opened his mouth and took her nipple and the surrounding breast inside the hot, wet cavern. Sylvie shuddered at the feel of his tongue flicking back and forth across the turgid peak. No one had ever kissed her breasts like this. Geoffrey had suckled there as a baby, but the feeling was completely different. Edmund's was the caress of a man, the desire of a man, pulling there, sucking there, and it was erotic and thrilling. It sent a wave of heat directly to her sex, where a hot gush of cream slid over the cooling wetness still there from before. She hadn't known, hadn't understood the depths of desire until today, until Edmund had touched her. She may be depraved, but it was a glorious depravity.

He sucked and bit at her nipple with a rumble of delight, as if it were a delicious treat, and Sylvie groaned as she scooted closer to the edge of the bench. Her legs widened as she tried to press her mound against Edmund—any part of him as long as she could ease the ache there. Her skirt had fallen to cover her as they had walked to the bench and was now too tight to allow her to spread her legs sufficiently. She growled in frustration, thrusting against air.

Edmund pulled off her nipple and languorously licked around it in widening circles, conscientiously making sure to leave no morsel of skin untasted. Sylvie cried out again, at the marvelous sensation of his mouth and tongue on her, but also in increasing agitation over her inability to press her aching sex against something hard, hot, and Edmund.

"Hmmm," Edmund sighed against her breast, causing tingles to chase down her spine. "Is there something wrong, my love?" His tone was innocent, but Sylvie knew very well that he was aware of her frustration and its cause.

"Edmund, please," she pleaded, and his hands lightly grasped her ankles, running up her lower legs just a few inches before trailing back down to her ankles. The caress felt good, but wasn't what she craved.

"Please what, my dear?" Edmund asked as he kissed her neck, and then trailed gentle kisses along her jaw. Her neck arched to give him more room there. It felt so good, he felt so good. Her body clamored for more.

"Please..." Sylvie was struck with panic as she realized she didn't know how to voice what she wanted. Edmund soothed her with a hand that ran slowly and lightly down the exposed skin of her back, his fingers bumping along her spine. She shivered as the innocuous caress sent waves of longing to her extremities, making her arms and legs feel heavy. She rested her forearms on his shoulders as her head fell back weakly. "Please touch me."

"I am." His voice was soft, uncompromising. He was going to make her say it.

"I mean, I...I want to touch you." That wasn't right, she thought, befuddled as his hand began smoothing in circles on her back, dipping lower each time to run under the crumpled edge of her dress at her hips, until he was able to dip one finger into the dimple at the top of the crease on her backside, just as she had done to him. The feeling made her writhe on the bench.

"You are," Edmund told her in the same soft, uncompromising tone.

Sylvie cried out in frustration. "Edmund, please, please! I want to press against you, my sex, please." She moved her arms and tried to pull up her skirts between them. Edmund stopped her with a firm hand.

"What you are trying to say, Sylvie, is that you want to press your wet, aching pussy against my hard cock, is that right?" His voice was harsh. "Say it, Sylvie."

"Yes, yes," she panted. "I want to press my wet, aching pussy against your hard cock." She didn't care about proprieties or moral sensibilities anymore, just satisfying her need, rubbing on him and touching him, coming with him again.

Edmund smiled wolfishly. "I have a better idea." His hands went to her ankles again and began pushing her dress up.

Edmund stood up, surprising Sylvie. She wasn't positioned properly on the bench. He took her hands and walked over to the side, pulling her around and over so she was balanced on the edge of the bench.

"What...what are you doing?" Sylvie asked, breathless and confused.

Edmund rapidly unbuttoned his jacket and peeled it off, turning it inside out. Then he laid it on the bench behind Sylvie, like a blanket. "Lie down," he told her gruffly, his hands gentle on her shoulders as he helped to lower her.

"Edmund, I told you, we can't..." Sylvie's voice was full of painful regret, and Edmund smiled inwardly. Today she said no, but give him a couple of days and it would be yes. She wanted to fuck him so badly she ached for it.

Edmund went to his knees between her legs, spreading them wide with his hands at the same time he pushed her skirts up all the way to her lap. He was struck speechless at the sight of her pussy. It was covered in dark blonde, tight, wet curls, the lips bright pink and swollen, the same pink as her distended nipples. Her entrance was open and weeping, just waiting for a cock to fill it. His own jumped at the sight. The soft inner lips were ruffled, like a lady's gown. How like Sylvie to have a ladylike pussy. He had to taste her, had to feel those ruffles on his tongue. With Sylvie breathlessly asking him what he was doing, trying desperately to pull her skirts down, Edmund leaned in and ran his tongue along the petal soft lips. Sylvie's cry was a muffled scream and she threw her head back against the marble bench with a loud crack.

Edmund pulled his head back sharply to look at her in concern. "Christ, Sylvie, are you all right?"

"Oh my God," Sylvie moaned, rubbing the back of her head. "Next time you plan to do something like that, please give me a little warning."

Edmund laughed. "Duly noted. Sylvie darling, I'm going to lick and suck this delectable pussy, and fuck you with my tongue until you come. Is that all right?"

"Edmund," she groaned. "God, if it feels as good as that first...yes, yes, it's all right." She ended on a moan. He hadn't waited for her permission, but had moved his mouth back to her dripping pussy even as he was speaking. God! She tasted so perfect, so wonderful. He'd always loved to lick a woman, the taste, the texture, the pleasure they received from it. But this was Sylvie, and that made it better than it had ever been before. He was instantly addicted to her taste.

Edmund grabbed her behind the knees and placed her legs over his shoulders so he could get closer to her. Her legs locked around his head, her ankles crossing along his back, and she thrust her hands into his hair to hold his face to her. He didn't care, he wanted to be that close, he wanted to drown in her. He grabbed her ass in his palms, squeezing as he lifted her higher, onto his mouth, his tongue. He found her clitoris and sucked it, laved it, nibbled it, and Sylvie was reduced to helpless sobs. He loved it, loved her complete surrender to the passion, to the moment, to him. Without warning she came, her sobs became a scream, and she pressed him hard against her. He thrust his tongue into her channel, so he could feel the muscles clench tight on it. He moaned as he worked her convulsing passage, rubbing the walls with the tip of his tongue. Sylvie writhed on the bench at the motion.

"Edmund," she cried, "God, yes! It feels so good. Don't stop, don't stop!"

He'd never heard sweeter love words. To have reduced the shy Lady Bartlebyrne to helpless begging was the greatest achievement of his life at that moment.

Her convulsions became tremors, but they went on and on. With each lick and thrust she moaned, her back arching and her hands clutching. She was the most responsive lover he'd ever had. Most women pushed him away after a climax, too sensitive to endure any more. Not Sylvie. She embraced the sensitivity, the shivering, aching need. Again and again she moaned and arched and begged for more. And he gave it. Twice more she reached a peak that made her cry out. She was soaking wet, as wet as he had ever felt a woman. He knew it would be so easy, so hot and pleasurable, to thrust his cock into that heated, soaking passage. The more he ate at her, and the wetter she got, the harder his cock became. It was becoming hard to focus on Sylvie his cock ached and jerked so much with each of her moans.

Finally he could take no more. He pulled back from her with a gasp, fighting against the grip of her hands and legs. She wailed in dismay as he left her and he grinned. "I've got to have relief, Sylvie," he rasped, licking his lips, running his hand over his face to wipe the excess that was dripping off his chin. He moaned at how wet he was from her. It was incredibly erotic. Sylvie sat up, a little wobbly, and Edmund put his arm around her to steady her. She looked as if she was barely able to focus, but she found his mouth and kissed him voraciously. She murmured in approval at the taste of her on his tongue.

"My turn, Sylvie," he murmured against her lips, "my turn." He stood, his hands on her shoulders, his cock jutting out of his open trousers. He aimed for her mouth, but she was too short, damn it, the bench too low. He pulled Sylvie up, and she came into his arms willingly, clinging to him, his for the taking. He held himself in check. If he did fuck her now, she'd be upset. He'd made her a promise and he meant to keep it. When he fucked her it would be because she asked for it. And she would.

He spun around slowly and let go of Sylvie once he was sure she could stand. Then he thrust his pants down over his hips, just enough to expose his cock and ass. Then he sat on the bench. The marble still held Sylvie's warmth, and was wet from her pussy. He rubbed his ass on it with a groan. That was what he'd wanted to feel, why he'd pulled his trousers down. He closed his eyes for a moment enjoying the feeling.

"Edmund?" Sylvie asked. "What do you want me to do?" She leaned over and reached for his hard cock, bobbing against his stomach. Jesus, he didn't think he'd ever been this hard. Not even a short while ago, against the wall. He grabbed her hands.

"Your mouth, Sylvie," he told her, his voice as ragged as his breathing. "Suck it."

Sylvie's head jerked back in surprise. "What?" she exclaimed.

Edmund groaned. He should have known Sylvie would not be familiar with sucking a man's cock. What the hell had she and that husband of hers done? The man had clearly been an idiot.

He leaned back, gripping the sides of the bench with both hands, his cock leaping toward her. "Kneel between my legs, Sylvie." At her hesitation he growled, "Do it."

She held on to his knee with one hand as she lifted her skirt slightly and kneeled before him. Her gown still gaped open, exposing her breasts, and she started to pull it up her arms.

"Don't," he ordered her, his voice harder than he wanted, but Jesus he was hurting. "I want to see your breasts as you suck my cock."

Sylvie gasped, but he saw the excitement in her eyes. Christ, she was so sensual, she loved these games. Why had no one played them with her before?

"Lean down and take my cock in your mouth, Sylvie. Do what you want to it, lick it, suck it. Take it deep, or just the head. Whatever you want, as long as my cock is in your sweet mouth and I can watch you."

"Oh my God," Sylvie said in a trembling voice. "I…is this normal? Do people do these things all the time? Your mouth…on me, and…and now this?" He smiled, although it was strained. She still had trouble with the words, even kneeling between his legs half clothed, her thighs soaked with her own cum as she got ready to suck his cock. The dichotomy of sweet innocence existing side by side with siren-like sensuality was an irresistible combination for Edmund.

"Yes," Edmund said, his voice low because he found it hard to speak as her eyes devoured his cock hungrily. "Yes, if they're smart they do. Suck it, Sylvie, go ahead."

She leaned forward and tentatively took the head into her warm, wet mouth, her rosebud lips stretched around its girth. His cock jerked at the first touch of her mouth on him, and she had to grab the base with one hand while the other hand stayed on his knee for balance. Edmund groaned at the sight and feel of what she was doing to him.

She was sexual abandon personified as she delicately sucked his cock and swirled her tongue around the head. Her hair was mussed, falling from its prim and proper style. Her cheeks were flushed, her eyes gleaming as she concentrated completely on what she was doing. She was a fast learner, her tender sucking and tasting making every nerve in Edmund's body quiver with hungry impatience. Her shoulders were gently sloped, her slim arms trapped in the fallen sleeves of her gown, impeding their movement. It was a gentle bondage that aroused him. Her breasts were not large, but they were very appealing, sloping deliciously from the top to the small hard points of her deep pink nipples to a full, round bottom that curved into her delicate sternum. His mouth watered as he remembered the way her breasts tasted. They swayed softly with her movements as her head moved on his cock, and the sight was almost as mesmerizing as his cock moving slowly deeper and deeper into her mouth.

"Yes, that's good, Sylvie," he praised her roughly. "Take more, yes, like that." She opened her mouth a little wider, he didn't think it could open much more, and he slid another inch inside. She gagged a little and he pulled back. "I'm sorry, darling, sorry." He was panting, the words harder and harder to get out. "I...relax, and just try to take as much as you can. I..." he chuckled breathlessly, derisively. "I don't think I'm going to last much longer, sweet. When I come, will you try to swallow it, Sylvie? It is so amazing if you swallow it." She nodded her head and Edmund groaned again, his head falling back.

His hips began moving of their own accord, thrusting his cock into her mouth. He ruthlessly controlled the motion as best he could. He didn't want to be too rough this first time, but God, next time she sucked his cock he was going to be on top fucking her mouth hard.

Sylvie was moving on his cock, up and down, licking and swirling her tongue. It felt so incredible he didn't think it could get better. Then she sucked hard without warning, long, sucking pulls that made his balls draw up tight as she sucked him as deep into her mouth as she could, practically to her throat from the feel of it.

"Christ!" Edmund gasped, and he grabbed the back of her head with one hand, his fingers tangling in her hair as he held her there, his cock deep, and she sucked and sucked. His hips jerked and he felt his climax coming. "I'm going to come, Sylvie," he said from between clenched teeth. "I'm going to come," and it was as if the words unlocked the orgasm from deep within him. The heat of his cum shot up his cock and out into her mouth, filling it, swirling around his cock in there before she managed a choking swallow. He knew it was too much, knew she was having trouble, but couldn't stop, couldn't pull out. It felt too damn good. Through hazy vision he saw her latched onto his cock, sucking and swallowing and the sight was so bloody fucking amazing he felt a second wave take him and he had to close his eyes to ride it.

When he could breathe again, he let go of her head and she pulled off, gasping. She didn't pull far away, and he could feel her hot breath on the incredibly sensitive head of his cock, and it made him shiver.

"I'm sorry, Sylvie," he said between deep breaths, "but God, it was so good."

Sylvie licked her lips, and one finger came up to wipe off a smear of cum in the corner. She sucked the cum off and Edmund's heart flipped over as it was pounding mercilessly in his chest.

"I liked it," Sylvie said quietly, her voice a little rough from his cock being rammed in her throat, he was sure. She smiled beatifically at him, and his heart squeezed. Much more of this and he'd have an apoplexy. "Is it all right that I liked it?"

Edmund laughed weakly, and leaned forward to kiss her softly on the lips. "Yes, it's more than all right," he whispered against that smile.

Chapter Four

ॐ

They dressed clumsily, trying to help one another with shaking hands which they laughed about. His jacket was a rumpled ruin, her hair impossibly tangled, and there was a rip in her petticoat.

"We smell like sex," Sylvie said with a sigh as she took his offered hand and gingerly stepped down the folly's marble steps to the path.

Edmund leaned over and sucked in a heady dose of the scent from Sylvie's neck, making her laugh. "Yes, yes we do," he replied contentedly.

They walked in silence for a minute, picking their way over summer's detritus on the path.

"I will come to you tonight," he told her matter-of-factly.

Sylvie stopped and looked at him, horrified. "You can't!" she cried, letting go of his arm. "The servants will talk already, Edmund. Please, you can't."

He gave her a long look and Sylvie began to panic. "You have one day, Sylvie, to figure out how we can do this without detection. But I will be in your bed tomorrow night."

Sylvie bit her cheek in indecision. She wanted this affair, desperately. Edmund had shown her a passion today that she hadn't known existed, not just within her but in the whole world. She craved more of it, more of him. She couldn't imagine doing those things with anyone but Edmund. She didn't even want to contemplate a life without them. But dare she risk it? She felt as if she'd been waiting a lifetime for this. Surely there was some way to be with Edmund without everyone knowing. Other people managed it, didn't they? She had to find a way.

"I will tell you tomorrow," she whispered, making a decision she hoped she wouldn't regret. "I'll think about how it can be done. I'll figure it out, and I'll tell you tomorrow morning when you come."

Edmund smiled mischievously. "I get to come again tomorrow morning? I like the sound of that."

Sylvie blushed at his innuendo and Edmund laughed. It was a sound she was beginning to crave.

They came out of the woods and started across the green just as Sylvie's housekeeper Mrs. Price stepped onto the terrace. She saw Sylvie and began walking toward them.

"There you are, my lady." She stopped at the bottom of the steps and looked at Sylvie suspiciously. "Are you quite all right, Lady Bartlebyrne?"

Sylvie laughed brittlely, and Edmund gave an inward sigh. She was right, she was horrible at subterfuge.

"I desired a bit of fresh air and a walk," Edmund told Mrs. Price with an innocent smile.

"Ah," Mrs. Price said, smiling back. "These youngsters, eh Lady Bartlebyrne? They quite wear us out, don't they?" She clucked sympathetically and took Sylvie's arm, helping her up the stairs as if she were infirm. "And you without a bonnet or shawl. You must be worn out, dear. We'll just have a lie down, hmm?"

She would be the first to go, Edmund thought, glaring at her unsuspecting back. The thought startled him and he stumbled. Was he really thinking of a future? Here? In Byrnham? No, he realized, watching Sylvie turn to wave goodbye as the housekeeper swept her into the house. Here, at The Byrne. And the thought didn't scare the wits out of him. As a matter of fact, it sounded damn good.

* * * * *

Two weeks later Sylvie showed Edmund to the door after their morning tea and pastries. "Are you going to see Mrs. Tilbury today?" Sylvie asked as they walked slowly.

"Yes." Edmund stopped and took his hat and gloves from Jernigan. "I've found her some work as a washerwoman and given her some funds from the parish, but I want to make sure she and the children have enough provisions. When she finally came to see me they were nearly starving. I'm appalled that she waited four months after her husband's death to seek assistance."

Sylvie shook her head and sighed. "It's very hard for some of the women to admit they need help. Accepting charity marks them in the neighborhood, no matter what you or I say or do. It is an attitude that is very pervasive here in the country, where people are expected to help themselves." Sylvie had to clutch her hands together to keep from smoothing Edmund's jacket across his shoulders after he put his hat on. "I do hope the work you're doing with the parish charity board will help. Prior to your arrival I was the only one calling for more assistance to the widows and orphans. Most of the others wish to keep the funds in case of an emergency at the parsonage or the church, and the last vicar quite agreed with them."

Edmund smiled at her, his eyes saying what he couldn't speak. The look was so tender Sylvie nearly gave in and touched him. Edmund turned and stepped to the door. Sylvie blushed at the knowing look he gave her. He knew she'd been about to touch him and he'd moved deliberately.

"I shall handle the board." Edmund's voice was hard as he said it, and Sylvie almost felt sorry for Sir Josiah Poole, who'd led the conservative board for years. "I hope more women will come forward if they are in need of assistance, and do not wait as long as Mrs. Tilbury now that they know the parish is available to help." His voice softened. "I shall give Mrs. Tilbury your regards."

Sylvie cleared her throat self-consciously. "Yes, yes do, please." She glanced out the door behind him. "I've had cook make up a basket for them. I believe it's waiting by your horse."

"I shall make sure they get it," Edmund said while looking out at the drive. He turned back and again his eyes said more than he could. "Thank you, Lady Bartlebyrne."

He tipped his hat and Sylvie stayed to watch, dreamy-eyed, as he mounted his horse and rode away, turning in the saddle to smile at her before riding out of the drive. She went back in the house, humming happily as she swayed to a tune in her head, the same tune Edmund had hummed in her ear last night as he waltzed her around her bedroom naked. She looked up to catch a smile on Jernigan's face. The butler immediately wiped his expression clean, but Sylvie felt herself blush, and she hurried back into her solar to escape.

Edmund had visited her almost every night for the last two weeks. The three nights he hadn't come had been interminable. They had kissed, licked and sucked every single inch of skin on each other's bodies, and Sylvie still blushed at the memories. He had even introduced her to anal sex, something she had never even dreamed of. Who could imagine that a man's cock there would feel so good? It was a way to fuck him without having to worry about pregnancy, and he loved it. She loved it. He'd brought her a gift, a "toy" he'd called it. A dildo made from jade. They had had hours of fun playing with that. She wanted him so much, every minute of every hour of every day. She knew it was foolish— eventually this affair would have to end. He would lose interest in her as she began to age more noticeably, and he would look for a younger woman to take to wife. The thought ripped through Sylvie's chest like a rapier, cutting out her heart. She knew she would leave The Byrne then. She couldn't stay here and watch Edmund with another woman. She had, in the supreme act of stupidity, fallen in love with him.

She sighed as she sank down on the velvet divan positioned so she could look out over the gardens. How she loved it here. It was only fitting that The Byrne was the backdrop for the great love of her life. It would make her memories of this beloved house even sweeter when she was an old woman.

There was only one thing marring her enjoyment of her torrid affair with Edmund—John the coachman. She'd been afraid to go near her own stables for almost a month, afraid of seeing him and the leering, knowing grin she knew he'd give her. She'd seen it. Several days after their horrid encounter she'd called for her coach and he had bordered on insolence. It had been intolerable, but there was nothing she could do. She had had sex with him! She deserved those awful looks. She put her face in her hands. What had she been thinking? No, she knew what she'd been thinking. She'd been thinking about Edmund and how much she wanted him but would never have him. She had touched herself until she ached and never been fulfilled, wishing it was Edmund's hands on her, Edmund's finger inside her.

It was on the way home from a dinner at Sir Josiah Poole's, in Edmund's honor, that it had happened. Sylvie had watched Edmund all night, watched the young girls flock to him as he smiled and teased them, knowing he would never be hers. By the time she left she was wet and aching from the sight of him, and desolate because she couldn't have him. When John had pulled the coach over on the dark road and climbed inside with her she thought she had nothing to live for, nothing to lose. No words had been spoken as he'd opened his trousers and shown her his hard cock. The sight had aroused her, the idea of a man hard for her. She'd said nothing when he'd roughly pushed her to the floor on her hands and knees and thrown her skirts up. But it was Edmund's face she'd seen as he thrust inside, Edmund's voice she heard in his grunts, Edmund with whom she came.

Sylvie shook her head to clear the images from her mind. She took a deep breath, resolved to deal with the situation, now, this morning. She wouldn't let the ugliness of what had happened with John ruin her happiness with Edmund.

When she got to the stables there was no one about. "Hullo?" she called out in a hesitant voice. The air in the stable was hot and dust filled, and the stalls needed to be mucked out. It should have been done hours ago. Sylvie looked in one stall and realized it hadn't been done for days. She was appalled. "John?" she called out sharply.

He came to the door of the back room in which he slept and leaned against the doorjamb. "You rang, milady?" he asked with a sly grin. He sauntered into the stable, his shirt open, looking disreputable and rather dangerous. Sylvie took a step back. She hadn't noticed John's looks much, not even the night he'd fucked her. He'd been a cock, that was all. She was ashamed at the thought, but it was true nonetheless. She looked at him now, surprised at his brutish good looks.

He was tall, as she'd known, with jet black hair that fell over his brow rakishly. His eyes were a startling blue, his other features coarse but attractive. He had a dimple in his chin and strong, white teeth. One of his front teeth was chipped, giving him almost a boyish appeal. But the muscular, hairy chest revealed by his open shirt belied that impression. Sylvie took another step back. As good looking as he was, she still got an uneasy feeling from him.

"I been wonderin' when you'd come for some more," he said insolently, rubbing his hand down his chest to his crotch, where he cupped the bulge there suggestively.

Sylvie gasped in outrage. "That is not why I am here! I have come to tell you that…that that can never happen again between us." John kept coming closer and Sylvie backed up until she was near the stable door.

"Ah, come on now, I knows ya liked it," he drawled lasciviously. "I sure did. My da was right, gentry cunt is fine indeed."

Sylvie felt ill. "Please, John. You must understand. I was...I was lonely, and not thinking clearly that night. I do not wish to use you that way."

John spread his hands in a magnanimous gesture. "Why not? I don't mind. Use me, my lady, all you like." He grinned as he ran a finger over his chin. "I love a good fuck, and you are that."

He feinted to the right and Sylvie moved to the left, but he was quick and she realized her mistake as he grabbed her arm. He laughed as he brought her flush against him, grinding his hard cock into her stomach. "Let's have a fuck now, my lady. You'll change your tune after you come on me cock again."

"No!" Sylvie cried, pushing at his chest ineffectually. He leaned in for a kiss, and Sylvie bit his lip hard, desperate to get away. With a yell he let her go and she scrambled to the open door while he cursed.

Sylvie was breathing hard, frightened. "You must leave here, John. I'm sorry, but you must. I shall give you a good reference, you deserve that much. I'm sorry." She started to leave but his reply shocked her into immobility.

"I deserve a hell of a lot more than that, your high and mighty ladyship, and you'll pay it. You'll pay for John to keep his mouth shut, or the whole village will know about you and me," he growled.

Sylvie spun back around to face him. "You wouldn't dare!"

John grinned, his teeth bloody from the bite she'd given him. "Oh yes I would. Ruin what you've got with the vicar, won't it? You tell him about our little fuck?"

Sylvie's chest felt as if it were crushing the breath from her lungs. "What are you talking about?"

John laughed cruelly. "I seen him, sneaking in the veranda door after the house is asleep, and sneaking back out afore dawn. I was tempted to try the same thing, but he's a horny little bastard, here practically every night. Wouldn't want anyone to know about that either, would you?" He grinned cruelly. "Then they'd all know the saintly Lady Bartlebyrne has a hot cunt for young cock."

"What do you want?" Sylvie was going to throw up. She knew as soon as she left the stable she'd throw up.

"Oh, just a little extra in me wages, I suppose," he said amiably, stepping toward her again. She backed away and his face was angry. "And some o' what you're givin' the good vicar."

Sylvie clutched her stomach and ran, John calling angrily to her from the stable door.

* * * * *

Sylvie took to her bed for two days. She sent a note round to Edmund telling him she was unwell the first night. She'd refused to see him the following morning, pleading a stomach illness, and he'd penned a note saying she should contact him when she was feeling better. She'd read between the lines. He was very concerned for her, and angry that he couldn't force his way in to see her. Last night John had stood beneath her window softly calling up to her in a chilling, singsong voice half the night. He thought he had her, that she would give in.

She'd cried out all her tears and made her decision. She would break it off with Edmund, and refuse to pay John his blood money. She wouldn't be in that kind of debt to him. She would have to leave here, of course, even if John didn't make good on his threats. She felt soul sick at the thought of losing Edmund and The Byrne. Before it had been a vague possibility in the back of her mind, now it was a crushing reality.

She wanted to tell Edmund at the vicarage, not here. That was not a memory she wanted to take with her from The Byrne. She dressed carefully in a sedate walking dress, proper respectable widow attire. Then she called for a horse, pointedly asking Jernigan for help mounting, ignoring John's smirking face next to the horse.

When she arrived in Byrnham she decided to walk for a bit, and left her horse at the town stable. She was so preoccupied she didn't notice the odd look the stable master gave her as he tipped his hat at the coin she pressed into his hand.

She stopped on the main street, looking in the dressmaker's window at some samples there, and she heard two women conversing boldly right behind her.

"There she is. Can you believe the nerve? I heard it was her coachman, a boy not even half her age! Disgraceful."

"Well, a widow married young, without a strong man to guide her, it's trouble from the start. No sense of propriety, of right or wrong! The poor lad, forced into such an abominable union." The woman clucked her tongue in shame.

Sylvie spun around to see two women a few years older than she. She knew them, Mrs. Smith and Mrs. Hopplewhite. She'd worked with them on the parish charity board. They had always been pleasant to her, if a little distant. Now they narrowed their eyes at her in disdain, and then spun about, giving her the cut direct. Sylvie was horrified. She looked about and saw several people on the street watching, some in horror, some with approval. She saw pretty little Alice Bauer, the baker's daughter next door to the dressmaker's, glaring at the women as they walked by her.

Oh God, did Edmund know? Had he heard already? Sylvie began to walk quickly back to the stable, unable to face the people of Byrnham for even one second more. By the time she reached the blessedly dark recesses of the stable she was running.

* * * * *

Edmund threw himself from the horse after he reined it harshly to a stop in front of The Byrne. Alice Bauer had come running to the vicarage not half an hour past to tell him about Sylvie's experience in Byrnham that afternoon. Alice had let it spill that most of the village knew he and Sylvie were involved, or as Alice put it, "head over arse for one another". She had ranted about Mrs. Smith and Mrs. Hopplewhite who, according to Alice, were jealous and spiteful because Edmund hadn't looked twice at their homely, unmarried daughters.

This had simply accelerated his plans, that was all. He had planned to enjoy the illicit nature of their present affair for a few more weeks before asking Sylvie to marry him. Common knowledge of the affair meant only that they would marry sooner. It need have no bearing on their relationship other than that, none.

So why was he so panicked? He could feel his heart trying pound out of his chest. He was panicking because he knew Sylvie. She was still so sensitive about their age difference. He didn't understand it. To him it meant nothing. She was his soul mate, no matter their ages — the woman he'd been waiting for. And he knew she loved him, he knew it.

It was the other rumor. She'd as much as admitted she'd had another lover. Was it true? Was it this young coachman? And if so, was it also true that she had a predilection for young men? Was he only one in a string of younger lovers?

Jernigan opened the door, the stoic butler for once looking discomposed. "Mr. James," he greeted Edmund, blocking his entrance.

"Hello, Jernigan," Edmund said, trying to get around the older man. "I must see Lady Bartlebyrne at once."

"Lady Bartlebyrne is not receiving today, sir," Jernigan told him, his distress evident.

Edmund narrowed his eyes and glared at Jernigan. "She will receive me." His voice was a low, angry growl.

Jernigan nervously cleared his throat. "I'm sorry, Mr. James, but she specifically said she was not home to you today."

"Sylvie!" Edmund's bellow echoed through the foyer. "Sylvie, damn it! Let me in!"

"Mr. James!" Jernigan gasped, shocked. He tried to close the door but Edmund shoved his foot in the way and pushed his shoulder against it.

"Sylvie!" he bellowed again.

"Let him in, Jernigan," Sylvie said quietly from behind the butler.

Jernigan opened the door and stepped aside. Sylvie was looking at him, sad and wan, from the hallway. She turned and walked back toward her solar. "We do not wish to be disturbed, Jernigan," she said, her voice breaking on the last word.

Edmund stepped through the door, noting the worried look on the butler's face. "Don't worry, Jernigan," Edmund told him flatly, "I will take care of it."

Jernigan sighed with relief. "Thank you, Mr. James."

"It's true," Sylvie said as soon as Edmund closed the door. He looked so upset, she didn't wait for him to speak. She couldn't bear to hear what he had to say to her. He must be so angry, feel so betrayed.

"Which one?" he asked in a low voice.

Sylvie spun back around to look at him. God, he was so beautiful. Her heart ached at the sight of him. For a short time he had been hers. His words confused her. "What? What do you mean?"

Edmund stalked across the room to stand in front of her. "I mean which rumor is true? That you and I are in love, or that you fucked your coachman?"

Sylvie gasped. "People are saying we're in love?"

Edmund looked as if she'd punched him. "Then it's true, that you fucked your coachman?"

The pain in his voice made Sylvie wrap her arms around her stomach and bend over, overcome with guilt and shame and a deep sadness. "Yes," she whispered, "yes, it's true."

Edmund's hands were rough on her shoulders as he raised her up, until she balanced on her toes, only his hold keeping her standing. "When? When did you fuck him?"

He was so intense, the anguish in his eyes so clear that Sylvie turned her head away, her eyes closed. "About a month ago, before you and I..." her voice trailed off.

Edmund shook her. "Before you let me lick me your pussy, and you sucked my cock? Before you made me beg for the chance to fuck your ass? Before that?"

"Yes!" Sylvie sobbed, and Edmund pulled her into a desperately tight hug.

"Then I don't care," he whispered brokenly. "I don't care, Sylvie. God help me, I love you so much. Whatever happened before I came into your life doesn't matter."

"You were here," she sobbed, determined that he know everything—determined to lay bare the extent of her perfidy. "You were here, and I wanted you so, Edmund. But I never dreamed that we would be together. After dinner at the Poole's that night, he...he pulled over and took me, and I let him. I wanted you, but I let him!" She was sobbing so hard she could hardly speak.

Edmund's arms fell away, and he pulled her over to the divan, pushing her down. It took her a moment to realize he'd gone to one knee before her.

"Marry me, Sylvie," he asked quietly, his gaze intent, his hold on her hand bruising.

"Wh-what?" she stuttered, unable to believe she'd heard him correctly.

"Marry me."

"But...but why?" She was dumbfounded. She'd never expected this, never in a million years.

Edmund smiled sadly. "For the usual reasons, at least on my part. I'm in love with you, you see, and in my world that means I want to marry you."

"But...but we can't!" Sylvie was aghast. He couldn't love her! He was throwing everything away, couldn't he see that?

"Why can't we?" His mouth was set stubbornly. Sylvie had seen that look before, when he was determined to fuck her ass, when he wouldn't let her say no. She'd given in then, and been glad she did. But not on this. She had to save him from his own folly.

Sylvie set her palm against his cheek tenderly. She sniffed, the tears still falling, but not quite so violently. "Dearest Edmund. I am too old for you. You are a young man. You deserve a young wife, who will give you children." She looked away. "One who doesn't have this kind of scandal in her past."

Edmund surprised her when he stood abruptly, cursing. "God damn it, Sylvie! I am so damn tired of hearing how old you are. You are thirty-nine, not eighty-nine! Although even if you were, I would still love you." He paced in front of her tugging on his hair in agitation. "You wear me out in the bedroom, Sylvie. You take all I can give you and then demand more, until I'm spent and utterly useless. If that is the sexual appetite of an old woman, I don't want a young one!" He spun to look at her, his eyes blazing with determination. "You are beautiful, desirable, witty, charming, intelligent, kind—in other words, everything a man could want in a wife." He fell to his knees again, his hands on her thighs, his look pleading. "Everything I want in a wife." He shook his head. "I know I am not a great prize, Sylvie. Marrying me will be a rather large step down for you, socially speaking. But I love you. I love you more than anyone will ever love you. Please, Sylvie, please."

Sylvie was weakening. "Children..." she said in a broken voice, but Edmund spoke over her.

"You are still young enough to have children, Sylvie. Lady Templeton just had twins, and she is forty-two."

Sylvie started in surprise. "Twins? Are you sure? I hadn't heard."

Edmund gave her a lopsided grin. "I have the best sources for gossip in the parish—my housekeeper and my mother's letters."

Sylvie smiled back, but shook her head. "You must think more about this, Edmund. And I must quit The Byrne. The scandal will reach London soon, and I must see Geoffrey before it does."

Edmund's chin turned stubborn once again. "Would you marry me if you were pregnant, Sylvie?"

Again, he'd taken Sylvie by surprise, and she answered without thinking. "Well, of course, Edmund, but we both know I'm not— What are you doing?" The last was asked with alarm as Edmund pulled her to the floor. He hands grabbed her legs and spread them, pushing her skirts up.

"I'm going to fuck you." His response was spoken conversationally, but his hands were hard and determined.

Chapter Five

80

"Edmund!" Sylvie cried as she heard her drawers rip, his hands strong and forceful as he tore them off. She couldn't stop the thrill that shot through her, the cream that immediately coated her sex at his rough treatment, at the thought of his cock in her. Edmund's hand cupped her pussy as his finger slid hard inside her. She moaned and arched her back and he grinned triumphantly.

"You are always so ready for me, Sylvie. Have you any idea how hard it has been to deny myself this for the past two weeks?" He thrust his finger in over and over, his palm grinding on her clitoris, and Sylvie writhed beneath his assault. "I'm going to fuck you, Sylvie. This," he fucked his finger into her and hooked it, rubbing up and down on the secret spot inside her that only he knew, the one that made her cry and beg, "this is mine. After today there will be no more barriers between us." Sylvie cried out, thrusting against his hand and he laughed, truly amused. "Even angry with me, even playing the martyr you are a siren, Sylvie. This pussy was made for cock, my cock."

Edmund pulled his hand out and began to roughly unfasten his trousers, his hands shaking. Sylvie was panting, wanting him desperately, but equally desperate to stop this madness, to get away before he did something he'd regret. As he worked the buttons on his pants, Sylvie tried to push back, bracing her feet on the floor and crawling backward. It was hard to get purchase he had her legs spread so far open. She hadn't gone far when he grabbed her ankle and hauled her back toward him, his pants open, his cock jutting out, angry and red and gorgeous. Sylvie felt a shudder rack her body as her pussy clenched in need at the sight of it. She kicked out at him, and he tightened his grip, grabbing both legs. He raised her legs until they were bent over his shoulders and he fell over her, so she couldn't bring them down, couldn't escape. His control over her drove her wild, her nipples so hard each brush of her chemise over them torture, her pussy so wet and aroused that she ached, actually ached, for his cock.

"Please, Edmund, please," she sobbed.

"What, Sylvie?" he whispered dangerously, braced on his arms as he fit his hips to hers, his cock rubbing in the cream that coated her nether lips. "What do you want?"

Sylvie shook her head in distress while her mind screamed, *You! I want you, Edmund!* She bit her lip to keep the words locked inside, hoping if she didn't say it, he would give up this insane idea. But also hoping he didn't give up, hoping against hope that he'd thrust his glorious cock inside her and fuck her until they collapsed, exhausted, and then fuck her again. She sobbed at her selfishness.

But she didn't need to speak. Edmund knew her better than that. "You want *me*," he growled as he thrust into her hard and deep. His penetration was powerful, rough, and felt so good Sylvie couldn't contain her scream as she threw her head back and arched into him. He thrust once into her and ground his pelvis against her sensitive clitoris and Sylvie came. She could no more control her reaction to finally being fucked by Edmund than she could control the tides. She sobbed his name and tightened her legs around his neck, holding his cock deep inside her while she worshipped it.

"Yes, yes," Edmund told her, holding his cock deep for her, letting her fuck herself on it, on him, her orgasm wild, out of control. When she fell back to the floor panting, he began to fuck her in earnest. "Now that that one's out of the way," he said roughly, "let's see how many more times I can make you come before I spill inside you, Sylvie." He thrust in and out in a hard, fast rhythm, different than when he fucked her mouth or her ass, where he'd been gentler, slower. This was a driving, furious fuck, full of passion and anger and determination.

Sylvie thrilled to it, devoured it and drove herself against his pistoning cock until sanity returned.

"No, Edmund, no," she cried, pushing him back with her arms. He grabbed both wrists and gathered them in one hand, pinning them over her head. She was completely at his mercy, and from the heat in his eyes he knew it. His thrusts gentled, became slower, deep and grinding, and Sylvie saw stars, the pleasure was so intense.

"Yes, Sylvie, yes," he answered her, but she had forgotten her earlier cry. She forgot everything but Edmund and the feel of him filling her, over and over, forcing pleasure into her until she was like a cup that overflowed, a never-ending fountain of pleasure.

"God, Sylvie," Edmund breathed as she locked her legs around his neck and opened herself completely to him. He leaned down and kissed her. The kiss was ferociously possessive, a claiming and a promise. Sylvie tasted her tears on his lips, and kissed him back with abandon. His cock glided into her pussy, the wet sound of flesh on flesh the only one in the room save their panting breaths. It was the most erotic thing she'd ever heard. Edmund's pace increased, his body straining. She knew he was going to come deep inside her, that his seed might take root there, that he wanted it to, and she selfishly urged him on with softly murmured words and with the lift and embrace of her hips and hot, wet passage.

"I'm going to come, Sylvie," he ground out, his hips pressed tightly to hers, unmoving. He held there until Sylvie looked at him, and triumph filled his eyes. His hips moved against her, once, twice, and she felt the delicious friction of his cock inside. As he began to come, his face contorted with pleasure, Sylvie was graced with another orgasm, a climax that reveled in the hot seed flowing into her, the strong, virile man fucking her so deeply, and the words of love that poured from his lips.

When it was over, Edmund gingerly lowered Sylvie's legs and she groaned.

"I may not be an old woman, but I may possibly be too old to do that very often," she joked. Edmund laughed, his spirit light.

She'd said yes. Not with words, but with her eyes, her face, her body. She'd accepted his climax inside her. Even now his seed might be bearing fruit. They were to be wed. Edmund rolled to his back, still buried inside Sylvie, pulling her on top of him. He closed his eyes against tears of happiness. And he felt like a complete idiot. He was not generally a poetic, romantic fool. But Sylvie, Christ. She was his.

"Edmund?" she asked, concern in her voice. "Are you having second thoughts?"

His eyes flew open to encounter her worried ones. "Only about ravishing you on the floor. I think my knees shall be bruised for a fortnight."

She straddled him more comfortably and leaned forward to rub her nose on his. The motion moved his over-sensitized cock inside her, and the sensation was a hot slash of pleasure. His back arched and he groaned. Sylvie laughed. "I shall make it up to you," she whispered as her mouth opened on his. Her kiss was tender and hungry, as Sylvie's kisses always were. He never grew tired of her insatiable hunger for him.

She trailed gentle kisses down his jaw as his cock softened and pulled from her warm sheath. "Tell me," he asked. She froze for a moment and then lay her head down on his shoulder. He could tell she knew exactly what he meant.

"I've told you, really. On the way home from the Poole's, John pulled the coach over on that lonely stretch of road near Harker's field. I didn't know what was wrong. Then he opened the door and stepped into the coach. He closed the door behind him, but even in the darkness I could see him unbutton his trousers and he was hard. I was so lonely, Edmund." She pressed her nose into his neck, her voice trembling. "I wanted you. I'd been burning for you every night, and had no hope of ever having you. I needed something to ease me. He was…" she paused, clearly distressed. "He was just a cock in the dark, Edmund, very like the dildo you gave me. Not real." She pushed off him and sat on the floor next to him. He rolled to his side to face her, and leaned on his elbow.

"I'm sorry," he said softly, seeing the shame and distress on her face.

She wiped the tears from her cheeks and nodded. She sniffed and looked up at him with trepidation. "That's not the end of it. When I went to tell him the other day that it couldn't happen again, that he would have to leave, he threatened me."

Edmund sat up then, alert. "What do you mean? Threatened you how?"

Sylvie sighed and gestured around them. "Threatened this—to tell everyone about him and me." She looked down and folded her hands in her lap. "About us. He knows about us, Edmund."

Edmund snorted. "Apparently most of the parish knows about us, Sylvie. But the other, it's unconscionable that a gentleman should tell tales of a lady."

Sylvie was shaking her head. "He is no gentleman, Edmund." She bit her lip. "He tried to…to grab me, in the stable. I had to bite his lip to get away." She was shaking, and Edmund felt murderous.

"I will take care of him, Sylvie. You aren't to worry anymore. When I am done, no one will believe his tales." She looked so upset that Edmund deliberately changed the topic.

"Hmmm," he said, taking her chin between his thumb and forefinger and turning her face this way and that. "I must be losing my touch."

Sylvie looked adorably confused. "What?"

"I have not fucked you insensible. I do not care to leave my lovers until they are insensate with pleasure." He grinned, but Sylvie's eyes filled with tears.

"Is that a way to get back at me?" she whispered. "To tell me of your other lovers?"

Edmund gathered her in his arms and lay down on the floor again with her draped across his chest. "No, my darling, it is my very awkward way of saying we both have pasts that are best forgotten. From this moment on there is only me and you, and no one else, ever." He buried his face in the curve of her neck, rubbing his cheek on the hair that had fallen there, breathing deeply of the scent that was pure Sylvie—pastries and sex.

"You mustn't say that, Edmund," she murmured, arching her neck to the side to give him more room as his lips began to roam.

He groaned and dropped his head to the floor. Christ, he thought she'd given up protesting. "Sylvie," he said, exasperated, "will you stop?" He lifted his head and glared at her. "You are not going to get rid of me, so you'd best get used to me."

"Edmund—" He cut her off with a kiss. If he fucked her long enough, perhaps she'd forget her foolish worries and marry him.

Sylvie kissed him back but he could feel her reservation. It was so unlike her he pulled away, lingering against her lips for a moment.

"Please don't worry, Sylvie," he whispered. "I will take care of you. I want to take care of you."

Sylvie smiled, the effort a little forced, and Edmund remembered his earlier feelings of panic.

"Well, I hate to be the one to point this out," Sylvie said, giving him a quick kiss, "but we are rolling around on the floor of my solar, fucking in front of the windows in the middle of the day." She pushed up on his chest with her hands and smiled wryly. "And Jernigan knows we are in here alone, with orders not to disturb us."

Edmund felt relief wash over him. Was that all she was worried about? He gave her a roguish grin. "True, but he also knows I plan to marry you." He grabbed her ass and squeezed and Sylvie yelped. "And I can't very well get dressed with a beguiling wench lying invitingly across my very interested cock."

Sylvie scrambled off him, to his regret, but she was right. This was not the time or place.

"Oh, goodness, Edmund, why didn't you say something?" Her hands flew to her cheeks, pink with embarrassment.

He laughed. "The day I complain about a warm, willing woman spread across me like a wanton blanket is the day they'll lay me in the ground." He adjusted his trousers as he lay there, closing them, and tried to tuck his shirt in.

Sylvie laughed delightedly. "You look like a dog scratching his back the way you're wiggling around down there."

Edmund gave up on his appearance and pulled Sylvie back over on top of him. She squealed with surprise. "Edmund! I thought we were getting up?"

He buried his nose in the warm hollow behind her ear and kissed her. "You were too far away. And besides, I'm decent now." She relaxed in his embrace, and let him kiss her. She was unable to remain passive for long and began to kiss him back, her passion rising. Edmund was considering moving behind the divan where no one would be able to see them through the window when an angry, insolent voice spoke from the terrace to their right.

"Well, now, sir, that's the problem there. As soon as you let a woman on top in the bedroom, so to speak, you're under her thumb out of it, my da used to say."

Sylvie gasped and Edmund rolled, placing Sylvie beneath him, his back to the room, protecting her. "What the devil?" he cried, looking over his shoulder. A young man, built like a laborer, with a shock of dark black hair stood in the doorway of the terrace glaring at them. He felt an unaccustomed spurt of jealousy. This must be the coachman, the one who fucked Sylvie. He was attractive in a coarse, brutish way.

"Glad to see someone's been scratchin' her itch for me, Vicar," the young man drawled as he leaned in the door. "Hate to think the widow'd let our little spat keep her from filling that hot little cunt."

Sylvie whimpered beneath him and Edmund saw red. "What do you want?" he snarled as he rose to his feet, keeping Sylvie behind him.

The coachman laughed, the sound ugly. "What I'm due, of course. I serviced 'er fair and square, and deserve my due."

"You little bastard," Edmund growled, taking a menacing step toward him.

The coachman laughed again. "What you gonna do, Vicar? Nothing, that's what." He scoffed in disdain. "You gentry, so afraid of what everyone thinks. Well I can make it better, can't I? Tell 'em what you wants 'em to hear." His look turned sly and calculating. "Or I can tell 'em what I just seen. You and the sainted Lady Bartlebyrne fucking like animals in the parlor. Cost you a livin', eh, Vicar?"

"You wouldn't dare," Edmund said, his voice throbbing with anger.

"Oh, ho, that's what the lady said to me, and I did it, didn't I?" He laughed as he said it. Laughed about the horror he put Sylvie through this morning. Edmund didn't think, he just charged.

"Edmund!" Sylvie screamed, but it was too late. He would only be satisfied with the little bastard's blood.

Sylvie was horrified at John's words, at the utter shame she felt for having put Edmund in such an untenable position. Then Edmund charged without warning and she screamed. She scrambled to her feet as the two men tumbled out the door onto the terrace. When she ran out after them she saw Edmund jump to his feet and race at John, still struggling to regain his footing. Edmund grabbed the front of John's shirt and punched him in the face, the impact spinning John's head to the side. The coachman grabbed the lapels of Edmund's jacket and threw him into the wall of the terrace, and the two men wrestled, brute strength against pure unadulterated rage. They rolled along the wall once, twice and then the wall abruptly ended at the stairs. Neither man was paying attention and their momentum carried them into the empty space before they fell and rolled down the stairs still grappling.

Sylvie screamed again as she watched Edmund hit the stairs, his descent rough and frightening on the stone steps. She heard the door of the solar burst open and turned to see Jernigan race into the room, two footmen behind him.

"Jernigan!" she cried. "Help him! Help Mr. James!"

She pointed to the green in the garden just as John landed a punch on Edmund's jaw, sending him sprawling. John fell on Edmund, choking him, but Edmund grabbed his wrists and forced his hands back, bucking until John fell off.

"You can have the bloody, cold bitch," John snarled, rolling to his feet gracelessly. "She weren't much of a fuck anyway, Vicar."

"You goddamned little guttersnipe," Edmund growled, circling the wary coachman. "You'll pay for that remark, and for everything else you've done to her."

John grinned evilly. "Well I certainly wouldn't pay for that fuck."

Sylvie sobbed and retreated to the back wall of the terrace covering her face with her hand. Oh God, everyone could hear him. They knew!

"She never let you touch her," Edmund snarled and Sylvie looked up in surprise, meeting Edmund's eyes. He was lying for her. She'd never loved him more than at that moment.

"What?" John yelled. "Is that what she told you? She's lying! I fucked her but good, in the carriage on the side of the road, like she weren't no better than she ought to be. And she was bloody panting for it, I tell you."

"You lie," Edmund growled, his voice low and contemptuous. "Do you expect anyone to believe that Lady Bartlebyrne would let scum like you near her?"

John's face contorted with rage. "You were just fucking her on the floor, you bloody lying pig!"

Before he could say any more Edmund tackled him. They went down and Edmund began to brutally hit the other man, who managed to block some of the punches and throw a few of his own.

"Jernigan," a calm, deep voice said from the doorway, "fetch me a gun."

Sylvie spun around to see her son Geoffrey standing in the door positively vibrating with rage.

"Mother, are you all right?" Geoffrey asked, sparing her a glance.

Sylvie cringed at the anger in his eyes. She nodded and he turned back to the brawl in the garden.

"Stay here," Geoffrey ordered, "I don't want you hurt."

Sylvie could only watch as he marched down the steps.

The gun went off right behind Edmund and he spun around in shock. A young man stood there, the smoking pistol pointed into the air. The damned coachman took advantage of his inattention to throw him off, but before he could launch himself at Edmund again, the young man spoke.

"The next time I fire it will be at you, coachman. You are easily explained away." His voice was clipped, but Edmund could hear the sincerity in it, and the bloodied young coachman froze.

"I was protecting your mum, your Lordship," he whined. "This one over here were trying to have his way with her right there on the floor of the parlor."

"You lying dog," Edmund snarled, scrambling to his feet. He froze when the freshly loaded pistol turned in his direction.

"You would be harder to explain, Mr. James, but not impossible."

"Geoffrey," Sylvie said quietly, her voice pained. She'd rushed down to them after the gunshot. "Please. May we discuss this inside?"

John's eyes turned calculating. "That's right, Your Lordship. We wouldn't want your mother's reputation getting any more tarnished than it is, now would we?" He smiled with a smirk. "I'd be more than happy to discuss how I can make sure that doesn't happen."

"You are fired." The young marquis's voice was flat. "Collect your things and go."

John's eyes widened with shock. "Now don't be hasty, sir—"

The Marquis of Bartlebyrne cut him off coldly. "Be grateful you leave here with your life and your belongings, cur." He motioned imperiously to Jernigan. "Have two of the footmen escort him from the property." He paused a moment. "Have them escort him out of Byrnham. He is not welcome there anymore, either."

John lost all semblance of courtesy or respect. "That whore begged me for it!" he snarled, pointing at Sylvie. "And then that bloody vicar come along and took her right out from under me nose! He's been crawling in between her sheets for weeks now, and all I got was one bloody fuck!"

Edmund didn't care if he got shot for it—he dove for the coachman and punched him so hard his hand exploded with pain. "You goddamned bastard! You are speaking of my future wife!"

He heard the collective gasp of the crowd that had gathered.

"Now," Lord Bartlebyrne said, his voice a low growl, "we take it inside." He walked over and kicked the coachman where he lay on the ground moaning. "Get rid of this offal." He turned furious eyes, the same soft blue as Sylvie's, on Edmund. "Inside, Mr. James." He turned and offered his arm to Sylvie, who looked frantic and scared and still lusciously rumpled from their fuck in the solar.

Edmund didn't think—he just reacted. He walked quickly over to Sylvie and fell to his knees.

"As God as my witness, Sylvie, I love you. I love you more than I can say. Please marry me, my love." She gasped and looked frantically between Edmund and her son. Edmund grabbed her hand. "I was nothing before you, Sylvie. If you cast me aside I will be less than nothing. I will be a shell of a man. My heart will remain with you, always, forever." His frustration got the better of him, and he gestured angrily to the coachman being dragged away between two footmen, who were staring agog over their shoulders at the spectacle he was making of himself. He didn't care. "That means nothing. His lies mean nothing. I don't care about the scandal." He kissed her hand fervently, noticing absently that he left some blood behind. He closed his eyes and held the back of her hand to his pounding forehead. "I need you, Sylvie. I care nothing about age or scandal, or what should be, or gossip." He looked up into her eyes, which were swimming with tears. "I just care about you, about us. You are brave and beautiful and brilliant, and I need you, Sylvie. Please say you'll take me. Marry me, Sylvie."

The young marquis snorted inelegantly. "Well, it's about bloody damn time someone noticed. I was beginning to think all the men around here were stupid and blind."

Epilogue

Edmund gasped and arched his back, taking the jade dildo deep into his luscious, firm ass. Sylvie couldn't resist leaning down and gently nipping one taut cheek. He was so wonderful, so sensual and desirable, and hers. She couldn't believe she'd had the nerve to ask him to do this. She'd wanted to do it forever, and tonight was supposed to be about her, about her pleasure. This was immensely pleasurable.

Suddenly Donald began to cry in the nursery next door.

"Don't you dare," Edmund growled, pushing backward until he bumped her hand still holding the dildo deep inside him.

"But…"

"This is why we employ a nurse." Edmund's voice was clipped, the strain of their interrupted games showing.

"But you know Jernigan hates when he fusses at night." Sylvie worked hard to keep the amusement out of her voice. She knew the baby was fine. He'd probably just kicked his blanket off, and nurse could handle that.

"Then let bloody damn Jernigan go in there," Edmund growled, and Sylvie felt the muscles of his buttocks clench tightly on the dildo beneath the hand she had laid on one cheek.

Sylvie glided the dildo out through those tightly clenched muscles and Edmund groaned in despair. Then she plunged it back into him and he cried out. "I have no intention of leaving you wanting," Sylvie purred as she leaned over his curved back and licked a path up the bumps of his spine.

Edmund shivered. "Christ, Sylvie." He was breathless with desire and Sylvie felt a triumphant thrill at her ability to still do that to him. They had been married for well over a year already. Even through her pregnancy, which had been very hard, he'd been faithful and loving and attentive. They had been reduced to pleasuring one another with hands and mouths for nearly all of their marriage. The doctor had advised them not to have sex after a frightening incident in which they thought she'd lost the baby. The delivery had been so hard that, again, the doctor had advised they wait. Donald was four months old. Sylvie felt fit, and the doctor agreed.

Sylvie had thought that Edmund would throw her to the floor again and take her wherever they were standing as soon as she gave him the news. He'd surprised her by insisting they wait another day, and he'd planned a night of scandalous delights for her. They had had an intimate dinner for two in their suite, all Sylvie's favorites, and then licked melted chocolate off various body parts for desert. It was heaven. But when Edmund had asked her what she most wanted, it was this. He'd been surprised, but enthusiastic, as he was with most things concerning sex. She knew he used to have sex with men, he'd told her, and she was worried that he missed that aspect of his past life.

He was on his knees on their big bed, his head and shoulders pressed into the sheets, his ass high in the air for her. She was pressed up against him, her hips right up behind him, moving with him. She pulled her hips back as she pulled the dildo back, and then thrust forward with both hips and dildo. It was extraordinarily erotic, almost like actually fucking him.

Edmund moaned and Sylvie laughed throatily, rubbing her breasts along his lower back. She watched the fine hairs on his arms rise with his growing arousal. "Do you like this, Edmund?" she whispered against his back between kisses.

"God yes, Sylvie," he moaned. "You are amazingly adept at fucking a man for someone who's never done it before." He wriggled his ass a little. "A little to the left, love. God! Yes, that's good." He shuddered with pleasure as she apparently hit the spot he wanted.

"Do you like it as much as…as fucking a man?" she asked quietly. She rushed on, afraid of his answer. "I mean, I know you enjoyed that before, and I…I don't want you to feel as if you've given up something…like that, for me."

Edmund froze in place, his breathing ragged. "Is that what this is about?" he rasped. "Is that why you wanted to fuck me with the dildo tonight?" He started to pull away, groaning as the dildo slid from him. Sylvie grabbed his hip to stop him, pressing it back in deep and he shuddered, thrusting back against her involuntarily.

"No, darling, Edmund stop," she entreated him softly. "That isn't why, not really. I just…I just wanted to do it. I wanted to see you like this, I wanted to give you this pleasure, and watch you take it, as you have me."

Edmund fucked up and back, the dildo gliding in and out as he breathed deeply, a small sound of pleasure escaping from deep in his throat.

"Tell me," Sylvie whispered as she snuggled up to him again and began to fuck him with hips and dildo. "Tell me how it feels."

"It's better, Sylvie," he whispered brokenly, "better than fucking a man, because you're doing it. I'd rather have this dildo with your hand guiding it than any cock, I don't care whose."

"Edmund," Sylvie breathed, overcome with tenderness at his confession. "I love doing this to you. I've dreamt about it, about watching you, listening to you, pleasuring you in such a decadent fashion." She leaned over and licked a patch on his lower back that was glistening with sweat. It was salty and she savored the taste of him. She glided the dildo in and out, varying the depth and speed of her thrusts, keeping Edmund on the cusp of his release, toying with him, and he moaned with pleasure. The muscles of his back and buttocks quivered with tension as he anticipated each new penetration.

Sylvie basked in her control over him, knowing his pleasure waited on her whim. It was a heady experience, and one she planned to enjoy often now that they'd crossed this line together. Never before she met Edmund could Sylvie have imagined doing the things she and he did. Every time he touched her she craved the basest desires, and he fulfilled them gladly. She realized that she had been an empty vessel waiting to be filled, and Edmund had come and poured passion and desire into her until she overflowed.

Suddenly Edmund pulled away roughly, the dildo sliding out of his ass. He groaned as it popped free, and Sylvie was mesmerized by his open, red, glistening entrance, crying out for her to fill it again. She reached for him, but Edmund stopped her.

"No, Sylvie. We are going to fuck each other now. I need you. I need my cock in your sweet pussy when I come. It's been so long, love."

Edmund watched Sylvie move as if in a trance, lying down on the bed and spreading her legs for him. She still held the dildo, shining with the lubricant they'd applied, and a shiver chased up his spine. It had felt so good to have her fuck his ass. Never had it felt that good before. Knowing his sweet Sylvie was wielding the instrument of his pleasure was so arousing that when she'd first penetrated him he'd almost come on the spot. Listening to her moans of pleasure as she humped against his buttocks with each thrust had pushed him closer to the edge than he'd ever been without falling off. Only sheer willpower had let him last this long.

He moved between her legs and reached down, spreading the lips of her pussy delicately with his thumbs. She was wet and hot, swollen with need, her ruffled inner lips red with arousal. She was as close as he from fucking him. He closed his eyes against the surge of lust that went through him.

On their next trip to London he was buying a two-sided dildo, so Sylvie could fuck herself and him at the same time. God, she was going to love it. He smiled at her wolfishly.

"Was there ever a man as lucky as I, wife? To have a woman who nearly comes from fucking him in the ass?"

Sylvie's face, flushed with passion, got redder as she blushed. "I liked it," she said softly, the understatement making Edmund laugh outright.

He nodded, still chuckling. "Yes, I noticed."

Sylvie smiled shyly at him and opened her arms, beckoning him. He lowered himself onto her, their hips meeting first, his cock stretched up along her wet slit, her juices coating him in seconds. He closed his eyes with a gasp. It felt so fucking, bloody good. "Sylvie," he moaned, unsure if she was ready for him. After so many months of abstinence, he didn't want to hurt her.

"Fuck me, Edmund," she whispered, surging against him, "now."

He needed no further encouragement. He raised his hips and slipped a hand between them to position his cock, and then he slid smoothly inside her. It was clear immediately that she was tight, as tight as the first time he'd fucked her on the floor of her solar. He had to fight for every inch he pushed inside her, and Sylvie arched her back and moaned as he did it.

"Yes, Edmund, yes, darling," she panted, "more. Give it all to me."

Her words sent a fire through his blood and he rammed home, hilting his cock, snug in her smoldering heat and drowning wetness. She felt so amazing, gloving every inch of his thick, hard cock like wet silk. Sylvie cried out softly as he seated himself deep within her with three or four short, hard strokes, until his balls rested against her upturned ass. He could barely draw breath, the tightness of her strangling him.

"Fuck, Sylvie, fuck," he moaned, unable to put a coherent thought together.

Sylvie laughed breathlessly, her hands coming up to rest on his waist. She still held the dildo, its slippery length against him, and he knew what he wanted.

"Fuck me again, Sylvie," he panted, pulling out and sliding forcefully back into her depths with a shudder that she matched. "Fuck me while I fuck you." He pulled his knees up a little, clasping an arm around her waist and raising her with him. She reached down and blindly ran the dildo down his crack, trying to find his entrance. Edmund groaned. "Down a little more, just a little." Then she hit the mark and thrust it home, the burn of the dildo's quick, hard penetration making Edmund see stars.

He became aware again as Sylvie let out a strangled scream. He was fucking her hard and deep, his cock pistoning in and out as she just held on, held the dildo inside him and let his own motions move it in and out. Her legs were wrapped around his thighs, and his ass was clenching the dildo tight, each thrust of his hips driving the dildo in, and then driving his cock into Sylvie. It was one of the most amazing rides he'd ever had.

"Christ yes, Sylvie," he panted, fucking her and the dildo ruthlessly. "God, it feels so good, don't let go, Sylvie, don't let go." He wasn't sure if he meant of him or the dildo, and didn't care. Neither one was acceptable right at the moment.

Sylvie moaned and he looked down to see her eyes closed as she bit her lip to keep her screams inside, pushing her sweet cunt against him, rubbing her clitoris on him with each thrust. God, she could fuck. He felt his balls pull up. No! It was too soon, too soon! But even as he despaired he rode the wave of anticipation and pleasure, his skin quivering with tension, every muscle taut with his impending orgasm.

"I've got to come, Sylvie, God," he gasped, and Sylvie thrust the dildo deep in his ass and his world exploded around him. He felt the intoxicating burn of his semen as it raced up and out of his cock into Sylvie's waiting, shivering depths and she froze for a moment and then flew apart in his arms, crying his name. They thrust against one another desperately, each holding the other deep, Edmund's cock jerking inside her at the same time his ass clenched tight on the dildo and the dual sensations rocked him to his core. He cried her name, hung his head as the waves of pleasure rode him. Sylvie gasped and trembled beneath him, holding him tightly, her hand still pressing the dildo deep, not forgetting his pleasure in the maelstrom of her own.

When it was over, when he could think and breathe again, he looked down at Sylvie. She was panting, her cheeks flushed a deep, rosy pink, her eyes sparkling as she grinned at him. "Am I the only one seeing stars?" she asked with breathless wonder. Edmund started to laugh, but it turned into a groan as Sylvie pulled the dildo out of his thoroughly fucked ass. She started to laugh until he did the same to her, pulling his cock out of her well-pleasured pussy.

They groaned together as Edmund fell to the bed beside Sylvie. He reached a trembling hand out and took the dildo, tossing it to the end of the bed. They'd deal with that later. He didn't think he could walk right now — perhaps not for a week, actually. Sylvie rolled over and snuggled up to him, her head on his shoulder and an arm and a leg draped possessively over him.

"Oh, Edmund," she sighed, "I'm so glad I found you."

Edmund looked down at her and raised an eyebrow in mock surprise. "Really? Well, Madame James, it certainly took you long enough to realize it."

Sylvie just smiled dreamily and rubbed a hand over his chest, grazing his nipples, still very sensitive, as she smoothed round and round. Edmund arched his neck, the pleasure almost painful. But then, that's how he liked it sometimes. With an ass aching from a good fuck, and a cock still leaking both his and her juice, he was a man well-contented.

Sylvie spoke softly, and he instinctively tightened his hold on her. "I was waiting, Edmund, my whole life for you, but when you showed up, you weren't what I'd been waiting for."

He smiled and kissed the top of her head tenderly, her unbound hair soft against his lips. "What? You weren't waiting for a lascivious, charming vicar? Why ever not?"

Sylvie's laugh was a soft breath against his chest, making him shiver.

Edmund turned on his side so Sylvie's head rested on his arm, her face turned up to his. He leaned down and kissed her, at first tenderly, but as usual with Sylvie, the kiss turned hot and hungry within moments. He would never tire of the taste of her, sweet and dangerously alluring, and all Sylvie. He hummed deep in his chest in approval and felt Sylvie smile against his lips as her tongue gave his a last flick and she sucked his lower lip into her mouth, letting go with a pop.

Edmund rested his forehead against hers, his breathing once again shallow. "What did you mean, my love, that I wasn't what you were waiting for?"

Sylvie pressed her entire length against him, wriggling her hips until they were tucked into his as her lips tucked into the curve of his neck. "I thought that when I married again, it would be to an older gentleman. One who was kind and settled in his ways, and my life would go on much as it had before. And then I would die."

"What?" Edmund exclaimed, pulling his head back to stare at Sylvie in astonishment.

Sylvie sighed. "I thought I was old, Edmund, and getting older. I know I felt old beyond my years. When you first came I thought my desire for you was sinful, that of a lecherous old woman for a beautiful young man, so full of life and vigor." She paused and licked her lips and she traced a teasing circle around his nipple, watching it pucker for her. "But before long, I felt young and vital and alive, and so full of passion. In your eyes I saw what you saw, a beautiful woman discovering her passion with you, for you. You made me young and beautiful again, Edmund." She shook her head. "No, not again—for the first time. I married an old man, too young." She looked up at him with eyes shining with tears. "I loved Christopher, but not like this. As his companion, I grew old with him. I never had a chance to be young and in love." She kissed him softly and slowly, a promise of the desire he could see burning in her eyes. "Thank you, my love, for being the young man I was waiting for."

At her words Edmund couldn't leave his lady waiting anymore. He showed her again and again how very much this young man loved her in return.

The End

IMPULSIVE PLEASURES
KyAnn Waters

യ

Trademarks Acknowledgement

Chapter One

ഇ

"Your father is an asshole."

"Mother, promise me you'll behave."

Jamie Cooper-Howe rolled her eyes and released an exasperated sigh. "Why is it you call me 'Mother', and your father 'Daddy'? Do you love him more?"

Ashley let out a snort and Jamie chuckled. The sound contrasted with her daughter's image of grace and beauty. Auburn hair was swept into a stylish twist while a hint of peach blush colored her cheeks and mascara accented her almond-shaped, hazel eyes. Along with a smooth and flawless complexion, Ashley was the spitting image of her mother. However, Jamie conceded, her daughter lacked laugh lines at the corners of her eyes. Okay, damn it, maybe they were wrinkles. But anyone who had put up with her ex-husband's bullshit was entitled to a few.

"I don't see how you can even socialize with him after what he's done to our family," Jamie continued.

"Mother, the divorce is over. Daddy has remarried. You have to let it go."

"I have let it go." Inhale, exhale, she calmed her agitated heart rate. Thoughts of her ex could still wreck a wonderful day. It wasn't the loss of a great love, but the betrayal. "I don't suppose he's leaving his breeding trollop at home."

Ashley wrapped her arms around her mother's shoulders. Jamie softened in the comforting warmth. She really didn't blame her daughter for remaining close to her father. Just because he'd fucked Jamie over when he started fucking his little secretary didn't mean her daughter had to bear the burden. Craig Howe had walked out of the marriage, not fatherhood. No, in fact, his little *slut*—Ashley remained determined to like her, but Jamie didn't have to—was expecting her first bundle of joy in a few weeks. Craig once again proved his virility. *Asshole*. His prowess in bed happened to be the only thing Jamie really missed. And even she could admit their sex life had become perfunctory.

A woman entered her prime in her forties. Sex was great, but a vibrator just didn't do the trick. However, neither did the men her age. Maybe she expected too much. Was wanting a man who took care of himself wrong? She wasn't looking for marriage ever again. That didn't mean she wanted to be alone…or lonely.

She sighed, smoothing her hands over her formfitting skirt. She kept in shape. Perhaps not everything was where it once was, but her breasts looked fabulous.

"Just be civil." Ashley kissed her cheek and stepped away. "It's my wedding and I want both my parents in attendance."

"I can be nice." She turned to her only child. Her baby was getting married. Tonight the rehearsal would be followed by a nice dinner at Bella's.

Jamie would have preferred Ashley pick a different location. There were too many memories tied to the expensive Italian restaurant. As a family, they had spent anniversaries, birthdays, and simple celebrations at Craig's favorite place. Because that's where Ashley wanted her rehearsal dinner, Craig offered to pick up the tab. Good, he could afford to spend the money. Amazing, considering she'd extracted a tidy sum in the divorce along with alimony for the next ten years.

"Why the smile, Mother?"

"Just thrilled my baby is marrying the man of her dreams. I really like Wes, sweetheart. You found one of the good ones."

"I just hope Wes' best friend makes it. Mark's flight should've gotten in hours ago. What point is a rehearsal if the best man isn't there?"

"Nothing will go wrong. I'm sure Mark what's-his-name," she waved her hand, "will be here any minute. He does know where the church is, doesn't he?" Stretching her fingers, she checked her Mystic Mauve nail polish for chips. The color complemented the two-carat sapphire she'd purchased eighteen months ago to replace the diamond she'd worn for twenty-two years.

"Mark Bentley. And yes, he knows. He grew up around here. He and Wes have been best friends since high school." She glanced at her watch. "We're fifteen minutes late."

"We have the church rented until tomorrow. Stop worrying." Jamie fluffed her hair and checked her image in the mirror. "Just think, tomorrow you'll stand here in your wedding dress." They stood in the bridal room in the same church where Jamie and Craig had married.

"Yeah, I know why you'll be happy. You'll finally have the house to yourself."

Jamie fought the urge to cry.

* * * * *

Mark Bentley checked his watch again as the plane taxied down the runway. Next time, he'd charter a flight. Not that there would be an occasion such as this again. A man hoped he only married once. Mark didn't plan to take the plunge—ever.

He grabbed his carryon and went to get the rental car. Fifteen minutes later, he was speeding twenty miles over the limit trying to make up time.

He glanced at the dashboard clock when he pulled into the parking lot of the church. He'd done fairly well not getting there too late considering he'd had to fly a thousand miles.

"Mark!" Wes waved from the bottom step of the church.

"Sorry. The flight was delayed." It had been a few years since they'd seen each other. Wes looked great. Same college boy good looks, blond hair, clean-shaven, he looked like an accountant. Seemed appropriate considering in college he majored in business right along with Mark. The similarities ended there. Wes got a job and started his climb up the corporate ladder whereas Mark, always the risk taker, had launched his own architectural landscape business. "Ashley must be good for you." Mark slapped him on the back in a friendly guy hug.

Wes laughed. "Very good for me."

"So you've said." He smiled. "No worries, brother. She'll never know how much I've heard. I can't wait to meet her."

"Come on. She's in the church."

Mark followed Wes. About twenty people milled about, some gathered near the minister. He glanced around wondering which young woman was the bride. Perhaps he'd entertain himself over the weekend with a bridesmaid. He hadn't slept with a woman in seven months and his dick was restless. An out-of-town, hotter than hell affair was just the kind of distraction he needed. Something temporary. Wes was getting a bride. Mark just wanted to get laid.

"There she is, with her mother, Jamie."

"That's her *mother*?" Mark raised an eyebrow. Ashley's mother was hot. However, married chicks didn't turn him on. Too bad his cock didn't agree.

Ashley and Jamie approached them. Wes put a hand around Ashley's waist and made introductions. "This is my future bride and her mother, Jamie."

Mark leaned in and gave Ashley a kiss on each cheek. "Wes is a lucky man." He turned to the mother. *And so was Ashley's father.* Mark took her hand, finding the skin soft under his fingertips. Instead of a handshake, he took a step closer and placed a kiss on her knuckles. "A pleasure."

"I told you. Mark's a charmer." Wes chuckled.

"Charmed by gorgeous women. I can see where Ashley gets her beauty." More than beauty, Jamie smelled like a woman. A subtle hint of perfume tickled his nose and her hair made him think of a chilly, fall evening. Smooth and shiny, it reflected the red and gold highlights of late afternoon sun coming through the stained-glass windows.

Their eyes locked when he stepped back. Fire blazed into his crotch. Moss-green edged with copper, her eyes held mystery. Her smile, however, hinted at mischief. He imagined those full pink lips, the color the same as a woman's inner folds, wrapped around his cock. He nearly groaned aloud. Damn, but it had been too long since lust had punched him in the gut.

"Mother, Daddy is here."

Jamie spun around. "And look, the little tart wore white."

"You promised."

"And I'm trying. Give me a little credit, Ashley. I'd like to run him over with my car in a dark alley. All I can legally do is give him the evil eye. Don't worry. I'm going to smile while I do."

"Here they come," Wes said. "You're enchanting when you smile, Jamie."

Jamie rolled her eyes. "Wes, I've been fed enough of that crap from Craig. You can say it. I'm being a bitch. I'm entitled."

Mark bit his tongue to keep from chuckling. Jamie's hip jutted forward in a defiant stance. She tucked her hair behind her ear, finger pausing to tickle a gold earring, and then briefly made eye contact with Mark again.

"I'm going to step away. I promised and I just don't think I can be nice." She gave Ashley a pleading look. "I'll be civil, but I can't pretend."

Mark noticed the provocative sway of her hips and the tantalizing curve of her heart-shaped ass as she walked away. When it was time to say hello to Ashley's father, he had to swallow twice. "Nice to meet you." He turned to Wes. "If you'll excuse me for a moment."

He hurried off in the direction Jamie disappeared, coming to a long hallway with a few doors down both sides. One door was open. He stepped into the room. Jamie stood at the window with her legs slightly parted, looking out to the parking lot. She had her back to him. Sunshine outlined her trim figure and revealed the slenderness of her thighs through the thin material of her skirt.

Mark closed the door. "Are you okay?"

Her shoulders stiffened. "He's an asshole." She turned around. "It isn't as if I'm still in love with Craig. I despise the way he looks at me. I don't need his pity." She put her hand on her forehead and turned back to the window. "I am so sorry. I shouldn't be saying this to you...or anyone else. Tomorrow is Ashley's wedding. I can do this. I will be nice. I will do this for Ashley."

"Is that your mantra?"

"Yes." She laughed. "But it's so much more fun to be nasty. How did I ever manage marriage to that pompous jerk for twenty-two years?"

Mark strolled across the room unsure of his motivation except that he wanted to see if he'd read the earlier sparkle in her eye correctly.

"Then you're divorced?"

Her breath hitched. Mark stood behind her. Warm breath fanned against her cheek. Gooseflesh crawled along her sensitized skin. Flutters filled her stomach. Jeezus, the best man was making her hot. Already wetness seeping from her pussy drenched her panties.

Jamie looked up into Mark's face. He stood well over six feet, with broad shoulders encased in a damn sexy, tailored, olive-toned suit. Contradicting the businessman was the youthful image he presented with a pencil line of hair along his jaw, a tight moustache, and thin strip of trimmed goatee. Dark wavy hair hung just below his shoulders. Thick brows framed heavy-lashed, chocolate eyes. His smile widened and revealed straight, white teeth.

Heat from his body radiated out to her, melting her core. She shifted from one foot to the other, nervous under the intensity of his gaze. The movement only caused her sticky panties to nudge against her clit. He muddled her mind.

"Your ex-husband is blind and stupid if he didn't appreciate what he had in a wife."

"I can't argue with his stupidity." She trembled on an exhale.

His fingers pushed her hair behind her ear, grazing her cheek as he pulled away. His touch sent ripples of awareness over her skin.

"God, you're beautiful."

She didn't know what to say. His statement stunned her. "They're probably... I mean, we should go back. The rehearsal is starting."

Jamie straightened and his hand blazed through her clothing where it rested against her lower back. She gave him a questioning look. Good hell, if she didn't know better, she might get the wrong impression that he was hitting on her. The best man. The best friend of her future *son-in-law*.

"Mark," she said, walking down the hall trying not to appear as though she was fleeing from his electrifying touch. "What exactly is going on here?" Glancing up at him, she narrowed her eyes.

"I'm going to help you turn the tables on your ex-husband." He put a hand on her arm and stopped her retreat. The pressure of his fingers changed and became a caress. "I rather enjoyed the way you looked at me when we were introduced. I could've sworn you were interested."

Mark backed her against the wall.

"Someone is going to see." She put her hands against his chest to push him away, but the moment she made contact with his silk shirt covering the chiseled muscles beneath, her shove turned into an exploration. Her thumbs brushed against his hardened nips and he sucked in a breath. She flooded with desire to rip his shirt from his body, throw him to the floor and satisfy the too-long denied fire in the center of her being. He even smelled like sex. Musky and spicy, totally male.

"That's the look."

Her nipples tightened to aching points beneath the sheer lace of her bra when his chest brushed against her. He leaned in, his breath heating her neck.

"Don't." She closed her eyes knowing his full lips were about to wreak havoc on her senses. Slipping out from between Mark and the wall gave her much needed distance. Blood pumped into her sex. Her pussy pulsed in tempo with the beat of her heart. She ran her fingers through her bangs, combing them out of her eyes, and then smoothed her skirt. There was nothing she could do about the breathlessness of her voice or the pounding in her chest. However, she could project outward calm. "This isn't happening. I could be your mother."

"No, you couldn't." His eyes glazed as he caressed her with a glance. "I'd never want to fuck my mother."

Chapter Two

❧

Jamie returned to the group, aware that Mark walked behind her. She looked over her shoulder. His lips turned up slightly at the corners. Yep, he was checking out her ass. She quickened her pace.

"Are you okay?"

Jamie took a tissue from Ashley. "I'm fine. Is it warm in here?"

"You do look a little flushed."

Jamie patted her forehead with the tissue. Oh, more than flushed, she was hot. The best offer she'd had in two years came from a man nearly half her age. And damn if she didn't want to blow off the rehearsal, maybe blow him, and definitely let him have his way with her.

Mark would be naughty. She'd had two affairs since her divorce and both had left her unsatisfied. Instinct told her Mark wouldn't let her walk away without an orgasm.

She smiled at Ashley and then headed for the minister. "Are we ready to begin?"

Jamie wished she wasn't so aware of Mark. No matter where he stood during the rehearsal, she could feel his gaze upon her. Excitement coursed through her. Would he follow her out of the room if she gave him another opportunity? Was she brave enough to try? She chose that moment to glance in his direction.

Mark winked. With a deep, steadying breath, she angled her body toward him and met his stare. A smile played on his lips. Energy buzzed between them and collected in the places she wanted his hands. Jamie barely heard the minister telling her where to stand. Dragging her eyes away from Mark, she focused on the instructions.

Even while she listened to Ashley and the minister discuss the positioning of people, she watched Mark maneuver around the room until he stood directly behind her.

"You aren't following directions."

He stepped in closer. The scent of his aftershave reminded her of their brief encounter in the hall. "If you're looking for someone who follows orders," he lowered his voice, "tell me what you want."

She turned around, facing him. Eyes striking in intensity caused her to lose her train of thought. "I think you're a naughty little boy who wants to play games—"

"Not games, but I would like to play with you."

"Tsk, tsk. You only just met me. What if I have sharp claws and a nasty disposition? Remember, I'm a woman scorned."

"Every time I look at you, I hope to God you're nasty. Claws I can handle as long as you scratch where no one else can see." He pinned her with a look. Barely able to breathe, she couldn't speak. "Spend the weekend with me."

Jamie laughed nervously. "You're young and good-looking. Don't you have someone at home expecting to hear from you?"

"This conversation wouldn't be happening if I did."

Jamie glanced around, afraid she and Mark were drawing attention. They'd captured Craig's curiosity. He openly stared at them from across the room. She meshed her lips together, refreshing her lipstick.

"We are spending the weekend together. We'll see each other tomorrow for the wedding."

"So the cougar is actually a kitten." Mark boldly put his hand on her hip and leaned in close. Soft and silky, wisps of his hair brushed her cheek. "Either way, I'm going to make your pussy purr."

Dirty talk in the church. She felt faint…and hot as hell. "You certainly have a way with words."

"There is plenty I'd like to whisper in your ear."

Damn, he was dangerous. And far too handsome to be interested in the mother of the bride.

A half hour later, the wedding party had gone through the motions and everyone knew the order in which to come down the aisle and where they were to stand during the ceremony.

"If we're done here, let's head over to the restaurant." Craig pulled his new wife close. "The mamma-to-be is getting hungry."

Jamie rolled her eyes.

"Well, the bride-to-be is hungry too," Ashley said. "Let's go."

Once in the parking lot, Wes asked, "Who's riding with whom?"

"You look hungry, Jamie." Mark put his hand on her back, gently propelling her to his rental car. "Ride with me."

"Ashley." Jamie waved to get her daughter's attention. "We'll meet you there. I'll show Mark the way." Butterflies fluttered in her stomach and heat radiated from between her thighs. Her panties were sticky with cream and she suspected Mark knew exactly what he was doing to her.

He opened the passenger door. "Get in."

"I thought you wanted to take orders, not give them."

He framed her in the open door with his arms. "Is it too soon to kiss you?"

Blood pumped hot and fast through her veins. A moment passed where she simply stared at him. The parking lot emptied of cars. "Someone will see. We've just met. It's fun to tease, but I don't want to give you the wrong impression."

Mark eased back and swept her body with his eyes. "Don't lie to me, Jamie. Do you know what they call what we've been doing since I walked into the church?"

She licked her dry lips. "What?"

"Foreplay." His mouth crashed into hers. Wrapping an arm around her waist, he pulled her close and crushed his hips against hers. He pulled away, breathing fast. "I've been hard for an hour."

Thoughts froze in her brain. She moaned, leaning her head against the edge of the open doorframe. Mark's tongue flicked her earlobe before gently nibbling, and then sucking it into his mouth. A string from her clit to her nipples tightened. She spread her legs as wide as her skirt would allow, nestling the full, thick, length of his cock in the V of her sex. A gush of fluid warmed her thigh. She was wet and ready to be fucked...in a parking lot.

The more she denied the attraction, the stronger it became. "As much as I'm enjoying your talented tongue..." his mouth opened over the sensitive skin where her neck met her shoulder. "This isn't the appropriate place for foreplay. Mark, we're in the church parking lot. Not to mention, Ashley and Wes expect us at the restaurant. Ohhh." His hand cupped her breast, stimulating the cherried nipple with his thumb.

"We'll get there...eventually."

Sliding his hands over her hips, he shimmied her skirt up her legs, revealing thigh-high stockings. Mark whistled, lifting the skirt to her waist. Panic weaved intimately with arousal. Her eyes darted around the vacant parking lot.

His palm cupped her mons. "Please get into the vehicle, Jamie."

She started to pull her skirt down.

"Uh uh. Leave it."

Jamie sat on the seat and scooted back. With Mark filling the space of the doorway, she wasn't visible within the darkened interior of the Escalade. Tinted windows blocked the sun.

"Spread your legs."

Pulling her bottom lip between her teeth, she did as he asked.

"Damn, you're wet."

Desire coiled, tightened, and threatened to snap. He clearly wanted to fuck her and she seriously contemplated letting him. They had just met, only her craving wouldn't let go. It held firmly, causing reckless thoughts. She crinkled her brows. Maybe she was suffering some type of midlife crisis because her baby was getting married. "Mark, we need to go."

"We need to come." He swung her legs into the car and slammed the door. Walking around the front of the vehicle, he then climbed behind the wheel. With a quick tug, he lowered the zipper of his slacks and his fist wrapped around the base of nine inches of skin stretching over a thick, steel bar.

Jamie stared at the enormous, mushroom-shaped head. Swallowing excess saliva, she watched his hand stroke the thick shaft, her breaths taking the same rhythm. He was too tempting. Offered such an enticing fare, she couldn't resist a taste.

Bending over his lap, she braced her hands on his strong thighs and put her mouth over the smooth, heated, velvet head.

Mark groaned his pleasure when her tongue swirled around the slit and traced the hard ridge of the crown. Pulling back, she lapped a bead of pearly pre-come from the tip. She hummed her enjoyment.

Mark lifted Jamie's hair. She turned her head, glanced into his face, and smiled. Then she parted her lips and took him fully into her mouth.

Mark hissed. "You're incredible."

Knowing he watched intensified her pleasure. She sucked and licked, pressing her tongue to the pulsing vein running down the underside of his shaft. As much as she liked giving him a blowjob, her body screamed for his touch. "Mark, you started this. Finish me, now."

"Sit back."

Jamie did. Mark reached between her legs and yanked her panties down. The elastic stung her skin when it snapped. Before she could catch her breath, he plunged two long, thick fingers deep into her dripping pussy. Flicking back and forth, he zeroed in on her G-spot. Uncontrollable pleasure flowed through her. Grabbing his wrist, she bucked against his hand, reaching for the prize of a powerful mind-numbing orgasm. And oh my, she was almost there.

"Kiss me," he whispered, continuing to finger-fuck her.

She leaned forward to reclaim his lips. His mouth moved over hers, devouring her softness with his firm lips. Shivers of erotic promises filled her mind when his tongue demanded entrance. Blood pounded in her brain with the same intensity as it beat in her core. In between, his tongue whirled with hers with erotic promise. Barely able to catch her breath, she submitted to the savagery of his reckless, fiery, possession. Her body tightened and her pussy clenched. Tremors built like a cresting wave waiting to crash against the rocky shore.

He nipped her lips. "You're coming, sweetheart. I can feel it." He slammed his fingers hard and deep into her moist, warm center. Twisting and turning. In and out.

"Oh...oh...oh!" He swallowed the rest of her indiscernible cries with another masterful kiss.

When the spasms ebbed, Mark pulled his fingers from her body, put them in his mouth, and sucked. Never had a man made her stomach quiver with such blatant sexual need. Whatever secret charm he used, he made her ignore the cynical inner voice cutting into her thoughts. She pushed aside the little whispers in her head reminding her of her age and his. Right now she was a woman and this man had her rapt attention. She wasn't too old to enjoy their encounter. Her heart pounded and her heated blood raced through her veins. She liked the feeling and wanted more. Maybe she was acting like a slut. Damn it, having Mark find her desirable felt incredible and so did his hands, mouth, and words.

Turning on the seat, he forced Jamie to scoot over until her back leaned against the passenger door. "How about another one?"

"I'll take whatever you want to give me." She spread her thighs wide while he penetrated her soul with his stare. One leg hooked over the seat and the other braced against the dash.

The heavy scent of her arousal hung in the confined space. Mark's nostrils flared. "You're so beautiful."

It wasn't as if she expected oral sex at the rehearsal of her daughter's wedding. Unexpected pleasures in the front seat of rental cars with gorgeous men not much more than half her age just didn't happen to her. She didn't have a clue why Mark had her panties off. And she wouldn't care. He obviously wanted her.

Jamie was glad she'd had a bikini wax when he bent his head and kissed the soft strip of hair covering her outer lips. Whiskers from his jaw tickled her inner thigh. She tunneled her fingers into his wavy hair and urged him closer to the rekindled ache centered between her legs. Anticipating his tongue, she sucked in her breath.

"Mark, I don't want to imply you don't know what you're doing, because it's clear you know exactly what to do. I'm on fire and I need more."

Using two fingers, she parted her curls and opened her pussy, exposing her clit. Mark accepted the invitation and burrowed his face between her legs.

"Sweet," he said, then licked the length of her pussy.

"Oh yes!" Straining her muscles, she lifted her ass off the seat. His tongue darted in and out. Then he sucked feverishly on her clit. "Right there." Flicking fast, he honed in on the sensitive bundle of nerves. Then using his lips and tongue, he explored and tasted her inner folds. "Oh Mark, make me come again."

"Yes, ma'am."

"Oh please, don't call me ma'am." She laughed. The last thing she wanted was a reminder of their age difference.

Mark grasped his cock in his hand. While he ate her, he stroked his shaft. The faster his hand slid up and down, the faster his tongue. Her thighs trembled. Tension built.

"Mark!" she cried, grabbing hair in her fists, her head thrashing against the window. Internal muscle spasms caused her to rock against his mouth. She heard him chuckle and realized she was pulling the hair knotted in her fingers, grinding her mound into his face.

"Shit. I'm going to come all over the seats." Mark sat back and continued to pump his cock with long, sure strokes.

Jamie giggled. "Stop." Lifting her leg from the seatback, she twisted until her ass faced the passenger window. On her knees, she leaned forward, pushed his hand out of the way, and swallowed his cock. His fingers furrowed into her hair, cupped the back of her head, and helped to set the rhythm. As she sucked hard, she could feel the increase of tension in his body. His chest expanded, pushing her shoulder against the steering wheel.

Swirling her tongue, moving her lips up and down, she felt his cock stretch, readying to ejaculate. His legs straightened, pushing his feet into the floorboards while his balls drew in tight.

He moaned. "Jamie, I'm coming." She took him deep as he thrust his hips. Every muscle tensed including his hands, which now fisted at his sides. Powerful spasms jerked his cock. Warm, salty come shot into her mouth. Savoring the taste, she swallowed, reveling in the sensation of his seed sliding down the back of her throat. Pulling her mouth to the tip, she licked the head clean.

"Damn, you are amazing. I'm lightheaded." He tucked himself back into his pants and zipped the fly.

Jamie sat up and found her purse on the floor. She pulled a tissue from the front pocket and wiped the corners of her mouth. Flipping down the visor, she used the mirror to freshen her lipstick and fluff her hair back into some semblance of style. "I hope you can drive fast too." She winked. He sure as hell knew how to get a woman to drop her panties and give him a blowjob in record speed. "We are going to be so late." She glanced in his direction, unwilling to hide her smile. Pleasure etched across his lips as well.

"Are you still hungry?"

She smirked. "Actually, I am. I've gone a long time without a meal."

"A happy meal." He chuckled.

"Mmmm. Very."

"Perhaps what you need is an all you can eat buffet."

"As appetizing as that sounds, I think I'll have to take a rain check."

"Then you aren't opposed to hooking up later?"

She was too old to *hook up*. Tempting as the fare was, she needed to put some perspective on what just happened. They caught themselves in a provocative game of cat and mouse that inevitably ended in mutual satisfaction. "Listen Mark, you have been an unexpected delight. But after the dinner, Wes and the guys are probably going to the titty bar. I'm sure the groom expects the best man to go. Ashley will be with her bridesmaids. And I will finally get a quiet night at home."

"Excuses." He looked both ways and pulled into traffic. "Do you know any shortcuts to the restaurant? Because you're right." He smiled at her. "We are going to be late."

"Take the next left. We'll tell them I got us lost. I'm old. People get forgetful with age."

Mark laughed. "They also become incredibly hot, passionate women. I want to spend the night with you, Jamie. Why don't you invite me over?"

She gave a snort. "Oh, you don't really think I'll want to get naked and dirty after you've been drooling over strippers at the bachelor party? No, that is not going to happen. Next right."

"I fly home the day after tomorrow. I'm not asking for anything more than a couple of days to enjoy each other's company."

She let her head fall back against the seat and closed her eyes. "You have no idea how tempting your offer is."

Chapter Three

ℬ

Mark leaned back in his chair and draped his arm across the back of Jamie's. He and Jamie had caused a few heads to turn when they strolled through the restaurant doors. Flustered, Jamie had done a convincing job of explaining their delay. Now she sat next to him folding and unfolding the napkin in her lap.

"I can't believe they waited to order. Now I feel guilty."

He picked up his water glass and took a long swallow. "Think of it as a guilty pleasure." He sat forward. His arm stayed on the back of her chair, but his other hand went to her thigh. "Like a decadent dessert. You can have it once in a while so long as you don't overindulge." He leaned closer.

"Mark," she said on a breath. "You're drawing attention to us."

"Invite me to stay at your place, Jamie."

"Sort of like a binge over the weekend?"

With every quick retort from her luscious lips, he doubted a weekend would be long enough to learn about this fiercely independent, divorced woman. Craig was a schmuck for not recognizing the passion in Jamie. Mark doubted she realized just how wild sex could be. He wanted to be the one to show her.

He could only assume her age, because he was sure she hadn't given birth at age ten. Considering Ashley's age, he guessed Jamie had to be in her early forties. What might appear to be a few years between him and Jamie was more likely fifteen. He didn't care. Cougar clubs were nothing new to him. He'd never gone himself, but he suddenly understood the fascination to older women. Some of the guys he worked with patronized establishments that catered to older women and younger men. He'd love to ditch the bachelor party tonight in order to plan a party for two with Jamie.

"You're not eating, Mark. Is there anything wrong with your dinner?"

Mark smiled at Ashley. "I'm not that hungry. I ate before I came."

Jamie turned her head to look at him and he met her stare. He raised an eyebrow and mouthed, *literally*.

Jamie started to choke beside him. "If you'll excuse me." She pushed back from the table. As a gentleman would, Mark stood and helped her with her chair. "Stay here," she whispered and hurried from the dining room.

"So Mark, I hope you're going to keep my groom from getting into any trouble tonight."

"Aw, baby, you don't want to give Mark that responsibility." Wes kissed Ashley.

"I'll make sure he's on his best behavior." Mark sipped his water, forming a plan. He wanted both Jamie and to fulfill his best man responsibilities. Mark was willing to work to have his way. Often all it required was subtle negotiation. "I went to the church straight from the airport. I need to check into a hotel and clean up before we head out. What time were you thinking about going?"

"Where are you staying?" Ashley asked.

Actually, he had a room at the downtown Hilton. He had the money to stay anywhere, except the one place he wanted to be—Jamie's bed and breakfast. "Downtown."

"Well, that's ridiculous. Stay somewhere close." Ashley punched Wes in the shoulder. "You should have him stay with you. He's your best friend."

"I offered," Wes said with a smile, rubbing his arm.

"You have enough to worry about without having to entertain your old buddy."

"My best man."

"Either way, I know you've got family in town." Mark glanced around the room. The wedding party was all seated in a sectioned-off part of the restaurant. Although they weren't all at the same table, the chatter and laughter revealed everyone having a good meal and conversation. Finally his gaze rested on Craig. Craig seemed to be the only one not smiling. They stared at each other for a brief moment. Then Craig excused himself and left the table.

Jamie washed her hands in the bathroom and calmed her rampant heartbeat. She'd worried everyone in the room was focused on her and Mark. Was she wearing the telltale sign of an O glow? She glanced in the mirror. Of course everyone would wonder. She had the look of a woman ravaged. Her cheeks were pink and her lips were red both from Mark's kisses and from biting into them while she'd sucked his cock. Her tummy swooped and her pulse spiked again. Their encounter had been incredible. And Mark wanted more.

She tucked her hair behind her ears. Standing back from the mirror she checked her clothing. Any outward signs now couldn't be helped. Her skirt was wrinkled and her panties were gone. A delicious ache still pulsed between her legs. She sniffed the air. "Oh hell." She smelled like sex.

Getting involved with Mark was crazy, especially this weekend. Ashley needed help with the wedding. It was her responsibility as a mother to be there for her daughter, to help Ashley fight wedding jitters by being a source of calming energy. However, inside she felt anything but calm. Mark had her nerves stretched tight. The best resolution to her condition would be more Mark. Quite the conundrum. Taking a deep breath, she walked out of the bathroom.

"Oh shit!" She put her hand to her heart. "You scared the crap out of me." Craig stood against the wall obviously waiting for her to come out of the bathroom.

"What's going on?" he demanded.

She pointed to the Ladies Room sign.

"I'm talking about you and best man. There's drool on his chin."

She wanted to tell him that it wasn't drool, but Craig spoke figuratively and not literally. Mark didn't wear any traces of their encounter, unlike Jamie. Her thighs still felt the wet effects of her releases. "That would be none of your business." She tried to walk past.

"I know the look, Jamie."

"And what look would that be?" She put her arms akimbo. "Oh, you mean the look of a satisfied woman. No, you wouldn't recognize that look on me so it must be something else." She tilted her head to the side.

Craig's lips pursed, he eyes narrowed, and he shook his head. "You're making a fool of yourself."

"Actually Craig, you are. Who I spend time with is none of your business." What, wasn't she supposed to have conversations with members of the wedding party? "Remember we're divorced now. Save your concerns for your little..." She smiled. "Trisha. I can take care of myself." She headed back to the table.

"You can't possibly think our daughter's wedding is the appropriate place for you to find a new boyfriend." He followed her down the hall.

"Who said I was looking for a boyfriend? Maybe I just want sex."

"And that's all he'd want."

"Is it that Mark's younger or that he's good-looking?" A lump formed in her throat. She swallowed before she allowed Craig to see his words had an impact. Truly she didn't want anything from Mark, but having Craig voice her thoughts still stung. Dammit. "Go to hell, Craig."

Mark stood when Jamie returned and held her chair for her. Craig took his seat at the far said of the table and whispered something to his wife.

"Mother, we had a brilliant idea while you were in the restroom. Why doesn't Mark stay with you? He can use my room since I won't be there."

"I wouldn't want to impose." Mark smiled when Jamie's eyes narrowed, scalding him with a scathing glance. "Really, I have a reservation downtown."

Craig coughed. "Mark would probably be more comfortable in the hotel, sweetheart."

Ashley turned to her father. "Don't be ridiculous. It's a great idea."

"But he has a reservation already." Craig took a drink of water then set the glass back on the table. "Hotels require a twenty-four-hour cancellation."

"Then cancel it," Ashley said. "You're practically family. Mother, tell him."

Mark targeted his stare at Craig. "The money isn't an issue." He turned to Jamie. "It's up to you." He'd told her earlier that he wanted to stay. He watched Jamie's eyes cloud with passion as her thoughts traveled in the same direction his had been since he'd set eyes on her at the church. They were just given an opportunity to act on their impulses. He waited to see if Jamie had the daring spirit he'd glimpsed in the car. Would she take the chance on a weekend full of fucking for the simple pleasure of it?

Her chest rose and fell with shallow breaths and her nipples puckered beneath her blouse. His cock twitched in his pants, knowing he'd stuffed her panties between the seats in the car and she was bare beneath her skirt.

"I suppose it doesn't make sense to stay in a hotel when I've got an extra room." The beginning of a smile tilted her lips.

"I don't like it."

"Daddy!"

Trisha nudged Craig and gave him a look of warning.

"Craig, if Mark staying with me makes you uncomfortable, I just might ask him to move in." Jamie picked up her water goblet and took a drink.

Craig bristled and Wes laughed, diffusing the brewing argument. "Give him your key," he said to Ashley. "Then he won't disturb Jamie when he stumbles in tonight."

Mark didn't reveal his intentions. He wouldn't be stumbling anywhere because he wanted command of all his senses when he spent the night buried balls-deep in the mother of the bride.

* * * * *

Mark checked his watch. Wes, his brother, and a handful of coworkers sat at several tables pushed close together. A woman on the stage, wearing thigh-high, patent leather boots, a g-string, and a tight, cropped tank climbed a brass pole, locked her legs around the cylinder, and humped in a frenzied gyration. Dark nipples and big breasts bounced, eliciting a round of applause and several dollars were tossed onto the stage. The woman slowly leaned back and plucked her nipples. Flipping up, her hair cascading to her ass, she unlinked her legs and slid down the pole like a fireman.

Mark had seen enough. His pole was hard as hell and it wasn't because of the stripper on stage. He looked at his watch again. How long was the best man obligated to stay at the bachelor party?

"Mark, you with us?"

Mark refocused on the group of men surrounding Wes. "I think I'll offer a toast to the groom and then bail on the party. It's been a long day and not even the excellent entertainment is keeping my focus." He lifted his soda glass. A few in the group were drinking beer. That was the downside of having the bachelor party the night before the wedding. No one wanted to see Ashley upset by a hung-over groom.

"I might be the best man in your wedding, but I might not be the best man to wish you luck in your marriage. I don't profess to know how to keep a woman content."

Wes chuckled. "Because you're always thinking of ways to cut them loose."

"True, very true. However, in my experience the hardest ones to shake are the ones who really like to fuck. So my advice is to never let your sex life become boring. Make her laugh and give great oral."

"I certainly wouldn't want a wife who didn't give a good blowjob." Wes' brother smiled while sipping his longneck bottle of beer.

"So in keeping with the promise I made to your future wife, I will have the groom choose a number between one and seven." The number of men at the bachelor party excluding him and Wes. "And that man," Mark waved to the woman standing to the side with breasts as large as cantaloupes, "will get to bury his face in this beautiful girl's tits and get the lap dance of his dreams." He handed the stripper a fifty. "Now don't stay out too late. You're getting married in the morning."

Wes stood and gave Mark a bear hug, slapping him on the back. "Someday it'll be your turn to take the long walk down the aisle."

"And if I do, it'll have to be someone as awesome as Ashley." His lips morphed into a smile. "And as hot." The smile grew wider. Marriage wasn't on his mind. However, making his feisty, sharp-clawed, sharp-tongued wildcat purr was driving him to distraction.

Mark hurried to the parking lot and climbed behind the wheel. Hell, he was bailing on his best friend's bachelor party. He'd feel guilty later. He took the panties from between the seats. Right now, he needed to finish what he and Jamie had started in the car.

Green lights and deserted streets heightened his anticipation. Only a few minutes passed before he arrived at the house. Pulling into the drive, he turned off the ignition, and stared at the darkened interior of the house. He tucked the panties in the glove box to save as a memento of his time with Jamie. He might just purchase the damn vehicle.

Taking the house key Ashley had given him, he unlocked and then opened the door. He felt on the wall for a light switch. Earlier, after the dinner, he'd dropped off his weekend bag. The house had been too chaotic to do anything but put his stuff in one of the bedrooms and then head out with the guys.

Finding the light, he left the keys on the hall table. Jamie lived well. However, it didn't compare to his place in Phoenix. Of course, his connections within the construction business helped. The economic boom fed the housing market, which lined his pockets. He'd done well in landscaping. He didn't just push a mower around. He brought in boulders with heavy equipment, dug holes for pools, and planned gardens for the wealthy. Hell, most considered him wealthy. He didn't need more money, but he wasn't a man to spend his time idle.

He loosened his tie and opened the top button of his cream-colored shirt. After toeing off his wingtips, he padded across the thick, beige carpet in his socks.

The house was quiet as he found his way to the kitchen. He took a bottle of beer out of the fridge and twisted off the cap. The yeasty flavor floated across his tongue and soothed his throat, parched from the smoke in the bar.

He hung his suit coat over the ladder-back kitchen chair. Stainless steel appliances sparkled in the glow of light from the hallway. His shadow cast dark against the wall. He considered how to go about getting into Jamie's bed. Until she invited him in, he'd be a gentleman. Mischievous thoughts crossed his mind. He'd be a gentleman only until she begged him not to.

Mark left his beer on the counter, turned off the lights in the living room, and climbed the stairs to the bedrooms. Taking the cracked door as an invitation, he pushed it open.

With his shoulder propped against the doorjamb, he watched her sleep in a king-size bed in the center of the large, elegantly decorated room. He was more earth tones and leather. Jamie was elegant comfort.

She stirred under the comforter. Sitting up, she didn't appear startled when she saw him.

"Mark." It sounded like a sigh from her lips. He crossed the room, beckoned by her sleepy eyes, soft mouth and bare shoulders. The sheet fell to her waist revealing the silky, transparent nightgown. Dark, erect areolas poked against the fabric. His cock pulsed in anticipation. Tasting her hadn't come close to satisfying his desire.

Jamie looked like romance. Only he knew her sharp edges promised more than a docile female, if their encounter in the car gave an indication.

"Is there something wrong?" She glanced at the clock beside her bed. "I didn't expect you back this early."

He crossed the room. "But you were expecting me?" He stood two feet away, staring down at her. "Are you going to invite me into your bed?" he asked while unbuttoning his shirt. "Or would you like to fuck on the floor?"

* * * * *

Jamie couldn't remember a time when a man had looked at her with such blatant sexual need. Mark stood next to her bed unbuttoning his shirt, revealing a tantalizing glimpse of sculpted chest. Her mouth watered thinking of him hovering over her, driving into her heat.

Rising up on her knees, she lifted her nightgown and inched it up her thighs. As she took the thin silk up her body, the fabric grazed her nipples. She sucked in a breath. The material brought awareness to her sensitized skin. She anticipated the touch of her lover's caress while she pulled the gown over her head and tossed it to the bottom of the bed. A smile tugged at her lips. Mark's lust-filled stare raked every curve of her body, infusing her with fervent desire. She ached to feel him inside—deep. On her knees with her thighs spread, she said, "Come to bed, Mark," and pulled back the covers.

A growl escaped his lips. After taking a couple of condoms from his back pocket and tossing them on the nightstand, he shucked his pants. His cock loomed large and tall thrusting from a thatch of dark, curling hair. She'd almost forgotten the tempting sight. Almost.

Reaching out, she wrapped her fingers gently around the girth and gave him a loving stroke. A hiss of pleasure from his lips made her smile wider. She understood the craving. Unable to resist, she pulled on his penis. He took a step closer so his thighs were flush with the edge of the bed. On her hands and knees, she took his hard, heated flesh into her mouth. She took him deep. Pleasure vibrated the back of her throat. Mark slowly pumped his hips, driving into her mouth and then as she sucked, he inched back.

Mark threaded his fingers into her hair above her ears. "Stay on your knees," he said, pulling his cock from her mouth.

"Are we back to giving orders? Tsk, tsk." Her stomach fluttered at the devastatingly sexy smirk on his lips.

"I'd be more than happy to take orders if you'd like to tell me what to do." He ran his hand over her hip as he moved onto the bed. "Would you prefer to be the teacher? Or the student? I know what I want to teach you. Do you think there's anything you could teach me?" he asked, interspersing his words with wet, tempting, little kisses.

She certainly didn't want to be reminded of the age difference by being the teacher. Yet knowing he desired her was a powerful aphrodisiac. Mark offered her a weekend where she could do anything she wanted. And what she wanted was to behave without consequence.

Taking a condom from the nightstand, Mark tore the package with his teeth. "Jamie, I'll take you places you've never been." His tender touch caressed the dip in her lower back. "If something doesn't feel good, say the word." Fitting the rubber ring to the head of his shaft, he unrolled the latex.

"Should I be scared?"

"Do you want to be?" He held her gaze, clearly expecting an answer.

"I don't know." In fact, she really didn't know anything about the best man except for the fact that he made her pussy throb. Initially her attraction to him might have been based on seeing her ex-husband with his new wife. At the rehearsal, she proved she could attract a man. Craig had noticed and that went a long way to softening the blow of being replaced. In one hour Mark had managed to do what she couldn't in the past eighteen months — piss Craig off.

Jamie scooted to the center of the bed. "Hurry Mark, I've wanted you to fuck me since you walked into the church."

Mark kneeled behind her. Searching out her center, he parted the moist outer lips of her pussy. She arched her back, encouraging him to probe deep inside. Wetness coated her inner thighs. She couldn't remember ever being this hot. Pressing her hips into his groin, she attempted to impale herself on him. His chuckled frustrated, yet heightened her awareness and anticipation.

"Is this what you want?" Her inner walls tightened around his finger. Pulling out, he then inserted a second finger, stretching her, sliding in and flicking back and forth.

"No, I want your cock." She glanced over her shoulder. "Mmmm." She quivered, expecting full penetration, but Mark barely breached her body with the head of his penis. "More." She tried to move, however Mark's hands on her hips held her still.

Inching ever so slowly, he pressed into her welcoming channel. "You feel so good." His deep voice filled the room, penetrating through the blood pounding in her ears. His strokes were slow and methodical. Pressing deep until his balls tightened and he nestled against her, he then slowly retreated.

"Mark?"

"Hmmm."

She glanced back at him. His jaw and teeth clenched. Muscles strained in his neck as he controlled his body's responses. She didn't want him in control. "My husband made love to me. I thought you wanted to fuck."

His eyes widened. "So the kitten has claws." He slammed his point home. Jamie cried out as he drove fiercely, jarring her body with his thrusts. Pressure built and her thighs trembled. "Are you going to come? Is your pussy ready to purr?"

"I'm going to come. Oh yes. Oh yes! *Oh yes.*" Sparks flashed behind her closed eyelids. "Oh yes!" Mark thrust two fingers into her ass, bringing on another wave of powerful aftershocks. With his cock pumping into her pussy and his fingers fucking her ass, pleasure rolled through her in waves. One crashing into the next. Before she could recover, he pulled his fingers from her ass and replaced them with the bulbous head of his cock wet with her cream. "Oh please, yes. Fuck me, Mark."

Slowly pressing into her tight little hole, he penetrated Jamie. He stretched her sphincter until she thought she'd split in half. Then in a rush of liquid heat, her body accepted his invasion. Smooth, hard strokes pushed her to heightened pleasures she'd never before experienced.

Arching her back, tossing her head, she cried his name into the darkened bedroom. Clamping her teeth into her bottom lip kept her from breaking into sobs of joy and pleasure. Heart racing, thighs and arms quivering, she grasped the sheets in her fists as another orgasm came upon her. Stronger than the previous two, it stole her breath.

A feral growl from Mark echoed in the room. His fingers bit into the flesh of her hips. She couldn't catch her breath. He thrust deep into her tight rosette and ground his pelvis against her ass. He tensed behind her, every muscle rigid while he exploded. Deplete of energy, he bent over her back, still buried full hilt, and rested his head. His chest molded to her form, offering warmth.

Jamie dropped her head forward. Her chin nearly touched her chest. She absorbed his weight, feeling wonderful in his embrace. His soft lips moved over her flesh from one shoulder blade to the next. Mark traced her spine with his tongue.

"You're an amazing lover," she whispered.

Mark slowly pulled from her body. She collapsed onto her stomach and he followed, lying on his back. "You know as well as I do that this is something different than either one of us has ever had." He turned his head. Their faces were only inches apart. His expression was serious but also disarming.

No, she didn't want to acknowledge that a man fifteen years younger made her ache for the years lost with her husband. She hadn't realized. She just hadn't known sex could be so damn intense. Jamie yawned. "We need to get some sleep. The wedding isn't until two, but there's so much to do."

Mark leaned over and kissed her quickly on the lips. "Red eyes and sleepless nights are expected with a wedding. We'll blend right in."

Chapter Four

හ

Jamie stood beneath the hot needles of the shower. Water sluiced over her whisker-burned skin. Never in her life had her limbs been weak from a night of fornication. And that was what Mark had given her, a heart pounding, wild night of sex. They hadn't made love, no, he'd fucked her well and good. And it was thrilling.

Turning off the water, she wrapped a towel turban style around her head. Technically, she hadn't overslept because she hadn't gone to sleep. In a little over an hour, she needed to be at the church.

She stepped from the bathroom. With his arms folded beneath the pillow under his head, Mark lay on his stomach in all his naked glory. His sculpted ass, tapered torso, and tousled hair nearly made her climb back into bed. The sheets were crumpled on the floor at the bottom of the bed and condom wrappers littered the floor. Her romantic boudoir looked like a dorm room at a sorority house.

"Mark." She ran her nails down his back and along the crease between his ass cheeks. "Jump in the shower and I'll start coffee."

She took his groan as a yes.

After Jamie had the coffee brewed, she took a steaming cup into her dressing room and sat at the vanity. Mark hummed a tune in the shower. She smiled because she hadn't thought of him as a morning person. There was too much dark mystery and sexual energy in his eyes.

"Morning." The sound of his voice behind her startled her out of the erotic reflection of his finer attributes. "I assume my tux is at the church."

She nodded. Water droplets glistened on his chest and dripped to follow the thin trail of hair to the edge of the towel wrapped low around his hips. Under her gaze, his erection grew, bulging beneath the towel.

"As tempting as you are, we don't have time. We cannot be late for the wedding. So put your weapon away." Her lips smirked into a smile.

"Yes, ma'am."

"Mark, I told you not to call me ma'am." She laughed at his retreating back. "And hurry."

She turned back to the mirror and cocked one of her eyebrows. Not bad for a ma'am.

* * * * *

Mark's mouth watered at the sight of Jamie in a cream-colored, silk slip of a dress. Sheer hose, high heels, she looked fabulous. He had a hard time keeping his eyes on the road as he drove them to the church.

"Mark, I'm going to need your help. Well, more of a favor." She glanced at him and then turned her gaze back to the window. "As lovely as yesterday was, it is still going to be difficult keeping up a degree of civility with Craig. Believe me, what has happened between us has definitely taken the sting out of having to spend today with my ex."

"Don't think about him. Just us." Mark reached over and took her hand.

"That's just it." She turned toward him on the seat and crossed one silk-covered calf over the other. "I don't want my family to know. The truth is that there really isn't an us because you're only here for the weekend. An unexpected delight, but then the real world will coming crashing in on Monday and I don't want any lingering repercussions."

"You don't want your daughter and ex to know you seduced the best man?"

She gave a snort. "I'm not sure who seduced whom. As for the ex, I'm sure he's figured out something happened between us." She told him about the exchange outside the bathroom at the restaurant.

"I suspected as much when he left the table."

"Thank you for not causing a scene."

Mark chuckled. Jamie didn't need him rushing to her defense. From what he'd seen, she didn't have a problem expressing herself. He found her honesty refreshing. And he told her so.

"This is a novel experience for me. However, I have no doubt you've developed an impressive reputation back home."

"Jamie, I'll admit that on the plane ride over I thought about spending the weekend fucking a bridesmaid. Then I saw the mother of the bride. I don't need entanglements in my life, which is why I haven't dated in a while. I haven't slept with a woman in months."

"Did I touch a tender spot?"

"No, in order to do that you'd need to touch here." He clasped her hand and pressed it against his raging erection.

"Shame to let it go to waste," she said.

"You'll let the cougar out of the bag with just one of those looks." Her eyes misted over with passion. He'd wondered if she'd be done with him after last night. Clearly she wasn't any closer to saying goodbye than he was. They had tonight. If she continued to stroke his cock through his slacks, they were going to have another round in the car. Jeezus, he needed to fuck her hot, moist mouth.

"Maybe we should just avoid each other at the wedding."

He groaned as her fingers traced the hard length. "Jamie, as much as I want to make you come, please, you have to stop or I'm going to." She smiled. Mark chuckled and said, "Or you can keep it up and I'll have you in the church parking lot again."

She snatched her hand back into her lap. "No touching at the wedding."

"Would it really bother you if Ashley found out? I get the impression you'd take sort of a perverse pleasure in confirming your ex's suspicions."

"I honestly don't know how Ashley would take it and I don't want to find out. Today is about her and Wes. Why should I cause a scene when you're leaving tomorrow anyway?"

"Because it would be fun to watch your ex."

Jamie's smile reflected exactly what she was thinking. "That would be the only benefit."

"Jamie..." He paused considering exactly why his stomach tightened at the thought of returning home to Phoenix. "I'd like to see you again."

The acknowledgement of the pleasure they could enjoy flashed in her eyes. "But you just said you weren't looking for an entanglement. And Mark, as delicious as you are, I'm certainly not looking for a long-term, long-distance relationship."

"I enjoyed being entangled with you last night. I think you did too." However, she was right. He wasn't looking for a girlfriend. He recognized the difference between a mature woman who wouldn't cling and the twenty-somethings back home who grated on his last nerve. Jamie didn't want or expect anything from him, and he certainly didn't need pandering from her. "Then you wouldn't be interested in seeing each other after this weekend?" Damn, his mouth spoke out of turn. He wasn't ready, yet fate seemed to lead him in a different direction. Jamie represented everything he found attractive in a woman—sharp wit, fierce independence and uninhibited sexual appetite.

"Actually, Mark, I'd love to keep you under my bed, bring you out a few times a day, and fuck you like my daily meals. Breakfast, lunch, and dinner. However, one night of incredible sex hasn't muddled my mind."

No, but maybe two might. He didn't care why. He just knew he wasn't going to be able to walk away after the weekend. Jamie didn't know it yet, but he intended the lessons to continue.

Several cars were already in the parking lot when they pulled up to the church.

A few men wearing black tuxes smoked cigarettes under a large elm. Peach taffeta ruffles blew in the breeze as two of the bridesmaids hurried back into the church. Out on the horizon, the morning skies darkened. Thunderstorms brewed.

"Ashley wanted to have most of her wedding photos taken outside on the church grounds. The rain is going to make that impossible."

Mark stepped from the vehicle and went around to the passenger door. The wind picked up, nearly pulling the door from his hand and slamming it closed. "Careful," he said, putting a hand on her dress to keep it from doing a Marilyn Monroe and blowing up around her waist. Just touching the silken texture caused his cock to jump with awareness.

Never had a woman commanded all his senses. Even with the heavy scent of rain in the air, he detected the subtle fragrance of her perfume. The wind kicked through her hair, tangling it around her face. He could've had his hands on her in the car. No one would have suspected anything. The wind was making a fine mess out of everyone's appearance.

They entered the church. The foyer was filled with beautiful flowers. A few bridesmaids flitted about, giggling. What had he been thinking? There was no comparison between the woman beside him and the gaggle of girls.

"There's still tonight," Jamie whispered, standing beside him. She'd obviously mistaken his expression for one of interest when looking at the jubilant frocks of taffeta.

He leaned close. "I intend to make the most of tonight." His eyes raked down her body. "Are you wearing panties?"

"I'd let you find out, but I need to help Ashley get ready for the ceremony."

"If you find yourself alone, will you do something for me?"

Mark wrapped his arm around her waist. At first she stiffened, her glance darting around the foyer. "Mark, someone will see." She tried to step away, but he held firm.

"If you find yourself alone, and I'm not around to do it for you, touch yourself."

"Mark." She spoke with the tone loud and clear even though her words were whispered.

"And then find me so that I can lick your fingers." He brought her hand to his mouth and flicked his tongue between her index and middle finger as if he were licking her pearly inner folds.

Her cheeks flushed with color. A sigh parted her lips. "You make me reckless. Why can't I say no?" She glanced down the vacant corridor.

He wanted to suck on her lips. He leaned in...

"You can't kiss me." Her voice was soft, yet full of promise. "Someone will see."

"Where?"

"Nowhere! We're in a church," she said, taking his hand and leading him down the hall.

Glancing around, he nodded. "Yes, we are in a church and it seems fitting since I want you on your knees."

Lightning flashed through stained glass. Thunder boomed.

"We're going to hell."

"No, we're going to heaven." He followed her into an empty classroom. Closing the door, he swooped down on her lips, thrusting his tongue in a rhythm his grinding hips

117

emulated. Velvet stroked velvet; she tasted fresh and of toothpaste.

Thunder crashed again.

Jamie pulled away, yet still angled her body to rub her clit through her dress and panties against his hard length. Damn, he felt the heat through his trousers.

"It's a sign," she whispered. "We should stop." Mouths open, their lips sealed again. He sucked on her tongue. Tension coiled in his gut. He had to complete the possession as much as he needed to take his next breath.

"No, the thunder is camouflage for your screams." He lifted her dress revealing her thigh-high stockings. "Do you have any idea how incredibly turned on I am? How am I supposed to survive the rest of the day knowing what you're wearing under this dress?"

"You weren't supposed to discover it until after the wedding."

He slid his hand into the front of her panties to feel the dewy wetness seeping from her honeyed core. "I want to fuck you, Jamie. Are you going to let me?" He kissed her.

She bit his lip. "All talk." She soothed the bite with a lick. "You've been efficient at everything. How fast can you make me come, because we've only got a minute?"

Mark opened the fly of his pants. His cock was so eager for release, it instantly snapped to attention the moment it had room to grow. Fully erect, he quickly sheathed himself in a condom. "Hold on. My lady wants a hard and fast orgasm. It's my honor to fulfill her every whim."

Mark backed Jamie against the wall, hiked her dress to her waist, and tugged the crotch of her panties out of the way. "Wrap your legs around me, sweetheart, and hold on with your claws." In one smooth push, he entered her hot, welcoming body.

"Oh God!"

"We're in church. You're supposed to say dear God."

"Be...good...Mark!"

He chuckled. "I thought I was." He slammed into her hot channel in quick but full strokes. Her body tightened, squeezing his cock in a silken glove. Lightning flashed. The lights flickered.

"Another sign," she said and laughed. "Oh...Mark...harder... Yes!"

The clap of thunder couldn't cover her cries. He kissed her mouth, stealing her breath. He had to do something. If her moans of pleasure didn't alert the wedding party to their tryst, his would. He felt like pounding his chest and releasing the call of the wild.

A knock on the door.

The handle turned.

"Mark!" He dropped her legs, hiked up his trousers, and turned to face the door just as it opened.

"Jamie?"

Mark heard her groan behind him as he blocked her from view. The door opened fully and Craig stepped into the room. Mark finished zipping his pants, his cock hard and still wearing the condom. With the smile stretching his mouth, he was glad Jamie stood behind him. He felt her forehead resting between his shoulder blades as she shimmied her dress back into position. Her body vibrated.

"Are you laughing?" Mark asked her.

"What in the hell is going on here?" Craig slammed the door behind him.

"Nothing *now*," Mark said. However, evidence of what had been going on hung heavy in the air, the musky scent of sex. Jamie rested her hand on his ass. He looked over his shoulder. "You okay?"

She nodded still smiling. She smoothed her hair and stepped around Mark to face her ex.

Red stained Craig's face. His hands formed fists at his side. "Jesus Christ, Jamie."

"Nice, Craig, we're in a church. Watch your language."

Mark stared at the toe of his shoe and thought about sad puppy eyes and focused on his aching dick. Damn Craig's timing. He'd been right at the precipice of rocketing off. Shifting the humor of the moment into irritation, he was able to keep the laughter from his voice. He asked, "What did you need?"

"Jamie, what would our daughter say?" Craig's eyes narrowed. "What are you thinking? He's half your age."

Jamie gave a snort. "Not quite. And how old is your little trollop?"

"Is that what this is about? Are you trying to prove something to me by having sex with him?" Craig pointed at Mark and then paced across the floor.

"You're an inquisitive guy," Mark said, slipping his hands into his pockets and leaning against the wall. "Do you really believe you have a right to ask?"

Not responding to Mark, Craig tilted his head and in a tone dripping with pity said, "I knew you had taken the divorce hard, but I didn't realize you were close to a breakdown. You've always been a cold-hearted woman. I never knew."

"Knew what?" Jamie's forehead scrunched as she arched an incredulous eyebrow. "What are you talking about?"

"You're screwing the best man in the church where we were married. You met him yesterday."

"I don't think it's any of your business why she's screwing me. But if you must know, I enjoy fucking beautiful women."

"Mark…"

120

"And you talk to me of watching my language. Jamie, is that what you want? To be a piece of meat to him? You're nothing to him, but an easy lay. You can't possibly want that."

"No, what she wants is to be fucked in the ass…only you interrupted before I had the chance to bend her over the desk."

"Mark! You aren't helping."

"He's a prick. Fuck him. What you do is none of his business anymore."

"Ashley will hear about this," Craig stated with a tone of authority.

"Craig, stop it. Don't…"

"Don't what? Tell our daughter her mother is a whore?"

Mark had heard enough. "Pull your head out. Jamie is an adult. And if you call her a whore again and I'll kick your ass. Remember I'm half *your* age, too."

Jamie chuckled then quickly squashed the sound.

"And where I fuck her is none of your business."

"What kind of sick game are you playing?" Craig's face twisted into a disgusted sneer. "She's twice your age."

"I couldn't care less how old she is." Rather the opposite. She was refreshingly mature and sexually his equal. Mark wasn't about to let Craig lay a guilt trip on her for acting on normal, if impulsive, pleasures.

"It's disgraceful."

Before Mark could defend Jamie, she took a step toward Craig. "You're a hypocrite. Did you think it disgraceful when you were banging Trisha on your office desk? So don't stand there and use that condescending tone with me."

"This isn't about me. It's about your behavior."

"Yes, and now I know why your secretary held appeal. There is something exciting about a young piece of ass."

"I'll take that as a compliment." Mark put his hands on Jamie's shoulders. "I don't know how you could walk away. I know I sure as hell won't."

"I'd like to know what that is supposed to mean," Craig said.

Jamie turned around. Her eyes widened and then narrowed seductively. "Are you saying you never leave the table until the meal is finished?"

"What does food have to do with this?"

"Nothing," Mark said to Craig. "I'm saying that Jamie is a fascinating, sexy-as-hell woman that I want to get to know a lot better." He tucked her hair behind her ear just the way she liked it.

She put her hands over his, brought it to her side, and held it. She stared into his face. "Mark?"

Shit, he didn't mean to announce his intentions in front of an audience. He wanted Jamie alone, naked and in his arms where he could be most convincing. He reached out and brushed a lock of hair from her face, gently grazing her soft and smooth cheek with the pad of his calloused fingertip. Both kitten and hellcat, she matched him perfectly.

"Jamie, can't you tell when you're being snowed? The man is going to profess his love to keep you in his bed."

Jamie's gaze didn't waver from Mark's. "Actually, I invited him into my bed." She glanced over her shoulder. "It was either that or get rug burns from being fucked on the floor."

Craig sucked in a sharp breath of air. Thunder boomed overhead and a cloud burst. The wind blew the pelting rain against the windows. Like a freight train the sound grew louder and louder.

"Craig, if you feel like you have to tell Ashley, at least wait until after the wedding ceremony," Jamie said. "The rain has already put a damper on her day."

Mark wrapped an arm around Jamie.

She glanced at him and then turned back to Craig. "Although I don't know why you should bother. All you'll do is stir up trouble. Mark is leaving tomorrow and it'll all be moot anyway. Beyond that, my sex life is none of your business."

"This isn't over." Craig stalked back to the door and threw it open. "Your daughter has been looking for you. I'm certainly glad I'm the one who walked in here. You should be thankful. I won't say anything until after the wedding."

"Exactly why do you care? You haven't cared about me in years."

Craig paused in the doorway. "That isn't true. We had a good marriage for a long time."

"Our marriage was boring and so were we. At least I'm enjoying myself. Listen, Craig, tell whomever you want. No one cares anymore. I'm beginning to wonder why I stayed in the marriage. I am only just beginning to realize we were sorely lacking in many areas."

Craig stormed from the room. Mark rubbed his hands up her arms. "Are you okay?" He bent to breathe in the scent of her skin. His lips brushed her neck. "You're shaking, but I don't think Craig noticed."

Jamie angled her head to keep Mark from kissing her. The way he looked at her, his lips, mouth, touch, all kept her from rational thought. Sleeping with him was a mistake, even if it didn't feel like it at the time. And pulling him into the classroom was the biggest one of all. He offered her a weekend tryst. No matter what he said to Craig, she wasn't going to ask for more. There were too many years between them. The novelty would wear off and then she'd be left pining for the best sex she'd ever had. No. They'd entered into the affair with a clear understanding of the duration. Yes, he created an unbelievable ache in her chest. When he left she'd feel the loss. Never had someone come into her life so suddenly and shone with such brilliance. He made her feel like a woman, beautiful, desirable and sexual. And it had been a long time.

"He's going to tell Ashley just to spite me."

"Deny it if you want. It won't matter. I know Wes and you know your daughter. Do you really think anything your ex-asshole—" He cocked an eyebrow. "Your words, not mine. Do you think Ashley is going to be bothered by anything he says? Craig betrayed you." Mark grew quiet and pensive, staring hard into her eyes. "I never would."

"Oh Mark." She dropped her forehead to his chest. "This was just supposed to be about sex. We've spent the night together and had unbelievable sex."

Hooking a finger under her chin, he lifted her face. "We've only just begun."

"We're finished." She pulled away and took two steps back. "We just had sex in a church." Her voice dripped with incredulity. "I should be helping my daughter get ready for the ceremony. And you should be with the groom. You're not even in your tux and look at me." She splayed her arms wide. "I'm a mess."

"I think you look sexy and well tossed." His mouth tilted into a crooked smile.

She put her arms akimbo. "Well Mark, that is exactly the problem. I need to find Ashley." She hurried to the door.

"Jamie—"

She glanced over her shoulder.

"It isn't just sex. You have wonderful qualities."

Oh yes, and the best part about her—she wore panties with easy access. "Mark, we were reckless and now I have to make sure Craig doesn't try to turn my daughter against me." She slipped from the room before he had a chance to convince her to stay.

For whatever reason, she couldn't control her lust for Mark. A bit of distance seemed in order. And since that wasn't possible during the wedding, she planned to stay in a crowd. A groan escaped her lips. That meant spending time in close proximity to Craig. She couldn't win.

Chapter Five

ᔆᑐ

Mark heard the boisterous laughter from inside the groom's room. What a mess. Pasting a spurious smile on his face, he knocked twice and opened the door. "Is there an extra monkey suit in here?"

"Mark, where've you been?" A round of laughs erupted. They'd really laugh if they knew he'd been in the bathroom, disposing of a condom and finishing himself off. The day kept getting worse.

"What'd I miss?" He hoped Craig hadn't come in here first and informed the wedding party he was fucking the mother of the bride. Not that he cared if anyone knew, but Jamie did. He didn't want to make dealing with her ex-husband any more difficult. Mostly, Mark was a good reader of people. Jamie had been upset in the classroom even though she'd done a convincing job of getting Craig to believe she wasn't bothered. Mark didn't want to scare her off. Just the opposite, he wanted to get her off. Again and again. She was good for him. It had been a long time since he'd felt compelled to enter a relationship. Yet that's what he wanted to explore with Jamie.

Wes came forward and slapped him on the back. "I'm sorry. I just know your reputation with the ladies. We were discussing which one of the bridesmaids had your attention." Wes wagged his brows. "Because you sure haven't been focused on the wedding."

Guilt stabbed at Mark's conscience. He needed to tell Wes about the incident in the classroom before he heard it from someone else. "Can I speak with you alone for a minute?"

Wes glanced at his brothers and his dad. Noticing the uncomfortable awkwardness, they excused themselves from the room. Once alone, Mark walked to the window. Staring out at the parking lot for a moment, he then turned and sat on the windowsill.

"Something has happened." Mark pushed his hair behind his ears, squared his shoulders and met his friend's eyes.

Wes took a chair across from him and rested his elbows on his knees, giving Mark his undivided attention. "I'm listening."

"You're right. I have hooked up with someone from the wedding party. Sparks ignited from the moment I saw her."

"Damn, you work fast."

Mark chuckled. In the past it had been a compliment. He wasn't sure Wes was going to see his prowess in a positive way considering the object of his affection. Best and least painless way to explain was to put the truth out there and hope Wes didn't have a problem with it. "I was doing your future mother-in-law, and your future father-in-law just walked in on us."

"What?" Wes started to laugh. "You were fucking Jamie here...at the church. Really?"

Mark nodded.

"Oh hell, what I wouldn't have given to be a fly on the wall."

"Hey, my sexual activities aren't for your voyeuristic fantasies."

Wes raised a questioning eyebrow.

"Not anymore."

Wes dragged his hands down his cheeks. "Well, I had meant watching that pompous ass find out his wife—"

"Ex-wife."

"Point taken. He's belittled Jamie since the divorce. I would have enjoyed the look on Craig's face as he watched his wife...ex-wife...where were you?"

"In a classroom. Craig didn't actually see anything. At least I don't think he did." Mark let out a sigh of relief. "Then you aren't upset? I know I just met her, Wes. But damn, this is different." He smiled. "I'm heading into the slow season at work. If I can convince Jamie, I want to take some time for us to get to know each other. Either spend a few weeks up here or convince her to come to Phoenix."

Wes leaned back in the chair. "You're serious?"

"On the flight here all I considered was a weekend fling. Fast and uncomplicated." He reflected on the shared moments with Jamie. "She can do fast...really well. But Craig just complicated the situation. We traded words. Craig threatened to tell Ashley."

"So what?"

Mark shrugged. "So it upset Jamie. She doesn't want a rift with her daughter."

"Jeez, Mark, are you serious about Jamie?"

"I don't know — maybe. However, I certainly don't want to be responsible for a quarrel if Craig causes trouble."

"He can try." Wes sighed and stood. "If Jamie's only concern is Ashley, I have some influence. Now put your tux on. I'm getting married."

Mark took the tux from the coat rack. "Are you nervous? Marriage. Big step, what if it's a big mistake?"

Wes chuckled. "Mark, the only difference between married and seriously dating is going to be getting laid whenever I want."

Marriage encompassed much more than that. Trouble was, watching Wes, Mark couldn't remember why he feared commitment. It boiled down to trusting the woman. Mark had never wanted to see past the moment. Twenty-four hours had made a serious impact on how he saw the future. For the first time, he could see a woman. Jamie.

Mark stripped off his shirt. He dressed quickly and then stood in front of the mirror to straighten his tie and cummerbund.

"I guess I'm ready."

"She's a great girl, Wes." Mark put his hand on Wes' shoulder as he took his turn in front of the mirror.

"Yeah, and so is her mom," Wes told him.

* * * * *

Jamie's heart pounded, her chest hollow. How could she be so stupid? Of course Craig would do anything to reflect an unbecoming light upon her. He knew he'd fallen from the pedestal Ashley had always kept him on when he walked away from the family. Ashley loved her father, but she didn't approve of how he ended the marriage. Craig's marriage and the little bun in the oven softened Ashley. He'd use Jamie's affair with Mark as one more way of justifying what he'd done. Sleeping with Mark wasn't the same as his infidelity, yet she still felt guilty.

"Hi, sorry I'm late." Jamie sucked in her breath sharply. Ashley stood in the center of the bride's room surrounded by elegant silk and lace. Her hair piled on top of her head adorned with white pearls. "You're stunning." Jamie crossed the room forgetting about her woes and focusing on the beautiful bride ready to begin the next stage of her life with the man she loved.

Tears streamed down Jamie's cheeks.

"Mother, you'll make me cry."

Jamie dabbed Ashley's eyes with a tissue and then wiped her own.

Thunder rumbled through the room. "Do you think it's a sign I shouldn't get married?" Ashley giggled, turning back to the mirror. "I'm just grateful. If bad weather is the only unplanned addition to the day, I'll be thrilled."

Jamie met Ashley's eyes in the mirror.

"Mother, thank you for being nice to Daddy."

Jamie hadn't been nice exactly. Ashley just hadn't been privy to the animated exchanges. Thank God. And Ashley wouldn't be if Craig would keep his mouth shut. A wedding day was meant to be about the bride. Jamie should remember that the next time Mark tempted her with his stirring words.

"I know it isn't easy, especially with Trisha hanging on his arm. Hey, you must be in a great mood. You didn't cringe when I said her name."

Jamie bit on her lower lip. She wanted to break down and confess what she had done. Soon. Just get through the wedding. Once the anxiety of the ceremony was behind her, she could focus on the anxiety of Mark. "I've realized I haven't truly been angry with your father for a while. I simply enjoy being a bitch to him."

"You're entitled. But it probably is time to let the divorce and all the ugly memories go."

"I am." Jamie calmed her nervous stomach. "I'll go get your father. It's time." No amount of deep breathing could quell the sudden escalation in her heart rate. Facing Craig would be difficult. It would need to be done eventually. Maybe she could reason with him. Although in all the years she'd dealt with him as wife to husband it was all about Craig. She had to be the perfect wife and what benefit did she reap? Nothing. After twenty-two years of devotion, her husband showed her neither respect nor appreciation for the years of wifely support. And since the divorce, his treatment of her had only deteriorated. Perhaps that's why she experienced such a quick fascination with the best man. He represented everything Craig opposed. Mark didn't want her hair perfectly coiffed. He wanted her hot, sweaty, and ready…in church parking lots and classrooms. With Mark around, she was in trouble.

Jamie found Craig mingling with guests in the foyer of the church before they were escorted to pews for the service. Five hundred invitations had been sent. Craig had an image to rebuild as the pillar of the community. His reputation had taken a near fatal blow when he'd left their marriage for his secretary. His daughter's wedding would be an event to remember, one to overshadow memory of his infidelity. Combined with the added scandal he intended to cause, Jamie would never forget tonight either.

"Craig." His initial sneer quickly morphed into a smile dripping with malevolence. "Why do you hate me?" She chuckled. "Never mind. I suppose we have reasons to hate each other."

He took her by the arm and hurried her down the hall. "Not in front of our guests."

"I only came to tell you it's time to walk our daughter down the aisle." She yanked on her arm. "And get your hands off me."

He released her. The door on the left opened. Wes filled the space with Mark standing directly behind him. Jamie's breath caught in her throat. Devastatingly handsome, Mark's tux fit to perfection. His hair hung loose around his shoulders. Lust snaked up her spine remembering the way the silky strands slipped through her fingers as he braced above her, filling, stretching, claiming her.

"Close your mouth, Jamie. Haven't you had enough?"

She glared at Craig. He said he would wait to say anything, yet at the first opportunity he made a comment to elicit a response. After the scene in the classroom, she didn't know how Mark would react.

Wes leaned a shoulder against the doorjamb, thereby blocking Mark. "Jamie," he said. "You look stunning. It isn't fair the mother of the bride look as beautiful as the bride."

"If you weren't going to be my son-in-law, I'd tell you what you can do with that line of crap." She tried to play it off as funny, but her skin tingled with awareness under Mark's gaze. Pulse racing, her flesh heated. Damn it, she wasn't going to let Craig bully her into a submissive mouse. She'd grown strong after the divorce and went after what she wanted. Right now, she wanted Mark. "And no, Craig, I haven't had enough."

"All right, Mom." Wes gave a nod of approval.

Mark pushed around Wes. "I told him."

Craig stiffened. Jamie doubted he'd have the balls to say anything to Wes. To do so might risk being at odds with Ashley. As if on cue, the bride's room door opened.

"What's going on?" Ashley flounced out of the room. Yards of white silk floated around her feet and trailed behind.

"Ashley, I was just coming to get you." Craig stepped away from the group. "You know, sweetheart, it's bad luck for the groom to see the bride before the ceremony."

"Daddy, what's going on?" She brushed past Craig and stood next to Wes. Great! Now the whole family stood in the hallway either wearing cheesy grins, like Mark, or sneers. However, no one was talking.

Wes trailed a finger down Ashley's bare arm. "You look beautiful."

Her eyes sparkled. "I love you... Now tell me what's going on out here." Her voice grew quiet. "Tell me Mother and Daddy aren't fighting again."

Wes shook his head. "No, it's great news actually."

"I'd hardly call it great news."

"Craig, you promised! I should know better," Jamie said on a sigh. "You don't keep your word."

"This isn't my fault. You were the one with your dress hiked up around your waist."

"Craig, it's none of your business." Mark wore an intimidating expression as he moved to stand next to Jamie.

"Would someone tell me what's going on?" Ashley pulled and tugged on her dress before stepping in the center of the grouping.

"I walked in on your mother and the best man in the classroom. It didn't take a genius to see they'd been screwing their brains out."

"Mother?"

Wes draped his arm around her shoulder. "Awesome, eh? The mother of the bride and the best man, I think it's great."

Jamie waited with bated breath. She could feel the heat of Mark's body beside her.

"Well...I guess." Ashley's brows furrowed. "You just met, though. I don't know what to say. I mean...it just happened?"

"Yes, here at the church, in the classroom. Your mother had her dress up—"

"Craig." Mark's commanding tone drew everyone's attention. "I don't think you need to give the details. That's Jamie's and my business. Not yours and not theirs."

"I agree. And I don't particularly want the details." Wes closed his eyes. "What I want is for my soon-to-be wife to disappear so that I can pretend it was only a vision of breathtaking beauty."

Ashley giggled. "Come on, Daddy." She tugged on Craig's arm. "I'm getting married," she squealed. Craig had little choice but to follow Ashley back into the bride's room.

"I'll leave you alone for a minute," Wes said to Jamie and Mark and then headed to the foyer of the church.

Jamie and Mark stood alone in the hall. "That was pleasant. How come you told Wes?" She surprised herself with the calm note to her voice. Between Mark's stunning good looks and the humiliation of the situation, her nerves were a wreck. He elicited both responses in her. She wanted to clobber him and then screw him. And the smug smile on his face revealed he knew it. "I thought we'd decided to wait until after the ceremony."

Mark leaned against the wall. "Telling Wes took the power away from Craig." He took a deep breath. "I didn't want him holding what happened between us over your head. I don't care what people think about me. I never have, but I won't let him attempt to tarnish your reputation."

"Why do you care?"

"The truth...I don't know," he growled, rolling his shoulders. "I'm the last guy to get pussy-whipped by a woman." His eyes narrowed, focused intently. She dizzied under his stare.

"All we have is fantastic sex."

He took a confident step toward her. "And in twenty-four hours, we've figured out we have similar appetites." He leaned in, lips close to hers, sharing the same breath. "Let me make love to you tonight."

"Love?" Damn, her pussy clenched in anticipation. Cream dampened her panties.

"Just say yes," he whispered.

"And if I do?"

"I'll take you high and make you come."

"And if I'm scared of heights?" Oh, but she enjoyed the way his voice caressed her ear.

"Jamie, I'll take you somewhere you've never been. All you have to do is say yes."

She had no doubt, both figuratively and literally. Since she'd met him, he'd taken her places she'd never been sexually. "Yes," she spoke on a breath and then closed the distance between their mouths. Hot, and wet, her tongue breached the barrier of his lips. He opened wide, forcing her head back in the aggressive response. He sucked her tongue.

Jamie put her hands on his hips, angled her head, and deepened the kiss. Mark groaned, but left his hands at his sides. He was letting her set the tone and tempo. He might have been the one to encourage their reckless behavior in the classroom. Here in the hall, Jamie decided how far to take it.

His lips were soft beneath hers. Tongues continued to stroke, taste, explore.

"Mmm." She pulled back and then brushed her lips against his warm mouth. "Until later."

"My balls are going to be blue."

Jamie giggled. "I don't think that counts as the something borrowed, something blue."

* * * * *

Jamie wore a smile and greeted guests. She repeated, "The ceremony was beautiful," like a mantra. Now and again, she'd feel Mark's hand against her lower back. They were both eagerly anticipating the end of the reception. It had already been a long day. The night's activities were sure to breathe renewed energy into their bodies.

"How exactly did you come to stand beside me?" she asked Mark during a lull in the receiving line. She should have been standing next to Craig. Some angel had maneuvered the line so she was sandwiched between Wes' dad and Mark.

"Can we step away and get a drink? Maybe if we break from formation, others will too."

Jamie glanced around the reception hall. Soon it would be time to cut the cake and then the newlyweds would depart for their honeymoon. Two weeks in Jamaica to explore each other's delights. All Jamie needed was one more night of discovery with Mark. "Sounds good."

Jamie tingled from his hand. It had to be clear to everyone in the wedding party that Jamie and Mark had developed, at the very least, a friendship. As they walked to the champagne fountain, he stayed near her side.

135

"I think it's time to toast the happy couple."

Jamie and Mark turned to see Craig at the microphone. Evidently the receiving line broke up as soon as they'd walked away. Waiters circled the room with trays of champagne flutes. Craig lifted his glass.

"Wes, I've had Ashley for twenty-three years. Now it's your turn. I wish you both as much happiness as I've found with Trisha."

"Isn't the best man supposed to offer the first toast?" Jamie's knuckles whitened on the stem of her flute.

Mark pried it from her fingers. "Easy, sweetheart."

"That ass actually toasted and wished our daughter a marriage like his. Is he insane?"

Mark pulled her close and kissed her lips quickly. "Best man's turn to toast the happy couple."

Before she could respond to the kiss or the statement, Mark made his way to the microphone. He lifted his champagne flute, winked at Jamie, and then turned to the newlyweds standing next to each other at a flowered archway where the cake would be cut.

"Wes, your wife is breathtaking." He winked at Ashley. "She looks like her mother, so you won't need to worry about her beauty fading."

Several people laughed. Jamie wanted to crawl under the table.

"This is a special day, a day for lovers." Jamie couldn't glance in Mark's direction for fear he looked at her. "Honesty fosters trust, trust builds love, and love inspires fidelity. Never forget that and never lose what you have today." He held up his glass. "Congratulations."

Everyone drank. Mark looked at his watch. "Now, I suggest we get this party started unless you plan to miss your plane."

The band started to play and the newlyweds were called to the dance floor for the first dance. Jamie watched Mark cross the room with purposeful strides until he stood before her. Breathing became difficult. In his tailored tux, long hair, and dark, mysterious eyes, he weakened her knees. Chills broke against her flesh as he took her hand.

"Will you dance with me?" He leaned in to sniff the skin beneath her ear. Moist, warm breath fanned her flesh where she dabbed her perfume. "I'd rather have my cock buried deep inside of you," he whispered near her ear. "Since I can't, I need to have my hands on your body." His lips brushed her neck. "Are you hot, Jamie? Are you thinking about what I'm going to do to you tonight?"

"Yes." She breathed the word.

"Will you trust me to decide what happens between us? Do what I ask even if you're not sure."

She didn't know how to answer when he had her thoughts muddled with brazen sexual desire.

"Honesty, Jamie. Honesty leads to trust."

She realized she had her hands on his hips, holding herself steady. "I trust you." She leaned into him. "And I want to dance." At the moment, she wanted a lot more than that.

While the cake was cut, several friends and family members took their turn at the microphone. Music played and Jamie mingled. However, she felt Mark's gaze often. She only had to glance around to find him nearby. He wasn't hovering or giving grist for the gossip mill.

"Mother? I need to speak with you in private," Ashley said.

They made their way to the rear of the reception hall, close to the kitchen. A few guests mingled about, but basically they were alone to speak candidly.

"Are you about ready to leave?" Ashley had changed out of her wedding dress into a loose pantsuit for traveling.

"Yes, I put my dress in Mark's vehicle. Mother, Daddy just spoke with me."

"Oh, good hell. My love life is none of his business."

"Daddy said you're having some kind of breakdown. A midlife crisis was his exact words."

Jamie rolled her eyes. "You are a grown, married woman now, so I'm going to speak plainly. Mark is a great lay. It's that simple. He came on to me yesterday and I thought, why not? My having sex has nothing to do with Craig. Ashley, I don't love your father anymore. I'm not pining for my lost marriage. Mark offered me a fun weekend of sex. I'm divorced, not dead."

Ashley pulled her into a hug. "That's what I told Daddy. I told him it's about time you let loose and had some fun." She pulled away and smiled. "Mark's hot."

"Yes, he is. Too hot. I am sorry about all that happened today."

"Don't be. This has been the happiest day. I'm ready to begin the rest of my life with Wes." She smiled, tears glistening on her lashes. "I'm married!" Ashley tucked her hair behind her ears. "Now it's time to take my half-drunk husband to the airport." She grabbed onto Jamie's arm. "I didn't tell you what Mark gave us as a wedding present."

"What?" Jamie noted the excitement in Ashley's voice.

"Membership into the mile high club." Ashley squealed. "He made arrangements for us to fly to Jamaica on a private jet."

"Wow, that is amazing."

"He's a good guy, Mother. He has money, so you know he isn't after yours. Wes said he's never been involved with a woman on a long-term basis. Yet Mark told Wes he wants more than a weekend with you." Ashley shrugged. "Just thought you should know you're the one who could hurt him."

"No one is going to get hurt. Both Mark and I know what yesterday...well, and today...meant. We're just having sex."

"Mother!"

"Hey, if we're going to speak as friends rather than mother and daughter, let's give it the full commitment. Mark is amazing in the sack."

Ashley sighed. "Wes told me."

"I don't need to know how much he told you. And I certainly don't want to know how Wes is privy to that information."

Ashley's lips twitched. "I guarantee you don't. He said Mark's kinky."

"Have fun on the honeymoon."

Chapter Six

ജ

The wedding wound down after the bride and groom took their departure.

"I'm ready." Jamie had her purse draped over her shoulder and a smile of anticipation on her lips.

Outside the sidewalks were still wet from the recent rain. Rainbow ribbons of oil reflected in large puddles in the parking lot. Mark held Jamie's elbow as he navigated their way to the Escalade.

He held the door for her and then went around the front of the vehicle. On the drive, he thought about a fast fuck on the foyer floor. Hard didn't come close to his condition, but he wanted to spend the night making love, not just a quick release giving mutual satisfaction.

A few minutes later, he parked in the drive. Still in possession of the house key, he unlocked the door, and then waited for Jamie to precede him inside.

Jamie flipped on the table lamp. "Do you want a drink?"

He closed the door, dropped the keys on the table and crossed the room. "I'd like to come up to your room and help you change your clothes."

"If you're looking for a way to get me out of my dress..." She lifted the silky slip over her head and dropped it on the floor. "All you have to do is ask." She reached an arm behind her back, unhooked her bra, and slipped the straps from her shoulders. The cream-colored lace dangled from her finger, then she dropped it to the floor.

"Take off the rest." He leaned against the wall and watched.

Jamie tucked her thumbs into the elastic waistband of her thong panties. She teased him a moment, toying with the edge. Finally, she shimmied them over her hips and down her thighs. She lifted one foot and then the other. "Do you want them?"

Jeezus. She stole his breath. Perfect breasts, small waist, and a triangle of auburn hair wet with desire. His cock jumped, filled, and then pulsed in his pants. He pressed his palm to the front of his trousers and rubbed roughly against his shaft. She stood before him in nothing but high heels and thigh-high stockings. Salivating at the sight, he had to have a taste. An appetizer before he feasted later in the night. "I want you." He took a step toward her.

"If you say please you can have me any way you want me." She trailed a finger from her neck, between her breasts and past her stomach. She paused before she touched her curls.

"Don't stop now."

She didn't touch herself. "I thought we'd have that drink first."

"I'd like that."

Jamie smiled and headed toward the kitchen. He followed, loving the way her ass bounced with each step. She pulled the vodka from the freezer.

"Straight or mixed?"

"Something lighter." Mark opened the refrigerator. Jamie's nipples puckered in the blast of cool air. He couldn't resist cupping the full globe and pinching the red, succulent tip. Mark grabbed the white wine from the door of the fridge. He pulled the cork from the bottle with his teeth. "Open your mouth, sweetheart."

Jamie stood nearly naked in the kitchen. She leaned her head back and did as he asked. Mark pleasantly plucked at one nipple while he put the bottle to her lips and carefully let a trickle flow onto her tongue. Bringing the bottle back to his lips, he took a hefty swallow. Their eyes locked, a moment passed, and then he dipped his head to taste her. Boldly thrusting his tongue into her mouth, he growled his pleasure. Cold blended with hot. Shifting his head, he took the kiss deeper, tweaking her nipple a little more firmly. She whimpered into his mouth, while her hands worked his tux shirt from his pants. The cummerbund and bow tie had long since been discarded. Mark sucked her upper lip while she bit on his bottom.

"Delicious," he said and then took another drink. This time instead of kissing her mouth, he latched onto her breast. The cool wetness of his tongue stroking her nipple caused her to moan. Clasping her hands to the sides of his head, she anchored him.

Mark lifted the bottle and poured wine over the milky smooth swell of her breast. Wine flowed into his mouth. He ate at her nipple and licked the flesh of her generous breast. Mark handed the bottle to Jamie. He lifted her up and set her on the granite island in the center of the kitchen.

"Lie down." She scooted onto the counter until she could rest her feet on the edge. Her stomach quivered under his touch. He spread her thighs and stepped between them. "You are so hot." He filled her navel with wine. Gooseflesh rippled her skin. Bending over her, he dipped his tongue, swirled around the edge, and then sucking, he drank the wine. "I could get drunk off you, Jamie."

Mark poured the wine over the wet, flushed lips of her pussy.

"Oh Mark." Her hands gripped the edge of the counter and her back arched. "Mark!"

He put her legs over his shoulders, bent his head and lapped at the wine, tasting the nectar of her arousal. He wrapped his lips around her labia while tunneling his tongue into the hot folds. Back and forth in quick bursts, he flicked the tip of his tongue against her clit. Intermittently he cooled her heated flesh by pouring more wine. Her essence was musky and sweet. Overwhelming need to bring her to climax crushed his chest. Her cries of pleasure fed his hunger.

"Ohshitohshitohshit."

He chuckled. Cupping her ass, he lifted. Thrusting into her hole, he fucked her with his tongue. Then he went back to her clit, pressing the swollen nubbin between his lips before drawing it into his mouth.

He moved his hands from her ass, leaving her on the edge of the counter. He grabbed the wine bottle and then poured the rest over her hot pussy. Wine dripped from her body and his chin onto the floor. "Would you like to be fucked?" Mark eased the neck of the wine bottle into her body. While he licked her clit, he pushed the bottle in and out, stretching her a little more with each stroke.

Her body tensed. "Oh Mark, I'm coming." First a spasm and then her thighs locked to the sides of his head. He could feel her orgasm against his tongue. Cream flowed from her cunt. He savored the essence, musky, sweet and tangy. Greedy for more, he flicked his tongue faster, pressed harder against her nubbin. Her internal muscles gripped the bottle and sucked it deeper.

Mark raked his eyes up her body and noted the quick shallow breaths causing her chest to rise and fall. Her head thrashed back and forth. Red hair fanned out on the counter. Good hell, she was the sexiest thing he'd ever seen.

He set the bottle on the counter and then tugged at his pants, freeing his cock. "Fuck!"

"What?" She leaned up on her elbows. Passion clouded her eyes.

"Condom."

"Come on me." She sat up and scooted forward.

Wrapping his fist around his cock, he stroked the length with a tight fist. Mark remained between her thighs. Before she could assist, he leaned his head back and shouted. Hot come spurted from his cock, landing on Jamie's thigh, her tummy and breasts. She rubbed his cream into her skin.

Mark took in deep breaths to calm his racing heart. Excitement coursed through his veins. He wrapped his arms around her hips and laced his fingers behind her back. "You make me feel sixteen."

"Oh Mark, please don't get any younger." She laughed, running her finger through his hair. Then she kissed his mouth.

"Does the age difference really bother you?"

She studied his face. "When I'm with you I feel like I'm in my twenties again." She sighed. "And then I look in the mirror and I have to acknowledge that I'm not young anymore. I'm not just getting older, I'm looking older."

Mark touched her face. She didn't look anywhere near her age, not that if she did it would make a difference. "You look great." *Perfect, in fact.*

She touched his face and trailed her fingers down his cheek. "So does twenty —"

"Nine." He lifted her and her legs wrapped around his waist. "I'm old enough to know what I want. And I just might miss my flight tomorrow."

"Mark."

He silenced her protest with a kiss. Lips sealed and his tongue slid into her mouth deep and penetrating. Tastes blended. His tongue caressed the soft tissues of her inner cheek. Emotions stirred in his gut. This was where he belonged. He pulled back so he could see to carry her up the stairs. "I'm not asking for forever, just tomorrow."

"And what about the day after that?"

He pushed open her bedroom door and crossed the room to her bed. "I want that too." He tenderly kissed her lips while laying her on the bed. "But I'll convince you of it later." After he spent the night making love to her.

SURPRISED BY DESIRE

Katie Blu

ಲ

Dedication

෩

To M, D, L and DP who said it couldn't be done.
And for S, G, A and A who believed it could be. Thank
you.

Chapter One

∞

He'd had a crush on her for years but finally he was at a place in his life where Jenna Michaels was fair game. His gaze lingered on her round ass as she leaned forward to get a good handhold on the slippery metal handrail coated in mineral water from dripping stalactites. She had not been in his family-owned caves since her college days. He considered it his personal lucky break she'd consented to her mother's demands for an old-time joint vacation exploring the property their two families shared, which linked some of the lesser-known branches in the Pennsylvania Caves network.

Jenna stretched farther, causing her denim jeans to pull across her hips. No panty line. Fuck. She had to be wearing a thong. He nearly moaned when his cock jerked to attention for the thousandth time since the tour began.

He breathed in the cool, damp air, steadying his nerves, wondering when would be the right time to make his move. Jenna had been driving him nuts way too long. She had a smile that spoke of hot sex and wicked fantasies. It started slowly, nudging her full lips apart like she shared a dirty secret, except Jenna smiled that way all the time. His libido didn't care — thought it was just for his benefit. He chose to agree.

If he could have one thing this weekend, it would be the curvy Ms. Michaels moaning beneath him, her huge brown eyes liquid with desire to have his cock buried deep in her slick pussy. Then maybe she'd finally notice him, see how much he loved her.

"Great guy, Jenna. Now that his divorce is finalized —" her mother droned on.

"Mother," Jenna bit out. "We're in a cavern. You know, a place where things *echo*? I think David's whole family knows you've been trying to set me up with him." And if she had to tell her mother one more time to put a sock in it, she'd scream. "Besides, I quit taking dating advice from you back in eighth grade. I think it's safe to say I can handle my own relationships in the twenty-odd years since, don't you?"

Sure he was attractive. At forty-four his black hair had begun the distinguished salt-and-pepper change along his temples and his moss-green eyes crinkled at the corners attractively but the guy had just got a divorce. He'd married his high school sweetheart when she got pregnant. Karen had reached a mid-life crisis and left David for another man. Jenna had no desire to be his first date since the split.

Jenna could hardly confess to her mother the slow simmer in the pit of her belly had nothing to do with David and everything to do with his gorgeous son Jason. But he was only twenty-five to her thirty-six and lusting after the young stud wasn't helping her concentration at the moment.

Her foot slipped and she slid backward directly into Jason. Her butt unceremoniously shoved his crotch. Again. Jason wrapped a long sinuous arm around her middle until she'd caught her balance. He'd been doing that all day and pretty soon he'd figure out she was sliding into him on purpose. But God, she could swear he had a boner in his pants and if it wasn't a boner that rubbed the seam of her jeans when he righted her, she didn't want to be disabused of the information.

"So Jenna, looks like your mom and mine coerced us both into this vacation. Seems like they want us to hook up." David winked at her. "What do you say we get a drink at the bed and breakfast when we get back tonight? It would give them something to talk about."

He was a nice guy. Really. But between her mother's insistence she find a nice man to settle down with and his mother Mona, who had been their neighbor since her mom and Mona were kids, Jenna had absolutely no interest. Now if they set her up with Jason, there'd be something to discuss.

She glanced from one man to the other. Jason had the same black hair and moss-colored eyes but his twinkled with mischief and his features were harder, more angular. Downright sexy. She couldn't help but smile back at him after his face broke into a huge grin upon hearing his father's words. Both men had the same lean, jean-clad physique. Impressive, truly.

Her gaze shifted to the third male in their party, Garth, Jason's twin. He grinned at her too but the effect was completely lost on Garth. His flame red hair and pale skin were his mother's contribution. Next to Jason and David, Garth's slimmer build and broad shoulders weren't packed with lean muscle and his hands on his hips made his elbows jut out oddly. The only thing the three men had in common was eye color and height. Oh and apparently a shared amusement of her mother's matchmaking abilities.

"I think my dad has the hots for you, Ms. Michaels." Jason dropped his large hands on his hips.

David chuckled and nudged him with his elbow. "At our ages we can't get picky with whom we settle down, son."

Jenna stared at him. Jason gave him a funny look too.

Suddenly the cave went dark.

"It's all right. Everyone stay where you are. We've lost power but if you don't move, you should all be fine. Power will be restored momentarily. Your patience is appreciated," the female tour guide—and the only one of the group not related to the two families—called out with a tremble in her voice. "Garth, you got it, right?"

"Uh, yeah, it'll take a few minutes to get it fixed." Garth's voice came from beside her. Hadn't he been a few feet away just seconds ago? "Take a deep breath, everyone," he said.

"Don't you guys carry flashlights on the tours?" Jenna asked.

"Normally," Garth said, "but this was about visiting with our two families so we didn't get the whole cave staff involved, or all the equipment out."

"Genius," she muttered.

"I'll take care of it for you, Jenna," he whispered, dropping a big hand on her arm.

Oh yeah, confidence inspiring *that* was. The pitch-black cave offered endless darkness and no whisper of light. The absolute black was probably one of the creepiest things she recalled about these tours. If she remembered correctly, the slope she'd slid from was to her back now with David, Garth and Jason in front of her. Small caves and indents dotted the walls of the huge central cavern they were in. That would put her mom and Mona above her on the plateau Jenna had failed to scale.

Jenna side-stepped toward the nearest indent. This close to the slope, she knew she'd stumble again without light if she stayed put. Her hand brushed against warm, hard cotton. A shirt, she supposed, based on the height. The sharp inhalation of breath from the owner of the shirt had her sending a whispered apology.

Her wrist was locked in the steely grip of a man's hand. Jenna was pulled forward with a jerk. Her body slammed hard into firm, flat planes of hot male from shoulder to hip. She gasped at the unexpected intimate contact. Her nipples beaded wantonly. His long, thick ridge of arousal pressed her abdomen but whose? Was it Garth? Jason? Or David?

She didn't have time to debate the issue. A hand fisted in her hair, dragging her to her toes. Warm, searching lips found hers. His tongue dipped inside to ravage her mouth and rub wickedly along her tongue. *Oh God.* Whoever's lips were plundering hers knew what they were doing. Heat coiled low and persistently, making her core quicken and moisture pool between her legs.

Jenna's sweet acquiescing murmur nearly buckled his knees. Fuck, she tasted good. Her hands curled on his waist and his chest. The contact sparked his pulse and throbbed the length of his cock. His tongue tangled with hers. Though she'd started off in surprise, her interest picked up. He'd made arrangements for the lights to be killed and intended to make the most of it.

His fingers caught her jeans button and snapped it open. Wiggle room, he thought. His hands trembled slightly. He released her hair, dropping his hand to her waist. He took his time stroking up her side until he covered her breast. Her nipple poked his palm through her shirt. He resisted the urge to groan. Instead, he sucked her bottom lip and dropped kisses to the spot where her neck curved to her shoulder.

Jenna shivered in his arms and her breathing sounded ragged. His thumb stroked over her pebbled tip. On another long hungry shudder, she pressed her forehead on his shoulder.

His other hand dipped easily inside her jeans, beneath the flimsy satin panties. Jenna struggled for only a second, stiffened and nearly pulled away. His fingers stroked her folds and her nipple simultaneously.

"Gotta touch you, Jenna. Gotta touch your wet pussy," he whispered in her ear.

Jenna stopped struggling.

His fingers found her slick pearl. Taking it between his finger and thumb, he rolled it, mirroring his actions with her nipple. Her mouth parted on his shoulder. Between her muffled panting and the moans he could feel against his shoulder, he rejoiced in giving her pleasure.

Jenna's hips thrust into his hand. He slipped his pinky into her slick channel. Her convulsions were beginning. He pinched her clit hard on a roll. Jenna gave a long low, audible moan that vibrated through him. His own hips jerked in response as he came in his jeans while her pussy wetly sucked his pinky.

"Oh God, Jenna," he murmured in her ear. "You made me come."

"Jenna honey? Are you okay? You didn't fall down and twist your ankle, did you? Sweetie?" Jenna's mom whined from on high.

"Fine, Mom," he heard her gasp.

"Are you sure? Sounds like you're trying not to cry. Are you scared? Honey, David's down there with you. Don't be scared."

He chuckled softly beside her ear. His hand left her sated folds and she could feel him lifting his arm, so close they stood. She caught the faint scent of her muskiness on his hand as it came near her face. Her secret partner inhaled sharply around a soft sucking noise. He moaned as though he tasted the sweetest honey. "Your pussy juice tastes good, honey."

Jenna shivered. "Fine, I said," she called to her mother.

"David?" her mother screeched.

Her lover stepped away from Jenna, separating himself from her delectable body.

"Here, Kathy. We're all fine down here," David said.

"Are you sure? Sounded like Jenna was whimpering and gasping."

Oh God, thought Jenna. Her cheeks heated. "I said I'm *fine*." If having the best orgasm of her life was fine. Her legs still felt like jelly. Feeling a little wicked, she added, "If I'd been masturbating, you'd be interrupting me right now."

"Jenna Andrea Michaels," her mother bellowed. "I swear, Mona, I raised her right but she has a mouth on her, that one. Once she marries your boy he'll keep her in line."

Jenna blocked her out. Had it been David who'd thoroughly gotten her off? Both he and Jason were on the same level with her. For that matter, Garth had been standing next to her too. If she could check their pants, she'd know.

Her stomach fluttered. She didn't know how she'd turned on any one of them enough to make him come just from coming herself. But damn if it wasn't hot to have been told.

Couldn't be Jason, she decided. Not with all his "Ms. Michaels" this, that and the other. He'd be more apt to say, "Ms. Michaels, do you mind if I put my hand in your pants and see what I can find?"

Garth? Could he have taken the risk to feel her up in the cave? She tried to imagine gangly Garth with his hand between her legs, kissing her like an expert. The image wouldn't form. Instead she got the picture of his russet head and wide, easy grin.

David? Did his broken-hearted divorced soul heat that quickly for another woman? For *her*? She had trouble seeing it. How the hell was she supposed to look any of them in the eye? Brought off by one while fantasizing about the other did not bode well for a future with David. She'd constantly be thinking of ways to get into Jason's pants. Great stepmother material she'd make. "Here, sonny, let's have a quick fuck before I set dinner on the table."

She snorted. The lights flickered on. Blinking in the sudden glow, she darted a look at the three suspects. David had his hands in his pockets. He winked at her. Jason was bent down tying his shoelace. Garth eyed her open jeans snap suspiciously. Damn, it had been David.

The tour was cut short and they went back to Mona's B&B where they were all staying. Jenna would have preferred staying in her former bedroom back home but Mom had insisted this was part of the experience. Late-night board games and horse rides during the day, just like old times when the Michaels and Nolans got together.

Would David be expecting that drink? She sure as hell hoped not. Jenna sneaked to her room, having lost David and their mothers in the foyer. She needed to think things through. The last thing she wanted was to peer over the rim of her pint glass and speculate about David's sudden lust for her. Or worse, listen to him prattle on about Karen's infidelity and betrayal. She'd heard enough last night.

Jenna slipped through her bedroom door. She dropped her key on the vanity counter and reached for the light switch. Thinking better of it, she pulled the drapes shut. Not like the cavern but dark. It occurred to her she hadn't heard the door latch catch and she glanced at it. Her heart thudded in her chest. The metal flip bolt was in the closed position, keeping the door ajar.

Her mind raced. Had she accidentally flipped it to block the door closure without thinking about it? Retracing her steps in her head, she was sure she hadn't, she'd been reaching for the light while tossing her key down. She could see the key on the edge of the vanity where she'd left it. Her throat tightened. Her gaze flicked to the corners of the room, the opening of the bathroom. Was someone in here with her?

She heard nothing. With a laugh at herself and a silent command to get her imagination under control, she went to the door to shut it properly. It was a family inn. Who was she afraid of? The cave episode must have fried her brain.

Jenna had just sealed the door when she was shoved forward into it and a travel sleeping mask dropped over her eyes. She tried to shove backward but her hands were trapped in a familiar steely grip behind her back. He was firm but gentle.

"Hi, Jenna."

Oh crap! He'd fondled her in the cave and she hadn't fought back. Did he think it gave him permission to rape her? She grunted and gave another shove. "Let go," she demanded.

Instantly her hands were released but he cupped the mask to her face and pinned her to the door with his hips. "I'm not going to hurt you, honey. I just like the idea of making you come without you knowing who is doing it."

Her pussy clenched. Apparently she liked the idea too. His sultry whisper in her ear didn't help her identify him either. It could be any of the three guys. But she'd seen David in the foyer. Had he made it up to her room so fast?

She almost didn't want to know if the stranger would revisit the same brand of eroticism he'd doled out in the cave. It was definitely one of the three. Was screwing around with one of the Nolans all that brilliant in the greater scheme of things? She didn't think so.

He rubbed his impressive cock against her bottom. "Can I trust you to leave the blindfold in place?"

"No." Well, it was true. Given a chance she'd rip the thing off and ruin the surprise. But knowing the identity of the man who'd made her come hard in the caves was a tempting prospect even if his last name was Nolan.

"Well fuck, Jenna. Guess I'll have to keep you pressed against the door."

He didn't seem to mind the prospect, she thought. His free hand moved around her waist and snapped open her button, eased down her zipper. Damn if her pussy didn't squeeze and leak for this. He pushed down her jeans one hip at a time, taking her panties with them until he could catch his foot on the crotch and shove them to the floor.

Cool air caressed her ass. He gently took one globe in his hand.

"I love this ass," he murmured.

Her nerve endings sizzled. She moaned with the rhythmic squeezing. Jenna splayed her hands on the door, not fighting him or trying to remove the mask. The not knowing made her pulse with need. The sensations from the cave taunted her and she shivered, wanting more of the same heated caresses.

She swallowed the urge to fight him. Her body demanded release only this man had provided. Jenna pushed her ass into his hand. "I won't take off the mask," she breathed.

With both hands on her, he massaged her butt, sliding his fingers to her inner thigh before "accidentally" brushing her pussy. His teeth grazed her neck, raising bumps on her body, making her already painfully tight nipples bud harder. She whimpered, spreading her legs for him. Silently she begged him to touch her pussy.

He left her ass and unbuttoned her shirt to throw it aside. He unclasped her bra but instead of throwing it too, he carefully used it to bind her wrists at the small of her back. She could easily free herself but she had no desire to do so. She was completely naked and from what she could tell, he was fully dressed. The realization pushed her nipples into the cool wooden door.

She swished her breasts against the wood. Her breath hitched.

"Fuck, Jenna, you have no idea what you do to me."

"I'm aching badly enough to sting," she confessed raggedly. The quiet rasp of a zipper filled her ears, then the crinkle of a condom wrapper. She'd forgotten about condoms. Jenna was heartily glad he'd remembered.

His fingers split her ass globes. She had the wicked sensation of cool air touching her pussy lips when he thrust up inside her hard enough to lift her to her toes. He was thick, huge. Her channel struggled to adjust to his size, burning as it did.

Jenna's pussy was fucking tight. He bit down on the back of her neck. She panted and squirmed.

"It hurts," she whimpered.

"I'm sorry, honey. I should have prepared you better."

She laughed then and he felt the vibration in his cock. "I was plenty prepared. I'm dripping." Jenna wiggled her hips.

He gritted his teeth to hold on to the orgasm threatening to take him before he'd even begun fucking her. "Can you bite me again?"

He barely heard her tentative question. But he did it. He caught her shoulder in an open mouth bite, enough to make her hiss, then slapped her ass. He loved the way her ass jiggled his balls. He did it again.

"I could get used to that." She swished her nipples on the door.

Did the lady have any idea how fucking incredible she was? Damn turn-on. He'd never imagined her to be an adventurous lover but he'd wanted her nonetheless.

"So, you going to fuck me now or stand here with your giant cock in my tight pussy?"

"Shit," he muttered. He pulled out and shoved back in. His hands circled to the front of her body, diving low between her legs. He caught her by her inner thighs, up high where his hold automatically split her pussy and opened it to the air. Both pointer fingers coasted over her clit on each thrust. Jenna squealed.

"Oh my God." Jenna thrust back on his cock.

Moisture slurped over him. The sound of her juices, her tangible arousal at what he was doing to her, shot straight to his balls. Fucking hell, he was going to come. He ground his teeth together and held back. Darts of pleasure plucked the fine string of his concentration.

"Oh my fucking God," she wailed louder.

She shoved back on him as hard as he pushed into her. Her gasps became high-pitched moans growing in volume and intensity with the wet slap of her pussy hitting the base of his cock. His heart slammed in his chest. He pushed in. Feeling her pussy swallow his cock made him dizzy. He wiggled his fingers, catching her clit between them as their bodies fucked together in a primal dance.

Jenna screamed, slamming backward in a frenzy to take his full thick length. Her pussy clenched around his shaft, drawing, pulling, sucking him with an intensity that made his eyes roll back and his brain stall. A shout ripped from his chest. His cock pulsed, shooting hot cum deep inside her tight well. Mindless, he thrust through wave after wave of spurting orgasm. "Fuck, yes." His heart burned like it would burst but his cock continued to pound in, out, in, out, until finally he was empty.

Running feet sounded in the hall. "Jenna?" She recognized Mona's voice immediately. "Jenna, are you okay?"

"It's all right, Mrs. Nolan. I killed it," Jenna called.

"Killed what, honey?"

"There was a huge spider. He's dead now."

"A spider? Oh dear! I'll call the exterminator tomorrow morning. I'm so sorry."

"Thank you, Mrs. Nolan."

"Oh Jenna, when Jason's done helping you in there, will you send him down to the kitchen? I have a trap out back he needs to take care of too."

She felt the lift and fall of his sigh at her back. "Sure, Grandma. Let me just clean up this mess in here. Ms. Michaels splattered the sucker everywhere before I could help her."

"No hurry." Mrs. Nolan's steps retreated the direction they'd come.

Chapter Two

ᏣᎳ

Fuck. He was screwed. It wasn't like he'd intended to keep his identity a secret from her forever but he'd certainly wanted to get her into a mind-numbing sexual haze so she wouldn't stop to question the age difference.

"Jason," Jenna said, her voice deadly calm.

He stroked his fingers over her clit, hoping to distract her. "Yeah?"

Her breath hitched and she shivered. "You're Jason."

"Yep."

"And the cave too?"

"Uh-huh," he agreed. Jason dropped a kiss on her shoulder. He stroked her pussy with featherlight touches. Her channel clenched around his shaft. Dragging one hand off her apex, he coasted his palm upward to claim her breast. His cock hardened.

She didn't say anything. Was she speechless or pissed? Only the sound of her breathing carried to him, otherwise she stood completely still. He was ready for her again. Knowing who he was might put a crimp in his desired sexual explorations though. He grabbed another condom from his pants pocket.

"Again?" she whispered.

Jason leaned forward, catching her earlobe between his teeth. "Where you're concerned? You could snap your fingers and I'd be ready for you."

The fingers of one hand curled away from the door. She pulled the mask off, dropping it to the floor. Then with deliberate flair, she snapped her fingers. The pop sounded loud in the room.

It took him a second to register what she had just done but he dragged his cock out of her, flipped her around. He grabbed the tissues off the vanity with a blind reach and switched condoms. Jenna's gaze darted over his face, her lips pursed.

Jason settled his hands on her hips. She sucked in a breath and her eyes widened as his cock pressed the tender flesh of her abdomen.

"Wait," she said, flattening her palm on his chest. He waited but not happily. Her head dropped back against the door. "We can't do this."

"I think I proved we could and very well." His eyes locked on her full lips. Lowering his head, he took her mouth. He relished the tangy heat of her tongue and kissed her as he'd imagined kissing her many times over the past years. He almost shook with his need to possess her.

How many times had he watched her lips curve into a smile, part with laughter, flirt with the edge of a wineglass? He'd lost count but tasting her had become a near obsession with him. He'd never dreamed she'd let him. Jason owed Garth a debt of gratitude. If Garth hadn't been sick of hearing Jason moon over her and insisted Jason take action when Garth programmed the lights to fail, Jason wasn't sure he would have worked up the nerve to approach her this weekend.

Jason cupped her face, deepening their kiss. Her arms circled his neck, pulling him closer. She arched her back. Her breasts cushioned against his chest. She gasped as her nipples rubbed his flesh.

She broke off with the same suddenness with which she had begun. "I can't. *We* can't. Your dad and your *grandmother*—shit, the whole family—" Her words broke off in a strangled mutter.

"We can, Jenna. You want to and I want to. As far as I'm concerned we're the only two people who matter."

She dropped her arms, planted her hands on his chest and gave him a shove. She shook her head and Jason saw the possibility of making love to her again dwindling before his eyes. "Jenna, I'm not fucking anyone else in the family. I'm fucking you and that's how I want to keep it. The rest of the family can mind their own business."

"Are you insane? You know Mona and Mom have been trying to get me and David together. How do you think they're going to take it that his son is screwing David's prospect?"

His jaw tightened. He stared hard at her, fighting the helpless stinging in his chest. "Do *you* want to marry my dad?"

"No."

"Then what's the problem?"

"The problem? Jason! I'm about to become the geriatric whore who split our families apart and seduced a young man by offering him big-boy candy."

"Big-boy candy?" He chuckled. "Well, you are definitely the best-tasting candy I've had. But I'm also able to make my own decisions. Right now, I'm deciding on you."

"It's not that simple. You have family dynamics to consider. How am I supposed to tell Mona and my mother that I'm corrupting Mona's grandson in her own home while she's planning my wedding to the boy's father?"

"The boy?" His green eyes seemed to frost over. His jaw, already tight, turned stony and his fingers gripped her hips. "Boy?"

She flushed. "I'm not saying I think you're a boy. I'm telling you how they would see it."

Doubt flashed across his eyes. His beautiful lips carefully formed his next words. "Jenna, am I a boy to you?"

How could she possibly mistake the man before her for a boy? Nothing about his form was boyish. His muscled shoulders displayed his sculpted chest, which tapered to a lean waist and narrow hips. His bronzed skin highlighted the rises and valleys along his torso to the black trail of hairs nesting around his impressive cock, which waited for her answer in its fiery impatience against her abdomen. His thickly corded arms held her firm and still within his easy access.

She wanted him back inside her immediately. Her breasts ached for his touch and she'd die if he didn't kiss her again soon. A boy? No. But he was Mona's grandson, David's little boy. So no matter what she wanted or how she saw Jason, those two impressions wouldn't change.

They would also see her as the aging woman, out of her prime and not able to deliver the required grandbabies. Forget that she didn't want children. Oh, she had wanted them in her twenties but she had moved past that once she'd settled into her life and realized how much fun being her own person was. No she didn't want children. She did want a life partner to share things. But Mona would see her as having ruined Jason's future, or worse, dominating him with seduction away from his true potential. And what happened down the road if Jason wanted kids? Or, and she swallowed hard at this, if Jason wanted a weekend fuck and not a future, they would have split their families for purely selfish desires.

She sobered. What *did* he want from her? Because it suddenly seemed very important to her that he want more than a weekend or an experienced woman to practice his moves on. She'd been hot for Jason since the year he'd graduated college and had decided to spend the summer in Uganda helping orphans. Who actually did that anymore? People talked about world impact but who ever actually altered their life for it? That summer her image of him as hot young stud had morphed. He'd grown in her estimation within seconds to a globally conscious man who took action.

Well, he'd certainly taken action today. But was she a summer of intense activity like his Uganda trip and then a lifetime of fond contributions and promotions? Would she become the next project for him? Occasional sex while he worked to score her a spouse? Part of his intense focus when he had a goal in mind?

"It doesn't matter what I think."

"It matters to me. I want to know if you think of me as a boy." He pressed his lips in a fine line. Jason grabbed her thigh, pulling it to his waist. His eyes burned into hers. He flexed his hips and penetrated her deep and sure. Jenna caught her lip, biting down to keep from moaning at the pleasure of his cock buried inside her. "Does this belong to a boy?" he asked, his breath rushing hard from his lungs.

"You want this now, Jason, but later you'll regret it."

"Never." He pulled out and thrust hard into her core, his balls thumping her bottom. "I won't regret you ever. I've wanted you too long to regret having you."

Jason grasped her breast, kneaded her with calloused hands that made her writhe against him. Catching her nipple, he pinched it hard. Jenna cried out, tilting her hips to grant him better access to her. She leaned forward and clamped her teeth down on his nipple. She pulled and sucked on him, her hands sliding to his back and stroking his spine, his shoulders, anywhere she could reach without letting go of her oral prize.

With a guttural yell, he crashed and ebbed into her, pounding a sensitive spot deep inside her until she clamped on his cock in wave after wave of orgasmic milking. Jason continued to thrust through the fog of need until his own climax took him, pulsing in sharp spurts inside her, spending him utterly.

"I'm Uganda," she panted softly.

"What?"

"Nothing."

"Don't tell me 'nothing'. What do you mean you're Uganda?" To her great disappointment Jason withdrew from her, cleaning himself a second time. His large hands gripped her shoulders and he propelled her backward onto the bed.

"I just mean…" She lost her words when Jason stripped in front of her, his eyes locked on her thirty-something body. What did he see when he looked at her? Did he see her not-as-perky boobs and the onset of cellulite on her thighs? Her tummy wasn't as tight and she needed to do crunches. Her upper arms were looser too and she could see that she was headed in the direction her mother had gone. Somewhere in the aging process her mother had grown wings under there. Would he still want her when her boobs dropped to her navel and her nether lips got prunie with age? He didn't see it now yet he'd feel trapped with her old body when his was just reaching his prime and younger women wanted him to warm their beds. Would he leave her for them?

His thick cock sprang from his groin, an extension of his hard, muscled body. Her breath caught sharply when she realized he was ready for her again. Ah, youth. "You just mean…" he encouraged.

"Uh. I just mean you have a passion for Uganda and spent a summer there committed to helping. And you've committed a lifetime to supporting the cause."

He grinned suddenly. "You're right. You're Uganda."

Jenna crossed her legs, locking her ankles together. "Exactly."

"Wait. I'm confused again." He crawled up the bed toward her, over her then lay on top of her. His naked body radiated heat. Jason swished his hips into hers, no doubt trying to settle against her sex but Jenna kept her legs together. "You're going to make me work for it this time. Okay."

"What? No! No, that's not what I'm doing. I'm trying to reason with you here."

"I'm already inclined to give you whatever you want, Jenna, so long as I get to be the one to give it to you."

She felt her cheeks heat. Locking her eyes on his, she couldn't mistake the twinkle of humor in his moss-colored eyes or the wicked quirk of his eyebrow. Jason's lips curved, showing the barest hint of even, white teeth.

"I love your smile, Jenna. It drives me nuts to see the way it curls around a naughty secret."

His look said he could devour her. Her heart pounded a demand to let him. How did he make her feel sexy with the smallest effort? "Uganda," she repeated more to remind herself than him of their conversation.

"You pegged me correctly if you meant you've become a lifetime obsession with me."

"Not what I meant. I mean, I'm your summer of effort, your lifetime of fixing."

"Fixing?" Jason lowered his head, teasing her lips with soft kisses. The tip of his tongue traced the middle of her upper lip along the seam and she parted for him, wanting him to make the connection. He obliged, caressing her lips with his, stroking the underside of her tongue and lightly rubbing against it. "God Jenna, you're perfect. There's nothing about you that needs fixing." His tone worshipped her even as his gaze scorched hot and confident into her own searching look.

"You'll feel obligated to keep an easy friendship. Worse, you'll think you have to set me up with someone so you can move on after this summer."

"That's what you think I do with Uganda?" The warmth in his eyes cooled.

She knew he took his work seriously. After that summer, he'd hooked up with a well-known international organization to help expedite adoptions and provide medical and agricultural visas for social workers. It belittled his work to call it "fixing" but she didn't want him to feel obligated to ease her romantic life once he had his fill of her either.

"No," she answered.

He stopped kissing her and she buried her hand in his hair to pull him back. He accepted for one kiss before pushing against her hand to stare down at her. She knew she wouldn't get out of this conversation without an explanation. Unnerved, she squirmed beneath him.

"Then what do you mean? That I'll find other men for you, provide their visas for them to come and plant your soil? That I'll adopt you out for other relationships because while I continue to love you, I can't bury my cock in you 24/7? You're saying I can't have you all the time but will feel committed to sharing you out, building you up for a different future without me? Because you need to explain your comparison before I form the wrong idea and get truly pissed."

He already looked pissed. His brows had drawn together and while the light in his eyes and the ridge on her pelvis told her he was still interested, he had an uneasiness to him she wished she could wipe away. Why couldn't she have left well enough alone? She'd lusted after him and had fucked him. She should lie back and enjoy the ride. When it was over move on and remember him fondly.

But there was a problem. Actually two of them that she could see. One, the superficial realization that she could never be the same around him, having completely enjoyed his fat cock and every friction-loaded inch of him, when their families would inevitably get together as they always did, over the next fifty years. And two, she could have dismissed her attraction to him as a passing phase and a long-shot. Not anymore. Not when she realized she'd fallen for him and by imprinting herself with his physical brand, she'd either have to have him or never show up for family functions. Seeing him with someone else would destroy her.

Where was the sense in that? He was young with his life ahead of him. He had a committed relationship with babies and club memberships in his future. He wouldn't saddle himself with a woman aging by the second, no family and a lifetime of wondering how different it could have been to marry someone his own age. She couldn't let him do it.

"Jason, think about this. I'm available and you're a sexually active man." His hips nudged hers and she licked her lips to hold a whimper at bay. If she spread her legs he could — *no, stop thinking that way and get back on subject, Jenna.* "I get to benefit from your obvious state of arousal but after this summer fling what happens?"

"Easy. You're going to marry me."

"What?" Okay, she hadn't anticipated that pronouncement. The butterflies in her stomach quivered to life and that little brain between her legs shivered happily, begging for more of Jason's attention to show its appreciation. "Wait. No. You don't want that. You want to get laid."

"Hell yes. It seems you do too as my balls are getting rather damp. Not that I'm complaining."

If he could get her to open her legs a little wider, Jason was convinced he could make her see reason. Why the hell was she protesting this? He'd never made a decision he regretted and he wasn't about to second-guess his instincts now. When she'd said she was his Uganda, he thought she'd finally understood he was committed to her for the rest of his life.

Then she'd switched it up again and made it sound like she was a pity fuck. When had Jenna Michaels ever been reduced to a pity fuck? Every sensual move of her body, from the widening of her big brown eyes to the red-nail-polished toes curling into the sheets when he'd thrown her down, kept him in a permanent state of arousal. Hell, her bubbly laugh could make him run to her from the next room and if she didn't quit wiggling beneath him, he'd black out from the loss of blood to his brain. There was a whole different part of him doing the thinking at the moment and her convoluted argument made it tough to follow along.

She blushed prettily and her dimple flashed. "Listen to me."

"I'm trying, Jenna, but can we speed up the explanation so I can show you how wrong you are?"

Oh shit. Irritation pursed her lips and she seemed to solidify her resolve to keep him out of her. "Jason Francis Nolan—"

He winced. Was she deliberately trying to make him think of his mom? That kind of talk could kill a perfectly good erection. To counteract her evil plot, Jason cupped her breast and massaged her nipple. He was rewarded with a gasp and slight glazing of her beautiful eyes.

"You are making a rash decision based on what you want right now. I'm not going to marry you and you will thank me for it. One day you will find a sweet young thing who will send you over the moon with love. She'll have your children and fawn over you. She'll be your perfect counterpoint. But that someone isn't going to be a woman past her prime, with no interest in having a family, no patience for sitting at home while you work through your dream job and has the potential for ruining your relationship with your father, brother and grandmother."

"You done?"

She opened her mouth to say more but Jason stopped her with a searing kiss. "Let me be perfectly clear. I want you, not a simpering brainless girl. I want a partner, not a panting puppy waiting on my every whim. I want a woman with a spine who knows her own mind and feels secure enough in her own identity to share it. I want a woman of passion who lets me know when she comes." He winked at her. "I don't want children. The world has enough of them. You are my Uganda. Not because I have to sit back and 'fix' you but because it's where I would be all the time if I could. Just like I want to be inside you, next to you, breathing your air, smelling your skin, tasting your lips. I want to think about you and know you are thinking about me. I want to come home and know that you want me there.

"My dad married his silly young girlfriend and she changed into a woman as all girls do. You, Jenna, are there. You know who you are and *that* is the sexiest thing I've ever come across. My family will have to deal with it and if they cannot, it won't matter because you will be my family."

Her pert mouth formed an "O" but no words came out. Jason rolled her nipple and caught her "O" in another kiss. He penetrated her mouth, taking her kiss and stealing her breath the way she stole his with every glance. He had seen her look at him in the caves but hadn't dared hope it was attraction. He didn't know how the confident, sexy Jenna could want him or how she could think she wasn't good enough to keep him. It held no logic but he was determined to fight for her, prove her wrong. If he was lucky enough to have attracted her at all, he wanted her to think long and hard before she tossed him aside.

He left her mouth to press sucking kisses on her throat and along her shoulder. Jason slipped down her body, tasting every inch of her he could reach. He pulled the crown of her full breast in his mouth, sucking her and flicking his tongue with eager laps over her distended nipple. The hard little bud teased him and he nipped it, rolled it, pulled on it until she arched madly beneath him. Her eyes closed, her mouth open, Jason thought he'd never seen a more sensual goddess and she was writhing for him. It gave him power and pride. It tightened his balls as the pressure built and he nearly lost it watching her pleasure at his hands.

His fingers skimmed down her ribs. Jason switched breasts with a noisy pop as he left one nipple for the other. His gaze locked on the flushed and damp breast he'd just left. Her nipple jutted firm and plump. He pulled on her breast as he watched the first one quivering and full inches from his eyes. Jason was lost in the way her breast swelled off her chest wall, the valleys and crevices, the rounded rise tipped with her aroused raspberry peak. It fascinated him, egged him on as he tasted and nipped the one in his mouth and heard her breath tremble in soft cries from her kiss-swollen lips.

Jason dragged himself from his feast, kissing her torso and laving his tongue on the softer belly flesh within the cradle of her hips. His fingers danced over the hip bones, dipped into her exquisitely narrow button and tugged on the diamond-studded barbell he hadn't known was there until now.

He scraped his teeth on her belly. Jenna moaned, buried her fingers in his hair. Her upper arms inadvertently pressed her glorious breasts together in her attempt to touch his hair and he groaned around a bite of her flesh. She shivered, finally parting her legs for him.

Sinking between her thighs, he hooked her legs with his forearms, spreading her open for him. Jenna made a small sound of protest but he ignored it. Her scent called him to taste but first he wanted a mouthful of her and he closed his teeth on her mound, lightly scraping her pubis. Jenna's fingers grabbed his head as she thrust her pussy harder to his teeth. Jason chuckled. Yeah, Jenna was definitely a passionate woman who knew what she wanted.

Still holding her with his teeth, he flattened his tongue inside her slit and gave her one long, forceful lick. "Oh God!" she cried.

Satisfied that he had her complete attention, Jason settled in for a delicious dinner. His leisurely strokes ran from anus to clit. When she picked up his rhythm, he altered it. Her hips lifted off the bed but he forced them back down. He pushed her wide with his shoulders, freed his hands and held her open to him. Jason closed his lips over her clit, flicking it with featherlight touches using the tip of his tongue. Then he dived lower to suck noisily at her channel, eating her, swirling in his tongue, rubbing his nose on her bud. Jenna writhed and begged but each time she came close, he backed off and went elsewhere until that new spot burned her to near-release.

Jenna couldn't make the torture stop. She bucked her hips, lifted, arched, twisted, anything to make him bring her off. His breath blew across her damp, parted pussy and she felt her body juice for him. His eager mouth sucked it up. She couldn't stand it. "Jason. *Now.*"

"Are you sure? I mean, only a *man* knows how to eat a woman to completion. Not sure you think I can do it."

"You can," she gasped.

"I'm dedicated to getting it right, Jenna. I never leave a project unfinished. Remember Uganda."

"Fuck Uganda."

"Not sure I understand. You said you were Uganda. Are you asking me to fuck you?"

"Yes. Please!"

Jason's lips crashed down on her clit as his tongue swirled around her straining pearl. His tongue flattened on it and rubbed with firm, quick strokes. Jenna arched, screaming into her pillow as the black behind her eyes splintered into burning shards of light and heat. Her pussy clenched and spurted. Jason made happy sounds, the humming setting off another explosive orgasm that had her bucking hard into his mouth and the fingers of one hand digging into his scalp.

He released the suction before she had come down. Jenna was vaguely aware of him sheathing himself. Her channel trembled around his tip. Thick friction filled her and made her mindless as she clung to him. He rocked in and out. Slowly he climbed to his knees, lifting her hips and legs off the bed.

Jenna opened her eyes to watch. Jason hooked her legs again and plowed into her. His cock plunging in and out of her like a wide piston with her pussy petals around him fixated her gaze. She slid her hand to touch them and then flattened her fingers above her hooded, erect clit, shoving it against his cock with each stroke. The pressure did good things for Jason too as he groaned and flexed on her nub. Jenna climaxed suddenly, her new orgasm taking her by surprise and clenching his cock with tight, wringing squeezes. Jason shouted as he came, filling the condom with thick, burning liquid that spurted hard enough for her to feel the pulses deep in her core.

"Do you get it yet, Jenna?"

"Get that you kind of like me?" She grinned at him.

"That I love you." He planted his hands on either side of her head and dropped a kiss on the tip of her nose. "If your mother told you to do something you didn't believe was right for you, like marry my dad, would you do it anyway?"

"No."

"Do you see me as a man who knows what he wants?"

Jenna thought about that for a moment. Even as a child, Jason had made careful but quick decisions. When he'd wanted to ride his bike, he'd learned how in a day. When he wanted a scholarship for the World Studies program to complete his masters, he'd obtained it with single-minded determination and finished his degree while working nights.

Garth was the clown, Jason the serious, driven twin. "Yes," she agreed.

"Then as a man who knows what he wants and, like you, who won't be talked out of it by people who couldn't understand, might you believe that I've thought about the repercussions to a relationship with you? That I have made my decision and the only other person whose opinion I care about is yours?"

Chapter Three

ℰ

"What about the age difference? There're eleven years between us. You just told me you didn't want to marry a girl. What happens when you develop more fully into a man as any twenty-five-year-old girl would develop into a woman?"

Jason rolled his eyes. "You're looking for excuses."

She didn't argue the point. Jenna knew she was exactly doing that. Could she have Jason? Really have him and not worry about their families? Mona would be less than ecstatic as would Jenna's mom. She didn't know how David would feel but after his comment in the cave about not being choosey, she didn't think love would enter the picture in his consideration of her relationship with his son.

Loud rapping startled them. Jason swung his head toward the door.

"Who is it?" Jenna called.

"Honey, it's Mona. Is Jason still squashing that spider in there or did you send him down already?"

Jenna opened her mouth to tell Mona Jason had left but Jason interrupted her. "I'm here, Grandma."

Mona jiggled the doorknob. Jenna held her breath. Jason turned back to Jenna and winked down at her. He lowered his body onto hers and with gentle touches, pushed her auburn hair back from her face.

"I asked you to come down as soon as possible. What's taking so long?"

"Isn't Garth down there?"

They heard her sigh with exasperation. "Well, yes but you aren't. And I want you downstairs immediately."

Jason cocked an eyebrow. Jenna shrugged. "I'm busy, Grandma."

"Jason Francis Nolan!"

Jenna started giggling.

"Grandmother, I'll be down when I'm finished," he called gently.

"You *are* finished. I think everyone in the inn knows precisely how often and when you and Jenna finished."

Jenna felt her face flood with heat. "Oh crap."

"We were going to tell them eventually. Or did you still want to debate the issue of whether or not I know I'm in love with you?"

She shook her head, a smile tugging her lips.

"God, there's that naughty grin again." Jason kissed her hard. He turned to the door. "Grandma, go on downstairs. We'll be down as soon as we get our clothes on but mind you, I'm not happy about the interruption."

Mona screeched and stomped away.

He nuzzled Jenna's neck. "If it were up to me," he whispered, "I'd keep you naked."

* * * * *

The reception when they got downstairs was anything but warm. Grateful the B&B had been closed to outsiders for the reunion of families, Jenna still felt a moment of trepidation. Jason grabbed her hand, linking their fingers. They entered the living room as a united front.

Garth was grinning, his green eyes alight with mischief. He propped on Mona's armrest as he surveyed the families. Jenna's mom was flushed with embarrassment and her eyes darted to any part of the room but where Jenna stood with Jason. David glared at Jason. Mona lifted her chin to the air and her lip curled with disdain. At least the tour guide from the cave wasn't around for this.

Jason released her hand and put his arm around her waist before pressing a kiss to her temple. "I love you," he whispered.

"All men profess their love when a woman parts her legs for them," Mona said with a snort.

Jenna's mother gasped.

Jason stiffened beside her. "I won't allow you to speak to Jenna that way."

"I'll speak to Jenna any way I want to," Mona countered.

Jason felt every one of his muscles lock up. Anger surged through his veins, drummed loudly in his ears. He didn't have to turn and look at Jenna to know that she was caving in on her resolve. Seeing the confident woman beside him weaken pissed him off royally. There wasn't any other circumstance he had seen her in where she'd faltered. But before the onslaught of Mona's judgment in the face of the two families she cared about, Jenna was ready to throw their budding relationship under the bus.

Even as he fumed at his grandmother for taking a verbal slap at the woman he loved, he was nearly as frustrated with Jenna for not bearing up under the scrutiny. What hope did they have if she wouldn't fight for them?

"No you can't, Mona," Jenna said, finding her voice as her words grew in strength. "I'm sorry you think it's necessary to hold a family committee over the appropriateness of my relationships but I don't answer to you and neither does Jason."

"Nope," Jason said, feeling himself smiling widely enough to split his face. He looked down at Jenna, whose shoulders seemed to firm before his eyes. Pride swelled his chest. "In fact, I see no reason to continue this conversation. It only humors you into believing you can change how I feel about her."

Jenna looked up at him. Her wide brown eyes reflected affection. Her gaze dropped to his lips and he could swear her breath caught. Did that mean he had the same effect on her that she had on him? God, he hoped so. Hope was a luxury he hadn't entertained until that moment. He'd be a very happy man if Jenna loved him half as much as he loved her.

"How do you feel about her?" Kathy said, her voice barely above a graveled whisper. She hadn't met his gaze yet but she studied her daughter's profile as Jenna looked up at him.

"That's easy. I'm in love with her."

Jenna's lips parted as the sexy smile he adored tipped the corner of her lips and set a seductive spark to life in the glimmer of her eyes. Jason felt as though she'd just sucker punched him, making him see stars and turning him slightly woozy. He should have been used to the effect of her attention on him.

"And you, Jenna?" Kathy asked her daughter.

"I love him too."

"How is that possible? Just this morning we were discussing your relationship with David. Who's next? Garth?" Mona snapped.

Jason saw the flash of irritation in Jenna's eyes before she leveled a look at his grandmother. "*You* were planning my future with David, not me."

"Mother, I was never going to marry Jenna," David said on a weary sigh. "I like her. Who wouldn't? But you'd have to be blind not to notice the chemistry that's been building between them since Jason graduated. It was inevitable."

"You're going along with this ridiculousness," Mona accused.

"It's easier than arguing with you, Mom," David shot back.

"Garth?" Mona beseeched her other grandson.

"Don't look at me. I think it's great." Garth was all grins.

"Kathy?"

Kathy shrugged. "You know, Mona, it's not so bad. Our families are still joining. Besides, look at them."

Mona sputtered her protest.

"Look! Look at them," Kathy nearly yelled at Mona. When Mona finally looked, Kathy continued. "Bob used to look at you like that. George never looked at me the way Jason is looking at Jenna. And I can tell you from personal experience what it feels like to see love in the people around you and never have it."

Mona folded her hands in her lap and stilled.

"I see the same look on Jason's face that I saw on Bob's when he was still alive. And I see Jenna glowing from it the way you did, Mona. I won't stand in their way."

"Neither will I," David commented.

"Well, that's good," Jenna said, "because I wasn't letting him go anyway."

"Music to my ears, sweetie."

Jenna shared another one of her hot-as-hell smiles.

"But she's so old," Mona offered weakly.

Jason started to protest but Jenna rose up on her toes and kissed him. He forgot whatever he had been going to say.

Garth met his gaze with a mischievous look of his own. "Well, damn, Grandma. How the hell am I supposed to introduce you to Gretchen now?"

"What do you mean?" Mona's voice rose in near panic.

Garth had the attention of both clans as he proceeded to discuss his love for a woman he'd met at the grocery store who had kids his age. Jason raised his brows suggestively at Jenna. Jenna whispered that she'd like to go back to the room. Garth pontificated over the virtues of older women and pronounced the love of his life was a young fifty. Mona went apoplectic, raging over cougars and their prey.

Jason took Jenna's hand and led her back up the stairs to her room. He shut the door behind them and Jenna suddenly put up her hand to stop him.

"Yes?" he asked.

"I love you. I didn't just say that for their benefit. I do love you. I also never believed you could love me back. You have your life ahead of you and you could have chosen to be with anyone."

"I didn't want just anyone. I wanted the best — the woman who stole my heart."

"I'm not giving it back, you know. It's mine now. Besides you're too freaking hot to be let loose on the singles market."

Laughter bubbled up in his chest. "Too freaking hot?" he mimicked. "Do you have any idea how insanely jealous I was when I thought Mona had a reason to hook you up with my dad? I thought she had inside information about a crush or something."

"I had a crush. It just wasn't on your dad."

"Garth?" he teased, bending to press a tender kiss just below her ear.

"Nah. That other guy. Garth's twin. He makes me wet with a single look."

"Shit!" Jason's laugh shook almost as hard has his hands. His eyes widened in disbelief. Did that mean she was wet for him right now? Time to find out, he decided.

It was the truth and if his look meant what she thought it did, she'd surprised him, pleased him with the admission. "Watching the way you stood up to Mona like that made me realize a serious miscalculation on my part," she confessed.

Jenna hooked her fingers in his jeans and popped the button closure. She grabbed a fistful of tee shirt and yanked it up his body to flatten her palm on his firm, packed torso. His skin heated her nerve-chilled fingers as she stroked the ridges. His stomach flexed beneath her whispering touch.

"What miscalculation?" he asked. His voice grew husky, shivering over her flesh and teasing her nipples to attention as though he had physically touched her.

His hands slid under her shirt, cupping her bare breasts. He swore softly when he discovered she'd left her bra off in the re-dress. Jenna kissed the taut cords on his neck. He was clearly trying to hold back, give her his attention while she talked. The restraint showed in every harsh breath, every carefully controlled motion. His flared nostrils and darkening green eyes quickened her desire. She arched into his palms. "I expected you to placate them. But you're more man than I gave you credit for."

"I've lived a lot in twenty-five years, Jenna. I've seen hard life and made hard decisions. I'm not an idealist, I'm a realist. Realistically, I cannot imagine my life without you in it. Don't ever accuse me of being a boy." To make his point, Jason kissed her, possessing her mouth and controlling her responses to him with the slightest pluck to her nipples, his hips thrusting at hers, his tongue mastering hers.

She dragged his shirt off over his head. Hers followed.

"I love looking at you," Jason said. He cupped her breasts, leaning back to look at them. Jenna looked down, seeing her breasts as he must have. Held in his hands, she had to admit they looked pretty good. His wide palms and long fingers, tanned against her pale skin, were a study of contrasts. His flesh was tougher and darker where hers was pearlescent, satiny. Her breasts looked amazing in his hands.

His long fingers petted her. His thumbs rolled her aching nipples. The wonder of his gaze matched the tender attention in his caress. "I'm not going to break, Jason."

"Just admiring."

"Can you admire a little rougher?" She caught his hands to her breasts and pressed, rubbing her nipples on his palms as she did so.

"After I look at every delicious inch of you."

The hell with that, she thought. Jenna cupped her hand to his groin, firmly massaging his swollen ridge. She was rewarded with his grunt of pure male satisfaction. It was an easy task to lower his zipper as his erection encouraged the downward rasp. His cock sprang forward into her hand. "That threat goes two ways, hot stuff. Looks like I'm not the only one who shorted the dressing process."

Jason stepped from his pants. He made quick work of her jeans as well, snagging her panties with his thumbs when he pushed them to the floor. He pulled their bodies flush to one another and she shivered at the intimate contact. Without conscious thought, she abraded her body with his, loving the sensual friction.

"You're driving me crazy," he muttered, reaching around her to cup her ass and lift her hips into firmer contact with his erection. "No regrets?"

"No regrets."

"Not about sex, Jenna. About the whole thing. Our families. Our future. I want a future with you."

Skimming her fingertips upward, she curled her hands over his shoulders and pushed. She walked him backward until the backs of his knees hit the bed. Then with a shove from her, he collapsed. Jason looked up at her. Trust shone in his eyes but it lingered with cautiousness. Jenna knew he meant to respect whatever decision she came to and for some reason that sealed her resolve.

She loved him. Until this weekend she'd thought her infatuation with him had been a heavy dose of sexual appreciation. But it went far further than that. It delved into her heart and locked with every memory of him and every realization that he had made more of his life than most men did by the time they retired.

No, Jason wasn't a boy. He hadn't been one for a long time. And the look on his face wasn't a boy's look for a girlfriend, it was a man's pure acceptance of his lover, his life-mate. He knew her. Knew her flaws, her setbacks, her body, her age, her successes. He knew her and he wanted her just the way she was. Not eleven years younger. Not eleven years more pert or innocent. And Jenna wanted him as he was, as her intellectual and emotional equal.

Yes, she was sure and she let her love for him shine through her eyes. "No regrets, Jason. Just us. Only ever us."

He had crawled back on the bed with a condom and Jenna climbed over him. She pressed gentle kisses to his chest and shoulders, his neck. Lifting his hands, she kissed his palms, hoping he could understand the feeling she had no words for. At a loss, she relied on her body to show him.

Jenna stoked her slit along his shaft from balls to tip, slicking him with her moisture, letting him feel for himself what his love did to her.

"Only ever us," he repeated. "Marry me, Jenna."

Her eyes met his. Taking his cock in her hand, she put the condom on before guiding it to her opening and lowered herself on him, sighing. "Yes."

"Yes you'll marry me, or yes that's what you wanted inside you?" he asked, his eyes glazing over on an involuntary thrust when her channel squeezed him luxuriously.

"Yes, I'll marry you. Yes, I want you inside me. Yes, I love you. Yes, yes, yes."

She punctuated each affirmation with the slide of her body over his. Jason groaned and buried his thumb between them, striking her wet pearl with deft, firm circles. Jenna shattered. "Too soon," she protested.

"No. I love watching you come. Your breasts turn pink and I'm the reason you hold your breath when you lose control." He rolled her clit again, pinching it gently.

Jenna spiraled higher, pounding him madly in her own insatiability. Finally her orgasm subsided and she collapsed against his chest. "You didn't come."

Jason rolled her swiftly onto her back. "I'm not done with you." His eyes glittered down on her with lust and longing. She couldn't help but grin. Jason mumbled something about orgasmic smiles when he grabbed her thighs and pushed them wide.

Jason removed his slippery rubbered cock from her pussy, leaving her bereft. He grinned at her and she couldn't miss the dangerous twinkle in his eyes. Sitting up between her legs, Jason leisurely examined her, stroking his fingers over the sensitized flesh still quivering from her orgasm.

"Come back," she moaned softly. Her hands reached up to cup her breasts, tweak her distended nipples. Spread so wide the muscles in her thighs ached, she realized it was a turn-on to be at his complete mercy. "Take me, Jason."

"In good time. I reckon you ought to know what you just agreed to."

"What do you mean?" she asked. Her breath hitched as she watched his thumb rub over her outer labia roughly. Jason took hold of her inner lips and pinched hard enough to make her hips buck. Her pussy flooded with renewed heat.

"You like that too, eh? Not just slapping on the ass, but rough sex?"

"So far."

"Don't worry, I won't hurt you." He dropped a kiss on her clit, flicking his tongue over the erect nub.

His calloused thumb dipped into her channel and pumped, coating his digit with her juices. Without warning, he circled her rosette and thrust his thumb inside her. Jenna closed her eyes, unable to do anything more than feel and tug on her nipples while he explored her body.

Jason eased two fingers into her pussy. With short strokes he rubbed his thumb and fingers together, heating the thin skin between her pussy and anus. His other hand massaged her lower lips until his thumb slipped into her channel. He rubbed the upper wall and Jenna nearly shot off the bed from the combined sensations. Tossing her head, she blindly grabbed the sheets and arched her hips. His thighs still forced her legs apart and she could not gain leverage to thrust against his fingers. She wanted more but couldn't reach him.

"Oh God, oh God, oh God," she gasped over and over.

As if it weren't enough, he rubbed his four free fingers over her clit in deep massaging strokes. He clamped his lips over her forgotten nipple and pulled hard. Jenna screamed. Black streaks shot through her vision as her climax stole her sight in a blinding flash that ripped its way over her flesh, tangling her nerve endings as it passed.

Jenna was still limp when he pushed in, bucking his hips upward as he did and jangling the nerves high on the inner wall of her vagina. Jenna saw stars, feeling the recent orgasm rebuild. With each forceful thrust against her womb, she dug her nails into his back and urged him on. Her legs wrapped around his hips, pulling him until his balls slapped wetly against her ass and her pussy pounded in a heady mixture of pleasure and pain. God she wanted him so badly.

She completely ignored the hoarse begging for more and high-pitched cries of passion. Surely they weren't from her.

Jason's chest rasped her nipples with each hop of her breasts on every thrust until she didn't think she could stand not feeling his seed spill hard and high into the condom inside her. "Jason, please come for me. I need you. Feels so good. Want to feel you come hard."

He growled low and hungry, shoving into her over and over. The headboard clacked against the wall in violent bangs.

On a final grind he came, spurting hard in consecutive pumps, jetting into her body. She screamed and everything went hazy. She felt her mouth pull into another smile. Jason's lips touched hers. His harsh breath fanned her face. "I love you, Jenna. Don't ever forget it."

"Impossible to forget."

"I plan to fuck you every conceivable way until the day I die. Still want to marry me?"

"Find the fucking minister. Now!"

TEMPTING TESS

Regina Carlysle

ഇ

Dedication

℘

*To Alisha Paige, Tessa Rae, Cindy Spencer Pape,
Judith Rochelle and Desiree Holt. Fellow authors and
sisters of the heart. For the fun, the belly laughs and the
strong shoulders when needed. I couldn't make it through
a single day without you.*

Trademarks Acknowledgement

℘

The author acknowledges the trademarked status and trademark owners of the following wordmarks mentioned in this work of fiction:

Alice in Wonderland: BKN International AG Corporation

Inn of the Mountain Gods: Mescalero Apache Tribe of the Mescalero Reservation, The Indian Charter Corporation

Pinot Noir : Wineland Ltd.

Spider-Man: Marvel Character, Inc.

Wizard of Oz: Turner Entertainment Co.

Chapter One

∞

Night had fallen to crisp cool temperatures in the beautiful Ruidoso Mountains and as the evening grew, turning into a deep incandescent blue, so did Tess Garrity's mood. Vacations were supposed to make one feel better, not worse, weren't they?

Nope, not happening.

At least not tonight.

She'd been here for a couple of days in an effort to reevaluate the vast wasteland that was her life. At forty-five, she was a widow and the mother of a grown daughter. Now here she was thinking things through, hoping for something, anything that could make her feel alive again.

Pathetic.

The wide back porch of her rented cabin was rustic, offering a panoramic view of a vast wilderness that called to something deep inside her. What that *something* was, she had no clue. Feeling a desperate sort of urgency grab her, she'd come outside with a bottle of Pinot Noir she'd picked up earlier today during her jaunt into town for groceries. She eyed the half empty bottle ruefully and walked over to pour herself a bit. Half a glass only. There was something really sad about drinking alone and she was already feeling a little tipsy.

Sinking down onto a comfy couch, she curled her legs under her and sighed. Glancing toward the cabin that sat to her right, she wondered briefly about skimming out of the nightgown she wore and changing into some jeans and a tee. Yeah, she could traipse over there in the dead of night clutching her half empty bottle of Pinot Noir and knock on the door of the sexiest, hottest man she'd ever seen in her life.

The very thought made her giggle.

Hastily she set her glass of wine aside and eyed it with contempt. Yep. Just a tad tipsy. Mr. Sexy would laugh his butt off, thinking she was making moves on his gorgeous young ass. The tall, rugged Latino would think she was pathetic.

Well, wasn't she?

Sobering instantly, Tess wrapped her arms around herself, hugging tight as she swallowed the lump that rose up in her throat. Not gonna cry. Not her. She'd been tough and strong for everyone. For years. This was her time of self-discovery. This was her time to be…

What?

Lonely as hell?

A great gaping emptiness rose up and threatened to steal her breath. She'd never been the kind of woman to feel sorry for herself but suddenly, alone, here in this vast wilderness she felt so small, so insignificant. Tears rose up but there was no one here to see so Tess gave in with a sigh.

They rolled across the surface of her eyes and dripped down her cheeks as she stared out over the beauty of the mountains and struggled to feel just the tiniest bit significant.

Raggedly, she gulped cold air, hoping for a return to sanity, but it was elusive.

Suddenly from around the corner of the cabin, a large dog ran into view. Tess recognized her neighbor's pet instantly. Milky moonlight gleamed over the coat of the golden retriever as he scampered up, bringing friendliness and comfort with him.

"Hey there, boy," she crooned as she stood and went to the top step of the porch. Sinking down, she brought him close and buried her face against his warmth. "Are you lost, sweetie? Lonely? I think I'm…um, feelin' kind of lonely myself."

The dog whined and leaned his big head against her shoulder and Tess just lost it.

Great gulping sobs broke from her throat. She cried so hard she shook with it. Maybe it was the wine but she didn't think so. She was lost. Alone.

Daniel Rios came out the backdoor of his cabin, skimming his gaze through the woods beyond as he looked for Bo. He'd let him out twenty minutes ago to take care of important doggie business but Bo hadn't returned. The night was quiet with only a faint whistling of breeze sifting through the pinon pines. Heading out across his back lawn, he peered into the darkness, hoping to head off a midnight squirrel hunt. It was getting late. He glanced across the way at the cabin he owned and rented out. This time to a beautiful woman whom he was dying to meet. A rental agency handled the details of stuff like this so, as of now, she was a stranger. Hopefully, she wouldn't be for much longer. To say the gorgeous blonde was intriguing was an understatement.

Daniel stilled and narrowed his eyes. It was late but her lights were still on. Should he go over and introduce himself? He snorted. Yeah right. What would he say? "Um…hi. I've been wanting to fuck you since the moment you moved into my little rental place. Yes, uh, you might think this is some kind of pick-up line but you look like an angel. A fuckable, delicious, sexy angel made just for me and I get hard every time I see you."

She'd think he was a nut.

He heard a sound. A faint one coming from the direction of the neighboring cabin so he headed that way, hoping Bo wasn't getting into a world of trouble. When he rounded the corner, he stopped dead in his tracks. The woman's face was buried in Bo's neck and she was sobbing like her heart was broken.

Daniel felt his heart tighten in his chest.

When Bo pulled away and took off to sniff around, she wrapped her arms around her slender body and shook like she

189

was caught in the midst of a tornado that threatened to tear her apart.

He just stood there watching her, unable to move. Bo ran up and Daniel gave him an absentminded pat on the head and sent him on his way. When he saw that the dog had gotten into his cabin by way of the doggie door, he turned back to watch the woman.

She was so lovely sitting there crying in the moonlight, he couldn't stand it another minute. Following instinct, he approached slowly and cleared his throat. He opened his mouth to say something, anything to offer comfort when she looked up and saw him.

Stumbling to her feet, she gazed at him with a dawning look of horror. Her hands went over her mouth as she choked back another sob. Her eyes were so blue they seemed a pale silver in the evening light. Tears floated across their surface and Daniel thought his heart would break at the sight.

He came closer and she didn't move, just looked at him. Finally he did the only thing he could. He wrapped her in his arms and drew her in. "Ah, *mi cielo*," he whispered against her hair, calling her darling, holding her close. "Don't cry. I can't fucking stand it."

She gasped against his chest and clutched his ribs with grasping fingers. Her breath soughed through his tee shirt, warming him. Impossibly, his cock grew thick and hard at the feel of her curves pressed against his body. He tightened his hold. "Talk to me."

"I-I don't know your name," she whispered on a shaky breath.

"I'm Daniel from next door. Just hang on, honey. Let me help."

"I'm Tess." She pulled back and looked at him with teary eyes and she knuckled the tears away but they just came faster. She broke his heart. He wanted to help her. Comfort her. "I'm just feelin'…um…so alone."

Her voice broke over the words and that did it. It just did it.

Daniel cupped her cheeks and bent low, breathing in her scent, the mystery of her. Using his thumbs, he swept away the dampness from her face and pressed his lips to hers. He'd intended to offer comfort but that instant warm connection threatened to bring him to his knees. Sweeping his tongue over her lips and beyond into the honey-sweet depths of her mouth drew an answering groan from the lovely, distraught woman in his arms. She burrowed in closer and he felt the pearling tips of her nipples stab relentlessly into his chest.

"Let me help you," he whispered.

"Yes. Yes. I don't know you but I want you. I want you now." Tess wound her arms around his neck and he didn't give another thought to lifting her up and carrying her inside the cabin. It seemed as natural as breathing when she clung to him and twined her long legs around his waist. The heat of her pussy burned through his shirt and against his belly. His shaft pounded hard against the fly of his jeans. He ached with the sudden, intense need of her.

Once inside, he pressed her to the wall and rubbed his hardness against her. A curling tingle started in the base of his spine as he raked over her warm pussy. His lips settled against her neck and he breathed her in. It was surreal. He felt alone in the world with her, wanting to protect, to help. Taking her became the most important thing he'd ever done but his mind rebelled. Taking advantage of weeping women wasn't his style.

"I can't do this," he gasped against her flesh. "It's wrong. You're upset. Damn."

"No. Don't say it." She grabbed his face and focused in. Dark desire, the want of human touch burned hot in her gaze as she pressed tiny frantic kisses on his eyes, his cheeks. She pressed her mouth to his, nipping his lips, stroking with her tongue. Her breath came out in a rush. "I haven't felt alive in a long time. Not until now. Fuck me. Take me."

Torn, Daniel made a rough sound and lowered his mouth to her breasts. Near violent with urgent need, he raked his teeth over her nipples, loving her gasp of pleasure. He pressed his heavy erection hard against her core and a cry tore from her mouth.

"Damn it, Tess. If you want to stop this, tell me now or I won't be able to stop."

"Don't stop. Don't ever stop."

"Shit."

He carried her through the dimly lit cabin and straight into the only bedroom. He'd built the place with his own two hands and knew every inch of it. Her bed was made so he reached down with one hand and jerked the bedspread down and out of the way. All the while, Tess clung to him, pressing kisses to his throat, nipping with her teeth.

The room was dark. Daniel lowered Tess to her feet and didn't hesitate. Not any more. He yanked the white nightgown over her head and tossed it away. He didn't take time to feast his eyes on her body limned by moonlight sifting through the blinds. He didn't take time to kiss her sweet, delicious mouth. Instead he filled his hands with her breasts.

Her nipples were stiff, prodding the palms of his hands, stabbing at the pads of his fingers. A hungry sound tore from his throat and he took one hard, swollen bud into his mouth to suck. Drawing deep, raking gently with his teeth, Daniel devoured it as if starved. He was a man who understood loneliness, who felt despair that his life was often more shallow than he'd like. No, he didn't know this woman who writhed in his arms but something about her was like a balm to feelings he'd buried deep. Passion for her brought it all to the forefront now as he sipped at her flesh.

Tess drove her fingers through his hair, held his head close and Daniel wanted more. More. He sent exploring fingers over her soft skin, touching her waist, her belly, diving into the curls between her thighs.

192

Daniel groaned low. "God, you're wet. Beautiful and wet. I'm going to fuck you with my fingers. Let me stroke this sweet cream."

She gasped and it fueled the heat that roared to life between them. Two sad strangers who met in a moment of need. Daniel sank his teeth gently into her shoulder as his fingers sought and found her distended clit. He strummed it lightly and Tess' breath broke. Her stance widened as she sought a firmer touch.

He gave it to her, diving his fingers deep into her cavern. She felt like warm, wet, satin and he wanted more, wanted it deep.

"Sure?" he murmured, knowing he'd die if she stopped him.

Tess' answer came with the brush of her hand against his cock as it pushed against the denim of his jeans. "Daniel," she whispered.

"Hell yes." Reluctantly, he withdrew his fingers from her depths and yanked his shirt over his head. He grabbed a rubber from his pocket before pushing his jeans down and tossing them aside. "No more waiting, honey. You're burning me alive." His head dropped back when her hand fisted around his pulsing cock. She squeezed lightly and he shivered. She moved her hand slowly down and up, spreading his pre-cum over the head of his cock with her thumb, and he wanted to roar. "God! You're sweet, Tess."

Daniel wanted her spread out beneath him. He wanted to take her, fuck her, suck her sweet clit into his mouth until she screamed.

Making his imaginings reality, he lifted her and spread her out against the backdrop of crisp cool sheets. She spread her legs. Her fingers were splayed across her belly. Beautiful.

Feeling savage, he clasped her knees and dragged her to the edge of the bed. She made a startled sound but he didn't want to give her time to think. He just wanted her to feel.

"Fuck! You're creamy and sweet," he murmured as he dipped his fingers into the hot silk of her pussy. "I'm gonna drink your cream, eat you like I'm starving and I am, Tess."

Bending low, he lapped her juices, sucked her clit, drank her down while his fingers plunged deep, sliding through the sultry damp heat. With his thumb, he circled her opening then dipped it low and back, to touch the bud of her ass in tantalizing strokes. Oh yeah. "Do you want it here? Want me to fill you everywhere, sweetheart?" Gently, he probed her ass with his thumb until it slid neatly inside.

"Daniel!"

"Feel full?" he breathed against her hot flesh. "Feel stretched? I wanna put my cock in you there. Fuck you in the ass until I come hard. How would you like that?"

But then she couldn't make a coherent sound other than to whimper as he started to eat her cunt again. Hot and deep, he took the strokes of his tongue, lashing her with pleasure until she trembled against her bed. Her fingers were anchored in his hair, her knees were pressed high against her belly as he pumped this thumb slowly into her ass and sucked hard then lightly on her clit offering twin sensations that would send her careening over passion's sharp edge.

Holy Christ!

And then she fell.

Daniel felt her stiffen with a moan, felt her body seize. She gulped a huge breath and screamed.

Something primitive roared to life deep inside him. It broke free, making him want to stake his claim on this lovely stranger. He wanted his touch, his taste imprinted forever on her mind.

Withdrawing his fingers from her body, he pumped his cock in his fist. Once, twice. Grabbing up the condom, he ripped the package open with his teeth and rolled it quickly into place. Taking her knees, pushing them high against her chest, he buried his length deep inside her wet heat.

It was Daniel's turn to cry out. His rough groan reverberated in the small bedroom, emphasizing the raw, sexual moment. He pumped his cock into her, pistoning hard as her cries grew apace with his. Reaching down, he took her clit with his fingers, pinching hard as he withdrew his cock and settled it at the rosebud of her anus.

He looked down and their eyes met, his silently asking permission.

"Yes," she whispered. "Fuck me. Fill me up."

With a low rough sound, he drew back and sent his fingers into her wetness, gathering her dew before bringing them to her rear entrance. One finger dipped deep in preparation and then he penetrated her, pushing slowly, carefully inside. Beneath him, Tess stilled and he saw her eyes go wide. "You sure?"

"Yeah."

"God!" He sent his cock slowly deeper and a dark thrill swept through him. His balls drew up tight as he felt her muscles tighten around his rock-hard length. "Oh yeah, darlin'. You feel so good. So hot and tight. Yeah, that's it. Relax for me. Let me get inside all the way."

Tess only gasped. Each breath she took seemed to blast a sensation through his hard, throbbing shaft. Nothing had ever felt so good. Once seated to the hilt, he began to move. His fingers went back into her pussy. Plunging in and then opening wide to stretch her. "You're as tight as a virgin, Tess. I need to stretch you." He used his thumb to tease her clit. And then the pleasure grew hot enough to set his hair on fire. His balls ached as he pressed his cock deeper, buried his fingers in the lush wetness of her sex.

Daniel looked down, saw the fine sheen of sweat that dampened Tess' shoulders and chest, and he suddenly knew he didn't want this for his first time with her.

Oh yeah.

Just the first time. Not the last. He wanted her again and again. She was definitely addictive and he wouldn't give her up. Not now.

Withdrawing slowly from her ass, he guided his cock home. Velvety vaginal walls clasped and clung, wringing a heavy moan from his lips. He leaned over her, propping his knee on the bed, and took it deeper. The head of his shaft bumped her cervix and it was like coming home.

Suddenly it was all too much. Beneath him Tess rocked against him, sent her body into motion as internal muscles milked his rigid length.

"Yes. Oh sweetheart, yeah!" Motion and lust propelled him as he pistoned into her. He stroked through sultry, clasping flesh, pounded hard as his fingers squeezed her protruding clit. It was suddenly too much, as sensation ran wicked fingers over his balls, up his shaft. Tickled them along the base of his spine and traveled to the top of his head. He blasted his seed into the condom as her orgasm sent him over the edge of desire.

Crawling up onto the bed, Daniel pulled her up against him. Tears fell from her eyes and he didn't know if they were because of the earlier emotional outburst or a result of a deliciously hard orgasm. They could even be a combination of both. But he didn't press her. Bending his head, he swept his mouth over her damp cheeks and heard her answering sigh. Her arms curled around him and her eyelids began to droop.

He didn't speak, just watched over her as she began to drift into an exhausted sleep. Tonight had been beyond bizarre and seriously, he couldn't ever recall something like this happening to him before. Tomorrow they would talk. She was such a gentle-natured woman, she would probably have huge regrets about jumping into hot, sweaty sex with a complete stranger but they'd talk it out. If he had anything to say about the matter, they wouldn't be strangers for long.

He must've dozed because he was jolted awake by the sound of a vehicle crunching through the gravel of the crude driveway he shared with Tess. Sitting up, he glanced at the bedside clock. Headlights flashed across the blinds and he moved away from Tess to look through the bedroom window.

"Shit." He whispered the word beneath his breath when he recognized Hillary Mills' car. She was an old girlfriend who had the annoying habit of dropping in unexpectedly at the oddest hours. It was over between them but she didn't seem to realize it. Like an angry pit bull, she clung to the hope there was a future for them.

Uh-uh. Not going to happen.

She was a party girl from the word go and they couldn't be further apart in what they wanted from life.

Tess rose up on an elbow and blinked sleepily. Yeah, she might be a good ten years older than him but it didn't take a rocket scientist to see she was a beautiful woman and right now, she looked like a sleepy young girl. Nothing would thrill him more than to crawl back into her bed and forget all about Hillary who was currently blasting the horn on her SUV as if celebrating her arrival.

After all Tess had been through tonight, she didn't deserve a scene and Hillary was the Queen of Scenes.

"Shh. Go back to sleep, sweetheart." He grabbed his clothes from the floor and then reached to run a hand along her bare arm. "Someone just showed up at my place."

"Really?" She looked at the clock and scowled. "It's three a.m. What kind of friends do you have anyway?"

He grinned. "Not very good ones, I guess. Right now, I think you're pretty much the best friend I've ever had."

Returning his smile, she lay back on her pillow again. "Mmm. That's nice. I kinda like you too, Daniel Rios. You need to go, don't you?"

"I'm sorry. You don't know how sorry I am, but yeah. Talk to you tomorrow?"

She sighed and watched as he pulled on his clothes. He bent to kiss her softly just as the horn blasted again. A car door slammed. Reaching down, he swept his finger over Tess' swollen lips and smiled. "I'll see you tomorrow, okay?"

"Yeah. Tomorrow. Good night, Daniel."

He'd just made it to the bedroom door but he turned when Tess called his name.

"For what it's worth, Daniel, this was a first for me."

"Yeah, I understand. It was a first for me too."

* * * * *

The whistle on the kettle went off with a blast of steam and Tess poured the boiling water into a mug that already contained the powdered hot chocolate mix she'd purchased earlier. Carefully she stirred and added exactly eight miniature marshmallows. She lifted it to her nose, inhaling the sweet scent, then once again, very carefully carried it over to the front window of her rented cabin.

She hadn't been quite so careful last night, had she?

Recalling everything that had happened between sexy Daniel Rios and herself during her wild moment of emotional crisis, she shivered. Her body ached in the most interesting places and regret rode her shoulders. Begging for sex wasn't her style, but she'd done it in spades. What must he think of her? She wrapped her hands around the warmth of the mug, closed her eyes and groaned, feeling like a complete fool. The whole hot scene replayed in her mind. The way he'd touched her, comforted her.

It had been so long since she'd been touched.

Everything she'd done for the past twenty-five years had been careful. Precise. She'd been everything to everyone. Nurturer, lover, supermom. Now it was just her and at forty-five it was time to ponder the great question of her personal universe.

What more was left?

Renting this rustic cabin in the mountains of Ruidoso, New Mexico, was a starting point for what Tess Garrity considered the beginning of her new life. She leaned against the window frame and stared out at nature laid out in all its glory.

Beautiful!

Pinon pines mingled with giant golden-leafed aspen that seemed to stretch all the way up to the hand of God, chilling in their majesty. In the distance, the Blanco Mountains rose high, a deep smoky blue, snow-topped and cloud-shrouded. Only a month or two and the snows would drift toward this lower level, blanketing hills and valley in a gown of white.

She'd only arrived in the tiny vacation spot a few days ago, driving in from Dallas with a quick stop-off in Lubbock where her daughter was attending college. Julie was thrilled that she was finally taking some much-needed time for herself but worried that she would be alone.

Right on cue, the landline in the small cabin rang and Tess smiled as she went to answer it.

"Hey, Mom! It's me. Checking up on you as promised."

Love expanded in Tess' chest as she flopped on the couch and curled her bare feet up beneath her. "Hi, cookie. How was the test?"

"Sucked. Think I did okay though. It's over now at least," Julie sighed on the other end and Tess heard the chatter of young women in the background. "Some of us are getting ready to go get a bite to eat, you know, celebrate Friday."

"Sounds like fun. Be careful, hon."

"Oh I will." Julie got quiet. "You doing okay, Mom? I hate to think of you vacationing alone. Are you sure you don't want me to drive out there?"

God love her. She'd raised a beautiful, loving young woman. Tess smiled. "No, Julie. I need this time alone. Everything at the shop has been so crazy lately and hell, I'm just so tired. I want to get my head together."

"You still thinking about selling Petal Pushers?"

Petal Pushers was a floral and gift shop she co-owned with her friend, Sassy Marshall. Tess hummed a little. "Yeah, maybe. Sassy knows I need a change but gosh, honey, what would I do with my time? It's a big decision and I don't know if I'm ready for anything drastic at this point in my life."

"Maybe it's way past time you did something drastic."

"Huh?" Yeah, Julie was sweet and supportive but was she psychic? Heaven help her! The last thing she wanted was for her impressionable daughter to know how low her mother had sunk last night. Middle-aged woman, desperate and needy, throwing herself at a younger man. Some role model.

"Listen, Mom, I know you don't need another lecture from me but you've got to start getting out there again."

"You mean dating?"

"That's exactly what I mean. I know you loved Daddy but he's been gone for two years and it's time to get the lead out and do something with yourself besides run that flower shop and worry about me."

Tess sighed into the receiver, wondering when her baby had become so wise. "Maybe that's why I'm here right now. I have some serious thinking to do."

"Do you have any neighbors out there in the boonies? Someone you could visit with if you get lonely? Have dinner or something?"

Laughing, she sent her gaze to the open front door of the cabin and shook her head. "Oh yeah, I have a neighbor all right. I'm looking at him right now."

Julie paused then gasped. "A man? Oh Mom, you've gotta tell me!"

Tess looked out into what passed for a front yard in this wilderness and tried not to drool. Six feet three inches of heaven stood a short distance away, tossing a small red ball to his gorgeous dog. Daniel was a real-life Latin hottie whose thick, black hair ruffled in the breeze, blowing back and then forward over a face that could've been carved by some wicked god. He laughed, the sound deep and husky, sending a chill over her arms. She hadn't heard that deep, dark voice since she'd come apart in his arms nor had she seen him since he'd walked from her bedroom afterward. Her heart thumped hard in her chest. She pressed her legs together hard to assuage the emptiness she felt between her thighs. That sharp ache of emptiness was sudden, catching her off guard.

Before last night, they'd only acknowledged each other a few times and exchanged smiles. Who would've thought she'd have an emotional crisis and end up in bed with a man like him? He was the kind of rough-hewn man who made a woman drool and Tess wasn't immune. Last night she'd begged for his touch, wanted his cock pounding her into oblivion and she still couldn't shake the memory of it. Dumb.

Just looking at him made her hunger for things she knew damn good and well she'd missed in her life and might never experience again. He conjured visions of mussed black satin bed sheets and the scent of sex and the touch of a lover who might fill her world with an eroticism she'd never known.

She blinked and looked away. She could forget about that. Today she'd gotten a very good look at the young woman who'd arrived in the wee hours of the morning. No doubt Daniel had forgotten about last night already.

"Not much to tell really," she finally said, lying her ass off. "We've waved a few times. He's gorgeous. And young."

"Ooh, how young?"

"Early to mid-thirties."

"Mom! That's not too young for you. Jeez. He's a grown man for cryin' out loud and you're a mature, drop-dead sexy woman. Heck, you look just like Michelle Pfeiffer. All my friends think so too and she's smoking hot. You should definitely go for it."

Tess had to laugh. Michelle Pfeiffer? Well, maybe a little. That aside, it was hard to imagine her delightful young daughter trying to arrange her sex life. "Uh-uh. Ain't gonna happen, sweetie. You should see the lovely young nymphette he has rooming with him. Simply gorgeous. Yeah, I'd say the man has his hands full."

Later, she unwound herself from the couch and disconnected. She stood and fixed one more cup of hot chocolate, placing exactly eight mini marshmallows on top, and went to the open front door of the cabin. It was dusk, cool but not cold, so she stepped into a pair of flats and went outside.

This was her favorite time of year in these mountains. She and Jeff used to vacation here during their twenty-three-year marriage. In the spring and summer, horse racing drew tourists by the thousands and in deep winter, it was a skier's paradise but she preferred Ruidoso's off-season. Fall brought crisp weather, turning leaves and few people. Perfect. Especially for a woman who was in the process of re-thinking her life.

Off in the distance between the two lone cabins sat a spacious gazebo. The deer in the area were tame enough to walk right up. Even now a doe stood guard over two fawns that nibbled at a nearby shrub. Another doe munched at a branch from a small tree near her neighbor's cabin. Clutching her hot chocolate in both hands, she gingerly walked toward the structure, not wanting to scare off the tiny creatures. Both babies looked up at her. "Ah, sweeties," she crooned. "Don't be scared. I'm not gonna hurt you."

Ignoring her completely, they went back to their dinner as she sprawled along the built-in bench of the gazebo. As she sat, relaxing, breathing the freshness of the air, a feeling of utter loneliness swept through her. Despair the likes of which she hadn't felt since the doctors had diagnosed Jeff's illness reached up with wicked claws and ripped at her heart. Sick to death of feeling sorry for herself, she blinked away the tears and sucked in a hearty breath. She'd never been a woman to feel sorry for herself and she wasn't about to indulge in a continuation of last night's pity party.

Suddenly she heard the sound of a door closing and she turned her head toward the cabin next door. Daniel stood there, much as she'd done earlier, drinking in the sight of the wild deer roaming the grounds. A tiny smile quirked at the corner of his sensual lips.

Dear God!

Daniel was the kind of man you might see on the pages of magazines and in the movies. Her nipples tightened at the sight of him standing there gazing over at her. Memories of what they'd done last night grabbed hold. Early this morning she'd heard his truck pull away from his cabin and she figured he was heading off to work, so though she knew it was inevitable they would talk again, nerves skittered down her spine.

God, his eyes were dark and liquid, his smile was as slow as his stride as he walked toward her. Beneath his boots, dry, brittle leaves crunched with every step he took.

Lord have mercy.

His shoulders were broad and his chest, covered by a tightly fitting thermal shirt that stroked those firm muscles like the hand of a lover. Tess swallowed hard. She could practically hear her heartbeat as it pounded in her throat. Between her legs, nerves long ignored thrummed to life.

He wore a flannel shirt unbuttoned over the thermal, and his worn jeans lovingly traced his cock, paler there as if hands had stroked the denim white in that one enticing spot.

White teeth flashed in his swarthy face and Tess noticed he held a bottle of beer loosely in one hand. "Cute, aren't they?" he said.

Shaking herself from the cloud of lust that had momentarily stolen her good sense, she sucked in a breath and smiled. "Yeah, they are. How are you?"

"Good. Been wanting to talk to you." He came closer and she realized she'd been pretty accurate about his age. Early to mid-thirties. He motioned with his hand at the bench. "May I?"

Tess straightened. "Oh yes. Please."

Keep things casual, she reminded herself.

He'd just started to sit when his dog came bounding into view. Leaves clung to his golden fur, making it obvious he'd been romping through the woods. Seeing his master, the dog trotted up and nudged Tess' knees.

"Stop that, Bo."

Tess laughed and stroked the animal's glossy hair. "Oh it's okay. I love dogs and you're a handsome guy, aren't you?" Bo panted a welcome and Tess looked up at the hottest, sexiest man she'd ever seen. He was frowning and shaking his head.

She grinned at him and he instantly returned her smile. Bo trotted off to chase the deer.

"You doing better today? I've been worried."

"Um. Yeah, I'm okay." She drew in a slow breath as Daniel sat and stretched out a big, bronzed hand. It immediately engulfed hers. So warm despite the evening chill that settled around them. Calluses ran across his fingertips and the pad of his hand. Beautiful hands. They were rough and so sexy, she immediately wanted to feel them rubbing against her face, her nipples, between her legs. She wanted to feel them roughly dipping into her weeping sex as he brought her to screaming orgasm. Oh yeah. Tess wanted those hands gripping her ass as he thrust repeatedly, deep and hard.

She almost shivered as awareness of this man and his blatant sexuality ripped through her hard-won composure. *Holy crap!* What was she thinking? Recalling the beautiful young woman who'd arrived last night, she mentally took a step back.

"Do you want to talk about it?" he asked in the face of her sudden silence.

Shaking her head, she struggled to remain calm. "No, I don't think so." She forced a smile and looked up at him. "Maybe we could just pretend it never happened. We could start over. I'm Tess Garrity."

"Daniel Rios and I have to confess something here." He gave her a steady look. "I already knew your name before last night. I'd asked around."

Tess frowned. "You did?"

He flashed that sexy white smile again. "Nothing insidious, I promise. Asked Pam, the leasing agent, about you. I own these cabins, built them a few years ago."

He'd asked about her?

Finally he released her hand and shifted on the bench slightly, turning more fully toward her. The intensity of his gaze whipped through her body like a steel blade. Those heavily lashed eyes might have been peering straight into her secret heart. Awareness trickled over her flesh, down her thighs. Her pussy throbbed to a pagan tempo. Carefully, she took a sip of her chocolate to mask the reaction. "You built these? They're gorgeous." Her face was burning and with her blonde coloring he was sure to notice.

"Actually, I've built a lot of cabins around here. Came to Ruidoso years ago with the construction company that built the casino over at the Inn of the Mountain Gods. I fell in love with the area and stayed. That's about all there is to it. So tell me something." He stretched out those long, muscular legs and crossed his booted feet at the ankles.

She arched a brow.

"Why are you here alone?"

Okay. Personal question here but they'd passed into the realm of personal with a bang last night considering she'd let him fuck her silly. She sighed. "I guess I just needed some time by myself."

"Divorced?"

Maybe Daniel was lonely too, since despite the woman in his cabin, he was out here with her asking questions. Younger people often talked with her about their troubles but with this man, the very air seemed different. She shrugged her shoulders. "Widowed. It's been two years now."

Tess sucked in a breath at the look he flashed her. Compassion filled his eyes. "I'm sorry, Tess. That must be hard."

Taking a sip of hot chocolate gone cold, she fought back memories that were always so close to the surface. "It is. Oh, it's better now. Jeff and I were together for twenty-odd years and had a beautiful, almost perfect daughter together. When he got sick five years ago, we thought he might beat it but—"

"But no."

"No." Tess blew out a breath. He seemed so gentle, spoke so tenderly to her. Despite last night's intimacy, handsome Daniel was a stranger but there was something so comforting in his rough, masculine voice. She stared him straight in the eye. "It was hard for a very long time. Getting over it, I mean. Jeff and Julie, my daughter, were my whole life and then suddenly, in a flash they were gone. Julie to college and then Jeff…well, just gone."

Daniel reached over and took her hand again. When had it gone so cold? The warmth of him seeped into her skin. It was comfort. Yeah, that was all.

"It's hard picking up the pieces, isn't it, Tess? That's what you're doing here in a mountain cabin all alone."

"Yes."

"Then I'll say it again, I'm sorry. Life shouldn't be so hard."

"Life is what it is, Daniel. I'm coping with everything, trying to adjust."

"All alone? Sounds pretty dismal to me."

"It can be," Tess stilled as his thumb brushed a soft path across her palm. "For the past few years, I've been trying to figure out how to be comfortable with myself again."

"And have you?" His eyes were hot, almost feral. "Maybe a little part of you is ready to move on now, let yourself reach out."

He released her hand and she felt the instant loss of his warm touch. Daniel's voice was deep and rich. Sexy as hell. He tipped back the bottle and took a drink of his beer. Waning sunlight shimmered through the leaves, dappling his hair, making it shine. Unexpectedly, desire slammed through her. Her fingers itched to dive into that silky mass, to feel it ghosting over her skin, between her thighs.

Memories of the night before, the hot, sexy fucking he'd given her, whipped through her mind and she fought them with every ounce of strength she possessed. Loss was there too and it made her ache. Last night had been a moment out of time. A mistake that wouldn't be repeated but one she'd never forget. That dreaded feeling of sadness drifted over her and sank into her bones.

She studied the man who sat quietly next to her, drinking a beer as the sun set low over the mountains, and regretted that she could never be anything more than a friend, a nice older woman whom he'd felt sorry for and felt obliged to fuck. He'd been kind. That was all.

But oh Lord, how she wished it could be different.

Oh yeah, she was truly losing it this time. A few years of celibacy could make a woman a little crazy. But was Daniel right? Was she ready to move on, reach out to someone? A man?

As if it was time for a reality check, the door to Daniel's cabin flew open and his gorgeous girlfriend gave them both a look. "Dinner's ready," she called. She shot a glance in Tess' direction.

Cool your jets, honey, she thought with a touch of regret. *I'm no competition for you.*

The lovely auburn-haired woman was roughly five years older than Tess' own daughter. Tall and shapely, she didn't have a sag or a bump and not a single tiny line on her very perfect face.

Daniel stood and frowned. "Listen, Tess. I know you don't want to talk about last night but I need to tell you—"

"Daniel?" The beauty in the doorway seemed to bristle with impatience.

Scowling, he looked back over his shoulder. "Yeah, Hill. Be right there."

Tess gave the younger woman a tiny wave and a smile. "Didn't mean to keep y'all from dinner. Sorry," she called out as she rose from her seat.

The woman seemed to relax. "That's okay. Come on, honey, dinner's getting cold."

Daniel started to turn away and then stopped and reached for Tess' shoulder. He gave it a small squeeze. A shimmer of awareness ran wicked fingers over her skin but she bravely smiled and gave him a questioning look.

"Would you like to join us, Tess? There's plenty."

Tess glanced at the other woman in time to see her stiffen. Nope. Not wanted there and not about to intrude. She shook her head. "Maybe another time. You kids go on and enjoy your meal." She'd used her *mother* voice. The voice that said she was a person of comfort, a woman in whom one could confide. It would be best all around to pretend last night never happened.

Daniel started to walk away and Tess watched him go, feeling a little lost and a whole lot alone, when suddenly he stopped and looked back at her. Within a moment, he was stalking back, his face was hard, his mouth no longer smiling. He moved close enough that she could smell the hint of beer and peppermint on his breath, the subtle spice of his cologne.

Bending low, he whispered in her ear, "For what it's worth, Tess Garrity, I'm not a kid."

Tess gasped and flashed her eyes up at him alarmed. "I didn't mean it that way."

Reaching up, he stroked a finger down the side of her cheek. "Yeah, I know. You can cut the *mother* persona with me. Things aren't always what they seem."

With that, he turned away and walked slowly toward the cabin. His girlfriend stared at her and then smiled a little before shutting the door.

* * * * *

"Bastard!"

Tess heard the scream in the middle of the night and bolted upright in her bed. The sheets pooled around her hips as she leaned over to check the time. Two a.m.

"I hate you! Creep!"

She heard a car door slam and rushed through the cabin, stubbing her toe on an end table. Gasping in pain, she made it to the window in time to see the redhead from next door rev the engine on her SUV and tear out down the winding graveled drive.

What the hell?

Daniel stood in the front, briefly illuminated by the flash of headlights, but it was so dark. Obviously, they'd had a fight. A big one. Peeking into the gloom, she saw him, a shadowy figure, standing some distance from the porch. Tess backed away.

Nope. Not her problem but she couldn't help wondering what on earth had happened to send the woman screaming off into the night like that.

Tess made her way to a floor lamp and turned it on before lifting her hands to rake her fingers through her disheveled hair. Jeez! There wasn't anything worse than being woken in the middle of the night like this. It brought back memories of Julie as a teen, out with friends. Every parent dreads those late-night calls…always bad news.

Shaken, her heart pounding, she started to curl up on the sofa when there was a knock on the door. Daniel! It could be no one else. He must've seen her light go on.

Drawing in a breath, she glanced down at herself. She was wearing a scoop-necked T-shirt with her loose, comfy flannel pj bottoms. Yep, decently covered.

Opening the door, she blinked up at Daniel standing there on the porch and damn it, blinked again.

Heavens to Betsy!

Bare-chested, he stood there wearing nothing but a pair of worn jeans and a frown. His hair was gorgeously tousled, drooping over his forehead and barely brushing those very wide shoulders. His feet were bare. When he shivered, Tess regained her composure in a rush.

"Daniel! Oh my God! You must be freezing. Come in."

"Thanks," he growled low as he came in. He ran those big, rough hands over his arms and stepped aside as Tess closed the front door. "Hell, Tess. I'm sorry about this."

"Don't you dare worry about it. Come in and let's get you warmed up."

Daniel flashed a look at her and she swallowed. Hard. Yeah, she was a practical woman. She wouldn't think about the flare of heat in those darker-than-sin eyes. The hard abs on his delicious belly practically screamed *stroke me*.

Uh-uh. Look away, Tess. Look far away.

"Sit down and I'll get a blanket. It's freezing tonight."

She rushed into the bedroom and lifted the lid of a storage trunk at the foot of her bed. Gathering up a heavy blanket, she went in and settled it around Daniel's shoulders. Thank God he was covered now. Maybe she could completely forget about the way his muscles bunched on that yummy chest or how his corrugated abs made her itch to lick every inch of exposed flesh.

"Thanks, Tess. I'm so sorry about this," he began rubbing the blanket over his arms and snuggling in. "Guess you heard Hillary screaming like a banshee."

Tess huffed a breath. "A deaf woman could hear her." Feeling a little safer with Daniel covered in the blanket, she sat beside him on the couch and curled her legs up. Propping an elbow on the back of the furniture, she looked at him. "Want to talk about it?"

"I owe you an explanation, at least." He settled back on the couch and turned his head. Humor lit his eyes. "She got mad so fast, I hardly knew what was happening. Like a dumb ass, I followed her outside. Hell, I didn't want her leaving in the dead of night. Morning would've been fine. And then the door shut behind me and I was locked out. Please know the last thing I wanted to do was get you involved in this crap."

Tess looked at him, absorbing his words. Curiosity reared its ugly head. From the sound of things, he'd asked her to leave. But why? The woman was beautiful and adoring, maybe just a little possessive but what woman wouldn't be just a little clingy with a man like Daniel Rios? He was big-time man candy. Finally she sighed. "I think we could both use a drink. Wine okay? I have about half a bottle of chardonnay in the fridge."

"Sounds fine." He shifted and tossed the blanket aside to stand. "Why don't I start a fire, Tess, and we'll talk."

She sucked in a gulp of air to steady her nerves as he loomed over her. Dominance oozed from every pore, a machismo that sent her nerves skittering wildly. Her heart thumped as she tried not to stare at that oh-so-lovely bare chest.

Daniel held out a hand to pull her from the couch and she caught her breath at how close he stood. For a man who'd been freezing his butt off a few minutes ago, he'd heated up nicely. Warmth fairly vibrated from the man. "Um. Good. I'll go get the wine."

Sheer nerves carried her into the kitchen where she poured the drinks. Looking back over her shoulder, she watched him build the fire. Stacking small pinon logs, striking a match. Muscles leaped to life on his long back and his arms bunched with each bit of effort.

He was the hottest man she'd ever seen. Jeff had been a handsome but rather ordinary man. Their life had been one of friendship and comfort. This moment with Daniel in the middle of the night was altogether different from anything she'd ever experienced before. Intimacy was ripe in the air and Tess wanted to shy away from it. She was afraid of what this man did to her. She'd been married to the same sweet, gentle man for years but she'd never felt the sheer magnetic pull that she felt with this stranger.

It scared her to death!

The cabin was shadowy, the lighting soft and it looked like Daniel would be here for the night. What on earth was she going to *do* with him?

Well, actually she could think of ten or twenty things she could do with him but, uh-uh, not going there. She wasn't one of those aggressive women who could just walk up to a guy and say, oh, um, by the way, you're the hottest, sexiest man I've ever met and I want your cock plunging into my pussy. Right fucking now! I want you to bang me into the mattress until my head threatens to explode. I want you to lick my cunt until I drown you in my cream.

Shit!

Terror zipped through her veins at all these crazy thoughts. She was a mother, for Christ's sake. She was at least a dozen years older than this hot stud. He'd laugh his ass off if he only knew what she was thinking.

Drawing her control around her, Tess struggled to regulate her breathing and went to Daniel who stood looking down into the fireplace. Tiny sparks were catching the dry wood, burning it into a delicate, cool blue mingled with hot yellow. Shadows from the growing flames seemed to dance along his torso like a sensual touch. Flicking, teasing flesh that was bronze and hard and so very tempting.

Suddenly he looked over at her as she stood there holding a wineglass in each hand. His eyes were hotter than the fire he'd built. Tess stood motionless, unable to speak.

"I want you to know something," he said. "I met Hillary a year ago. She was vacationing here with friends and I took her to bed. For some reason, she got it in her head that I wanted more. Wanted a relationship."

"You didn't."

Daniel shook his head and made a sound of disgust. "Hardly. She's not my type. Good for a one-night stand but that's about it with a woman like that. She's a party girl and I've had my fill with it. Outgrown it. That's not what my life is about anymore."

Tess pressed a glass into his hand, sensing his need to talk. She was a good listener. Always had been. "You told me this evening that you're a man, not a kid. You're right about that."

He speared her with a glance then took a sip of the chilled wine. "Got that right. I'm into women, not girls."

"I see." Tess looked down into the fire, watched it catch and grow. Burning, fragrant and clean.

"I doubt you do. I had no idea she was coming here, Tess. The whole thing was unexpected. After I left you, I told her she needed to leave but when I came in from work she was still here. She started making demands, talking about a future."

"What happened?"

Daniel shrugged. "I told her I wasn't interested in something serious with her and that I wanted her gone, it was over between us. I mentioned I'd met someone else and she got pissed off and left. It's a good thing. Right after I told her to leave, she grabbed my cock through my jeans. She started stroking me, tried to get me hot for her and I pushed her hand away. Everything can't be solved through sex."

"Some things can," Tess whispered, almost to herself. Her gaze shot up when she realized she'd spoken the thought aloud.

His eyes narrowed then focused on her lips for a split second. "Tess."

She shook her head and rolled her eyes. "God! Dumb. I don't know where that came from."

Daniel took her glass and set it along with his on the mantle. He turned to face her squarely. His hands, those marvelous hard hands, settled on her shoulders. A calloused thumb traced the exposed line of her collarbone and a shiver of awareness sank deep into her bones. "You can say anything to me. Anything at all. Ask me about the woman, Tess. Ask me about the woman I met."

She drew in a shaky breath as expectation hummed in the air. She shouldn't ask because she already knew the answer and this answer could land her in a world of heartache. A wisp of fear mingled with anticipation lashed wildly through her body. It couldn't be. Things like this didn't happen to her. The flesh between her legs throbbed like mad, moisture pooled, thick and heavy in the crotch of her panties. Muscles, little used over the past few years, pulsed to life.

"Okay. Who is she, Daniel?"

"I told her I'd met you, Tess. I told her I'd met you."

Chapter Two

ဢ

Was he kidding? God, he had to be kidding.

"You can't be serious. Things like this don't happen to me," she whispered, knowing no truer words had ever been spoken.

"Now it's my turn to be surprised. Bet men try to pick you up every goddamned day and don't you dare tell me you're too old for me, or that you have too much good sense to let me fuck you." His gaze burned with intensity. Truth rang loud and strong in his voice. "I've been hard enough to pound stone since the moment I set eyes on you. This has been on my mind since what happened between us last night. I assure you, Tess, I couldn't be more certain."

She barely had time to gasp when he reached out with both hands, cupped her face and kissed her. Pressure, lightly applied by his thumbs at her jaw, forced her mouth open but force wasn't necessary. His tongue was right where she wanted it.

Over and over he plunged, stroked, taking the kiss deep, ghosting over the walls of her cheeks, whispering lightly across her teeth and her tongue.

Delicious.

He was an utterly delicious man.

Changing the angle of the devastating kiss, Daniel plowed his fingers through her hair, dipped his hands to her neck and stroked the rapidly beating pulse at the base of her throat.

When had he moved closer?

Oh God! His scent wrapped around her like a wicked dream. *Please, never let me wake up. Things like this aren't supposed to happen to widows, to mothers.*

"You're not just a mother, Tess. You're not just a widow. You're a woman," he whispered as if he'd read her thoughts. He formed the words against her lips as he drank her breath with rapid gulps. He panted like he'd been in a race and she realized he had been. He wanted her enthralled by his touch. This man didn't want to give her a chance to escape from his plans for her.

Tess felt the touch of denim brush against worn flannel. His gaze flashed to hers and she noted the thick curling black lashes then the sharp slashes of his cheekbones. Helplessly, her eyes fell to his mouth. Had lips ever seemed so sensual? No, never.

His hands dipped to her ass and he gripped her hard as he thrust his cock against her and Tess suddenly hated the veil of fabric that kept flesh from stroking flesh. A low moan broke the plane of his lips as he made a sensual slide against her core. He had to know she was wet, dripping with lust. He dry fucked her, sliding over and over, barreling between the lips of her sex, pressing the damp heart of her. His touch was electrifying against the distended bud of her clit.

She panted, gripping those firm muscular shoulders, and something wild broke free from deep inside her as he raked that delicious hardness against her.

First and foremost, she was a woman with needs and desires that had been tucked away for far too long.

"Daniel," she breathed.

"Damn. Too many clothes. I've got to get inside you, sweetheart. I've thought of nothing else for days." With a savage look, he gripped the hem of her T-shirt and yanked it over her head. He flung it away and stilled.

For one miniscule moment Tess wanted to cover her breasts but then she caught the glint of steely pleasure in his eyes. Her nipples pearled, peaked. A little thrumming pulse skipped through the sensitive flesh. "I want your mouth on me, Daniel."

Daniel groaned. "Hands first." He reached out and plucked the hard buds with his calloused fingertips. Transfixed, she watched, her mouth going dry as he scraped the pad of his thumb, then his nail across the distended tip. A moan broke free and she gasped as he plucked, pulled, each tiny tug growing stronger and harder.

Her panties were soaked, sopping wet.

"They look like strawberry ice cream," he murmured in that deep, mesmerizing voice. "My favorite flavor."

"Oh God. Yes. Yes, Daniel."

Daniel wrapped an arm around her waist and yanked her closer. His dark head bent as he drew a nipple deep in his mouth. The sucking action had Tess rocking against his erection. His face seemed carved from stone as he pressed against her core. Slid. Rotated. "Shit, yes. You're sweet," he crooned, transferring his attention to the other nipple.

Tess rubbed her clit against his cock. Ah, so good, so fucking good. Had it ever been this way for her before?

Never.

Every practical thought she'd ever had flew from her brain as she let desire for this stranger sweep her away. As he sucked strongly at her breast, his hands swept the bare lines of her back, then he dipped them past the drawstring waist of her pajama pants to grip her ass.

"Panties," he whispered against her flesh. "Don't wear them again, Tess. I want to think of you naked there. Naked and ready for me to take you."

Before she could blink, he drew away and tugged at the drawstring of her bottoms. Soft flannel fell down her legs to pool at her ankles and she stepped out of the fabric and kicked it aside.

"Don't hide yourself from me. Not ever," he commanded in a brusque tone. Reaching out, he moved her hands from her breasts, leaving her standing there in only a pair of very drenched panties. "Take them off."

Tess swallowed, catching the predatory glint in his eyes. It was part of a game, she knew. His touch had been nothing but gentle yet the sound of his rough voice demanding she remove every stitch sent a thrill of expectation shivering across her hot flesh.

Biting her lower lip, she reached down and pushed the miniscule panties down her legs, maintaining eye contact the entire time. She stepped out of them.

"Pick 'em up, sweetheart. Hand them to me."

Tess obeyed and felt her face burn. The tiny blue panties were drenched with her juices and she jerked when Daniel's hand brushed her own. A knowing look glittered in his beautiful eyes as he held the undergarment gently and brought it to his face. "Smells like you, Tess. Like a warm, living, breathing passionate woman. How long had it been since before last night, honey? You were so damn tight."

Breathing evenly was futile so she finally gave up. She gasped for air, her heart thundering in her chest. Her knees went weak. Embarrassed, she shook her head. "I-I can't…"

"Yes, you can, darling. How long?"

Tears of shame burned behind her eyes. She couldn't answer. She wouldn't.

Daniel's face softened. He threw the panties aside with a vivid curse and stepped up to her. "I'm sorry. Not my business. Not yet."

He kissed her again, gently, nipping her lips, teasing with his tongue, gentling her with a touch that was tender and warm. Rough hands teased along her spine and gripped the cheeks of her butt. She gasped against his mouth as he dipped his fingers deep between the globes to probe and touch. Daniel groaned loudly against her mouth then suddenly released her.

"Enough."

Grabbing the heavy blanket from the couch, he spread it out before the fire and turned to her. "Come here, sweetheart. Let me touch you."

The cabin was chilly but where Daniel stood, holding out his hand, it was warm. Sensation sang in her blood as he drew her close to the fire's warmth. The blaze from the fire was nothing compared to the heat that roiled through her veins. She'd had a good marriage, a comfortable marriage but Jeff had not been a demonstrative man. Sexual adventures were completely alien to his nature.

Oh yeah. This was a first for her.

Go for it, Tess, her mind encouraged. *You'll live on it forever. Enjoy him. Take him and let him take you.*

The tempting, wicked voice had her smiling at this ruggedly handsome, younger man and the daring imp inside her grinned with satisfaction.

She let him draw her down, spread her out. Supine she lay before the fire while Daniel stood over her. Intensity radiated from his big body and he reached for the snap on his jeans. Tess heard the soft rasp of a zipper.

Oh wow! Commando!

He didn't wear a smidgeon of underwear beneath those soft-as-butter jeans. With a flick of his hands, they dropped from his hips and he kicked them away. Tess' mouth opened on a gasp of delight. It had been so dark last night, only vague impressions remained.

Huge! Oh yeah, honey. Come to mama.

That naughty imp in her brain giggled with delight. Lust burned hot and wild through her body as she took in his massive erection. Proudly it rose from a nest of black hair at his groin. Nearly waist high, it was thick and long, pulsing with color at the broad plum-shaped head.

Holy shit!

She found her mouth watering at the sight of him and involuntarily, she arched her back in invitation. From above her Daniel made a growling sound that sent moisture to rain once again between her legs. Her upper thighs were damp from the passion he called from her.

Tess reached out, reached up.

Daniel shook his head. "Not yet. If you touch me now, I'll go off like a rocket." He came down on his knees between her spread thighs. "Raise your arms back. Yeah, like that, honey. Keep them stretched above you that way. I love the way it makes your breasts rise as if hungry for my tongue. Are they hungry, Tess?"

"Um…yes. Yes, Daniel, please put—"

"Shh. Be patient, darling. I've been waiting for days to get a look at this lovely body. Let me enjoy this. I promise you will too."

She'd never felt more exposed. She wasn't an eighteen-year-old hardbody anymore and she was certain she couldn't possibly compare with the younger women he'd had in the past. But suddenly, it didn't matter. Nothing mattered but the dark heat that burned in her lover's eyes as he looked at her body. His gaze lingered on her face before zeroing in on her breasts and waist. One fingertip stroked her from sternum to navel, leaving her shivering in its wake.

He stilled. With one finger, he lightly stroked the straight line that stretched above her mound from one side to the other. His gaze flashed up.

"C-section," she murmured.

One side of his mouth kicked up then he bent and stroked that scar with his lips. His fingers glided through the damp curls just below. "Sweetheart," he whispered against her belly.

Stunned, Tess watched him rise over her again. His hands were firm on her knees as he lifted them, held her open. Totally exposed to him, she watched as he stared as if mesmerized. "So pink. Beautiful. Like a dark pink rose with petals opening just for me. God, Tess."

She knew she was dripping, could feel it, warm and wet on the insides of her thighs, drenching her labia. He saw it too. Daniel's sensual bottom lip was slack and he reached down to run his fingers over her sex, dipping into the moisture. His jaw flexed, a muscle working.

She jerked at the first touch.

"Shh. Easy."

His fingers swept through the heavy dew, spreading her labia. A thumb dipped into her sweet center and through it all, he watched, his expression hard with lust.

Tess watched the play of firelight on his dark skin and ached to touch him. She'd been told not to move her arms so her fingers could only twitch helplessly as he played.

Held captive by the command in his voice, she watched him, jerking as he plunged two fingers deep inside her pussy. Muscles, unused for years, contracted, expanded, clenched. Tess gasped at the invasion. Dark pleasure wound as tight as a coiled spring. Thrusting his fingers deep, he placed his other hand over her mons, pressing, holding her still. "Ah, that's it, honey," he said as she writhed. "You're so tight. Can't wait to send my cock plunging through this tight, pink, flesh. So pretty."

Keeping his fingers inside her, he began to torment her with the other hand. His fingers slipped through tender layers of flesh, found her clit with unerring accuracy and strummed upon it.

Tess cried out, tension holding her tightly as he plucked and pulled the morsel. Waves of pleasure lashed up and out, spiraling through her belly, hardening nipples that were taut and exposed to the cool air in the cabin. She became a writhing mass of nerves, unable to stop quivering.

With a raw curse, Daniel withdrew his fingers and went down between her spread thighs. His tongue stabbed hard and repeatedly deep inside her, tasting her fully, and she arched to meet his mouth. Her thighs were firmly clutched in those devastating hands and then he increased the pleasure by taking her clit in his mouth to suck, returning his fingers to her sheath. He held them still for just a moment, letting her absorb the impact of his sucking mouth, his lapping tongue, the breath he whispered over that ultrasensitive flesh.

Tears rolled from her eyes as she looked down at his dark hair splashed across her pale belly. Once, he looked up at her, his chin was wet and glistening with her juices. His smile was wicked and filled with knowledge.

When he returned to her cunt, he raked gently with his teeth then pulled the throbbing little knot into his mouth. He plunged his fingers deep repeatedly and Tess' body reacted violently. She pushed against his mouth, writhed against the thick blanket.

"Daniel. Oh God. Oh honey, yes. Please, please, please." The begging wouldn't stop. Nor the pleading. It was too much and not enough. His mouth opened wide to engage her pussy fully and his plunging fingers suddenly stilled. She could feel the contractions begin and she simply shuddered as pleasure rocketed through her. Her feet flexed, her thighs tightened. Her hips jerked. Daniel's beautiful hair was silky against the insides of her thighs.

Feeling swamped her, took her under as she came against his eating mouth. A wild pulsing set up in her nipples and chills cruised over her flesh and across her scalp. Her cry of completion was loud and wailing as she jerked and writhed, falling from the sharp blade of pleasure into a fire so hot she thought it might consume her.

And then Daniel's mouth was there. Against hers. He tasted of her sex. Her pleasure. He buried his mouth against her shoulder as the aftershocks hit her and then he latched onto a tender, throbbing nipple and tugged with a gentle sucking motion that threatened to send her teetering again.

"Not finished," he whispered. "Not by a long shot."

He drew back to his knees and reached for his jeans. Plucking a condom from the pocket, he opened it and within seconds rolled it over his straining erection. Tess closed her eyes quickly, tried to catch her breath but nothing helped. Her eyes flipped open to take in his beauty. She didn't want to miss a moment of this. Being here with Daniel this way was pure fantasy and she wanted it to last.

Taking his cock in his fist, he stroked himself. His eyes fluttered closed before he stared down at her as if he wanted to devour her whole. No one had ever looked at her with such primal intensity before and she shivered in reaction. Moving over her, he swept the broad knob of his sex across her pussy. Down, up and down again. She gasped as delight tore up through her once more. Glancing down, mesmerized, she saw the condom was wet from her fluids. Groaning, he dipped his cock up through the cheeks of her ass where he pumped slowly, then moved that heavy head against the entrance to her body. A dip, then two.

His shaft was thick and Tess felt it pulsing with life as he stroked her labia, the silken, wet tissues of her sex. It circled and teased at her throbbing clit, pressing until she squirmed.

Growling low, Daniel reared up and clasped her knees, bringing her legs up and out. With a rough sound, he began to enter her. Looking down at her, he stilled. His jaw was clenched tight and a muscle worked furiously.

"How long, Tess? You're so tight, honey. So tight."

She shook her head. "Long, long time."

"Shit." He plunged further, working in by tiny increments until, with a low growl, he was seated to the hilt. He pressed against her from knee to chest. The hard muscles of his chest, the thatch of curling hair on it, further abraded nipples that were ultrasensitive.

"Touch me, Tess. I need your hands on me."

A second invitation wasn't needed. Gratefully, she settled her hands on his very broad shoulders, cruised them over the muscles on his upper back. God, he felt good. Strong and capable and sexier than any man should be. Daniel lay above her utterly still as her body became accustomed to his invasion. Wanting to hold him closer, she looped her legs around his hips, drew him tighter with her heels pressed against his lower back.

Propped on his elbows, he looked down at her. "You're like a virgin. You're so tight." His hands sifted through her hair and lingered.

"I feel like one. This feels like the first time."

Daniel's eyes closed briefly as he started to move. Tess gasped. "Ah. Yes, Daniel. Oh yes."

Slow and strong, he moved, thrusting through vaginal walls that were sensitized from her climax. He bumped the entrance to her womb with each stroke and Tess felt her body clench around him. She'd never felt so full before, full to bursting. Stretched tight around him, she felt him change the angle of his powerful strokes with electrifying results. The head of his cock rubbed her G-spot and suddenly she knew what all the talk was about. Feeling roared to life deep inside her body and she cried out, burying her face against Daniel's sweat-sheened chest.

"Shit." With the sharp curse bursting from his lips, he disentangled himself from her clutching arms and reached back to remove her legs from his waist. Sitting back on his knees, still completely engaged, he draped her quivering thighs over his and started thrusting again.

A low moan broke from her throat as each devastating plunge raked that ultrasensitive spot deep within her. He thrummed her clit, pinched it lightly, stroked harder.

She wanted to watch.

Lifting her head seemed impossible in the midst of such mind-blowing pleasure but she managed it. The sight of Daniel's heavy shaft plunging and retreating held her transfixed. His cock was dark red with color, shimmering from her flowing juices. She gasped as the thrill curled up tight in her belly. Her legs were sprawled wantonly across those muscular dark thighs looking pale and fragile.

Tess was completely at his mercy.

More than anything, she wanted to touch his balls, fondle them. She knew they had to be hard and drawn up tightly against his body. It was useless from this position. Frustrated, she flopped back and took her nipples in her fingers to tease herself.

"Yeah, Tess. Do it. God, you're beautiful." Daniel plunged again and it was as if she could feel everything. His thickness, his strength, the flanged head of his erection scraping tissue that cried out for his touch. A low groan broke from Daniel's throat as he increased his speed, thrusting wildly. Breath whooshed from her chest as the sensations built apace with her racy heartbeat. Frantic need tore up, reaching out with tender claws, and Daniel squeezed harder at her pulsing clit.

Suddenly the wave broke over her, within her and she tensed. Reaching for what had always been so elusive seemed suddenly the easiest thing she'd ever done. Crying out, sobbing his name, Tess rolled over that steep edge as sweet contractions shook her to the core.

His strokes picked up in pace as he reached out with her. With a wild cry, he plunged hard and strong, deep inside her trembling sheath and Tess felt the gathering come down upon her again. Oh hell. Again? No, it couldn't be.

"Yes." She moaned the word, then cried it out as Daniel pumped and rotated his hips. Sweat beaded his forehead and ran in rivulets down the side of his devastatingly handsome face. Tension made the lines of his body jerk as he pounded deep and hard. White teeth flashed, seemed to snap, as he growled low and then his entire body jerked.

Gasping, Tess came with him, squeezing his cock with muscles that had sprung to life under his touch. Never had she felt such earth-shattering pleasure. Still buried deep within her, Daniel came down over her, kissing her gently, crooning Spanish words that she didn't understand. But they were beautiful.

Oh yeah, she knew they were tender and loving as he rained kisses over her damp cheeks, over her temples and against her throat. At the start of this adventure the things that had happened between them seemed just some weird kind of faraway dream but now, oh now, everything was different. She was different. Something had changed deep inside her with Daniel's loving and she never wanted to let it go.

Regret tore through Daniel as he pulled out of her limp body. He'd gone at her like an animal. God, she was pretty and sweet and sexy. A woman like Tess Garrity needed a gentle man, a considerate man but hell no, he'd let lust take him over that line between gentleman and savage. Had he hurt her?

Though he'd had her the night before, her body was almost virginal. Sweet and tight and he knew Tess wasn't a woman who had a string of lovers. Swallowing harshly, he looked down into her big blue eyes and pushed her damp hair from her face. "Was I too rough?"

Tess smiled.

A man could get lost in that gentle smile of hers or in the knowledge that shone as brightly as a beacon in the depths of her eyes. To him, she was perfection and everything a woman should be. Smart, sexy, gentle and kind.

"No, Daniel. It was perfect. Has anyone ever told you that you come on like a steamroller?"

He frowned. "I'm sorry."

She shook her head quickly. The firelight caught the shimmer of her pale hair and he wanted to run his fingers through that shining stuff. He wanted to see it draped across his thighs as she sipped at his cock. "No, I'm kidding you. The orgasm was mind-blowing and I want to do it again and again." She frowned suddenly and Daniel's heart clenched. "I mean, that is, if you want to."

Her uncertainty in the face of what had happened between them shook him. He grinned down at her. "You can count on it, honey. Don't you know how perfect you are?"

Tess snorted and rolled her eyes. "Hardly that. Just ask my daughter or my business partner or any one of my friends."

He didn't want to let her go but the floor was beginning to get uncomfortable so he got up and reached down a hand. "Come on, Tess. I can't stand to think of you lying on that floor one minute more."

A hint of uncertainty flashed in her eyes. She was wondering what happened next. She was thinking too hard and Daniel didn't want that. When she lifted her arm, he gently hauled her up and wrapped his arms around her. Kissing her forehead, he delighted in the feel of her naked and warm in his arms. "Let me take you to bed."

No words were needed. The bedroom was dark, the sheets mussed from her interrupted sleep. The scent of her perfume lingered in the air and his eyes fell on the small, silver vibrator setting on her nightstand. Inwardly, he smiled. Oh yeah. He knew just what to do with that naughty little toy.

He was sorry about the scene with Hillary but not a bit regretful about what had happened later. From the moment he'd seen her unloading her luggage several days ago, he'd wanted her. Those feelings only intensified when he'd stumbled across her sobbing in the moonlight. Once he'd taken her there'd been no going back.

There was a calm self-assurance about her movements that entranced him. She was a woman, not a girl, and the knowledge that sparkled from those gorgeous eyes was a turn-on for a man who'd had bad experiences with flighty women. Tess was a woman who'd faced the fire and walked through it fearlessly. She was strong but with a vivid sense of humor and innate sweetness that sent him to his knees. And she was beautiful with her delicate build, blonde shoulder-length hair and that classic bone structure.

Daniel watched her slide into the bed and followed her down, wrapping her in his arms. She felt so good there, like she belonged. Burying his face in her hair, he inhaled the fresh, clean scent of her. Her long legs slid against his but she still wasn't close enough. He clutched her gorgeous ass and dragged her closer.

The damp curls of her pussy were wet from him, from her, pressing against his thigh. Unable to get closer, to touch enough, he dipped his fingers between the firm globes he held in his hands. Tess shuddered in his arms, sighed against his chest.

"Daniel." The sound of his name whispered there made him hard and hungry again. Recovery wasn't an issue with this woman. He wanted her with every breath he took. There was just something about her that touched him deeply and he found he wanted her all over again. Nothing would make him happier than to test her limits. String her out on the sharp edge of lust and watch her react to every little thing he wanted to share with her. Naughty images flickered through his brain. Daniel wanted to do all those wicked things and more.

He pressed a kiss to her damp forehead and drew away.

"Where are you going?" she murmured.

"Starting a shower." He stood beside the bed and looked down at her. "Join me, Tess."

Chapter Three

ഐ

He wanted her. Again!

The evidence of his need stood out strong and proud from his body. Tess' heart rose up in her throat as she followed him into the small bath and watched him turn on the shower. Such a beautiful man and he wanted her.

Yep, again.

Still trying to absorb what was happening to her, somewhere deep inside her woman's soul, she decided it was time for action.

No more wondering. No more feeling sorry for herself. She wasn't an old woman to be relegated to a rocking chair dangling grandchildren on her knee. She was vibrant, strong and willing to take a chance on something more than she'd ever had before.

Daniel was offering her a trip down the road to self-discovery and she was smart enough to hold on for the ride.

He turned to her and she caught her breath as his eyes raked over her nudity. Something dark and dangerous flashed in those smoldering eyes and Tess felt her body respond to the demand in them. Her pulse quickened causing her body to ready itself. Sensitized flesh throbbed for more of what Daniel had to offer. Taking his hand, she stepped into the shower enclosure as steam curled warm and delightful over her body. Pulling her back against the front of him, Daniel turned her so they faced the gentle rush of water. It sluiced over her nipples like tiny pinpricks, ran in rivulets down her torso and Daniel filled his hands with her breasts. His cock prodded her ass from behind and she felt it slick over her pussy, between her legs. The flanged head rasped her, teasing until she gasped and leaned her head against the mounded muscles of his chest. "Ah Daniel."

Those delicious rough hands released her breasts. He trailed them leisurely over her ribs, her belly. When his fingers dipped into her drenched sex and thrummed her clit to a fever pitch, she began to tremble. Sensation assaulted her from every angle.

"Hand me the soap, Tess."

Blindly she reached down for the bottle of fresh-smelling liquid soap she brought from home and flipped open the lid with her thumb. She dripped some into Daniel's palm and watched him bring his hands together. As lather built, he applied his soapy hands to her breasts. It felt like heaven but then he stoked the fires of hell inside her as he pinched her nipples between his thumb and index fingers. He circled the areolas, teased the taut points before working his hands lower and lower.

A sharp sound crossed her lips when he tugged her clit then smoothed his finger over the spot. Unable to resist, Tess reached down her soapy body and touched the head of his cock, which was hard and probing, brushing back and forth against her cunt.

It was Daniel's turn to groan when she stroked that huge head, pressing it deeper, harder. A little more. Ah yes. Bending slightly forward, she reached out for his balls. They were hard and full, pressed near her gate and she smiled, stroking, squeezing, playing with the tender flesh. Daniel thrust up, his cock sliding against her wrist as she gently explored. "Tess. Oh sweet Tess, yes," he whispered. His voice was low and rough, sending pleasure to spike along her body. He took her shoulders then and settled her against the wall of the shower. "Let me wash you. If you keep touching me like that, it'll be over too soon. I won't have a chance to enjoy this luscious body like I want."

Tess wanted to climb up his body and sink her pussy down over his throbbing, pulsing cock. Moisture that had nothing to do with the shower and everything to do with lust dripped from her cunt. Closing her eyes against the wild impulse to follow thought with deed, she felt his hands work lather into her scalding flesh. His hands rubbed her breasts, her belly, between her legs.

She knew the moment he realized how much she wanted him, because she heard a rough sound. Going to his knees, he parted her labia and whisked knowing fingers over her trembling skin. He dipped a finger into her slick passage and sucked her clit until she writhed against the wall.

Daniel gripped one thigh to hold her still and lifted her other foot to prop on his sturdy shoulder. The arch of her foot dug in against that hard muscle as he ate her pussy as if he couldn't get his fill.

"You're delicious, Tess," he said against her cunt before he nipped her there.

Crying out, she arched against his lips and felt heat whip up and over her. His strong sucking brought her to the edge of orgasm and grabbing for it, reaching for it, she fell over that cliff, shuddering against his mouth.

Finally, he stood before her and Tess smiled. He was panting hard, his face tense with unspent passion, and she took charge. "My turn, big guy."

His eyes widened then slammed shut as she pressed him back against the shower wall. Down on her knees she went but unlike Daniel, her eyes weren't shut. Dragging her hands from thick base to pulsing head, she drew them up and over each inch of flesh. God, she loved the look of him, the steely strength, the vein that pulsed sharp and red over his cock. His heavy balls were drawn up and tight.

Exploring him, she cupped his sac, caressed it with her fingers until he groaned and shifted his stance against the wall. Reaching back, she found the cluster of nerves just at the base of his balls and pressed that spot with her thumb. Her lips stroked over his shaft from base to tip.

"God!" The prayer burst from Daniel's lips and Tess glanced up to see him looking down at her. Dark fire flashed from his eyes, water beaded on those ultrathick lashes.

Power rose up through her. The very image of bringing this strong man to his knees made cream seep from her pussy. Tess opened her mouth on him and felt him quiver.

Yes.

Yes.

Oh. My. God. He tasted like heaven, thick and powerful against her tongue. Gripping him at his base, she ran her tongue up his mighty length, stopping to suck and nip until she reached the broad head of his cock. She dragged her tongue along the slit, sipping at the pearled drops that gathered on his scarlet head. Holding his balls in her hand, she teased along the crease and over the head several delicious times before drawing him fully into her mouth.

"*Fuck!*"

Daniel roared the word and she sucked hard and long, just at the head of him. She tasted the pulsating spot, stroked it with her tongue then took him deep. His hands speared through her wet hair, holding her still as he plunged strong and slow within her mouth. His balls hardened in her hand, she pressed behind them and felt him shiver, then gasp out loud.

"Goddaaaaamn."

Empowerment flooded her senses that she could bring this ultrasexy man to his knees with pleasure. Her tongue went wild on him as she teased, making it last, making him tremble and shake. Finally releasing his balls, she wrapped both hands around him and dug her fingers into his hard ass. The tip of his cock brushed the back of her throat as he gripped her head and gasped for breath. "Shit. I'm coming. Oh God. I'm coming, honey. Yes."

Tess felt him stiffen then blast his cum into her mouth. Roaring his release, trembling with reaction, he held her head in his big hands.

In the aftermath, she lapped softly at his cock, gently touched his balls. Daniel's hands rubbed through her hair and above her, he sighed before taking her shoulders and drawing her up.

"Hell," he whispered against the top of her head. "You are the most responsive, giving woman I've ever known."

"I like to think I can give as good as I get. I loved tasting you, Daniel. I adored fucking you with my mouth." She lifted her face, strangely calm considering she'd just had wild monkey sex with a man she hardly knew. Reaching up, feeling fearless and strong, she stroked his bottom lip then kissed him. "Maybe we can do this again sometime."

"You damn well better believe we will, sweetheart. I don't think I'll ever let you go."

* * * * *

Later, Tess curled up in Daniel's arms, smiling a little. He smelled like her soap, clean and flowery. Yeah, he'd hate knowing that. Daniel Rios was as macho and manly as it got. He was asleep, curled like a warm blanket around her, and she studied his face, suddenly re-thinking her position about that.

Nope. This was one supremely confident man. He wouldn't let a little thing like smelling like a rose keep him from being one hundred percent male. Tess shivered a little and let herself sink into him. Best to enjoy the moment, she thought. It might never come again.

I don't think I'll ever let you go.

The words he'd said in the shower rolled over her like a dream. He couldn't mean such a thing. He was young and virile. She was rapidly approaching middle age. Crazy. Men like Daniel didn't mean such things. Surely it was the afterglow of great sex talking.

In sleep Daniel curved his arm around her and wrapped his hand over her butt. He stroked her, squeezed her. Tess yawned widely, feeling comfort slip over her in the aftermath of what had been a cataclysmic night. Morning was fast approaching and she'd return to the real world soon enough. She let herself go and drifted off in the arms of her young lover.

"More," he whispered. "Give me more."

The dark, seductive words swirled through her dreams then brought her slowly awake. "Daniel."

"I'm here."

She felt the curve of his chest brush her back as his lips settled at the crook of her neck. So sensitive. His teeth nipped her there then his tongue followed to tease the spot. Groaning low, she shifted, feeling his cock prodding the crease of her ass. With an easy move, he slipped the thickness deep between the globes and she gasped softly. He dipped deep then retreated as a rough sound escaped from his mouth to brush her flesh. Their legs were entwined and God, he was warm, so warm. "Touch me," she whispered in answer.

In the pre-dawn hours, she watched his dark hands come up to cup her breasts. He palmed them lightly, then with a firmer touch. He plucked her nipples into hard, puckered peaks then pulled, sending a shaft of pleasure from those two points to blast through her belly and settle deep in her core. The swollen tissues of her pussy throbbed. She felt the moisture he called with his touch saturate her tender folds.

"Yes. Beautiful." His praise made her shiver and she felt the stroke of his rough palms brush over her ribs and her belly, felt his fingers stroke gently through the curls between her thighs.

Making a low sound, Daniel shifted to raise her outside leg with his knee, opening her wide. "Don't move. Stay like this. I'm going to play with you, Tess. Wanna come again, sweetheart?"

His fingers were buried in the warm, wet flesh of her pussy and when he took them away, Tess wanted to weep at the loss.

The covers had been shoved to the foot of the bed at some point and the crispness of the morning mountain air swept over tender flesh. She was hot there and the contrasting temperatures made her gasp. A familiar low humming broke through the sudden quiet. She stilled.

Her vibrator.

Daniel continued to move his thickness against her, sometimes prodding the pucker of her anus, and though she tried to move, he held her still, kept her open. She saw the flash of silver as he reached out with the vibrator and drew it slowly from sternum to belly. Then he dipped it lower and she sucked in her breath. Held it.

"God!" she burst when he pressed the end to her clit. Shattering vibrations moved from that hard little knot to her opening. She felt her vaginal walls tighten and contract, needing more, wanting a firmer touch. "More!"

Daniel laughed softly. "Oh yeah. Your pussy's dripping with cream." He emphasized the statement by sinking the small toy deep into her cunt. Helplessly she tightened around it.

Daniel kept it there, moving it slightly, working her deep, then shallow.

Tess writhed against the pleasure of the vibrations that sang through her body and Daniel kept pace, stroking between the globes of her ass, whispering hotly against her neck.

"Fuck. You're so damn hot, Tess."

Suddenly he flipped her to her belly, making her cry out. He stuffed a pillow beneath her until her ass was tilted up, leaving her totally exposed. She felt his fingers delve deep into her pussy and move as if searching. He crooked his index finger and brushed the sensitive spot behind her pubic bone and Tess felt tears slip from her eyes.

Too much pleasure. Too much. Too much.

Repeatedly, he stroked until she threatened to fly apart but then he stopped and withdrew his hand. She heard a tearing sound, felt movement behind her and knew he'd covered himself, protecting them both, but she was frantic with need.

"Let me come. Oh God!"

He gripped her ass and bent low to press a kiss at the base of her spine. "Shhh. Okay. Let's do it." The buzz started again as he dipped the vibrator into her pussy, gathering moisture. Above her, he made a satisfied sound and trailed the toy higher, drawing the cheeks of her ass open.

Tess was so hot she thought steam could rise from her body. His finger probed her hole but then he slowly began to push the vibrator deep inside. "Easy," he crooned. "Relax."

He didn't have to tell her twice. She went still as dark, heavy vibrations tore through her. Daniel pressed more and she shivered. The head of his cock brushed lower, she felt him take his shaft and drag it erotically over her pulsing flesh. She burned, she ached. Unable to stop herself, she began to cry from the force of her pleasure as he pressed his heavy erection deep into her cunt.

"Fuck," he growled low from behind her. His thumb held the vibrator in place as he plowed repeatedly into her. Vaginal walls clasped him tight, held him. She felt the muscles of his thighs clench as he brushed her with each heavy thrust. She felt the heavy weight of his balls and knew she'd never forget this dark, heady pleasure.

Tess came hard as the pleasure spiraled high and long, thrusting her upward, blasting through her senses. Screaming her pleasure, hearing his answering roar of release, she felt her body go boneless against the sheets. Tears seeped from her eyes and she shook from head to toe.

Moments later, when Daniel collapsed by her side and drew her into his arms she sighed against his chest, breathed him in and thanked God for bringing Daniel into her life. If only for a moment.

* * * * *

A hazy day greeted her through the bottom of the curtains at the window and Tess looked around herself as events of the night past crashed down on her. Her face burned at each wicked memory but she wasn't ashamed. Just shocked that such a thing had happened at all.

It was crazy.

Naked, she sat at the side of her bed and felt the emptiness of the small cabin. Daniel was gone just as she knew he would be. Groaning, stretching overused muscles, she dragged her fingers through sleep-mussed hair and then spotted the note lying on a bedside table. Tess picked up the paper, noting the heavy masculine scrawl.

Dinner. Tonight. Seven sharp. Be there or I'm coming to get you. D.

Clasping the note, absorbing the sense of expectation shimmering to life in her body, Tess shrugged into old sweats and a T-shirt. Holding the note to her chest, she stumbled into the main part of the cabin. The blanket from last night was neatly folded on the couch and a freshly lit fire burned slowly in the fireplace, sending the scent of pinon pine through the room. She also smelled fresh coffee and her eyes widened. Near the coffeepot sat a clean mug.

What a surprising man!

Later that morning, freshly showered and aching in the most delicious places, Tess got in her car and headed out for a shopping tour of the tiny town of Ruidoso. Winding her way down the mountainous inclines, she reached the valley and drank in the scenery, as always amazed at the quaint beauty of this town. Colorful shops lined the thoroughfare and she stopped at a cute little restaurant for a quick bite. It was near lunchtime and clusters of people strolled the sidewalks, pausing at shop windows, enjoying the crisp autumn day. The sun had finally broken through and Tess sat at her table near the front window nibbling on a club sandwich.

A young family occupied the table next to her and she smiled, watching the mother carefully cut a hamburger in half for her five-year-old while the father lifted a whimpering toddler from a booster seat and held him. The scene brought back memories of those exact kinds of moments she'd shared with her husband while raising their daughter. They'd been crazy years but good. Honest and decent times when they'd grown together as a family.

Sighing, settling back, she wondered what Jeff would think of last night's naughty sexual adventure. Julie had said go for it. Live a little. Wise girl. Tess sipped her iced tea and realized that Jeff's thoughts didn't matter now. He wasn't here and she was the one who had to go on. Well, last night Tess had busted loose and set herself free and there was no going back.

Just thinking of Daniel sent awareness zipping through her body. She'd never been more sexually responsive. Was it Daniel and the ways in which he'd touched her or was it something within her that had been dying to break free and fly? No answers were forthcoming and Tess had never been the type of woman to think things to death. She'd always been pretty damn decisive and in this matter of Daniel she'd made her decision.

She shopped her afternoon away, chatting with storekeepers and picking up the odd item she thought Julie might like. It was a fun day all in all, but Tess wasn't one who enjoyed solitary shopping. It was always more fun to ooh and ahh with friends. Spotting a little gift and floral shop on a busy street corner, she crossed over and went inside. The charming store smelled like a bit of heaven, the scents so familiar she wondered again at the wisdom of selling Petal Pushers to her business partner. Sassy wanted to expand the place in a manner that Tess was uncertain of and that was what had led to this whole business of selling out. She had a very good business in Dallas but Sassy was friends with an interior decorator who wanted to set up shop there. To Tess' way of thinking, mixing these businesses could make them grow in ways they weren't prepared to handle. Bigger wasn't necessarily better.

"I love your store," Tess said, smiling over a display of pricey bric-a-brac artfully arranged near the front of the place.

The woman who stood nearby nodded her thanks. "I opened this shop many years ago and I hate having to sell."

"Sell?"

"Yes. My husband passed away recently and my kids are anxious to have me close by now that Dennis is gone," she sighed and smiled a little. "Guess it's time for something new for me."

"I'm sorry," Tess said. "I lost my husband a couple of years ago."

"Does it get any easier?"

"Not really. It just gets different. We're women, we adapt. That's what it's all about."

Later, Tess got in her SUV and tooled down Main Street. She stopped at an out-of-the-way coffee shop and selected some great-smelling coffee beans along with several pieces of homemade fudge then headed back down the main drag again in search of a gas station. Time to top off the tank.

She'd just stopped at a red light when she looked over and saw a new building going up. Looked like a new hotel. Fresh lumber stretched across the stark blue sky like some sort of skeleton and men were hammering away. The sound of saws buzzing rang through the air.

Daniel stood there, clipboard in hand, talking with several men and Tess stilled, her senses going on red hot alert. The brilliant afternoon sunlight streaked through his blacker-than-sin hair, making it shine. His muscular arms and chest were covered by a light jacket but she could appreciate the sight of his sturdy, long legs encased in worn denim. Reaction to him tightened low in her belly and memories of last night's sexual romp played through her mind. Nerves in her clit thumped to life at the sight of him and her panties grew damp as if his big fingers were stroking her. Tess twitched a little and thought of the night ahead. Nervously licking her lips, she'd barely had time to blink when Daniel looked up and saw her.

He stilled and nodded in her direction. The other men were looking too, so Tess just waved and pulled into the nearby gas station. She'd just climbed from her car and zipped her gasoline card through the machine when she saw Daniel loping across the street.

Oh my.

There was only one word for Daniel Rios.

Hot.

She stood there stupidly gawking, holding the gas nozzle as he came up to her.

"Tess."

"Um...hi." God, so lame! She swallowed as her body reacted instantly to the heat he generated. She might've been all of sixteen and facing her first crush with the way she was acting.

Intensity shone from Daniel's dark eyes as he raked his gaze over the front of her body. Today she wore black leggings, boots and a tunic-length sweater that was casually belted at her hips but she might as well have been nude considering the look that leaped to life in his eyes. He reached out and took the gas nozzle from her hand.

"Here let me."

Tess watched him fill her tank and thought of that *other* tank he could fill. Shit. When had her thoughts landed so firmly in the gutter? That wicked imp in her subconscious snickered at her. "Thanks."

Daniel tossed her a look after he put the nozzle back. "I've been thinking about you all day."

"Me too," she whispered. "Thanks for the fire in the fireplace and the coffee. For everything."

"Figured it was long past time someone did something for *you* for a change."

Tess felt her heartbeat speed up. She licked her lips. "Got your note."

"You'll be there?"

How could he doubt it? Tess nodded, taking the leap. "I will."

Daniel moved close, crowding her against her truck. His gaze dropped to her lips as he dipped his broad hand to the nape of her neck. Then he kissed her, taking it slow, making it deep and Tess forgot she was in a public place, forgot he was at least ten years younger. She forgot everything but the scent of him, the delicious feel of his tongue in her mouth.

Shouts and hoots reached her through the sexual haze and Daniel pulled back. A tiny smile quirked at one corner of his delectable lips. "For what it's worth, honey, my crew thinks you're hot."

"Me?"

"Oh yeah. You. I'll see you tonight. If you're not on time, I'm coming to get you."

His words, low and rough, sent a chill over her flesh. What would he do if she was late? Spank her? Jesus! A fine trembling set up in her thighs and her nipples hardened at the thought. As if he understood the wicked notions swirling through her brain, he laughed wickedly. "Don't tempt me, Tess. I'm just itching to punish you."

Before she could do more than blink, Daniel leaned close to whisper in her ear. "I want to drape you naked across my lap and spank your sweet ass red, watch you squirm. I want to dip my fingers in your juices and play for as long as I like. You'll let me too, Tess. Won't you?"

He breathed deeply then stroked his tongue over the rim of her ear. Tess shivered, her pussy gushing at the imagery he'd painted. "Um."

"Won't you, honey?"

Tess knew what she wanted and she was sick to death of waiting for it. Gathering her nerve, reaching for what her secret heart of hearts desired, she pulled back and stared unflinchingly into his smoldering eyes.

"Yes. Oh yes, Daniel, I will."

Chapter Four

Night had fallen by the time she reached the cabin next door. Nerves skittered along Tess' spine as fallen leaves crunched beneath her casual shoes. Hanging on Daniel's front door was the colorful wreath she'd made earlier. Fall leaves, pine cones and angular cinnamon sticks gave the door a seasonal look and was very pretty. Was it too much?

Unable to resist doing something for him, she'd gone back to the floral shop she'd visited earlier and asked the owner, Karen, to stock her up with the makings for the wreath but now she felt dumb. Men didn't appreciate things like this as a rule. Would Daniel?

Lifting her hand to knock, she heard the strains of soft music coming from inside the cabin. She sucked in a breath and rapped twice in quick succession. The door opened immediately and Daniel stood there, his big body filling the space. Tess caught her breath at the sight of him.

Dressed casually in jeans and a sweater, he drew her close and kissed her. Desperate longing zipped through her senses, making her catch her breath. Her defenses crumbled as the whip of his tongue lashed deep into her mouth. She sucked it and practically climbed up his big body. He grabbed her knee and held it high against his hip as he spun with her, pressing her to the door frame. "I want to fuck you hard. Right now," he growled against her lips.

"Yes."

"Let's take the edge off." Daniel lifted her, cupped her ass in his hands and kicked the door shut. Pressing her against the wood, he ground that hard bulge against her over the seam of her jeans.

"Oh yeah." She was gasping, breathing hard as he raked his huge cock over her dripping pussy. "Daniel."

"Thanks for the gift," he murmured. "Can't remember the last time someone thought to do something like that. It's pretty."

Odd time to mention the gift, she thought as he pressed himself against her, raking slowly but precisely, rubbing her clit with each pass. The zipper, pulled tight across his erection, teased her further and she felt the silken walls deep in her channel contract as if in expectation. Gradually, he released her to make a slow, sexy slide down the front of his body. God! He was hard everywhere. Still, he pressed her against the wall as he began to tease.

He bent to kiss her throat but growled at the soft cashmere turtleneck. With a curse, he pushed the fur-trimmed vest she wore down her arms and lifted the hem of the sweater and tossed it aside. Daniel filled his palms with her breasts, thumbing the nipples through her pale, sheer bra. His thumbnail abraded her pulsing flesh, sending the fabric to scratch across each nipple. Gasping at the sensation, she writhed against his cock and lifted her leg to wrap around the back of his thigh. Pressing him closer, frantic to feel him skin to bare skin, she hummed a little when he flipped open the catch of her bra. He peeled back the edges, leaving her exposed to his hungry gaze. Tess felt her nipples tighten, a relentless torture. Popping a throbbing bit into his mouth, he sucked, tonguing her hungrily.

"I can't wait to get inside you, Tess," he breathed against her taut nipple. He blew lightly, causing her flesh to draw tight as a bowstring. "I wanted to fuck you in front of God and everybody today. Wanted to yank down those leggings and pound you into the side of your truck. Damn, woman, you make me burn."

Tess could only gasp as he worked the zipper of her jeans and thrust them down her legs. She kicked out of her flats as he pulled the denim off and tossed it aside, leaving her wearing only her panties and a whole bunch of naked skin. He looked down her body and scowled at the flimsy slip of beige at her hips.

"Thought I told you not to wear panties around me, sweetheart."

The endearment was an oddity coming along with the fierce expression on his face. He flipped his gaze up to her and the breath caught in her throat. Oh dear. A game. She sensed it coming as he grabbed her hand, drawing her from where she'd been pressed against the wall.

She barely noticed anything about his rustic cabin, even the music seemed to come at her as if from a great distance. All she could hear was the pounding of her own heart as he sprawled into a big comfy chair and flopped her, face first, over his thighs.

"What are yo—"

"Shh. You'll learn, Tess. Don't fool around with me," he crooned. His hand caressed the silky panties over her ass. He spanked her, his big hand rising and falling. Tess jerked at the sting.

"Daniel!"

"I told you to be quiet." His hand descended again, this time a little harder and she jerked again as the tiny sting spread fingers of lust through her belly. Her pussy clenched tight as his hand rose and fell, delivering sharp smacks to her flimsily clad bottom. Squirming against the denim, she parted her legs a little. Her naked breasts brushed against his leg and Daniel reached down to clasp a nipple and pinch it hard.

Tess gasped and helplessly opened her legs farther. She was drenched with juice, saturated with pleasure. Daniel slapped her ass several more times before dipping his broad, calloused hand beneath her panties and sliding them off.

"Ah yeah. You're red, honey." His hand cruised a path over her pulsing, burning ass and she whimpered. "Hot as hell, Tess."

Anticipation poured through her trembling body and she stilled, waiting, Finally, she sighed deeply as Daniel drifted his fingers through the crack of her ass to probe her lightly. Dipping them farther, he sank his hand into the flood of moisture that pooled between her thighs. Stroking, separating her, he filled her with his fingers and Tess clenched her body around the invasion.

"Yesss. Ah Daniel. Yes."

The bud of her clit throbbed for attention and finally he pressed her there, plucked lightly, rubbed with the pad of his thumb until she was a writhing mass of nerves against him. "Naughty girl. Want more?" His voice was rougher than before, made thrilling by the fact she couldn't see his face, read his expression.

"More. Give me more."

"Oh yeah." His hand spanked her again, on the insides of her thighs where she dripped with cream. Interspersing stroking and playing at her cunt, he brought her to the very edge of orgasm. Left her hanging. Left her wanting.

"Holy shit," she cried.

Daniel's laughter was husky and low. "I second that, gorgeous. God, I could spank this beautiful ass all day."

Suddenly, he reared up and brought her, trembling, with him. Tess found herself on all fours on the rug in the middle of his living room floor. "Stay there. Don't move," he ordered.

Tess heard the sounds of clothing being stripped away, discarded, the clump of his boots as they hit the floor. She heard the faint sound of foil tearing and knew he had rolled on a condom. Feeling completely exposed, she jumped as his hands gripped her hips.

Oh God!

She jerked at the feel of his mouth at the base of her spine. His tongue swept naked flesh then those wicked white teeth nipped at her burning ass.

"Jesus. God!"

246

He made a harsh sound as he spread her ass cheeks and she felt his face caress her there. The stubble of his whiskers abraded tender flesh. Something dark and utterly delicious sang through her brain and she felt his breath sweep forbidden flesh. His tongue stroked and circled her hole, stabbing lightly before dipping lower to drink the juice that dripped from her cunt.

"Fuck me, Daniel. Oh God. Fuck me now, honey."

His hair swept across her burning ass as he engulfed her gushing pussy with his mouth. Sucking hard and deep, he ate her with relentless precision until she just lost it. Exploding, coming against his mouth, she arched and pressed against him. Tess trembled like a racehorse at the starting gate as Daniel came up behind her and plunged the pulsing, huge head of his cock deeper than she'd ever known a man could go.

"Fuuuuck." The words left her lips on a wail. Every bit of her body shook as he plunged repeatedly, hard, thrusting, sending her body into a forward motion she couldn't stop. His arm wrapped around her belly to anchor her as she whimpered and cursed like a sailor. Trembling, throbbing tissues grabbed hold and refused to let go and it was Daniel's turn to curse.

"Christ! That's it. That's it."

The mental image of the feel of his cock planted deep inside her channel speared through her brain. She felt everything. Every delicious inch. The hard, thick stalk, the pulsing flared head.

Daniel Rios was moving her through an erotic tango over which she was still learning the steps but, shit, she was becoming a fast learner. Close to the edge of insanity, Tess reached down under her body and grabbed his heavy balls in her hand.

A low animal growl rumbled over her. Daniel took her bare shoulder between his teeth and nipped with a rough touch that sent her over the edge. Something dark and wicked was delivered into life as she met him stroke for stroke. His fingers squeezed her clit, his cock pounded hard into the wet heat of her.

Daniel shook and roared his release and Tess fell with him. The jet of his cum filled the condom hot and steady, as she squeezed with inner muscles she didn't know she possessed.

In the aftermath, she could only slump face first into the rug. Yes, he'd fucked her into the floor. If she could've moved, she might have rolled over to see if he'd been as affected but she wasn't a fool. She knew he'd been taken as well. With hands that trembled, Daniel stroked her bare back, rubbed her sore, stinging butt. His mouth settled on her shoulder. "Don't move, honey. I'll be right back."

Tess could only sigh as she closed her eyes. Bliss stole over her and then she felt Daniel lifting her, drawing her to her feet. Shakily, she leaned against him as he drew a soft, warm black robe over her body. The feel of the soft velour against her bare skin was heavenly. Risking a glance at Daniel, she blinked at the soft look that had stolen like a thief into his deep, dark eyes. Tenderly, he kissed her lips before donning an identical black robe.

Tess laughed a little. "I don't know what they put in the water in these mountains but I must remember to take some back to Dallas with me."

Daniel whipped his head around. His lips firmed. "Don't talk about that yet, Tess."

Okaaay. No references to her leaving and returning to the real world. If that's the way he wanted it, then all right.

For the first time, she got a good look around and loved what he'd done here. The cabin was very much like her own but lots fancier, bigger. Not a vacation getaway but a beautiful home. It suited him with its rugged lines and heavy leather furniture. A blaze crackled low in the fireplace and nearby, Bo lay on a doggie bed having doggie dreams. In the distance a small table was set for dinner. Squat candles burned low on a rustic sideboard in the dining area and on the massive coffee table in the living room. Stairs led up to a loft bedroom that was visible from down below.

"Is your bedroom up there?"

Daniel shook his head as he filled two glasses with dark, rich red wine. "No. It's actually the master bedroom but I keep it ready for my sons when they come to visit. They think the loft bedroom is cool."

"Your sons?"

Daniel's face softened as he handed the glass to her and then sampled a bit of the wine. "Yeah. I have a picture or ten. Want to see?"

"Oh yes."

Together they walked to the heavy sideboard and he motioned to a picture of him posing with two smiling young boys. Tess' heart melted at the sight. "They're darling."

He snorted. "I don't know about that but they're good kids." He stroked a finger over the glass-covered faces. "This is Michael. He's seven and Jacob is five."

"Divorced?"

"Yeah, hell, we were just kids when she got pregnant with Michael. We got married thinking everything would be okay but it wasn't."

"I'm sorry. Things can be tough for young couples under any circumstances."

"Yeah." He replaced the picture and took her elbow. "Come on. Let's eat. I promised dinner and you're going to get it, followed by more sex, of course."

She had to laugh. Spoken like a true man. "Of course. Everything looks great."

The rough-hewn oak table could've been in a fine dining room in any restaurant in town. Chunky candlesticks, three in all, were grouped in the center of the table and Tess watched while Daniel lit the candles and then gave her a smile. He'd gone to quite a bit of trouble to entertain her. Oh yeah, he knew how to show a woman a good time, that was for sure. Even now, she ached in the most delicious way.

"Let me pull dinner from the oven."

"I'll help."

He lifted his hand. "Nope. Sit before you fall down. That was quite a sexual exercise we just went through. I want you well rested for later." Daniel wagged his black brows to emphasize his promise.

That naughty little imp deep inside her subconscious hooted with wicked laughter. Tess saw the teasing glint in her lover's eyes and obeyed. *Her lover*. What a weird but titillating concept when applied to her boring self.

Within moments her taste buds sat up attentively. Daniel carried a small platter of some kind of herbed chicken surrounded by crisp steamed veggies. He sat the platter down between them along with a basket of fresh-smelling rolls. "Oh my God! Daniel? Did you make this?"

He smiled as he filled a plate for her. "Hell no! My favorite restaurant delivered this to me."

"Aren't you lucky?"

"The waitresses all think I'm hot. They'll do anything for me."

Tess had to laugh at the naughty glint in his eyes. The food was delicious and well-prepared, conversation was light with an underlying hint of tension. They both knew what they'd be doing later and that *knowing* sent a frisson of expectation humming through the air. She bit into a soft buttery roll that fairly melted in her mouth.

"How often do you get to see your boys? I assume they live primarily with their mother."

Daniel refilled his wineglass and ran a long finger down its stem. "I get them every other weekend, every other holiday and every summer."

"You miss them."

"Like crazy. Their mother is a good woman though. She's remarried and living in Roswell so the boys are close by. Janine married a nice guy. He's good to the boys and to my ex."

Tess shook her head. "Crazy. Relationships are crazy. I'm glad things have worked out well for you though. This could be a bad situation but it's not."

"You're right about that. Things have worked out well for me. Almost." He started to gather up their plates and Tess helped him carry things into the large, roomy kitchen. Gosh, his place was unexpectedly big. Big place for a big man.

"Can I ask you a question?"

Daniel looked at her. "Sure. Anything."

"How old were you when you got married?"

A smile widened on his face. "Is this a roundabout way of asking how old I am?"

Heat blasted up her neck and over her cheeks but she was honest. "Yeah, I guess so."

Holding out a hand, he laced his fingers with hers and led her into the living room. He tossed more logs on the dying fire and settled in beside her. "I'm thirty-five, Tess. Like I said that first day, I'm a man. Not a boy."

"I think I got that part."

Wrapping his arm around her shoulders, drawing her in, Daniel chuckled. "I love your sense of humor."

"Yeah, yeah, I'm a funny chick."

"An honest one. I haven't had a lot of experience with honest women, sweetheart, but I feel I can tell you anything. I've been divorced for over four years. Fucked a lot of women but never really gotten close, you know?"

"Once burned, twice shy?"

He laughed. "Something like that. Just seemed easier to keep everything nice and neat. Most of my women have been like the world-famous Hillary who wanted way more than I wanted to give. Does that make me a prick?"

"No. Not at all. You're gorgeous and smart, as sexy as hell. You have the right to be picky."

A deliciously wicked grin split his face. "You trying to flatter me so you can get in my britches?"

Responding in kind, she ran a finger over his chest where the soft, black robe parted. "Is it working?"

"Like a charm. I have a permanent hard-on around you, sweetheart. Seriously, you don't even have to try, Tess. There's a beautiful, natural sensuality about you that's a complete turn-on."

If anyone had the right to be as picky as hell it was Tess, he thought as he drew her closer, inhaled the clean fragrance of her hair. Even after he'd jumped her the moment she'd entered his house, she smelled as fresh as a spring rain. Her scent, the feel of her, called to him on a primitive level he'd never understood before now.

He ran his hand over the length of her arm and felt her soften against him. The first time he'd laid eyes on this woman, he'd wanted her and he knew it wasn't just Tess' classy movie-star looks that attracted him. To him, she seemed so genuine and real. She was accepting of him in every way.

And sexually?

They were a perfect match.

Yeah, she was unsure of herself in that arena but he was a very good teacher. Just thinking of all the ways he wanted to fuck this woman made him hard. But he wanted more than that too. Ruidoso was a chiefly Native American place and mysticism seemed to permeate the very mountain air. He'd always figured it was mainly bullshit but now he wasn't so sure.

Daniel felt a mystical connection with this woman whenever he looked into those soft baby blues.

"Tell me about your life, Tess." A log in the fireplace burned in half, falling to send sizzling sparks into the air.

She sighed deeply and to his satisfaction snuggled deeper. Her hand settled on his thigh, sealing the intimacy of the moment. "Oh, same old, same old, I guess. Nothing special. I got married pretty young and Jeff and I had a daughter together. Julie is twenty and in college. That's about it."

"Uh-uh. You don't get off that easily."

"No?"

He could hear the smile in her voice. "Nope. Spill it."

"Pretty much a fairy tale life for the most part. Jeff loved me and he was a sweet man until the day he died. He taught math at one of our big Dallas high schools and I'm a florist. I have a shop back home."

"Ah, that explains the wreath on the door. You made that?"

"Yeah, dumb huh?"

"Not dumb. I've never met a woman who would've given me something like that. As far as I'm concerned you are unique."

"Mmm. I like the sound of that. Never thought of myself as being different from any other woman."

Daniel trailed a finger over her bottom lip. "Oh but you are. How many women would've hung around taking care of a sick man? Hanging tough? Sticking it out?"

"Quite a few, I would imagine."

"You'd be wrong. You've stuck it out for everyone."

"It wasn't hard to do that for Jeff. I cared for him."

"Did you love him?"

Tess raised her head and looked him dead in the eye. Her mouth was set in mulish lines. "Of course I did. I mean we...um...we had a strong, traditional marriage."

"Sounds pretty dull."

It was as if the air left her lungs and suddenly Daniel was sorry he'd pressed her. "It was a little. I mean everything was so safe. Dinner at six, Monday Night Football. Those aren't bad things."

"Tess, honey, they are only bad if that's all it ever was."

Tess was silent for a very long time and Daniel would've kicked his own ass if he could've. These were messy memories that were better left alone but, damn it, he wanted to know everything about her and she was shutting him out. "I'm sorry," he finally said. "I shouldn't dig into stuff that's not my business but, honey, I've got to say this. You were almost like a virgin when I had you. You haven't dated at all, have you?"

"No. I mean, some friends have tried to set me up but those men were all like—"

"Like Jeff?"

Tears pooled in her eyes and she knuckled them away but not before he saw how shaken she was. She sighed and leaned her head back against his arm. "Yeah, maybe," she whispered. "Jeff was always so safe. Well, damn it, maybe I'm sick of *safe*. I'm forty-five and I don't want to go on another day without knowing what else is out there for me. I don't want to stop living just because my husband did. God! Does any of this make sense?"

Daniel felt his heart clench in his chest, squeezing tightly. She was more woman than he'd ever known before. More beautiful too but she'd never believe that. She didn't realize that she had things to offer him that no one else could.

Fuck!

He didn't want to feel this way. He hadn't wanted to let himself be drawn into the life of this beautiful, sexy widow.

Still, it had happened. The gentleness of her nature, her tenderness, the way her sweet body responded sent an ache through his lonely heart.

Nope. Daniel Rios didn't want to go through life solo anymore. The problem remained how to convince this lovely woman that she belonged right here in his arms.

Chapter Five

ဢ

"I've come to a realization," she said, taking in his chiseled masculine face softened somehow by the shadows that danced in the room.

Daniel turned to face her more fully and brushed a length of her hair behind her ear. Despite his being such a rough, big man, his touch was infinitely gentle. Her heart clenched in her chest and she could feel her body's response to his nearness. "I've come to one of those tonight too but go ahead."

"I guess the thing is, I've always taken care of everyone in my life. Very good care. It was my choice to put everything into their lives, to make them comfortable and happy." Because she couldn't resist, she parted the front of Daniel's robe and let her fingers sweep the firm mounds of his chest. He liked it, she knew. His breath soughed from his lips and she noted the tent his full erection made beneath the black velour. Tess licked her lips. Her mouth watered for another taste of him. "I came to the mountains to reevaluate things and I've come to some conclusions."

"Yeah?"

She didn't let herself think. Or worry. Or hesitate. Reaching down, she tugged at the tie in his robe and opened it up. Taking what she wanted, she gripped his cock firmly in her fist and moved it up and down, over and across. Savoring him, she let her touch linger slowly over his swollen flesh. Her thumb shaped the broad tip, finding moisture beaded there. She smoothed it, rubbed, delighting in the sound of his indrawn breath. "I want to *take* now, Daniel. I want to be a woman who grabs what she wants with no looking back. It's my time. Now. My daughter is grown and my marriage, as sweet as it was, is over."

Daniel's eyes grew darker, more liquid, that penetrating gaze centered on her lips then flipping to her eyes. "Good girl. Take it then, Tess. Let yourself be tempted by life and adventure. Take what you want but fuck, take me too."

Tess laughed, the sound breaking through her, setting her free. "Oh I plan to, honey." Suddenly she stood and let her robe drop from her shoulders to slide to the floor where it pooled at her feet. Excitement thrummed her senses to living, breathing life. Her nipples pearled, as hard as diamonds, and she reached up to pluck them hard between her fingertips. Palming her breasts, she watched Daniel's hands go to his own throbbing cock. So big. So hard. It was lush and full and she watched the distended veins coursing over the thick shaft begin to pulse faintly.

"Touch yourself, Tess. Show me what you do when you are alone in your bed."

She let her hands trail slowly down her body. Between her legs, her pussy throbbed, cream slid warm over the insides of her thighs but she didn't rush in her flight to pleasure herself in front of his man. As her fingers stroked down her torso, Daniel pumped his fat cock in his fist slowly.

Her mouth went dry. Daniel groaned, the sound seeming loud in the quiet cabin. His steady gaze was riveted on the movement of her hands so Tess dipped them lower to spear through the wet curls coving her mons.

"Yeah, Tess. That's it. Do it."

Reaching low, she spread her labia and widened her stance, knowing he watched, waited. Yesss. Oh God! She couldn't believe she was doing this but a dark thrill weaved through her body, intoxicating her.

Unerringly, she found her clit and teased it with her fingers, stroking, stunned to hear her breath break over the pounding in her heart. A dark flush stained Daniel's cheeks as he watched. He teased his balls then zipped his fisted hand up over his stalk, then down again. "That's it, sweetheart. Shit. Dip your fingers in your cunt. God, it's juicy, ripe."

Tess obeyed, slithering her drenched fingers down and up until they slid deep but it wasn't enough. Just touching herself would never be enough again. She wasn't going to settle for masturbation when Daniel sprawled there like some Aztec god.

"I'm taking you. Right now," she snapped. "Fuck this."

Daniel's eyes flared wide. He released his cock from his fist and shrugged jerkily out of his robe as she approached slowly. He took a condom from the pocket, opened it quickly and rolled it onto his shaft. His breath was heavy and hard, his abs flexed as he settled back against the couch, offering his body. With a knee planted on either side of his open thighs, she rose up over him and looked down.

Hot, dark eyes gone lambent with desire speared her as he grabbed her ass with both hands. "Tess." Daniel squeezed the globes, speared his fingers into the shadowy cleft. He drew her belly against his mouth.

Opening his lips over her flesh, he nipped her there in that soft place as he probed the pucker of her anus with the tip of a finger, circling, circling, entering slightly. A moan broke from her throat at the touch of his fingers, his hands, there but she wanted more. Cream drenched her when he nipped her belly again. Releasing her ass from tender captivity, he gripped her thighs then moved to other softer ground. "I love your pussy. So wet and liquid." He plunged his fingers into the deep, dark pink of her cunt and worked her until she cried out. Pleasure spiked sharply, making her wild.

"My clit! Touch my clit!"

Growling an answer, he thumbed the distended knot of nerves, pressing until she trembled with reaction. Her hands gripped his shoulders and squeezed repeatedly. When he removed his wet fingers, she suddenly felt the very tip of his cock brush over her steaming flesh. The broad head rubbed slowly, languidly over pulsing tissue, making her hunger for more.

No. Not yet.

Determined to tease, she lowered her body fractionally, taking just the head of him into her depths. Daniel made a sharp sound as she rotated her lower body, squeezed and flexed over the pulsing knob. Each time he tried to thrust deep, she shifted elusively.

"You'll pay for this."

"Yeah, honey, make me pay," she crooned, running her hands over the cords of his neck and into his damp hair. "I'll look forward to it."

"You're beautiful," he gritted out. "I'm going to spank that gorgeous cunt and then deny you."

His words sent her reeling and when he pinched the bud of her clit sharply, she cried out, arching against the torment, swirling her sex over that delicious head. Without warning, it was too much.

Tess sank upon his shaft and wailed at the feel of him stretching her. He went so damn deep, she had to rise again and hover before sinking again, going for what she wanted most. Her clit, swollen and pulsing, raked against his pelvis bone with each downward movement and she rubbed it there as delicious torment made her shiver.

Lust throbbed through her veins and then Daniel sealed the deal by latching onto her rock-hard nipple. Sucking in a sharp, stabbing rhythm, he finally broke free from the torture she'd visited upon him and thrust high and hard inside her.

She felt everything, oh God, just everything.

The flared head raked vaginal walls, stroking that bundle of nerves just behind her pubic bone. Dark heat lashed her as she quivered there, suspended on a blade of pleasure. His hands clutched high on her thighs as he thrust and pounded and Tess met him stroke for stroke as delicious pleasure held her high on its seductive edge.

At last it was too much but, paradoxically, she knew it would never be enough. Never. Release blasted through her body. Pleasure zipped through her blood like wine. Shivers stole over her skin. Her cries rose up, high and sharp, as the man beneath her stiffened, roaring an answer. His cum jetted in a hot blast as she sank gasping against his sturdy chest. Daniel's arms clasped her hard against him as if he'd never let her go.

Once they regained their breath, he unseated her from his cock and stood over her, a savage look on his face. "I'm not done with you, Tess." Daniel swooped her up with a growl, Tess laughed and wound her legs around his lean waist. He buried his face against her throat. "Feeling adventurous, Ms. Garrity? Hm?"

Tess tossed her head back and looked at him, flashing a quick grin. "I'm always up for a challenge. Color me ready for anything."

"Anything?"

"Oh yeah. Give it to me."

Laughing, he carried her into his bedroom. It was big and dimly lit. Daniel kissed her deeply then laid her out on his bed and looked at her, suddenly serious. "I'm hungry, Tess. I want to do things to you. Promise to tell me if you don't like it or it makes you uncomfortable."

A shiver raced down her spine. She blinked but knew she wasn't afraid. He would never do anything she didn't want. A dark-edged thrill made her breath break. She'd lied to him before, well, sort of, when she'd presented herself as a sexually adventurous woman. Uh-uh. For most of her married life, she'd pretty much been missionary all the way with occasional forays into *woman on top* with some oral sex thrown into the mix. She'd never done anything remotely spontaneous as she'd done tonight.

She'd wanted to change her life and Daniel was offering it to her in spades. Well, she'd damn sure never been a fool! She wasn't about to start being one now.

"I'm ready, Daniel," she breathed, looking straight into those serious dark eyes. "I'm ready for anything."

A smile curved his lips. He reached down and drew his hands slowly over her body, touching her breasts, her belly, her thighs. "Trust me," he said.

"Yes."

Daniel walked naked to an armoire across the room and opened the doors. When he turned, he held a black case. Curiosity hammered through her brain. Suspicions grew. He set it down on the end of the bed and opened it before giving her a quick look.

Tess' eyes widened when he withdrew two sets of velvet-lined handcuffs and several flexible straps. She flicked her gaze to him and he gave her a slow, sexy smile. "Scared, Tess? Wanna call it a night?"

"Hell no."

She said the words so fast, Daniel laughed as he snapped a cuff into place around her right ankle.

"What are you —"

"Just a minute," he murmured, intent on his task. He looped one strap through the empty cuff and tied it high on a post of his four-poster bed. The action caused her leg to splay high and wide, away from her body.

Willing to see it through, Tess bit her lip against the questions she wanted to ask and watched as he hoisted up the other leg. In minutes, her legs were spread wide and high, attached to the posts. She'd never felt more exposed but this was her moment of self-discovery. This was adventure. She kept her mouth shut and watched to see what he would do next.

Daniel stepped back to admire his handiwork, his face hard with lust. He ran his warm hands over the insides of her thighs. "I love you like this, Tess. God! You make me hot."

He didn't linger but quickly snapped her wrists together over her head and, using another long strap, looped it through the cuffs and tied the ends to the posts at the head of the bed.

"Kinky," Tess said suddenly, laughing at the image of how she must look trussed up like a Christmas turkey. "I think I like kinky."

"Oh yeah." Daniel's gaze swept her and his returning laughter was low and sexy.

He started to come toward her but she stopped him. "Daniel! Wait! Um...I'm not...um... I need a shower! Damn it."

A slow, gentle smile lifted his lips and he lifted a finger. "Don't move."

"As if!"

She watched him go into his bathroom, heard him chuckle and call her a *smart ass* under his breath. She heard water running and in a moment or two he came back with a warm, wet cloth. Tess wanted to weep at his thoughtfulness and at the feel of the cloth pressed against her pussy. She was swollen from earlier play but he was gentle as he washed her. Tender. Careful.

He swiped the cloth through her folds, cleaned her thoroughly. Even her rear entrance was tended and then he tossed the cloth aside. When he finally stood at the foot of the bed, his eyes were stormy with lust. A muscle worked in his jaw. His gaze ran the length of her from top to toe and lingered on her vulnerable flesh.

Wicked pleasure zipped through Tess' body. He liked what he saw. Nope. He didn't like it, he loved it! His tongue flicked out to lick his bottom lip and he swallowed as if his mouth had gone dry. Tess had never felt sexier in her entire life.

"You're the most delicious thing I've ever seen," he said, reaching out for a black jar.

Curious, she watched him remove the lid. The scent of mint filled the room. "What is that?"

"Nothing dangerous. It'll make you feel good. Make your orgasm stronger."

Tess didn't speak as he brought a dollop to her exposed pussy and drew it gently over her tender skin. Immediately she began to tingle but not in a burning kind of way. It was pleasant and warm. "Mmm. I think I like these games," she whispered, closing her eyes as the pleasant warm cream was applied to her nipples too.

Finally she opened her eyes to see Daniel close by, looking down at her. "And I think I like, no love, looking at you like this." His gaze flicked to her nipples and lingered. "I love the way your back is bowed on the bed just a little and the way your nipples are puckered as if they ache for me to suck them."

His words brought a flood of heat to her pussy and her inner muscles clenched tight in response.

Daniel ran his warm hands over her arms and down to her chest where he stopped to play. Her nipples burned deliciously. Tingled and throbbed. A low moan broke from her lips. "Daniel," she whispered.

"Patience, Tess."

Patience? My God, he was burning her alive. She wanted his mouth, his tongue, his hard, heavy cock pounding her to mindless orgasm. Unable to resist, she writhed against the light bonds and Daniel laughed low.

Moving to the foot of the bed, he bent over her fully opened cunt. His breath was hot, his tongue stroked intimately, lapping her cream, sucking the juices from her ripe body. Tess cried out and jerked against the bonds that held her. Daniel seemed oblivious to her frustration, taking his time, eating her out like she was melted chocolate and he needed a candy fix. "Mmm. You're delicious, Tess," he whispered against her flesh. "More."

His tongue trailed lower and he stabbed repeatedly at her body's entrance then further to deeper, darker places. He hummed as he swept it to her rectum and circled slowly, eating her thoroughly and stabbing again, lightly. The tingling sensation started again. This time at her hole. She was deliciously warm and thunderously turned on.

Daniel stood and looked at her. His chin was damp with her juices and he licked his lips. "Delicious."

"Jesus! Daniel!"

"Not finished." He bent and took her clit, eating hungrily as he plunged his finger into her ass. More fingers slid into her opening as he mouth fucked her and brought her. Higher. Higher. Longer. Stronger. Holy fuck! She was coming.

Tess opened her mouth and screamed as she flew apart, shivering, jerking against the bonds that kept her from bringing him into her arms. Gasping, she opened her eyes and saw Daniel had straddled her torso with a knee on either side of her. Muscle corrugated his body, lined his abs and she wanted to touch him so badly she ached.

"Wanna...touch...you," she whispered brokenly.

"Not yet."

"Crap."

Daniel chuckled. "Like I said, I'm not finished. I'm still hungry. I want your breasts. Wanna see if they are as delicious as your pussy."

She didn't know her nipples had ears but they perked right up. Oh yeah.

Daniel bent and drew one into his mouth, sucking hard. Once again, Tess jerked against her bonds as he nibbled, scraping his teeth gently across the puckered surface. By the time he'd turned his attention to the other nipple, she was ready to do a Spider-Man and start climbing the walls.

Writhing against the bonds, moaning his name, Tess lost all semblance of control and resorted to begging.

The cream he'd rubbed into her flesh tingled until she was almost uncontrollable with lust. Passion made her wild and when she nipped at his shoulder, Daniel laughed with wicked delight. "God, you're hot," he said before taking her mouth in a wild, crazy kiss that made their toes curl.

"Put your cock in my mouth," Tess demanded. She was sick and tired of her loss of control. Damn weary of it. Needing to give as good as she got, she glared up at him, noting his amused expression. "Right now, damn it!"

The smile died on his lips as he groaned and brought his body over her. His steely length speared in front of her face and she swallowed hard. The head was violently purple, broad and thick. Wanting to make him as needy as she was, Tess opened her mouth over the rigid head and took him deep in her mouth. Daniel's curse was ripe. Music to her ears. Opening wider, she sucked and pulled, knowing deep down she had very little control of things considering her hands were bound. It didn't matter. She wanted to torture him with pleasure. She wanted him to remember her days from now, when she was back in Dallas, long gone from these mountains.

She wanted to be unforgettable to him.

Oh yes.

Tess sucked him deep, licked, flicked and fucked him with her avid mouth. Above her, Daniel began to pump but she knew he was being oh-so careful not to send his cock too deep. When he finally began to shake, he yanked his cock out of her mouth with a hurried gasp. "No. Not like this. Not this time. Goddamn it, Tess."

It was clear now that Daniel was as out of control as she felt. Cursing, he pulled away and gave her a hungry look. "Sick of waiting, honey. No more."

Daniel moved between her widely spread thighs and grabbed a rubber from the end of the bed. He rolled it on and gripped her ass just seconds before he plunged home. The feel of his hot shaft entering her body threatened to send her into a screaming orgasm but then her eyes widened as she realized the minty cream he'd rubbed on her was now inside, heating her further. She pulsed and throbbed, squeezed tight around his cock, wanting more, more, more. And he gave it to her.

Gasping, her back bowed sharply on the bed, she delighted in the trip she took with Daniel. A trip straight to Oz and back. Or was she Alice who had fallen into a Wonderland of sex and passion and a night filled with hot, screaming wild-monkey sex?

And as her body seized and spasmed, she screamed her pleasure and brought Daniel to frickin' Oz with her. This might have been her best moment yet.

Kisses rained over her cheeks, her neck, and Tess slowly woke, realizing she was in Daniel's bed, warm and cozy, after having slept harder than ever before. She never wanted to leave this cocoon of warmth and pleasure.

She never wanted to leave this man.

"Um… What time is it?" she murmured sleepily. Opening her eyes, she saw gorgeous Daniel leaning over her, smiling.

"Late. I let you sleep."

"Aren't you sweet?"

"I can be." He flashed a grin. "Come on, honey. I have plans for us and I don't want to waste a minute."

Plans? Sounded yummy to her.

Tess shifted up and lolled against the fluffy pillows, taking in his room. Needless to say, she'd paid very little attention to it last night. She'd thought of nothing but having Daniel and his very delicious heat buried deep inside her. God! She was such a slut! That naughty little imp in her subconscious did some cartwheels!

The room was large as was his bed. A row of big windows provided a beautiful view of the mountains. Native American artwork dominated the rest of the walls. Her gaze fell on a beautiful bronze that featured a nude Indian couple sharing an embrace. It was seductive and entrancing. A sensual rendering of eroticism. Through the windows, she spotted a large patio and several rough-hewn pieces of furniture.

She returned Daniel's smile. "What do you have planned for us?"

"Mmm. I'll tell you in a minute but first, you might want to call Julie. She might be worrying about her mama."

Oh my God! How could she have forgotten? The man was full of surprises. Thank the stars Daniel was thinking because her own brain had apparently turned to mush. "Good thinking."

He motioned to the phone near the bed. "Help yourself. I'll be right back."

Tess watched him leave. Completely naked and apparently very at ease, he walked through the door and she just had to lick her lips. That tight ass had her mouth watering for a bite. As if he could read her mind, he turned at the door and flashed a wicked grin.

Sighing a little, she dialed her daughter. Julie was sleeping in this morning, after all it was Saturday morning and Tess knew well the habits of college girls so she didn't linger on the line. A quick hello. All is well. Having a great time.

When she finally hung up, she sighed deeply. She hadn't said a word about meeting Daniel but, truthfully, it wasn't her daughter's business. For the first time, Tess allowed herself to be completely selfish.

Even now her body felt awake, alive and refreshed. She wouldn't trade these last few days for anything in the world. Being here with Daniel made her feel complete for the first time in years.

Tess crawled naked from the bed, dashed into the bathroom and ran Daniel's brush quickly through her hair. After splashing water on her face and soaping her body, she used the brand new toothbrush he'd left for her near the bathroom sink then returned to the bedroom. Helplessly, she grinned. The scene of the crime.

Later, she greeted Daniel with a smile when he came back into the room. "Hey, gorgeous."

"Mmm. You stole those exact words from my brain." He held out his hand. "Come on. I have a surprise for you."

"I've had quite a few of those lately. Don't know if I can take much more."

"Oh, you'll really like this one."

Tess grabbed Daniel's hand and naked she padded with him across the bedroom. He opened a door leading to the patio and the quick nip of cold made her gasp. "If we hurry, it'll be okay," he said.

A few yards away sat an enormous sunken hot tub. Bubbles gurgled enticingly against the walls of the dark navy blue fiberglass. The scent of something clean and soapy mingled with the rising steam. On a ledge sat a pitcher of orange juice, an iced bottle of bubbly and two frosted glasses. He'd already poured two mimosas. They were beautiful, trimmed with slivers of orange. He'd gone to a lot of trouble to please her. It worked. Her heart melted at the thoughtful gesture and she turned, despite the chill in the air, to loop her arms around his neck. Her kiss landed at one corner of his smiling mouth. "This is wonderful."

"I aim to please."

Tess laughed and kissed him again. "Oh you do. I promise."

Once they'd settled deep into the warm water of the tub, he placed a drink in her hand and reached for a platter that she hadn't noticed before now. On it were wedges of fruit and quartered bagels that had been slathered with some kind of pink cream cheese spread. She plucked a wedge of pastry from the pottery tray, tore off a piece and popped it in her mouth, not realizing until now how hungry she was.

"Um, this is wonderful," she said around the bite and then she smiled when he held out a big chunk of pineapple and put it between her lips. Jeff had never been a really romantic man and Daniel's actions floored her. A shiver that had nothing to do with the morning chill shook her. She sipped her drink and watched Daniel look out over the mountains. "You really love it here, don't you?"

"Can't imagine living anywhere else." He turned his head, giving her an enigmatic look. "What about you, sweetheart? Does Dallas have your whole heart or could you see yourself moving someday?"

The question took her by surprise. She'd lived in Texas her entire life. She looked at Daniel then out over the mountains, took in the stately aspens, turned golden in the morning light. Her heart flipped in her chest. A wisp of an idea curled through her mind. What if?

"I've never really thought about it. Yeah, I have friends but they were friends I had with Jeff. Couple friends." Daniel reached across the lightly churning water and wrapped his sturdy arm around her shoulders to draw her closer. She leaned against him with a sigh. "Oh, they're all sweet. Such good friends but we don't really have that much in common anymore. It's funny. When you lose a spouse, it seems people just kind of tiptoe around you. It's uncomfortable. So I just go off to work every day, keep myself busy and head home to a book or some television."

"Doesn't sound very fulfilling." He pressed a kiss to her hair.

"Now that I really think about it, I guess it's not. Its part of the reason I'm here right now. I'm trying to think things through."

Daniel took her glass and set both their drinks aside. Steam curled off his warm skin as it touched the chill air. He advanced steadily, caging her in against the tub. Bending close, he kissed her then pulled back to whisper against her lips. "Why don't you think about this instead?"

Once his firm lips claimed her mouth, every thought, every worry fled her mind and instead she thought of his taste, the dark thrill she felt leaning naked against his chest as warm, bubbly water whispered over their skin. Tess writhed against his broad chest and heard him catch his breath. His fully erect cock prodded her belly, making her ache for a firmer touch. Using the buoyancy of the water, she lifted from the built-in seat and wrapped her legs around his hips to draw him closer. Her curls rubbed the length of his erection and she went closer as his arm wrapped tightly around her lower back. Her parted flesh cruised over that delicious warm length, making him curse. She nipped the corded column of his throat.

"I could eat you up," she whispered, lapping at the droplets of water that settled at the base of his neck. "You're better than chocolate, Daniel, an aphrodisiac I'm not sure I can do without."

Daniel groaned and buried his face against her throat as he raked his cock over her center. "Let me fuck you, honey."

"Oh yes, please." Tess trembled as he gripped her waist, lifted and feasted on her breasts like a man starved. Stabbing her nipple with his tongue, he spread her legs open wide and she gasped sharply as the heavy jet behind her pulsed against her throbbing flesh.

Daniel stilled. A wicked glint leapt into his darker-than-sin eyes. His teeth flashed white and strong.

Before she could draw another breath, he turned her back to his front and drew her tight against him. He reached past her for a condom and quickly covered himself.

"What are yo—"

"Shh. Let me."

270

Then Tess could do nothing but moan, a deep burning sound that simply tore up from her chest to curl out from her lips. Daniel had positioned her clit in front of the blasting jet and a quick trembling set up in her limbs as the decadent sensation tore through her. "Feel good?"

Shit. She couldn't think much less respond and then her naughty lover plunged two fingers deep into her slick channel.

Jesus!

Tess arched back as Daniel sank his teeth into the damp flesh of her shoulder. The tiny, teasing pain sent pleasure shooting through her like stars burning out of control. Still the pulsing jets teased her until tears rolled down her face. When he finally withdrew his big fingers, she cried out, bereft at the loss, but then he replaced that touch with another bigger, stronger, firmer touch altogether.

The head of his cock breached her gate and he plunged inside the sweltering heat of her pussy. Instantly, she clamped down upon him, gratified to hear his breath gush from his lungs.

"Tess!"

"Yes. Oh yes," she wailed as he pounded inside while the steady pulsating water pounded her sensitive clit. Shivering, wailing out, she came hard, leaning back against him as he let her come and enjoy the pleasure that raked wicked claws through her body.

She melted against him as he whispered hot, naughty words in her ear. He teased her breasts and tenderly stroked her swollen clit. He was still hard inside her, bigger than before and it was as if at this moment she could feel everything. Every dip and groove, every pulsing vein and warmth spread through her body in response.

"More," she whispered at last. She felt like a starving woman at a feast. Tess wanted to fall for Daniel and he'd been tempting her all along. His ploy had worked. She fell hard and fast and wanted to give him everything she had and more.

Daniel murmured a dark curse then whipped his arm around her middle, lifting her almost completely from the tub. Steam rolled from her arms as the damp air touched them. She didn't care. She didn't care about the chill when her hot nipples settled against the chill fiberglass or that she was sexually involved with a man ten years younger. Not anymore.

Coming up behind her, he plunged deep and strong into the wet core of her. Her legs were spread wide against the seat as he pounded hard and strong, bringing her to the edge of another climax. It rolled down her spine, arrowing straight to her clit, the silken vaginal walls and climbed straight into her heart. Her heat pulsed against his cock. It was Daniel's turn to fall apart and she was there with him in pleasure as the orgasm spiked. He pumped hard, thrust repeatedly until he stilled and roared his release into the bright morning sky.

Chapter Six

ഗ

Four nights later, Tess held the land phone to her ear and stared dismally at her nearly packed suitcase. Almost ready to go. She felt her throat tighten at the prospect of leaving but Julie's voice brought her back to the present.

"Mom? You sound funny. Are you sure you're all right?" her daughter said.

"Sure, I'm okay, sweetie. It was just such a good vacation and I hate getting back to the grind. That's all."

There was a pause. "Somehow I don't believe you. I've talked to you every day this week and each time you sounded better than the time before. You laugh more often too. And now you're getting ready to come home tomorrow and you sound all crappy and sad."

Tess lay back on the bed on which she sat and stared at the ceiling, feeling like her heart was breaking. "Ah, honey, you're just imagining things."

Julie's voice sharpened. "Don't do this, Mom. Something's got you all upset and I hate it. I want you to be happy for once."

"I am happy."

"Bullshit. You've never lied to me before. What's happened?"

"I-I can't."

"Stop crying right now or I'm getting in my car and coming to you."

Surprised, she reached up to feel the tears on her face and realized that she really couldn't hide anything from her very smart daughter. "Don't be silly, Jules. I'll be okay."

"Talk to me. Right now."

Should she? Could she talk to her daughter about something like this? Giving in, she sighed into the phone. "I met someone, honey."

"Oh Mom! Really? Oh please, please tell me it's the hunky guy from the next cabin."

Tess gasped out loud. Oh my. How perceptive. "Um...well...yeah."

"Yessssss."

Tess imagined Julie's habitual fist pump accompanying those words. "You're not upset?"

"Upset? God, no! Mom, you've spent your whole life taking care of me and taking care of Daddy when he was sick. This is your time. You rock, Mom. Don't you know anything? You look like a frickin' movie star and you're cooler than anyone I know. You deserve to be happy."

"He's younger than me, cookie."

"Um. How much younger?"

"Daniel is thirty-five."

"Oh my God! He's grown, Mom. A real live man and you're acting like he's a teenager and you're some old lady. That's just not the case."

"Yeah, I know it's not but—"

"But what? What, Mom? Are you scared?"

Was she scared? Hell yes, she was terrified of the things Daniel made her feel. She was so afraid to trust that this had been anything more than her personal sexual awakening. But it was. She'd fallen in love. Again. And this time with a man who made her toes curl and her body heat with a passion she hadn't known she possessed.

Tess blew out a breath. "I guess I am a little scared."

* * * * *

Later that evening, she ran around the cabin tidying up in preparation for the next day's departure. She'd just taken a small load of dishes from the dishwasher and tucked them away in the kitchen cabinets when there was a knock at her door.

Daniel.

Shaking with nerves, she wet her lips, smoothed her hair and opened the door. Daniel stood there solemnly holding a bottle of wine in one hand. Tess waved him in and lifted a brow. "A farewell drink?"

"Cut it out, Tess."

"Cut out what?"

He shrugged and took off his jacket, tossing it on the couch. "You can stop all the 'oh we're just casual fuck-buddies' thing."

She shook her head. "That's not what I'm trying to do. I'm just being a realist."

Daniel stalked to the kitchen and removed two glasses from the cupboard. After pouring them each a glass of chardonnay, he handed one to her and held his own loosely in his hand.

It seemed odd to her they would have this "good-bye" talk in the middle of the kitchen floor. But Daniel leaned against the counter and pierced her with those ultradark eyes. "We need to talk."

Tess sipped her wine and looked down at her feet clad only in a pair of socks. "It was fun, Daniel. I had a wonderful time."

"Wonderful time?"

She looked up in time to see a brow lift mockingly over one eye. "It was more than fucking wonderful and you know it."

"Okay," she said, surprised at the breathless quality of her voice. "It was more."

Daniel set down his glass and the sound of it hitting the tiled countertop sounded loud in the sudden quiet. For a minute he hung his head, causing his thick black hair to fall gracefully over his forehead. "I have to talk to you about something important."

When he looked up, she saw the stark sincerity in his eyes and her throat went dry. "Okay."

Daniel moved close and gripped her upper arms. He blew out a heavy breath. "I'm just wondering how you're feeling about us. I love you, honey. I've never in my life loved a woman as much as I love you."

Tess' world reeled. She gasped and stared him straight in the eye. "Daniel, I'm ten years older than you."

He laughed, a full-bodied sound that sent a shiver racing through her blood. "I think I've already established that I'm a man and not a boy."

Her answering smile bloomed and she reached up to stroke a hand along the buttons of his shirt. "Yeah. I think I got that. But Daniel, are you sure about this?"

"I've never been more sure about anything, Tess. Tempting you to come back to life has been the best thing I've ever done. I've been thinking, sweetheart. I could sell the company and move to Dallas if you want. We could be together."

His face could have been carved from stone as he watched her, waited for her answer but Tess was so shocked she could only stare. "Daniel, your boys are here. Yeah, you could find plenty of work in Dallas but why would you sell everything you've built here and follow me to Texas? It's crazy."

Suddenly Daniel swooped in and took her in his arms. He stole her breath with his kiss, a kiss full of passion and love and all the good things. Shaking, she drew away and looked at him. Her eyes were swimming in tears but she didn't give a damn. Let them fall.

"You'd give up everything you've found here?"

"In a heartbeat. If you want me, Tess, the way I want you."

Like the sky opening above her, the answer to all her questions about what she would do with the rest of her life suddenly became so very clear. "I do want you, Daniel. It's crazy but I feel I've known you forever. You've taught me how to open myself up, to be true to myself. I've never known a man more generous and loving."

"More generous and loving than Jeff?" He ran a hand through her hair, touched the high curve of her cheekbone.

"I loved Jeff for a very long time but it was a different kind of love from what I feel for you. With you the world is magic and sex and affection and so many other things, I couldn't begin to name them."

A smile broke over Daniel's face as he laughed and scooped her up into his arms. Swiftly he carried her into the living room and settled on the couch with her in his lap. God! Had a more romantic man ever lived? Tess didn't think so.

"You can't come to Dallas, Daniel," she whispered leaning against his chest, loving the feel of him. "Your boys."

"There is such a thing as planes, honey."

"Yeah, I know but it's not the same. You have a life here. A home. People here care about you. Now, me? I'm not so sure I'd be leaving so much if I just moved here."

"Are you serious? Would you do that for me?"

Tess laughed into the front of his shirt and then looked up into his beautiful face. "I'd do anything for you, Daniel. For us. I love you. I don't know when I've loved anyone more. Sassy wants to buy me out and if you're sure about this, I think I'm just going to let her. I happen to know of a really nice little floral shop for sale here. Prime location too."

Daniel drew a breath and bent to her. Tess tasted love and acceptance on his lips and fell into it as her heart soared into the stratosphere.

"Ah, honey," he whispered between kisses. "Tempting you to sin with me was the best thing I ever did. For me."

"And for me too."

When Tess met his kiss again, feeling, sweet and pure, blasted through her heart. To love again was magic and she planned to enjoy it every day for the rest of her life.

DR. FEELGOOD

Alice Gaines

ഔ

Trademarks Acknowledgement

∞

The author acknowledges the trademarked status and trademark owners of the following wordmarks mentioned in this work of fiction:

BMW: Bayerische Motoren Werke

Chapter One

ಬಾ

On the other side of the one-way glass from Dr. Sarah Dalton, the machine gently masturbated the latest experimental subject. All of the men agreed to being observed but it intimidated some of them enough that they couldn't maintain erections. This one managed nicely though and his penis thickened and elongated. He had a beautiful organ. Large and evenly shaped with a huge head. Very much like another one...

Watch me.

Would she never get that day out of her head? This same room, an older apparatus. A young man stretched out on his back while the mechanical fingers stroked his sex. He'd stared at the glass the entire time as though he could see through to her.

Watch me.

Heaven help her, she hadn't been able to look at anything but his eyes and his swelling cock. She'd messed up the experimental protocol completely and had to junk the session.

In the other room the bell went off, the sound traveling through the speakers into the observation booth. The man pressed a button on the panel next to him and the read-out appeared on her screen. Moderate arousal. He was fighting his response, just as she'd instructed.

Watch me.

The other man had resisted that day too. He took so long to climax, she'd almost gone in to check the equipment. Finally he'd erupted into the most violent orgasm she'd ever observed. What a shame she couldn't use the data.

She had to forget that day or ruin another research session. Dragging herself back to the present, she increased the lubrication and pressure and watched his responses. The tape would record the length of time it took for him to reach orgasm, the amount of ejaculate and the speed with which it shot from his body. But it took a well-trained human observer to gauge the objective intensity of his climax. His reports would tell her how it felt from the inside.

The bell went off again. He moaned and pushed a button. Much more intense arousal this time. How long could he last?

She'd observed hundreds, if not thousands, of orgasms and she ought to be used to it by now. Any normal person would but she could hardly call her own sexual drive normal. Even at forty-one, her libido had scarcely slowed at all. Despite her years of dealing with almost overwhelming sexual needs by facing them head-on in her work, she hadn't found real relief yet. She sighed. After the party tonight she'd dig her favorite vibrator out from underneath her sweaters and work the edge off. Again.

Right now she'd study MAp08-15's reaction to the suction that slid up and down the length of his organ, grazing the head with each upstroke. If only he didn't remind her of that other man who'd so wrecked her detachment she'd looked up his name in the institute's records.

Rick Wilson. Mercifully he'd moved five years ago, preventing her from doing something completely unprofessional. She'd never gotten him out of her dreams — neither the day nor night variety.

She reached for the controls and advanced the settings one more step. On the other side of the glass, the man responded with a loud groan of pleasure. She almost whimpered herself. He looked so much like Rick.

"Oh yeah," a male voice said behind her. "I remember that machine."

No, it couldn't be. She turned and found him standing in the doorway. "Rick?"

His face broke into that smile that curled his lips into something wicked and forbidden. "You did know my name. I always wondered."

"What are you doing here?" The words came out breathless. The voice of a woman aroused. If her pussy had felt fluttery before, the clitoris hardening, it raced past that now into fully blown need.

"I work here."

"You left five years ago. I haven't seen you in all that time."

His smile broadened. "Did you miss me?"

"What do you mean you work here?"

He pointed toward the glass. "You're supposed to be watching, right? He's going to come in a minute and you'll miss it."

Damn but the man rattled her. She turned back to her work but the man in the next room barely registered in her consciousness. Rick had come back and he hadn't changed one bit.

Wrong. He'd filled out. Become more muscular, less gangly. Where he'd been all arms and legs—a brand new graduate student earning his way through school in her experiments—now he had strong shoulders and a broad chest. Even the sports jacket he wore with his slacks couldn't hide that. She did some basic math in her head. He'd be thirty now, thirty-two tops. Just the right age for fantasy and too young for her reality. What in hell did he mean he worked here?

He joined her at the console. Not close enough to touch her but near enough to share body heat.

"Would you like to explain the 'work here' remark?" she asked.

"You hired me for your research team," he answered.

She looked at him out of the corner of her eye. "No I didn't."

He shrugged. "Your colleagues did. You were in Europe on sabbatical."

Yes they had hired someone. She'd consulted by phone and e-mail. Hardly necessary. Dr. F. H. Wilson was a rising star in the field. Everyone read his papers on the female orgasm. Her lab had managed quite a coup to steal him away from his tenure-track position at UC.

He even had a nickname everyone knew but no one used in professional settings. Dr. Feelgood. Rick and Dr. Feelgood were one and the same. "So you're—"

"Frederick Harold Wilson," he answered. "I've never felt like a Fred so I go by Rick."

"But you were studying microbiology or something similar."

"You knew that too?" His smile grew smug. "I switched fields."

"Why?"

He nodded toward the glass. "Don't you think you should finish that poor bastard before he goes nuts wanting to come?"

"Of course." The man's cock had taken on a crimson color and a white droplet at the head showed he'd approached orgasm. She turned up the controls and his groans grew louder.

"If he's like most guys, he's imagining some woman sucking him deep into her mouth right now," Rick said.

"Is that what you did?"

He chuckled but the sound had more lust than mirth in it. "I pictured you in here fingering yourself so that we could come together."

Her skin heated from her cheeks to the roots of her hair. Blushing, damn it. "You shouldn't say such things."

"Did you ever do it?"

"Never." But she'd wanted to.

"Too bad."

On the other side of the glass, the man's face contorted and his body stiffened. His groans became a shout as his hips jerked upward and semen shot out of him. One of the more powerful orgasms she'd ever observed. Again like Rick. Only this time, Rick stood beside her and watched with her. Finally the man relaxed and she turned off the machine.

If only she could relax too. But she hadn't climaxed and the man of her fantasies stood only inches away.

"Aren't you forgetting something?" he asked.

Of course. She opened the microphone that would project her voice into the next room. "Fill out the questionnaire please."

While the man reached to the bedside table and grabbed the clipboard, she turned off the microphone.

"I used to do that too," he said. "Deliberately forget the paperwork. That way I always found out if it was you in the booth."

She turned to him. "Why would you do that? Why did you come back here now?"

He leaned a hip against the counter and crossed his arms over his chest. "That should be obvious."

She stood and stared at him—at the strong jaw and sensuous lips. The dark hair that brushed his ears. The green-blue eyes, so clear and deep. He'd been handsome before. Now he was temptation personified.

He let his gaze wander over her and his nostrils flared. "I want you, Dr. Sarah Dalton. I have for over five years."

"You switched disciplines because you want me?"

"I also took an interest in the work. Not much holds more appeal than figuring out what gives a woman a really good orgasm."

Of course. Dr. Feelgood. In only a few years he'd earned an international reputation in the field. That had impressed her staff the most about him. So many researchers discounted the female orgasm — and not all of them men. He'd carved out a niche for himself and had gone on to fill it brilliantly. Dr. F. H. Wilson had an excellent understanding of what excited women. Rick Wilson had all the equipment to put theory into action. Her knees almost buckled at the thought.

"So I switched disciplines, changed schools and got my Ph.D.," he said. "After that, logic sent me back to the world's best lab in the human sexual response. And to its head researcher."

"Me." Her voice had gone breathy again. Damn, how would she get it under control?

"We have a lot to work through, Sarah. I'm going to enjoy every minute of it."

No, this was insane. He couldn't mean an affair with her. He was a young man, just approaching the prime of his life. She kept herself fit but her forty-one-year-old body couldn't compare to the younger women on her staff. Her staff? Dr. Feelgood could have any woman he wanted with his good looks and the sex appeal that radiated off him. Add to that the fact that he'd made it his life's work to study how to satisfy a lover and that he was probably the most attractive man on the planet. He couldn't possibly prefer a woman old enough to have been his babysitter.

He gave her a look that would melt a lesser female. "So you're throwing a party for me tonight."

Crap, she was. A welcome for Dr. F. H. Wilson. The entire staff would be there, along with spouses and assorted significant others. Rick Wilson would visit her in her own house while dozens of people watched. Her colleagues. People with whom she had to maintain decorum. Even authority. If only she'd known. She could have arranged someplace less intimate than where she lived.

No help for it now. She glanced at her watch. With everything she had to do, she wouldn't even have time for her vibrator. Damn, damn, damn.

"Earl gave me directions to your place," Rick said. He grasped her wrist and turned it until he could read her watch. "I'll see you there in about two hours."

She pulled her hand back and straightened. "Until then."

He pushed away from the counter and walked to the doorway. When he got there he turned back briefly and stared at her. A feral, hungry look entered his eyes, as if he couldn't decide whether to smile at her or devour her alive. The smile won out—for the moment. Then he turned and left.

She absentmindedly rubbed her wrist where his fingers had touched while she willed her breath back to normal. No man had any right to be that sexy.

* * * * *

Rick adjusted his jacket to hide the fact that he was getting hard again. Just as he had when he'd found Sarah Dalton in her lab. She'd hardly changed. The lustrous brown hair she kept fastened at the nape of her neck had some gray. Her body was lusher now. But she still had the high cheekbones, deep amber eyes and full lips. The same lips he'd dreamed of around his cock.

He reached up to ring the bell. After a minute the door opened and she stood before him. She'd dressed in demure, almost innocent, clothing. A peasant blouse with the drawstring neckline pulled tight so that only her collarbones

287

and a bit of shoulder showed. A mid-calf skirt flowed over her hips. No one could make that outfit sexy except Sarah. Her soft curves accentuated by the way the fabric clung to her. The straps of sandals encased her otherwise bare feet. No pantyhose, just bare skin under the skirt all the way up to her panties — if she was even wearing any.

A casual smile curved her lips but the flutter of her breath gave her away. She felt anything but casual. Good.

"Rick, do come in." She stepped aside and opened the door fully. "Almost everyone's here. Can I take your jacket?"

Some devil tempted him to whisper to her that giving up his jacket would show off his growing erection but he resisted. She'd find out about the state of his cock when the time was right.

"I'll keep it," he said.

"Of course. Come in."

He entered the front hallway and kept going until he stood in her living room. Pretty much what he'd expected to find. Everything in good taste but not extravagant. She could have made a mint writing popular books about her studies but she didn't go for sensation. It would have lessened her stature in the academic community.

Earl was the first to greet him, shaking his hand and then indicating a small woman at his side. "This is my wife Jan."

She also took his hand and stared up at him with some interest. Most women did once they learned about his work. And his nickname. "Nice to meet you, Rick."

"Same here."

"You'll remember Doug, Lynn, Stew," Earl said.

Rick nodded to each in turn. Lynn rose from the couch and approached him, finally tucking her arm under his. "Let me show you where Sarah's hidden the wine."

"If the sideboard in the dining room counts as hiding," Sarah said. She'd walked up to them and was busy pretending she didn't notice Lynn's arm snaked around his.

"Come on, Rick." Lynn tugged at his hand and led him into the dining room. Sure enough, several bottles of wine stood open on a marble-topped sideboard. The necks of the whites peeked out from coolers but the reds were at room temperature. He picked one up and studied it—a Sangiovese rather than cabernet. Sierra foothills, outside Sacramento, rather than Napa Valley. He showed the bottle to Lynn. "Can I pour you some?"

"I'll help myself to some white," she said.

As she served herself, he found a goblet and poured a bit of the red. After setting the bottle aside, he swirled the Sangiovese for a moment, tilted the glass to inhale its perfume and tasted it. An unusual varietal, and very, very good.

Lynn sipped at her wine, looking at him all the while over the rim of her glass. "You know what you're doing."

She meant more than wine tasting. She was cute enough. Probably in her first years of graduate school—not that much younger than him, when you got right down to it. Grad students who worked together routinely had affairs. As the youngest faculty member at the institute, he could indulge himself with her without raising too many eyebrows. Too bad she wasn't nearly as interesting as the boss. Desperation fucks weren't his idea of a good time, although his aching cock would sure appreciate one right now.

Nope.

She eyed him, obviously looking for a reaction. He gave her a noncommittal smile. "Once you've lived in Northern California for a while, you learn a bit about wine."

"Wine." She lifted her glass in a toast. "So you're Dr. Feelgood."

He managed to swallow his wine before he choked on it. "You heard about that."

"Ours is a small research community."

"It was a joke among the students at my last job."

Her smile broadened. "A joke?"

"I don't mess with my students."

That ought to have dimmed her enthusiasm but she just kept smiling at him. He looked around the room and his gaze fell on a curio case in the corner. That sort of piece normally would hold teacups and crystal glasses and the like. This one displayed statuettes. He walked to it and checked out the contents. Erotic sculpture, all of it. Various cultures and periods. Several appeared to be European prehistoric Venuses. Plush, female bodies—downright fat by today's standards. No clothing. In fact they consisted mostly of breasts, bellies and labia with little in the way of other body parts.

"Sarah has quite a collection," Lynn said. "She finds them all over the world."

Here and there among the female forms stood male figures—all of them with prominent erections. Some appeared to be African woodcarvings. Others made of clay looked as if they'd come from India.

Lynn opened the glass door and reached inside.

"Should you do that?" he asked.

"Sarah won't mind." She picked up an odd piece. Blown glass by the looks of it. It didn't even have a body but was no more than a huge phallus with a scrotal sac attached.

"This one's my favorite." Lynn caressed it, suggestively rubbing her thumb along the underside of the head. "So smooth and large."

"And fragile."

Her lips parted in a sinful grin. "I'm always very careful with it."

Sarah's head and shoulders appeared from the entrance to the kitchen. Somehow she'd gotten from the living room in there without him noticing. Had she witnessed Lynn's obvious attempts to get his attention?

Maybe not because she noticed the younger woman fondling a glass cock for him and her shoulders stiffened. She recovered quickly and gave them both a phony smile.

"Dinner's served on the deck," she said and then disappeared again.

Lynn placed the phallus in his hand and smiled at him. "Later."

Not in this lifetime. He didn't say it though. He'd just avoid her.

She left, swinging her hips a little too much. Once she was gone, he slowly blew out a breath he didn't realize he had been holding and carefully returned the glass piece to its place in the cabinet. As he shut the door, one of the African pieces grabbed his attention. It had an erect cock way out of proportion to the rest of his body.

"I know exactly how you feel, pal," he muttered before heading toward the deck himself.

* * * * *

Sarah couldn't stand another minute. With Lynn's constant attempts to get Rick's attention and the looks he sent Sarah's way, her head felt like the ball in an emotional game of ping-pong. None of the others seemed to notice but he took every opportunity to give her a sleepy-eyed smile that belonged in the bedroom. Of course none of them knew about the conversation they'd had that afternoon.

While he'd submitted to the machine years ago, he'd imagined her stimulating her own clitoris to share an orgasm with him. He'd deliberately made his observer speak to him so he'd know when she'd looked on.

He'd known she was in the booth that day when he'd stared at the glass the whole time.

Watch me. See what you do to me. Do the same to yourself.

Damn, he was looking at her that way now. He knew the effect he had on her and he didn't care that their colleagues surrounded them. Just a stare could make her want him.

She shifted in her chair but couldn't get comfortable. He smiled. Satisfied with his power over her body, curse the man. She grabbed her dessert plate and stood quickly.

Jan looked up. "Do you need help?"

She needed help all right but nothing Jan could do for her. "I'm just going to tidy a few things."

Jan went to stand but Sarah put a hand on her shoulder. "Enjoy your cheesecake. I'll only be a minute."

Before Jan could protest, Sarah turned, crossed the deck and slipped into the kitchen. At the sink, she rinsed the plate and set it aside, then stared out the window, clutching the edge of the counter.

God, she was hot. Her pussy throbbed in rhythm with her accelerated heartbeat. Her most sensitive flesh would be erect now, her panties wet. She had to get some relief. It would only take a moment. A brief encounter with her vibrator and she'd be able to go back to the party. She'd go to her bedroom where no one would hear the buzzing and guess what she was doing.

She walked to the front of the house and climbed the stairs to her bedroom. She quietly closed the door, went to the walk-in closet and turned on the light. After pulling out the bottom drawer of her dresser, she rummaged around in the bottom until her hand found the battery-powered shaft. Before she could take it out, a tingle raced down her spine. She straightened and turned. Rick stood on the threshold to the bedroom.

His eyebrow went up. "Looking for something?"

She put her palm on her forehead. "Headache."

He nodded toward the dresser. "You keep your aspirin in there?"

"It's not so bad. I'll go back to the others."

She tried to walk past him but he reached out an arm and caught her around the waist. "I know about that kind of headache. Let me make it better."

He pulled her close to his body. Too close. His scent overwhelmed her—aftershave and his own musk. His heat penetrated to her bones and she nearly slumped against him. "Rick, I—"

"I know how you feel. I can fix you. Trust me."

She stared at his face, at the light in his eyes, the curve of his lips. He was sin incarnate but he could definitely ease the ache between her legs. She nodded.

"That's my girl." He pulled the louvered door of the closet closed and guided her to the dresser. After placing her hands on the top, he eased her legs apart and pressed himself against her back. A hard ridge pressed against her buttocks. He was fully aroused.

"Now then..." He gathered her skirt up in his hands, baring her legs. Scarcely daring to breathe, she let him run his hands over her thighs and then between them. When his fingers brushed her lips through the silky fabric of her panties, she couldn't suppress a whimper of need.

"You're so hot, baby." His voice was unsteady, full of lust. "So wet."

He slid his hands inside her panties and touched her directly. Her whole body trembled and she clutched the dresser for support.

"I've wanted to do this for over five years," he whispered. "Do you remember the day I stared at the one-way mirror the whole time?" *Watch me. I'm going to climax. Just for you.*

He slipped two fingers inside her wetness and pumped. She closed her eyes and pictured his beautiful cock entering her. Slowly, while she begged for more.

"I knew it was you on the other side of that glass," he went on. "I could feel you, like a charge in the air around me."

He withdrew his fingers and circled them around the spot where she most needed it. Her universe contracted to that eager point between her legs. Her most sensitive flesh. In a moment, he'd push her over the edge into orgasm. Damn, but she needed it.

"I fought that climax as long as I could," he said. "I imagined you doing this to yourself."

His fingers went inside her again, making wet sounds as they plunged between her muscles. Her pussy took on a life of its own, contracting around him. Squeezing, reaching for maximum friction. He bent so that he could penetrate her more deeply and run his thumb over her clit.

It was too much and yet not enough. He could take her apart with his fingers. Would she come back together again when he finished? Did she have any choice? She was going to come and she had to surrender.

He groaned. "I held out that day. I waited until I could hear your cries in my mind. I could smell your arousal. I could feel you shudder when you came."

"God, Rick, yes!"

"Now, baby. Give it to me. Now." He pushed her past the brink. His fingers stretched while his thumb rubbed. Harder and faster. Until she couldn't breathe.

The orgasm washed over her with a force that made her shake. Deep inside her, the spasms started and coursed all along his fingers. He didn't stop until he'd drawn every bit of response from her and she almost collapsed.

When it finally ended, he turned her around on shaky legs and rested her against his chest. Damn. He'd made her helpless in the face of her lust. She always responded too hotly. With him, it was even worse than usual. Before she could stop it, a sob escaped her.

"Sarah?" He lifted her chin and looked into her face. "Tears?"

She swiped the wetness away. "Nothing. Foolishness."

He didn't believe her, obviously, as he stared into her eyes, his brows knitted with concern. Wonderful, a man ten or more years younger than she, worrying about her. First she'd let him take advantage of her weakness and use his hands to make her wild while her entire staff would have to wonder where they'd gotten to. Now he made her feel stupid.

She pushed out of his arms. "I need to get back."

"You'd better change your panties." He turned around but didn't leave. Oh hell. They'd been intimate enough. Pretending modesty would only make her look more foolish. She shucked off her wet panties and dropped them to the floor then found another pair in a drawer and put them on.

"Maybe we shouldn't reappear together," she said.

He didn't turn back to her. "I'll be along in a minute."

She nodded, even though he wouldn't see it, and left the closet.

* * * * *

Smart move, dumbass. Rick stood in Sarah's bedroom closet, struggling to catch his breath. He'd been so determined to get his fingers on her clit and hear her sighs of pleasure. So intent on feeling her pussy clench in orgasm that he'd forgotten the effect she had on him. His cock hadn't forgotten though. Stiff as a crowbar, *this* hard-on wasn't going to go away on its own.

For a moment, her tears had distracted him—what the hell was up with that anyway? Now the scene came rushing back in all its lusty glory. How he'd found her bent over, her gorgeous butt tempting him, while she searched for something in the bottom drawer. If he looked in there, he'd probably find some sex toy. She'd obviously been aroused all evening, although the others wouldn't have noticed as he had. She was a cool customer on the surface but he'd seen enough women ready to come—and not all of them in his research. She'd run up here to blow off some steam and he might as well find out exactly what she used to turn herself on.

He pulled open the drawer, lifted out some sweaters and found the thing. Holding it up into the dim light, he checked it out.

Pink latex in the shape of a cock. A pretty big one at that. A little rabbit was attached near the base, its long ears running parallel to the shaft. Not unlike the device his subjects rated as delivering the most pleasure. He twisted the knob at the bottom and the whole thing moved. The shaft gyrated and the rabbit's ears fluttered where her clit would be once the vibrator was buried in her pussy.

He groaned. Great. Now he had to picture her on her bed, her legs spread as she slid the latex shaft inside her. He had to listen to the motor's hum while he imagined her skin flushing and her breasts pushing up against her peasant blouse.

This was *not* good. Not good at all. He'd lost control of his own body and he couldn't join the others in this state.

He couldn't sneak away from his own damn party either. He'd have to take care of business on his own. He reached to where his erection rubbed against the cotton of his pants and stroked himself. Just that contact nearly did him in.

He bent and returned the vibrator to its rightful place, put the sweaters back on top as neatly as he could manage, then closed the drawer.

With no other alternative, he opened his fly and took out his throbbing cock. Bracing himself with a fist on the dresser, he began to stroke the length of his shaft.

Shit, he'd never wanted a woman the way he wanted Sarah. Five years and he'd never gotten her out of his mind. Even with other women, he'd fantasized about Sarah. How he'd take charge and show her what real lust felt like. How he'd be in control the next time they met.

Yeah right. Now here he was jerking off like a randy teenager. For crissake he could still smell her arousal.

Wait a minute. He had good reason to detect her scent. Her soaked panties lay on the floor where she'd dropped them. He stopped stroking himself and picked them up. They were still warm from her body and wet with her juices. The perfume of her arousal permeated the cloth.

He should drop them again or put them on the dresser where he could stare at them as he came. He wasn't going to do that though. He was going to do something she'd absolutely hate. Well, she'd never find out. No harm, no foul.

Clutching the sodden material in his fist, he curled it around his cock and resumed stroking. Hot and wet like this, the fabric made him imagine her pussy all around him. He rested his fist on the dresser again and closed his eyes as he increased the pressure. All the way from the head of his cock down to his balls, he rubbed her wetness into his skin. He was going to come in the same panties she had and he was going to come hard.

Next time he'd be inside her for real. He'd plunge his member deep inside her and listen to her cries get louder. He'd fuck her until neither of them could stand it anymore and then he'd turn her over and fuck her some more. He'd screw her night and day until neither of them could walk. After five years of waiting, he'd make it last.

This wasn't going to last though. This was going to be over in another minute. Already his balls were tightening as his body got ready to come. He stroked harder and faster, spreading her moisture everywhere as the inevitable happened. He hit the point of no return and couldn't hold back.

His hips bucked as the explosion built in his cock. He came in searing waves, barely staying upright as his come spurted into her panties.

Shit, it was good. So damn fucking good. He milked the last drop out of him and used the silk to wipe himself off. Finally he returned to the real world and looked down to find his cock getting soft surrounded by Sarah's panties.

He'd better find a laundry hamper somewhere. Amazing what the woman could do to him. Next time he'd have all of her.

Chapter Two

ɷ

The next Sunday, Sarah found Rick on her front lawn, holding her newspaper in his hand.

"Where've you been?" he asked.

"Did I invite you here and then forget?"

He didn't budge but stood, holding the paper out to her. She walked toward him and took it, even though she had to tug at it to make him let go.

He pointed to her mug. "Is your coffee as good as your cheesecake?"

"What do you want?"

"I want to know why you haven't been at the lab for three days."

"I have been working at home, writing my latest paper, if you must know."

He grinned. "I think you're avoiding me after that little grope we had in your closet."

"Oh for heaven's sake." She looked down the street to where Mrs. Glass was rolling her trashcan to the curb. "You'd better come inside before the neighbors see me talking to you in my robe."

"That's my girl."

"I'm not your girl." She turned and led him back into the house.

Once he'd gone into the living room, she shut the front door and walked by him into the kitchen. After setting her coffee aside, she pulled down a mug. "Cream and sugar?"

"Black's fine."

She poured him some coffee and turned to find him standing almost on top of her. He smelled of the same aftershave he'd worn to the party. The pleasant, masculine scent had surrounded her as she rested against his chest in her closet. Her pussy clenched at the purely tactile memory of his fingers deep inside her while his thumb played her hot point like a delicate instrument. He had a master's touch, she'd give him that. She *wouldn't* give him another chance to demonstrate it on her.

He looked down at the mug in her hand and one eyebrow went up in challenge. As if he'd read her thoughts. Her cheeks burning, she shoved it toward him, almost sloshing some onto his chest.

Now grinning wickedly, he raised it to his mouth and took a sip. "As good as your cooking. Seems you do everything well."

She stepped back and pulled the tie of her robe tighter. "All right. Why are you here?"

"We have unfinished business."

"We did what we did," she said. "It's over."

"What we did…correction…what you did was amazing. I want to know why it made you cry."

"A silly, emotional reaction," she said. "It didn't mean anything."

He set the nearly full mug on the counter. No surprise there. He hadn't really come for coffee. She'd slipped up and let him see her vulnerable. He'd come for more of that. Why couldn't he be a typical man and go after Lynn? Hot, young and flirtatious, Lynn ought to be more his type than a woman in her forties.

He studied her now, no hint of amusement or self-satisfaction in his gaze. "A woman's tears always mean something. I want to know what yours meant."

She stared back into his blue-green eyes. Just like that day in her lab when he'd focused on the glass, daring her to look into his soul while the machine stroked his cock. He'd laid himself open to her. If only she could afford to be that honest.

Oh well. She wouldn't lie to him. "Sex is complicated for me."

"It's complicated for everyone."

"Not for young men. It's slam-bam-thank-you-ma'am."

A hint of anger flashed in his eyes. "Is that what you think of me?"

"You signed up for research that allowed other people to observe you climax."

"I needed the money," he said. "There was only one part I enjoyed."

She hugged her ribs. She wouldn't ask which part he enjoyed. She wouldn't want to hear the answer. He'd probably tell her anyway.

He took a step closer to her. Not enough to make her back away. Just enough to remind her of how right it felt to have his arms around her.

"I only enjoyed imagining that you were watching me," he said. "That you wanted me as much as I wanted you."

"An ethical researcher doesn't become involved with her subjects."

"I'm not your subject anymore." He took another step toward her, now much too close. She ought to move. Back away. Put enough space between them for her to think. To breathe. But her feet wouldn't move. She would have stumbled if she tried.

Now only inches from her, he took her chin between a thumb and forefinger and tipped her face up to his. "I've never kissed you. Not after coming dozens of times in front of you. Not after the other night when you climaxed in my arms."

"Rick, don't."

"No other woman has ever responded like that," he said. "You went up in flames the minute I touched you."

That was the problem. Her damn hair-trigger. It had plagued her since puberty. She'd only confessed that to one man…a boy, actually. The confession had cost her. Rick had discovered her secret on his own, damn him.

"What would you do if I kissed you?" he said.

"Please…" The word came out like a plea. She'd meant please don't. Why had she begged for a kiss instead?

Still she couldn't move away. Not while his eyes drifted closed. Not while his head lowered. Not when his lips finally…finally…brushed over hers.

When their mouths met, a jolt went through her. Only by leaning toward him and grasping at the fabric of his shirt did she keep upright. He groaned and pulled her against him while his lips explored every inch of hers. Tender and insistent. Innocent and explosive. Everything in his caress demanded a response from her and she gave it. Running her arms around his neck, she answered, parting her lips in welcome. Soon they were straining against each other. Giving, taking, needing more.

When he offered his tongue, she touched it with her own. Heat coiled around them and they clutched each other close, fingers in hair, lips battling. She pressed herself against his length and found the hardness she'd felt against her buttocks the other night. When she ground her hip against it, he growled and pushed her away from him.

"Not like this." He took an uncertain breath and then another. "I've dreamed of making love to you for over five years. I want it right."

She stood there and let his hands on her upper arms support her. She had a perfectly good bed upstairs, as he well knew. She wouldn't fight him if he tried to take her up there right now. Heaven help her, he'd aroused her to the point where she could deny him nothing. With just a kiss, he'd won her body over. In another moment, he would have reduced her to begging. Despite her strong sex drive, no one had ever managed *that* before.

"Come away with me for a long weekend," he said.

"I have work to do."

"Take your laptop. You can write your paper there. I'll do the same."

She pushed away from him and rubbed her arms. "It isn't wise."

"Damn it," he shouted. "You made me come over and over while I fantasized about you. You've driven me to the edge again. You owe this to me."

"It was research."

"It didn't have anything to do with research and you know it," he said.

Oh hell. Why didn't she just say yes? Her body wouldn't give her any peace until it had him.

"Say you'll go, Sarah," he said, "or I'll keep at you with my fingers and tongue until you do."

"All right." She threw her hands up in the air. "All right, I'll go away with you."

He nodded, looking relieved. As if he'd thought she *could* resist him. "Pack for three days. I'll pick you up in the morning."

* * * * *

Sarah sat in the passenger's seat of the BMW and watched the scenery fly by. The Pacific Ocean on one side and redwood forests on the other. Nothing could be more breathtaking. They'd followed the Coast Highway for most of the day. Taking the inland route at least part of the way would have gone faster but wouldn't have provided the same drama. Rick had planned everything well.

Rick looked like a Greek god in sunglasses as the sunlight poured into the convertible. Her own hair would take half an hour to untangle after the ride but who cared? Practicality didn't fit with a day like this. By the end of the evening, he'd be her lover. Her boy toy, if only for a week.

"Where are you taking me?" she asked.

He smiled but kept his attention on the road. "You'll see."

"I'm not going to try to escape. You can tell me."

He shrugged. "It's only a few miles away. I guess I can."

He didn't though. He kept smiling and didn't say another word.

"So?" she prompted.

"A modest little villa overlooking the sea. Two bedrooms, three baths, deck with spa, professional kitchen."

She sputtered. "You call that modest?"

"Nothing but the best for my Sarah."

"How can you afford a place like that?"

"It belongs to my friend Sybil," he said.

Sybil. A woman. That figured. "What does she do for a living?"

"She's a sculptor."

Wonderful. A rich woman friend. "She must be very successful."

"She is. It doesn't hurt that her husband Tom is a high-powered corporate attorney."

"She's married."

He glanced at her and that expressive brow came up. "You care?"

She crossed her arms over her chest. "I'm sure it's none of my business."

"Right." He barked a laugh. "And yes, we were lovers. We parted as friends."

"Are Sybil and Tom going to be there?"

He laughed again. "You really are something, you know that?"

"You seem to enjoy whatever it is I am."

"More than you know." He guided the car off the highway onto a private lane. "We're here."

The road twisted and turned as it climbed a hill toward the sea. At the top, the pavement gave way to gravel and a house came into view.

Modest indeed. It was a multi-level redwood palace with skylights studding the roof. The sound of waves crashing in the distance promised a view of the ocean. Rick stopped the sports car in front of the house but kept the motor running while he fished around in the glove compartment for something.

He had to almost lean into her lap to do it and she balled her hands into fists to keep her fingers from digging into his sun-warmed hair and skimming over the muscles of his shoulders. She'd have plenty of time for that later.

Finally he straightened, holding a garage door opener. With a flick of his thumb, the door raised to reveal plenty of space for two large cars. Empty. Of course.

Rick drove inside and shut off the engine. "Sit tight. I'll get your bag."

Normally she would have climbed out of the car without assistance but he'd been playing the gallant all day. Opening doors, putting his hand at the small of her back to guide her through. He'd constructed a fantasy around the whole trip and she'd played along despite herself. It felt damn good to have someone else take charge of things for once.

The BMW's trunk closed and then Rick opened her door, her bag in his hand. After helping her out, he shut the door again and bent to pick up her makeup case. "This way."

He opened a door at the back of the garage and waited for her to go first. It led to a staircase with plush carpeting. She climbed silently upward, turning once at a landing, and found herself in a tiled hallway. Straight ahead of her lay a sunken living room with more of the same carpet. She walked to it and descended the stairs.

On the opposite side a wall of windows soared all the way to the beams of the roof. Almost thirty feet, if her guess was right. A redwood deck ran the length of the house on the other side of the windows. It had a panoramic view of the ocean.

She turned back to Rick, who stood several feet behind her, still holding her luggage. He smiled. "You like it?"

"I'll give your modest villa a modest wow."

He pointed to a cast-iron spiral staircase that led up to a balcony overlooking everything. "Bedrooms up there."

"Give me a minute to absorb this first."

"It's something, huh?"

"Very nice. I should have gone to law school."

He chuckled. "Not your style."

She looked around at the furniture. Modern but not stark with cushions everywhere to make things comfortable. The artwork was incredible. Paintings and, of course, sculpture. One piece in particular caught her eye and she walked to it. As tall as she, it resembled some kind of fantastic tree made of bronze. A mobile floated around the top, representing leaves and tiny birds. When she touched it, the figures moved and gave off a sound not unlike wind chimes. "Sybil's work?"

"She's very good," Rick said.

First modest. Now good. Rick had developed a tendency toward understatement. She looked around one more time. "I'm ready for the bedrooms."

Heat flared in his eyes, turning the normal deep green-blue even darker. Did he plan to start the weekend with sex right off? Would she ask for more time if he did? Or would she let him take her still half-dressed on the bedspread? Did she really care either way?

He indicated the spiral staircase with a motion of the hand that held her makeup case and she walked to it and climbed upward.

At the top, he led her toward the front of the house to an open door. When she crossed the threshold, she found herself in a room almost as magnificent as the one below. A skylight poured sunshine down onto a huge bed covered with brightly colored pillows and a matching comforter. More artwork, with small pieces sharing shelves with dozens of books. Mirrors banked a long dressing table and across the room stood a chest of drawers, again modern but not severe.

She turned to Rick. "Should we be using the master bedroom?"

"This is the guest room." He set her things on the bed. "Check out the bath."

She didn't move but stood and looked into his face. "You've been here before, I take it."

"To visit Sybil and Tom." He paused. "Alone."

"I shouldn't have asked."

"They always told me I could use the place. They even gave me a key and the remote for the garage door. I never wanted to until now."

That shouldn't have pleased her. As good-looking as Rick was, he must have had dozens of lovers in his lifetime. But he'd never brought one here. That mattered even though it shouldn't have.

"I'm sorry," she said. "I'm not normally possessive."

He didn't look upset. In fact he looked entirely too pleased with himself. "Check out the bathroom."

She walked to the bathroom doorway. Hitting the switch just inside revealed a dressing area with brightly lit mirrors. On the other side, a tile floor beckoned. Once there, she found gleaming marble and brass fixtures. This room also had a skylight, which allowed dozens of plants to grow around the enormous sunken tub. Jets along the sides indicated a whirlpool. A separate shower was more than big enough for two.

Hands touched her shoulders and she started, flinching at the surprise.

"Easy," Rick crooned into her ear. He continued massaging her, turning tense muscles into mush. "That's more like it."

"Everything's beautiful, Rick," she said, her voice not much more than a whisper. "Thank you."

"You'll thank me all right." He pulled her against him until she could feel the hardness against her buttocks. She'd felt him the same way the night of her party but she still hadn't seen him for more than five years. It didn't seem that he'd lost anything.

"Make yourself comfortable." He nuzzled her neck and then nipped gently at the skin. "I have to go into town for supplies."

Of course. The BMW wouldn't hold much with both of them and their luggage in it. She'd take a long hot bath and wait for him to return.

Suddenly the warmth at her back disappeared and his hands fell from her shoulders. By the time she turned around, he was gone.

Supplies. She'd need some fortification for what would come next.

* * * * *

Sarah awoke in the tub. The bubbles from her bath had long ago faded and the water had started to cool. She turned off the jets of water and stretched. She could get used to this bathroom.

Sunbeams now slanted through the skylight. Late afternoon. It would get dark soon. What a shame to sleep a day like this away.

She climbed out of the tub and took a bath sheet from the rack. The terrycloth warmed her skin everywhere she rubbed it, especially between her legs and over her breasts. They'd been sensitive all day in anticipation of Rick's fingers and his mouth. His stiff shaft inside her. Finally, she hung the towel on a bar and turned to study herself in the mirror.

Not bad for forty-one was the best she could conjure about her body. She'd hated her small breasts when she was younger but at least they hadn't sagged as some women's did. Her belly and thighs had lost some of their firmness though. Though not pocked with cellulite, they appeared squishy rather than tight and they were entirely too rounded for fashion. Overall she looked exactly like a healthy woman past her prime.

She groaned. What on Earth had Rick been thinking? He had to know she was forty-one damn years old. Was he remembering her at thirty-six? Hell, he probably had no idea what a thirty-six-year-old body looked like either.

What if his face fell when he saw her naked? What would she do then? What if he decided they were better off as colleagues after all? She'd laugh it off or pretend to. She'd sleep on the couch and ask him to take her home in the morning. Then she'd have to find some way of facing him every day in the lab.

Damn it all! Why hadn't she thought this through?

Nothing to do about all that now. She took a fluffy robe from a hook on the back of the door, put it on and went looking for him.

Out in the bedroom, his bags sat next to hers on the bed. Sounds wafted up from the floor below. She padded out barefoot and descended the spiral staircase.

The room below stood empty so she looked until she found the kitchen. It was half the size of the huge living room and gleamed with slanted sunlight bouncing off stainless steel everywhere. Rick stood at a butcher-block table that filled the center of the room. His back was to her as he worked something on the table with his hands.

"What are you doing?"

He looked over his shoulder and smiled. "Hi there, sleepyhead. Have a good bath?"

"The best. What do you have there?"

He held up a lump of dough of some kind. "Pasta."

"That's pasta?"

"Flour, egg, water, a bit of olive oil and salt. Pasta."

She pointed to it. "They sell that stuff at the grocery."

"Not like homemade."

She stared at the incongruous lump some more. "They sell the fresh kind too."

"I like my own." He turned back to the table. "Come here. Let me show you."

She joined him and he sprinkled some flour on the surface in front of her and handed her the dough. "Knead."

She'd kneaded other kinds of dough often enough but this was different. It was pliant but so firm it seemed to snap back after every pass of her hands.

"You need to work it a bit harder," Rick said. He put his hand over hers and pressed down and outward. The dough responded to his greater pressure and soon the two of them were working it together. Pressing, folding and pressing again.

"I can't believe a cook as good as you has never made homemade pasta," he said.

"I never had the time. This is a lot of work."

"Worth it." He inclined his head toward a small, stainless machine with a hand crank. "The roller will help."

Working the dough was fun though, she'd have to admit. It had a sensual rhythm to it with Rick's larger hands over hers. They continued in silence, so close their shoulders rubbed. As always his nearness washed over her. His heat. His scent. The extra tingle of awareness in her private places. He seemed affected too, as his breathing grew more rapid, hot puffs grazing her cheek. The kneading wasn't enough exertion to cause all that.

He stopped finally and she found herself breathless as well.

"Now for the rollers." Rick grabbed the machine and fixed it to the work surface with a clamp. "You catch while I crank."

After adjusting the settings, he pressed the edge of the dough between the rollers and turned the handle. Now smooth, the pasta turned into a ribbon about three inches wide and it stretched out in length and tumbled into her hands.

With each pass and each adjustment, the pasta got thinner and longer.

"See how smooth it feels," he said, his voice a caress against her ear. "Silky. Tender. Like your skin."

"Rick—"

"Shh. Don't talk. Just feel."

It did feel like silk as it glided through her fingers. Cool and supple. When the ribbon got too long, he took kitchen shears and cut it into four parts. Then the two of them worked those parts. One at a time. Always through the rollers. Always falling into her hands. Becoming more and more delicate as they worked.

"Cooking should engage all the senses," he said. "Smell and taste are important but so is touch."

He wasn't really talking about pasta any longer but about touching. He was so close she could feel him along her side. Sleek muscle everywhere. His young body was so perfectly formed. Big, but in proportion. Once an appealing youth, he'd grown into a splendid man and he'd get even more glorious over the next few years. Her own body thrummed in response to his. Still they worked in silence, connected at the hip and shoulder, spinning flour, egg and water into silk.

He moved the crank to the cutting blades and slipped a section of the dough into it. Now the pasta slipped into her fingers as recognizable fettuccine. He followed that with the other sections of dough and set them aside on the floured surface of the table.

He picked up a towel, brushed the flour from his hands and then did the same with hers. His actions made her feel small and helpless, like a child, but a protected and well-loved child. Had she ever felt that when she had been a child?

She looked up at him. "Now what?"

He set aside the towel and took her into his arms. His eyelids lowered as his face neared hers. She closed her own eyes and reached upward to him until their lips touched.

They kissed for a moment. Softly, slowly. Not rushing. His lips were soft, his mouth teasing rather than pushing. She leaned against him and ran her arms around his neck.

Heat enveloped them, pulling the tension out of her body. She melted on the inside, surrendering to the building need inside her.

She couldn't help but moan into his mouth.

"I know, baby." He pressed small kisses along her jawbone to her ear. "God, you make me hot."

"Rick…"

"Hmm?" His breath hummed in her ear.

"Oh! Um…the pasta?"

He took her earlobe between his teeth and nibbled. "What about it?"

"Doesn't it…"

He tugged her robe open and ran his hands inside. Over her ribs, pulling her hard against him, the outline of his erection pressing into her belly.

"Need something?" she breathed.

He moaned. "You bet I do."

"I meant the pasta."

"Right." He straightened and gave her a lazy smile. "The pasta needs to rest an hour. I think that'll give us enough time."

Chapter Three

ଚର

Rick's cock would have burst through his pants in another minute. He'd spent hours in the BMW with her, anticipating this exact moment. He'd come back from town to find her dozing in the tub. He'd almost lost it right then. Almost stripped and joined her, sliding his rock-hard member inside her before she came fully awake. Down in the kitchen, he could have happily hoisted her onto the work table, parted her legs and buried his face in her pussy until she gave him another one of her amazing orgasms. Only sheer willpower gave him the strength to lead her up to the bedroom and remove their bags from the bed so he could take her fully as the last minutes of daylight spilled in from above them.

She'd tied the belt to her robe again and now she held the ends in her hands. Shyness. The combination with her obvious heat was endearing. He ought to feel frustration at her fear of revealing herself after all she'd done to him over the years but instead going slowly and watching her open like a flower would be a lot more fun. If only his throbbing member would allow him that patience.

He walked to her and reached for the belt of her robe but she clutched it in her fingers.

"We need to get naked to do this right, baby," he said.

She nibbled her bottom lip — her full and luscious bottom lip. "I'm forty-one you know."

"I figured something like that."

"How old are you?"

"Thirty."

She sighed. "I wish you could have seen me when I was thirty."

"I would have been nineteen. Not a good match," he answered. "Besides at that age, I would have gone off like a bottle rocket if I'd even touched you."

"That's not funny."

He kissed her briefly. "I'm not laughing."

She had no answer to that but just stood staring at him with wide brown eyes.

"Sarah, I saw you asleep in the bathtub. I know what you look like."

"The whirlpool was on. You couldn't have had a good look."

Well shit. What a time for her to worry about the age difference between them. He kissed her again, pulling her hard against him so that she couldn't mistake his state of arousal. If he couldn't convince her brain that he wanted her, maybe he could show her body. Her body always seemed to be on his side.

The ploy worked this time too and soon she was kissing him back with all the hunger she'd shown in the kitchen. She was one hot-blooded lady and she knew how to set a fire under him too.

Finally she pulled back and looked up into his face. "All right. Just promise—"

"God, baby, anything. I'm at the end of my rope here."

"Total honesty. You won't say anything about how I look that you don't mean."

"Deal." He grasped the knot in her belt again and this time she let him untie it and open the terrycloth, baring her to his gaze.

And what a body. Long, graceful neck and collarbone. Small breasts, nicely rounded. Her torso tapered past her ribs

315

to her waist and then flared outward in feminine perfection. Lush hips and thighs.

"Damn, baby," he whispered. "You're beautiful."

"Do you mean that?"

"Honestly," he said. "When a man sees thighs like those, he can't wait to have them pressing against his ears."

She let out a long breath of relief. "Your turn to get naked."

"In a minute. There's something I want to do first."

"Not fair. I want to see you."

"You'll see all of me you can take." He cupped one of her breasts and squeezed. The nipple hardened against his palm and she let out a whimper. She wouldn't complain once she understood what he had planned for the next couple minutes. Bending, he ran his tongue along the underside of the other breast. While he teased the first with his fingers, he took the second nipple deep into his mouth and sucked. Her whimper became a gasp and her fingers burrowed into his hair to hold his head against her.

The scent of her arousal floated to his nostrils. The same perfume from the other night in her closet. On her soaked panties as he'd emptied his lust into them. It had the same effect on him now, slamming into his gut and making his cock twitch in his pants. Damn if she wasn't already near climax. Amazing.

He lowered himself slowly, running his tongue over her ribs and then into her navel. She shifted, parting her legs and the evidence of how hot she'd grown became even more obvious. He touched her inner thigh and found moisture there. Already she was wet and he hadn't even touched her there yet.

No time like the present. He dropped to his knees and grasped her hips so that he could bring her sweet pussy to his face. She opened to him, just the way he'd hoped. With no hesitation, she gave him access to her most intimate depths. Here, with his nose buried in the curling hairs at the apex of her thighs, her scent became intoxicating. He took a moment to savor her perfume, her vulnerability, her need.

"Rick, please," she gasped.

"I know, baby." He slipped two fingers inside her and felt her muscles squeeze around him. Slick and hot, she'd welcome his desperate cock soon. She'd grip him while they both reached their peak.

"Please," she said again. "I need…"

He removed his fingers and instead probed her with the tip of his tongue. She shuddered and gave him a mewling cry. She was so hot. So close.

Finally he tongued her clit. It was fully distended, a tight pebble of nerve endings. Flicking, he rubbed it gently and then with more pressure. Her hips moved, pressing herself against him in a silent plea for more. His heart swelled in his chest. Satisfaction that he could give her so much pleasure. Tenderness that she could let him know her so completely.

Her cries grew louder and her fingers dug into his shoulders. Time to end her torment.

He took her clit into his mouth and sucked and she immediately came. Her hips bucked and he quickly put his fingers into her again to feel her spasms. Strong and rhythmic, she grasped him in powerful convulsions. He drew it out as long as he could until she sighed. She'd finished but her pussy still fluttered with aftershocks. Unbelievable.

When she swayed, hanging onto his shoulders, he rose and scooped her up into his arms. She sighed and ran her arms around his neck. "I can walk."

"None too steadily."

"Really, Rick." But she didn't move a muscle and lay limp against him. That had been one hell of an orgasm and he'd given it to her. He could muster a lot more where that had come from and he'd feel the next one around his cock. Buried deep inside her.

His balls tightened at the thought. He'd waited so long for this moment. His mind wanted to savor it. His body had other ideas.

He walked to the bed and lowered her onto it then moved their bags to the floor. Now, alone on the comforter and cushions, she stretched, raising her arms above her and pointing her toes. A purely sexual move, one that might be made by the goddess of love herself. He sat beside her and stroked the side of her face. Without warning, she turned her head and took his index finger between her lips, sucking on it rhythmically. His cock didn't miss the message. It throbbed in time with the movements of her cheeks as if she'd taken his shaft into her mouth. Damn but he needed to fuck her.

He quickly removed his shoes and socks and tore off his shirt. After tossing it aside, he rose and reached to the buckle of his belt.

She watched him as he stripped, her eyes heavy-lidded and her lips parted in a smile. As he lowered the zipper and shucked out of his slacks, her breath caught. Now he wore nothing but briefs and they clearly showed the outline of his erection.

Smiling himself, he took those off too and stood for her inspection.

"Oh my God," she whispered. "You're even bigger than I remember."

"I can honestly say I've never been harder."

"Fuck me, please."

"I'm going to make love to you. There's a difference."

She opened her arms in invitation. "Whatever you call it, please do it."

He joined her on the bed and took her into his arms for a kiss. When their lips met, a searing heat exploded between them. Naked together for the first time, he pressed himself against her, pushing her down into the mattress as their mouths locked. Lips, tongues, teeth, they explored each other.

Her skin felt like silk against his. Her moans heated his blood. This was a coming together of two souls, each hungry for connection.

As the passion built, she rolled him onto his back and launched an assault on all his senses. Still kissing him, she slid her body down his. Her nipples pressed against his chest, her pelvis arching against him, bringing her thigh against his cock with each movement. Her hands went everywhere, from his face, over his shoulders and down his sides. No woman had ever touched him like this and his body responded. Demanding more. Needing more. Until he nearly lost his mind with lust.

Her mouth left his finally and she slid lower along his body. When her tongue swept over his nipple, he couldn't hold back a groan. Damn, what she did to him.

She moved to the other nipple while her hand went wandering. Over his belly and into the nest of hair that curled around his cock. She took his shaft into her fist and pumped and he nearly came off the bed. Then she moved lower and the knowledge of her intentions hit him in the groin. She planned to give him head.

He caught her face in his hands. "Don't, baby."

"Want to. Please."

"I'll lose it, Sarah. I swear."

"I need to." She shook him off, moved downward and caught the head of his hard-on in her mouth.

Damn. Shit. He had to stop her. His balls were ready to explode and there she was sucking him deeper. Making him wild with her tongue.

With his last scrap of sanity, he caught her under her arms and tossed her onto her back. Biting his lip for control, he plunged two fingers into her pussy and worked her clit with his thumb. He needed to prepare her because, God help him, when he finally got inside her, he wasn't going to be gentle.

"Hurry, Rick," she gasped. "Please now."

"Need to make you ready."

"I am." Her cry came out like a sob. "Can't wait. Can't."

Her pussy exploded in orgasm, grasping at his fingers. He moved quickly and entered her with one thrust.

She screamed and her climax continued. Racking her body while the muscles of her sex clenched and shuddered around him. It seemed to go on forever as he surged into her. Now hard and fast, he drove her on until he couldn't hold out any longer.

He came with a fury that felt as if it took the top of his head off. Thrusting wildly, his cock emptied into her, semen shooting from him. Even when it had finally ended and he lay on top of her in boneless satisfaction, her contractions continued all around him.

Finally he found the strength to lift himself and look down into her face. Into the face of a thoroughly loved and satisfied woman. What a sight she made.

Then it hit him. "Shit, baby. I forgot the condom. I brought a whole box of them."

She didn't open her eyes but smiled. "I won't get pregnant."

He kissed the tip of her nose. "We're okay then. I got tested before I started working in the lab. I knew we'd end up together."

Her eyes opened. "You're mighty sure of yourself."

"Nope, I was sure of you."

"Well, I haven't been tested."

"We'll do that when we go back," he said. "I'm sure we're fine."

Her eyes narrowed. "That's a lot of 'we's'."

"We're definitely a 'we' now." Although softened, his cock still had enough stiffness that he could move it inside her. "In case you hadn't noticed we're still joined."

"I didn't agree to that, Rick. I only said I'd spend a weekend with you."

He couldn't help but grin. "At the end of three days you'll never want to be away from me again."

She groaned.

"Honestly, Sarah, you make me feel like a king. You're an amazing lady."

She started to move from under him but he kept her right where she was. "You come like no other woman I've ever known. It seems like I hardly have to touch you."

She stiffened in his arms. "Please don't."

"All right. What's up? You act as if that's something bad."

"I can't tell you now." She nibbled her lip for a moment. "Not while you're still inside me."

"If something's wrong, I need to know."

"I'll tell you. I promise." She wriggled out from under him and he let her go this time. She sat at the edge of the bed, looking away from him. "Just not now."

He stroked her back. "Okay. Don't stress it."

She turned to him, smiled and nodded. "Hey let's cook that pasta. All of a sudden, I'm famished."

* * * * *

After dinner they sat on the deck and watched the reflection of the moon shimmer on the waves of the Pacific Ocean. For the first time in longer than she could remember Sarah's body gave her some peace. Soon enough she'd need more of Rick—more of his hands and mouth and cock. For now his cooking satisfied her stomach and his lovemaking satisfied her sex. Even the wine was perfect—a buttery Chardonnay that balanced the *Frutti di Mare* sauce he'd made for their pasta.

He reached across the tiny distance that separated their chairs and stroked her free hand with his fingers. "Ready to talk?"

"As ready as I'll ever be, I suppose."

"I'm ready to listen."

"I didn't realize I was different until my junior year in high school." A silly place to start the story, really, but her problem had become so urgent then. "I thought all girls had the same urges I did."

"All girls do."

"Not like I did. I always masturbated. When I was little, it just felt good but didn't accomplish much. Then puberty hit."

He curled his hand around hers and squeezed.

"I started waking during the night in the middle of orgasms. Deep, bone-melting ones. I didn't know what was happening to me."

"They must have explained your sexual response in school," he said. "Health ed or something."

"They taught us about pregnancy and protection. How to say no to boys. They didn't teach us about pleasure."

He frowned. "Your parents didn't say anything?"

"My father couldn't have gotten the words out and my mother was too shy. But I found her stash of books one day and, oh boy, did they open my eyes."

His eyebrow went up. "Pornography?"

She had to laugh at that. "No, you silly man. Romance novels."

"You mean the kind they sell in the supermarket with the half-naked people on the cover?"

"They're very good books, most of them. I have my own secret stash now."

"I don't believe it." He chuckled. "Dr. Sarah Dalton, leading researcher in human sexuality, reads romance novels."

She pushed his hand away. "You'll read one too when we get back. Sooner if I can find some good ones in town."

"Okay. I'll try anything once."

She took a breath. "They at least explained what was happening with my body."

"Fabio did?"

"Rick, you're making yourself sound really ignorant on the subject."

He raised his hands in surrender. "You win. Tell me about them."

"There's always courtship. Breathless kisses. Progressive intimacy and finally consummation. Both partners reach orgasm. Always. I recognized what happened to me in their responses."

"Interesting," he said. "I'll have to figure out a way to introduce that into my research."

"Your subjects are already reading them. I promise you."

"Go on."

"Then I figured I was perfectly normal and I only had to find the right man and I'd live happily ever after. In the meantime I experimented."

He grinned. Or, better put he leered. "Now *that* sounds interesting."

She groaned.

"Okay I'm being bad. But you promised to tell."

She took a breath. "I got better at masturbating. I'd come home after school, hot for a boy in my algebra class, and I'd lock myself in my room and give myself some relief. If an erotic dream woke me up in the night, I'd stimulate myself to orgasm. At least then I could go back to sleep."

"There's nothing unusual about that," he said.

"But I did it so often. I needed it so much. I finally found an understanding partner."

"The kid from algebra class?"

"A girl. Cynthia Grant." She looked down at her hands. "She came out to me as a lesbian. She had a crush on me and I used her."

He took her hand and squeezed it again. "Aw, baby. You were young."

"Young and selfish and still it didn't help. I discovered that Cynthia took a lot longer to reach climax than I did, even though she loved me." She looked into his eyes, at the concern there. Not pity. Please not pity. "I was a freak, Rick. I still am."

"That you're not." He set his wineglass on the deck and leaned toward her, his gaze intent on her face. "You're a gift."

"Don't humor me please."

"Look. When a guy comes too fast, it ruins everyone's fun. When you come fast and hard...and often...it gives me extra pleasure."

"That's not how my first lover saw it."

He continued staring into her eyes. "Okay, tell me about that."

She finished her own wine and set the glass aside. "Stewart Morrison. One of the popular kids. So good looking, I couldn't believe he was interested in me. He wasn't. He just wanted to get laid."

"Typical guy."

"As sweet as Cynthia was, I knew there was something on a man's body that could give me pleasure," she said. "I had to have it."

"Lucky Stewart."

She briefly shut her eyes but that only brought back images of the backseat of Stewart's sports car. Of groping in the tiny space. Of her first encounter with an erection. She rested her elbows on her knees and put her head in her hands. "Even though it was my first time, I climaxed the moment he got inside me. God, it was humiliating."

He stroked her back. "It couldn't have been that bad. You got some pleasure from it."

"He told all his friends. I mean *all* of them. They told their girlfriends and they told all *their* friends. Pretty soon the whole school knew I was Slutty Sarah."

"Shit."

"I'll never forget the look on Cindy's face when she confronted me," she said. "I broke her heart."

"Aw, baby. Come here. Let me hold you."

She looked up to find him patting his knee. He meant for her to sit in his lap. What an absurd notion. And yet, when his arms spread wide, she went to him and let him tuck her head under his chin and hold her against his chest.

She was a decade older than he and his superior at work. Now here she sat like a child. The heat of his body warmed her through, keeping away the cold of the ocean breeze. The sounds of the breakers below felt like a lullaby. She couldn't allow herself to act helpless like this but it felt so good.

After a moment, he kissed her hair. "So after all that, why did you go into your area of research?"

"I've asked myself that many times."

"Come up with any answers?"

"Several reasons." She sighed. "Not all of them nice."

"Let me guess the not-nice one." He paused, sitting in silence for a bit. "You got to control a bunch of guys instead of the other way around."

She nodded. "Until you. You knocked me for a loop because I couldn't command you."

He lifted her chin and gave her a quick kiss. "Baby, you owned my cock from the minute I first set eyes on you."

"How could that be?"

"There you were. So professional and detached, your hair always tied back. Underneath I could sense your passion. I kept waiting for you to snap."

She groaned again. "Slutty Sarah."

"Sensuous Sarah. Sexy Sarah. I wanted to be the guy who melted your ice."

"You almost managed." Almost? He'd managed very nicely or she wouldn't be sitting on his lap, feeling—naturally—his cock thickening and getting hard.

"So what other reasons?" he asked.

She looked up at him. "Reasons?"

"For your choice of work."

"Oh… Well…I guess I thought that I'd conquer my fears by facing them. On my terms of course. And then…" Her skin got hot. She knew she was blushing but most likely the dim light would hide that from him. "And then my deep and abiding fascination with the human penis."

He chuckled. "Mine's at your complete disposal while we're here. Any time you want. Any place you want. Any way you want."

"I'll take you up on that." She would too. And soon.

* * * * *

During the night Sarah woke up, aroused by a dream she'd already forgotten. Only vague images remained. She'd straddled some beast while an impossibly huge object thrust up into her. They'd galloped that way, her need building with every hoof beat. Silly and yet perfectly capable of turning her on.

A hard back pressed against her own. Finely muscled and hot. Rick had said she could have him any time she wanted. She might as well take him up on that offer.

She rolled over and kissed his shoulder. "Are you awake?"

No answer came except for his even breathing of deep sleep.

"Rick?"

Still nothing.

Damn. She could try to go back to sleep but that likely wouldn't work. She could slip her fingers between her thighs and finish what the dream had started but it'd be pretty embarrassing if Rick woke and found her doing that. She could get up and go somewhere else to finger her clit but then she'd have to leave the warmth of the bed and his body.

Or she could do what he'd promised. She could wake him up and tell him she wanted him now and here. The how didn't matter much.

She reached around him and found his cock. It wasn't completely soft and as she stroked it, it lengthened and grew thick.

"Ah," he said. "Sarah."

The words came out slurred. Still not awake, his first response was to say her name.

She continued pumping him, stroking the tip of him with her thumb on each pass. That roused him finally and he rolled onto his back and opened his eyes. "Find something interesting?"

"You said I could have it whenever I want it."

His eyes flashed in the moonlight coming through skylight. "It's all yours."

"Good, because there's something you wouldn't let me do before."

"Oh God," he moaned. "Oral sex?"

"You've done it for me."

"You really want to do that?"

"Watch me." She pushed the covers away to find him fully erect. Already moist, her pussy grew wetter, readying itself to accept his bulk. With any luck, the proper use of her lips and tongue could make him even larger.

Still grasping his shaft, she lowered her face and took the head of his cock into her mouth.

He moaned, a dark and sinful sound that connected with her own body. Whatever pleasure she gave him, he'd give back double. She took him deeper into her mouth and sucked. He did get larger and harder, so big she could only take part of him. She used her hands for the rest. One to grip his shaft while the other cupped the sac at the base.

"God, you know what you're doing," he gasped. "You're getting me so excited."

She lifted her head. "I want you excited. I want you as aroused and hungry as I am."

"You're playing with dynamite."

"I like living dangerously." She squeezed him with just the right pressure to hold off his climax so that she could take him higher when he finally came. His body went stiff and a white droplet appeared at the head of his cock. Poor baby was suffering now but he'd get his reward.

She resumed exploring him with her mouth, sliding her lips down on him as far as she could manage. Oh-so gently, she scraped her teeth along the underside of his cock on the upstroke. His fingers tangled in her hair, guiding her in the rhythm he wanted while his hips rose upward to meet the movements of her mouth. He couldn't take much more and yet she lingered for another moment, savoring the feel of his hard flesh against her tongue.

When his groans got louder, she released him, sat up and swung a leg over him. Immediately, his hands went around her waist to hold her over him. Grasping his cock with one hand, she used the fingers of the other one to spread her lips and then guided herself down onto him.

"You're tight, baby," he said.

"I'm fine. You're just so big."

"God, I love being inside you."

"I want to feel you move, Rick," she said.

"You move. Slowly so I can feel every inch of you." He'd taken the edge off for her earlier and now she could let herself take her time. She moved on him, her pussy muscles stretching to take all of him. First a little and then more. Lower and lower until her pelvis met his and he was completely embedded inside her. Both of them remained motionless for a moment. Joined as lovers. His body fit hers perfectly, his hardness pulsing inside her. No, that was her heartbeat racing through her until she throbbed along with it. Of all the men she'd known in her life only Rick made her feel complete. She wasn't Slutty Sarah with him but simply a woman with needs that matched his own.

"I wish you could see what I'm looking at," he said.

"A horny old lady?" she answered.

"Stop that. You're not old."

"But I am horny."

"I like you horny," he said.

"Oh Rick, you feel so good."

"Enjoy."

She began to move, gliding up on him and then down again until she'd impaled herself on his cock. Each contraction of muscle that lifted her also grasped him. Tightening, bringing more friction on the down stroke. Heaven.

He reached up and took her breasts in his palms. Squeezing and using his fingers to toy with her nipples, he gave her another set of sensations. Her flesh grew hot and heavy. Overly sensitive.

Rick knew how to play her body, drawing out her pleasure. With him, she could relax and let the arousal build without allowing it to rule her. She did that now, taking note of all the textures of him. His hardness, the satin of his skin, the crinkling of the curling hairs that met her own. She bent and kissed him and tasted the honey of his lips without breaking the rhythm of their coupling or the pressure against her breasts.

When he started moving with her, she sat up and closed her eyes. All the better to concentrate on his thrusts as they met hers. Still neither of them rushed but kept up a steady pace as he slid in and out of her depths.

"I feel as if I could do this all night," he said.

"I wish," she whispered.

"I can try."

"Wicked man."

"Insatiable woman."

Oh yes. No matter how hard she tried, she'd never get enough of this. The sheets under her knees, the way his hands roamed over her body from her breasts, over her ribs and finally to her hips as he urged her up and down. When his thumb traveled to her folds and parted them, it found her clit hard and eager for his touch. She surrendered to that too, letting him push her higher. With her eyes tightly closed, she let the sensations wash over her. Passion and need and yet not overpowering. It was natural for Rick to make her feel this way. It was right.

"That's it, Sarah," he said. "Enjoy."

"You always know how to touch me."

"And I'll always learn more."

"Oh God. I can't hold back."

He stroked her clit harder and faster. "Let go. When you're ready."

"Oh yes. Oh yesss."

Already her muscles were clenching around him, seeking more friction. Her whole body throbbed, ready to burst. She moved faster, frantically reaching for the ultimate. Up, down, taking him deeper inside with every stroke until she felt as though he'd split her in two. Still it wasn't enough. She could find something more if only she could hit on the right stroke, the right tempo. Almost there. Almost.

His movements grew wilder as he pounded up into her. "Shit, I thought I could do this all night. You're too much."

"It's all right, Rick. Whatever you need."

"Not without you."

"I'll come. I always do."

His thumb drove her clit while his cock slammed into her pussy. He worried that she wouldn't climax? Impossible. The feeling of inevitability swept through her, from her pelvis, to her breasts, to her heart as it hammered in her chest.

"Now, Rick!" she shouted. "Don't stop. Don't...stop!"

Another powerful thrust and another and another and he roared as he came. She joined him, gripping him over and over as she climaxed. They stayed that way, their juices mingling at the moment of perfection.

Finally she fell against him and his arms went around her. His chest rose and fell under her cheek, the ragged beat of his heart in sync with her own. When his fingers stroked her cheek, she felt a tenderness no man had ever shown her before. They could make heaven together. They'd almost gotten there tonight and they had days to keep trying.

Chapter Four

ಐ

When Rick returned from the boutique, he found Sarah sitting on a bench near the BMW.

"I thought you were going to check out that gallery," he said.

"I finished fifteen minutes ago."

It had taken him more time inside than he'd estimated when he'd told Sarah he had an errand to run and he'd meet her at the car. After all you couldn't rush picking out the exact dress in exactly the right color. Now she spotted the bag in his hand—way too pink for anything a guy would buy for himself—and her eyebrow went up.

"Just a little something," he said as he stashed the bag behind the driver's seat of the convertible.

"Even the 'little somethings' around here cost a lot of money," she said.

He shrugged. "What can I say? It's a trendy artists' colony up here."

"I'm sure whatever *that* is is lovely but you shouldn't be spending so much money on me."

"I spent it on myself."

Her forehead crinkled.

"Well, you'll wear it but it's really for me."

She smiled. "You're impossible."

"And hungry. Let's get some lunch."

He joined her on the sidewalk and took her hand. When she rose from the bench, he didn't release her but interlocked his fingers with hers. She looked down at them and then up at him.

"I'm playing possessive," he said. "Go along."

She *tsked* but didn't pull away and he led her down the street and turned the corner. On a weekday, they had the town pretty much to themselves except for the merchants. One couple approached them though. In their fifties by all appearances. The woman wore a pants suit that even his mother would declare dowdy and her shoes matched her purse. She looked at where his hand held Sarah's and she bristled with disapproval.

Sarah noticed and stiffened. She tried to pull her hand back but he held on. He smiled and nodded to the woman. "Nice weather."

She didn't answer but picked up her pace and walked around them, pulling her husband behind her.

"Uptight old biddy," he muttered.

"Quiet," Sarah whispered. "She'll hear you."

"Do you care?"

She sighed. "Honestly, Rick."

"Here we are." He led her to The Civilized Omnivore, opened the door and guided her inside. The bell rang for a second time as the door swung shut again. Only a few customers sat at a table in the corner. When no hostess greeted them, he took Sarah to a booth. She selected a seat and he slid in next to her. From here he could touch her easily as they ate.

A waitress appeared with water glasses in her hands. The young woman put them down and filled them. She checked Rick out briefly and smiled. "Do you need menus?"

"That would help," he answered.

She turned and walked way, her hips swinging inside her tight jeans. Much the same way Lynn had come on to him at Sarah's house and Sarah noticed just as she had that night too.

"Another admirer," she said.

"Really? I hadn't noticed."

She *tsked* again and this time she rolled her eyes too.

"I don't care about her or Miss Manners on the street either."

"They can all tell I'm older than you."

"So?"

The waitress returned with laminated menus. She placed them on the table and pulled a pad and pen out of the pocket of her mini-apron.

Sarah looked at the selections for a moment. "I'll have the house salad."

Rick took her menu, added his and handed both to the waitress. "I'll have the Omni Burger with cheese."

The woman wrote that down. "Fries or onion rings?"

"Onion rings."

The young woman studied both of them, curiosity in her expression. Rick stared right back at her, daring her to make a comment about Sarah and her age. Finally the waitress blushed and walked away.

"Well, that was fun," Sarah said.

He took her hand and squeezed. "Don't let it get to you."

"I could see the arithmetic in her head. I wasn't old enough to be your mother but too old to be your lover. You were holding my hand so there was something there. I'd probably bought myself a boy toy."

"Let's not get carried away."

"We should have stayed at the house."

He brought her hand to his mouth and kissed the palm. "Nuh-uh. I have the sexiest woman on Earth and I'm going to show her off."

"Please let's not make a scene."

"Scene?" he said. "A scene would be standing on the table demanding that anyone who disapproves tell me why."

"Rick—"

"I'll do it if you want me to," he said.

"Keep your voice down."

The waitress reappeared with their food. She set the salad in front of Sarah and the burger platter in front him, finally tucking the bill under his plate.

He picked up the Omni Burger and bit into juicy beef, crisp vegetables and a piquant sauce. Delicious as usual. He chewed and swallowed. "So I had an idea of how we can work on what you think is your problem."

She choked on the tomato wedge she'd just put into her mouth and then coughed. "You're not going to talk about that here."

"In general terms only."

"I'd rather we not talk about it at all."

"We have to talk about it."

"Eat your food."

He picked up an onion ring and held it to her lips. "These are great."

She pushed his hand away. "I have my own lunch."

"Bird food." He put the onion ring against her lips again. "Eat."

She bit into it—delicately—and then took the ring from his hands. "Very good."

"That's more like it." He ate his burger for a moment. Taking Sarah away for three days of romance and sex had been the best idea he'd had in his entire adult life. The sex had blown his mind—and hers too whether she wanted to admit it or not. The romance still needed some work but he had a few ideas in that department too. The two things belonged together and as soon as he could get her past her hang-up about her healthy sexual appetite she'd see that too.

She thought she was oversexed. What a laugh. Any guy would kill to have a woman like that. With any luck, he wouldn't have to kill anyone. He'd just have to fuck her brains out. Nice work if you could get it.

"All right, what's going on in there?" she said.

He opened his eyes wide and put his hand over his heart. "Who? Me?"

She tapped the side of his head. "I can see the wheels turning."

He ate another onion ring for fortitude, wiped his fingers on his napkin and took her hand. "I've been toying with an idea for a new experimental protocol."

"We could have discussed that back at the lab."

"I thought the two of us might give it a dry run," he said. "But I need your permission first."

She looked pointedly at the people sitting at the other table and then around the restaurant. Then she leaned toward him.

"What is it you want to do?" she said in a near whisper.

"I'm interested in the effects of prolonged arousal. Delaying orgasm."

She removed her hand from his and placed it against his mouth. "Rick…"

He moved her fingers away. "They can't hear us."

Just to make sure of that, he glanced over at the other table. The couple continued their conversation as they had since Rick and Sarah had come in.

He turned back and moved closer to Sarah. "I'm guessing that putting satisfaction off will feel frustrating at first but will lead to more powerful climaxes."

Her skin flushed. Embarrassment or arousal? She didn't move away though and her breathing got shallow and irregular. Arousal.

He put his lips right next to her ear. "I'm thinking that if I did that to you, you'd learn that you have some control over how quickly you come."

She bit her lip and nodded. "That could work."

"Then I have your permission?"

"Sure." The word came out like a sigh. He'd turned her on with just the idea of long, leisurely lovemaking. Hell, the idea had turned him on too and he could already feel his member thicken and swelled in anticipation.

"It could get pretty intense and you'll probably want to kill me."

"I'd already like to kill you for any number of things."

"That's my girl."

She rolled her eyes and groaned.

"You want to try this?" he asked.

She nodded.

"Good," he said. "But I'm going to order you a burger first. You're going to need your strength."

He pressed a kiss to her ear and then turned to look for the waitress.

* * * * *

Sarah reclined in the tub and let the jets of water play over her body. Per Rick's instruction, she closed her eyes and imagined the currents were his fingers and mouth caressing her breasts, her sex, the backs of her knees. All the way down to the soles of her feet.

She allowed her body to become excited. Even though he hadn't suggested it, she pictured him entering her. His beautiful, big cock slowly pushing into her, withdrawing and then filling her again. She didn't touch herself though. Not even her breasts, although they tingled in anticipation. She'd take this slowly. Wait for as long as she could before moving to the next level.

What a sensual treat. A full stomach from that delicious hamburger. The feel of the hot water sluicing over her. The memory of how he felt inside her while they made love. The word "sex" didn't reflect the devotion he gave to her pleasure. The care he took to satisfy her every need. He'd asked for her trust for this new exercise. She hadn't realized the implications of what she'd promised to do with him until the trip back from town. She hadn't trusted a man—not really—since her very first experience had turned out so badly. She had to trust Rick now or she'd never know what true communion with a lover would feel like.

He'd satisfied her before and he'd do it again. Only more completely this time.

Ready for the next step, she turned off the jets, opened the drain and climbed out of the tub. As she rubbed the towel over her body, she pictured Rick's tongue following the terrycloth. Along the back of her neck and then down her spine. At her bottom it became his hands, cupping her buttocks and kneading the flesh. She continued, bending to dry each leg and then upward between her thighs. When she reached her mons, she allowed herself to linger, pressing against her pussy lips. Her clit responded to the movement and a shock of excitement went through her. A moan caught in her throat and she stood there for a moment, her eyes closed so that she could focus on the sensations. Moisture collected there—her own, not from the bath.

Slow down. Not so fast. Make it linger.

She willed her hands to her sides, one still clutching the towel. Breathing evenly, she opened her eyes and stood for a moment to collect herself.

Damn but this was going to be hard. If she were at home she'd get her vibrator, apply the warming gel and slide it up her eager pussy. She'd let the rotating shaft take her closer and then turn on the vibrating parts to play against her clit until she came. Today she needed to fight the rising heat inside her. Rick waited for her downstairs. She'd made him a promise and she'd keep it.

She finished drying herself, taking extra care with her breasts. One at a time she lifted each one and stroked the towel along the underside. Then she used the soft cloth to stimulate her nipples to hard peaks. Finally she hung the towel on its rod and turned to look at herself in the mirror.

Her skin glowed pink from the heat of the water and the friction of drying herself. An extra flush covered her chest and continued all the way up to her face. Sexual excitement. And Rick hadn't even touched her yet.

She reached to the bag he'd carried out of the boutique. She was to wear only the things she found in there and nothing else. Her fingers met something hard, so she pulled it out. A crystal decanter of perfume. Heavy and expensive, with a finely cut swan adorning the stopper. She opened it and raised it to her nose.

If a scent could embody sin, this one would. Rich and intoxicating, it smelled like warm rain on a summer night. Underneath that lay something muskier. The scent of lovers coupling.

She dabbed a little behind each ear and at the insides of her elbows. More went under her breasts and in the valley between them. After she'd finished by scenting the backs of her knees, she was surrounded by a cloud of its musk. Subtle and seductive. He'd chosen well.

She set the perfume aside and searched the bag again. This time she found a garment. A dress. The fabric felt like cashmere. It was pale pink in color with silver threads that made it shimmer. Finding no zippers or buttons, she guided it over her head and let it slide down over her body.

The dress fell to her ankles but had side slits to above her knees. When she moved, it would expose most of her legs. The neckline went low in the center and showed the curve of her breasts. Cap sleeves left most of her arms bare.

She took a few steps to test the feel of the dress against her skin. Soft like a lover's kiss and yet the metal of the silver threads seemed to set up tiny currents of electricity against her skin. Her nipples responded until they poked prominently against the cashmere. She tweaked them to full hardness and smiled at the effect. Her breasts had never seemed so large and full, the peaks begging for attention.

Her body was ready for Rick now and for whatever he had planned for it. It felt like ripe fruit ready to burst. The time had come to offer it to the man who waited for her downstairs.

She left the bathroom and crossed the bedroom to the front hallway. At the edge of the balcony she looked down into the living room.

Rick stood at the opposite side, looking through the huge windows at the sea. He wore a robe of a deep-blue fabric that looked like silk and hugged his broad shoulders. His dark hair curled around his ears, giving him a roguish look. His bare feet and the muscles of his calves suggested power.

For a moment she tried to remember the intense young man who'd so confounded her five years ago. He'd seemed dangerous then — to her equilibrium and her professional detachment. He was a far greater danger now but if she didn't face the risks, she might never feel whole as a sexual creature. Or as a human being.

He stiffened as if he'd sensed something and turned around. When he found her, he gave her a smile. "That's exactly how I'd hoped you'd look."

"You have excellent taste."

"It's easy when you're dressing a goddess."

"Silly man." She descended the stairs, letting herself savor the cool metal beneath her feet. Her toes curled into the carpet as she crossed the room to him.

When she reached him, he took her hands in his and kissed her forehead. "You ready?"

"As ready as I'll ever be."

"What I'm going to do is arouse you and then back off," he said. "I'll let you rest and then start again. Do you understand?"

"Is that what you plan to do to your subjects?"

He actually blushed at that. "Not me personally. I use mechanical stimulation as you do."

She'd known that of course. But hearing him confirm it could save her the trouble of getting jealous of some faceless female or other. Jealousy. What next?

"Each time I'm going to take you higher and then stop again," he went on. "You need to know I'm not abandoning you."

"I know that."

"All right. We'll start with a kiss."

He leaned toward her, his lips approaching hers while still leaving space between their bodies. She stepped toward him but he put his hands on her shoulders to hold her back. Separated like this, she could concentrate on his mouth as it covered hers and explored.

How unbelievably sweet. Gentleness personified. He let his lips play over hers, flicking his tongue at the corners of her mouth and then taking her bottom lip between his teeth to nibble. She rested against the strength of his arms and put her soul into answering him. Never had a kiss touched her this way — making her heart sing and her spirit soar.

He straightened, his mouth leaving hers. "Open your eyes."

She hadn't even realized she'd closed them but she did as he asked and looked into his face. His eyelids looked heavy, his lips moist. "Nothing terrible happened because we stopped, did it?"

Only that the best kiss of her life had ended. "I guess not."

"We're going to kiss thousands of times and each one will be different."

"Thousands?" She tried doing the math in her head but her brain had gotten too fuzzy for complex thought.

He ran his thumb over her lips. "Hundreds of thousands."

"That would keep us pretty busy."

"Night and day."

That would take years. Lots and lots of years. What was he trying to say?

"Catch your breath and then we'll move on," he said.

She took a few breaths and became more aware of her surroundings. The carpet between her toes, the whisper of cashmere against her skin. He'd opened one of the doors to the deck and the distant sounds of the ocean came through the screen. Gulls cried and waves crashed against the rocks below. All her senses came alive.

Why had she never allowed herself to experience the world this way before? Because of Rick? Because she could make herself open to him as she'd never done with a man before?

He watched her the whole time, as if memorizing her face. "I feel as if I'm seeing the world through your eyes."

"Impossible."

"Only if you have no imagination." He took her hand. "Let's go outside."

He led her to the deck and opened the screen door. While he shut it behind her, she walked across the planks and gripped the railing. In an instant he joined her, standing behind her and wrapping his arms around her. The cashmere of her dress met the silk of his robe with a sensual rustle.

"Tell me everything you're sensing right now," he murmured into her ear.

She melted back against him and closed her eyes.

"Sarah?" he prompted.

"You're warm behind me but my front is cool from the ocean breeze. It's making my nipples hard."

"Like this?" His hands cupped her breasts and toyed with the sensitive peaks.

"Oh God," she breathed.

He nibbled at her earlobe. "Tell me what you see. What you hear."

"That feels so good."

"Do it, baby."

"All right." She forced herself to open her eyes. "Um... There's a tiny island not far in the distance. The currents seem to eddy around it."

His lips traveled along her throat. Hot kisses to where the curve of her neck met her shoulder. "Good. More."

"Each third wave seems louder than the others. No, that doesn't make any sense." How could anything make any sense when he was leaving a trail of fire against her skin?

"It doesn't have to make sense."

"Rick, I need—"

"Okay." His own breath seemed labored. "A little break."

He moved to stand beside her and rested his hand over hers on the railing. "We're doing fine."

"Are you sure you want to do this?"

"Are you chickening out on me?"

She shrugged. "It seems kind of pointless. We can have perfectly good sex without the trouble."

He took her jaw in his hand and turned her head to face him. "It isn't trouble."

He'd made a simple enough statement but his gaze questioned her. Seldom had anyone ever looked at her in quite that way. As if he could see inside her. Read her fear. Dear God, yes. He frightened her. This wasn't sex any longer, at least not the way she'd always known sex. It went beyond lovemaking too. He expected her to open herself completely to him. Too much. How had she let things go this far?

"Are you cold?" he asked.

"No. Well, a little." That would explain her trembling. Let him think that.

"We'll get in the hot tub in a minute."

"In our clothes?"

"No, silly," he answered.

"I just got out of a tub," she said.

"I wasn't in there with you."

"I'll turn into a prune."

He laughed. "Silly, sillier, silliest."

She couldn't help but chuckle too. A moment ago, she'd been ready to melt into a puddle of lust and now she could look into his face and share a goofy joke. He'd rekindle the fire again soon, until then she could just be with him and enjoy the contrast of the cool breeze with the warmth of the sun on her shoulders.

"I like the way you look right this minute," he said.

"And how do I look?"

"As if you're comfortable in your own skin. As if you're not worried about yesterday or tomorrow."

"A philosopher."

"A lover," he corrected.

"Then love me." Damn, that wasn't what she'd meant to say. L as in lovemaking was one thing. L as in love was quite another. Too many years separated them. Too much emotional baggage in the lab if they became a couple.

His expression grew serious. "Always, Sarah."

"I didn't mean it that way." She put on the best casual smile she could manage. "The word slipped out."

"Now that it has, I'm going to hold you to it."

"We don't have to discuss it now." She turned to him and took his hands in hers. "Aren't you supposed to be working on my problem?"

"I just realized this *is* your problem. You use sex to protect yourself from love."

"Please." Curse it, that didn't sound casual at all. Far from it. "This isn't the time for psychoanalysis."

"All right. Later."

"Good." She smiled up at him. "What do we do now?"

With no further explanation, he bent and kissed her again. This time he pulled her hard against him, while his mouth captured hers for a searing caress. Her body pressed against the length of him, her breasts against his chest. She slipped her arms under his so that she could slide her hands up along his back. He was solid male everywhere and the muscles around his shoulder blades worked as his fingers found their way down her spine to her ass. He cupped her buttocks, just as she'd imagined earlier, molding her pelvis to his. The ridge of his erection pushed against her belly. Long and thick. Ready to take her.

His tongue parted her lips and darted into her mouth only to retreat again. She angled her head to kiss him more deeply, offering her own tongue. When the two touched, she whimpered into his mouth. How she craved him.

He pulled back a bit. "Easy, baby."

Easy? Easy for him to say. Or perhaps not, as his breath came in hot puffs against her cheek.

"Slow down a bit," he said.

"I don't want to slow down."

"I know. Just a little." He eased away from her but before she could protest, his hand traveled up her arm and across her chest to where the neckline of the dress barely closed over her breasts. He stroked the backs of his fingers over the curve there and then slipped them inside to touch the sensitive skin. Rough and gentle all at once, his touch set her heart to racing.

Her flesh seemed to swell into his hand, pushing the aching nipple against his palm.

"Don't stop," she gasped.

"You want more."

"God yes."

He pushed the fabric aside and bent to put his mouth over her breast. Sucking, he pulled the nipple deep. Her head became too heavy to hold up and she leaned back. He switched to the other breast and gave it the same reverence. The pressure connected with her heart and sent shockwaves along her nerves. Deeper and lower. Her pussy grew damp, sending moisture along her inner thighs. She swayed and might have fallen if she hadn't clutched his shoulders.

Groaning, he straightened and held her against him. He'd stopped again. He'd told her he would and she'd agreed. She'd been thinking rationally, not allowing for how her body would scream for his. With no choice now, she'd have to trust him.

They stood that way for a while, each clinging to the other as her heart slowed. A cloud of the perfume he'd given her floated around them, released by the heat of her skin. She burrowed her fingers under the silk of his robe to stroke his chest. Just beneath the skin she felt his heart beat. Rapid and strong. She pressed her lips over the spot.

He sighed. "Time for the hot tub."

Just as well. Her juices would soak through the cashmere of her dress in another minute. And now she'd have him naked. Another step toward the coupling her pussy craved.

He bunched the dress up in his hands and she lifted her arms so that he could pull it off. He looked at it for a moment. "I almost hate to take it off you. You look so damn beautiful in it."

"It's gorgeous. Thank you."

He carefully folded the garment and draped it over the back of one of the chairs. Now the sea air washed over her. Cool but exhilarating.

She reached to the tie of his robe. The knot resisted opening but after a moment she managed to untie it. The silk parted to reveal his chest and belly. And his cock. It stood straight out from his torso, stiff and heavy. She curled her fingers around it, savoring the feel of his velvet. He closed his eyes and his expression went slack with pleasure.

"Do you want me, Rick?" she said.

"You know I do."

"I want you too." She knelt and stroked him then took the head of his rod into her mouth. A slight tang of salt greeted her tongue as she sucked him. He grew harder and thicker, his skin taut along his length. She took him deeper and sucked until his hips started to move.

"Oh no." He reached down, caught her under her arms, raised her to her feet. "Won't work, baby."

"I was enjoying myself."

"You were driving me crazy so that I'd fuck you. We're not ready for that."

"I know something about the male sexual response," she said. She could even add that she knew a lot about his sexual response. "You're ready."

"You're not."

"You're impossible."

He shrugged out of the robe and laid it on the chair. "Hot tub."

She walked to the redwood tub and climbed in. The water heated her skin as she lowered herself to a seat. He joined her, lifted her into his lap and turned them so that they looked out to sea. Her hip rubbed against his cock and she reached down to stroke the tip.

He caught her hand and brought it to his mouth for a kiss. "Not yet."

"Spoilsport."

He chuckled and lifted her again, this time spreading her legs and guiding her to straddle his legs, her back to his front. Now that glorious hardness pressed into her back. His hands went to her breasts, cupping them and kneading them. Still ultra-sensitive, the nipples drew up into tight knots. He fingered them gently, circling them and then stroking them with his thumbs.

Her sex throbbed and she would have squeezed her thighs together if it weren't for his legs between them. So she leaned forward, searching for some friction against her clit. She rocked back and forth but it wasn't enough. She needed more. She needed him to stroke her there as he continued to rub her nipples. Hard and throbbing, the bundle of nerves at the entrance to her core demanded attention. Now.

"Rick, please," she gasped. "Please."

That got his hands to moving finally. They smoothed over her ribs and down to her belly. He'd touch her now surely. He couldn't be so cruel as to leave her hanging here on the edge of bliss.

Lower and lower they went. Damn him, if he didn't help her soon, she'd do it herself. She'd stroke herself to climax as they sat here. To hell with his experiments.

When his fingers parted her folds and touched that burning spot, she cried out. It felt so damn good. *More. Please more.*

She leaned back against his chest and concentrated on that spot between her legs. He knew exactly how to touch her, exactly the right pressure to urge the maximum response. She floated in heaven while he drove her higher and higher. Another cry escaped her and he stopped.

Stopped!

She had to struggle for breath. "What are you doing?"

"What we agreed."

"It's not fair." Damn, it wouldn't take much more for her to come. How could he torture her like this?

"Come on, Sarah. We need to break through your barrier. You agreed."

"I didn't know it would be like this."

"Yes you did. You're a sex researcher, remember?"

Lord, did her subjects go through such hell? None of them complained. How could they stand it?

"It'll be worth it, baby," he whispered into her ear. "You'll see."

"That's easy for you to say. You're not suffering."

He pushed his erection against her buttocks. "I'm aroused. I can hold off for your sake."

Put that way, the whole situation took on another light. He was doing this for her. He knew how women responded to sex. He sure as hell understood what made her tick. She needed to take a chance.

"Okay." She took a few breaths and opened her eyes. "You're right."

"Good girl."

He hugged her ribs, holding her tenderly, while he nibbled at her earlobe and then along her neck. She hung helpless in a haze of need, her body thrumming with arousal. She willed her muscles to relax, her pussy to stop clenching. In her lab, she'd seen how delaying gratification made for orgasms that shot her subjects into the stratosphere. She'd read their responses—descriptions of climaxes that felt like out-of-body experiences. Some of them reported losing consciousness all the while being aware of every inch of their body. Why had she never tried for that herself? All these years of either going for the instant pleasure or giving up on men all together in favor of her vibrator.

Rick had it right. She'd been defending herself from intimacy and betrayal. She couldn't defend herself from Rick. She'd come too far to turn back now.

His hands went back into motion, sliding over her torso down to her outer thighs. He rubbed her from her knees up to her hips—a sensuous massage. She sighed and leaned her head back against his shoulder, looking up into the darkening sky.

His hands went to her inner thighs, still rubbing upward and downward. On each circuit, he neared her mons. The lips felt swollen, her clit throbbing. Finally he touched her there too, the heel of his hand pressing against her pubic bone.

She didn't cry out. He'd stop again if she did that. She bit her lip but a little whimper escaped anyway. He didn't stop but kept pressing. Not touching her clit directly but applying pressure nevertheless.

She closed her hands into fists so tight that her fingernails dug into her palms. The pain distracted her, helped her hold onto her sanity while her body demanded release. She would last. For Rick's sake and her own.

"I want you to take me inside you now," he whispered into her ear.

"I can't," she gasped. "I'll come. I swear."

"You won't. You can do this."

"Damn it, Rick."

"Trust me." He moved his hands to her waist and lifted her from his lap. "Open your pussy and take me inside. Slowly."

She nodded. With one hand, she parted the lips of her sex while her other hand reached between her legs to find his cock. He felt like satin over steel—rock-hard and perfectly huge. She had to stretch to take the enormous head inside her. But oh! What heaven when she did accept him. Better than any fantasy. Hotter than her most erotic dream. Nothing like she'd ever experienced with another man.

She lowered herself slowly, savoring each inch as it swelled up into her. More and more—he never seemed to end—until she'd impaled herself on him all the way to her core.

"Damn," he gritted. "Ah shit, you feel good."

She moved, her pussy grasping at him as she rose and lowered herself again.

His fingers dug into her waist, holding her still. "Don't, baby. I'm having control issues of my own."

Good. He was as hot as she. As close to the edge. Soon he couldn't deny himself any longer and he'd have to let her climax too. For now, she'd settle for the feel of his cock inside her. The fullness, the heat.

They sat that way in silence as the sun met the ocean at the horizon. The air chilled and steam lifted from the heated water around them. No frantic coupling. No hurried thrusting. No rushed orgasms. Just perfect connection, him deep inside her.

"You're doing great, Sarah," he said after some time. "Ready for the final challenge?"

"What is it?"

"You'll find out," he said. "Just remember...no matter how hard I am on you, I'll make it worth the wait."

That sounded bad. Still, she'd made such progress. If this was the final challenge, her reward would follow. "I'm ready."

He lifted her off him and rose. Her inner muscles contracted, seeking the contact they'd lost. Bereft, aching inside, she sat and watched him climb out of the hot tub. He bent and in a moment he stood again with a pair of towels in his hands. One he placed on the edge of the tub then wrapped the second around his waist. As rigid as any tent pole, his erection pushed against the terrycloth. What would she have to endure before she could have all that hardness inside her again?

He held out a hand toward her and she took it and let him help her out of the tub. After retrieving the second towel, he used it to dry her. The cool night air gave her gooseflesh and her nipples peaked into tight buds but the friction of the cloth against her skin warmed her as he stroked her everywhere — over her breasts and belly, finally bending to dry her legs. When he'd finished, he rose, put the towel over her shoulders and guided her inside.

Shutting only the screen door, he let the sounds of the ocean float into the living room. He took her hand, walked her to the area before the fireplace and helped her down onto the carpet. A fire burned brightly but he added a log and used the poker to send the flames higher. That done, he set the poker aside and removed the towel from his waist.

He stood there and let her study him. Though there was some faint light outside still, in here most of the room lay in darkness but the firelight made him visible. Sleek muscle and shadows, he seemed almost unearthly, the light of passion in his eyes. Broad shoulders, narrow hips, strong legs. And that cock — long, thick and stiff. He made a powerful male specimen. All hers, at least for the long weekend. After that who knew? Tonight she'd command all that power and when he'd finished, he'd own her completely.

Just for tonight, these three days, no more.

He came to her then. He spread out his towel and lifted her hips to pull her onto it. Kneeling, he spread her legs and bent her knees to place her feet flat against the carpet. He stayed there, staring at her pussy as though he wanted to devour it.

Oh no. He couldn't mean to do *that*. Oral sex — and he expected her not to come? No way that was possible.

"Rick, you're not going to — "

"Shhh." He reached out and touched her, parting the lips to slip a finger inside her. Her hips lifted and hot juices spread out of her over his hand and the apex of her thighs.

"I can't," she gasped. "If you eat me, I'll shatter."

"Not much longer, Sarah. I promise."

"Please no. Not that."

He pumped his finger a few times, the movement making liquid sounds. She burned, her level of arousal almost painful. She needed to come. Now. She'd done everything he'd asked. No more. Please no more.

He removed his finger and lowered himself between her legs. Resting on his elbows, he pulled her hips forward until her sex met his face. With her every nerve ending on fire, even his breath felt like a caress. Then his tongue came out, playing over the lips of her pussy, and she almost screamed. No one should have to endure this. She'd let herself climax and that would be that. Still, if she could hold out a little longer...

The wicked man seemed to know exactly how much she could take and he gave her that and no more. Hot passes of his tongue over her swollen flesh, each just grazing her clit before moving downward again. Over and over until she could scarcely breathe. The tension built, coiling in the pit of her belly. Ready to break free.

Then he stopped again. Damn. Damndamnfuckingdamn. She gasped for breath and squirmed. Writhing, twisting, anything for more friction.

"Just a little longer," he said.

"Damn you!"

"Relax. Listen to the fire."

"Fuck the fire."

"Do it, Sarah."

She took a breath and held it. Fighting the orgasm that waited at the edges of her reality. The fire roared in her ears or maybe that was her heart. The blood rushing through her veins.

"All right. Now the last." He bent to her again and this time he stroked her clit with his tongue and took the aching flesh into his mouth.

She counted backward by threes. One hundred...ninety-seven...ninety-one...shit...ninety-four. No use. No use.

"Please, Rick," she cried. Damn, she was sobbing now. Begging. Every inch of her body ached, stretched past endurance. Her clit throbbed. Her pussy ached for him. "Please, Rick. *Please!*"

He pulled back. "Okay, you did it."

She lay there, helpless, burning up with need. He'd said he wouldn't leave her. *Please!*

Then he moved over her. Positioned himself between her legs and entered her with one deep thrust. She arched her back and screamed.

"That's it, baby. Whatever you need."

Trembling from head to toe, she raised her hips, taking him as deep as she could. He moved with her, lunging forward then pulling back out. Deep thrusts. Pounding into her. Beneath her palms his muscles bunched as he drove her higher and higher. Past control, past sanity, past everything except his hardness filling her. Now faster and more savage, each thrust brought pressure against her breasts, inside her pussy, against her clit. Again the tension coiled inside her and this time she let it loose. She came with a force that shook her free from reality. She screamed again as the eruptions started and continued to build. One after another, cresting over each other, while her muscles clenched around him in massive contractions.

Her world became a blinding fire of passion so intense, she almost missed his roar of completion as he thrust into her one more time and emptied himself inside her.

They clung together for one long moment of perfection before the darkness closed in on her and the world slipped away.

Chapter Five

ॐ

After a while Rick regained full consciousness and he rolled off Sarah and flopped onto his back, his chest heaving. Not very gallant but all he could manage. If sex with this lady got any better, it'd kill him.

Beside him, she struggled for air, her breath coming in ragged gulps as if she'd run a mile at top speed. "Oh," *breath*, "my," *breath*, "God."

"You got that right," he whispered. "Baby, you're incredible."

She didn't open her eyes but smiled. "Oh Rick…"

He looked over to find her eyes were closed and her expression pure bliss. He'd seen some satisfied women in his day. None like the treasure that was Sarah. His heart swelled with…something. Pride, yes, but a lot more too. He loved her.

Mentally he smacked himself on the forehead. He'd never find the strength to do it for real. Of course he loved her. He'd loved her from the very beginning. Otherwise he would have moved on when he first left her lab. He'd been too young to see that five years ago. Now he couldn't miss it. He'd found the woman he loved.

He pulled her to him and rested her head on his shoulder, breathing in her perfume. The stuff from the bottle he'd bought but her own scent too. Soap and warm female.

"That settles it." He kissed her forehead. "We'll get married."

Her eyes flew open at that. "What?"

"Married. You and me. Husband and wife."

"Impossible."

"Not only possible. Inevitable." He rolled her onto her back and lifted himself onto an elbow so he could look down into her face. "As long as I'm alive, no other man will ever touch you."

"Stop acting the caveman. It doesn't become you."

"Oh no. You're not joking your way out of this."

"Who said I was joking?" she said.

He stroked the side of her face. "After sex...no, lovemaking...like that, can you doubt we belong together for life?"

"It was really good."

"Nuh-uh. 'Really good' doesn't cut it. It was cosmic, Earth-shaking, beyond belief."

"Really really good," she said.

Bullshit. "I've never felt anything like that and I'm pretty sure you haven't either."

She didn't answer but bit her lip.

"Have you?" he prompted.

"No."

"When a man has sex like that, he knows he's found the woman he wants to spend the rest of his life with."

She sat up, presenting him her back. "It won't work."

"Sarah, we belong together."

She sighed. "I know."

"Well then?"

"We have to figure out how to deal with this."

He sat up too and put his arm around her shoulder. "Simple. Marriage."

"Rick, you're really sweet."

"Fuck that shit."

Her jaw dropped and she stared at him. "Where did that come from?"

He counted one on his index finger. "First of all, I'm not sweet."

"But you just knocked yourself out to give me great sex."

"That wasn't for you. It was for us." He counted two on his middle finger. "Second, you're not going to give me the 'I love you but I'm not *in* love with you' crap."

She rubbed her forehead. "This is ridiculous."

"We're in love, Sarah. Serious love." At least he was. No cancel that. She was too. No woman gave herself like that to a man she didn't love. Her brain might not have admitted it yet but her body sure had.

"It doesn't matter," she said.

"Like hell. When a man falls in love, he wants the woman to be his wife and the mother of his children."

"You're making my point for me." She got up, picked up the towel and wrapped it around her body, finally tucking it inside itself to fasten it. "I'm too old to start having babies."

"Women give birth over forty all the time."

"Not a first child—maybe others do, but not me."

Oh hell. Maybe she was right about that. It didn't matter. "There are other ways to get children. Lots of kids need good homes."

She crossed her arms and glared at him as if he was an idiot. "Sure. Men just love raising some other man's child."

"Don't tell me what I want. I want to marry you and I'm going to do it, damn it."

"How could I possibly refuse such a heart-felt proposal?"

Oh for crissake. "I'm sorry, baby. You drive me nuts sometimes."

"Tell me about it," she answered.

He rose, walked to her and took her into his arms. "Let's not fight."

She melted against him, her body resting against his with only the towel between them. Damn, but she fit him perfectly.

"I just had the best sex of my life with the woman I love," he said. "Can't we have a little afterglow?"

"Do you really love me?"

"You know I wouldn't lie about something like that."

She sighed. "I guess not."

"You love me too. Admit it."

She pushed herself out of his arms and hugged her ribs. "Why did I come here? How on Earth could I have thought time with you would be an innocent fling?"

This didn't make any sense. Women were supposed to want commitment. Here he'd offered himself to her in sickness and in health and all that. He'd given her his heart and any fool knew that came with his soul as well. Couldn't she look the least bit happy about that?"

He crossed his arms over his chest. "What's the problem, Sarah? What did I do wrong?"

That honestly seemed to surprise her because her eyes widened. "You didn't do anything wrong."

"Then what's the issue here? Why are you acting like the final act of a Verdi opera?"

"It's complicated."

"Then explain it to me. I have a Ph.D. I think I'm bright enough to understand," he said.

"I never planned to get married at all."

"Change your plans."

She put her hands on her hips. "Do you want to understand or are you going to issue orders?"

"Sorry. Go on."

"It's difficult for a woman in academia," she said. "You have to work harder than a man to get half the recognition. It means long hours with little time for family."

"That's why I'm perfect for you."

Her eyebrow went up and she looked at him as if he'd suddenly started talking gibberish. He took her hand. "Come sit in front of the fire with me."

She nodded and he led her to the place where they'd made love only a few minutes before. It almost felt like days ago now, except for the sated feeling that still left his limbs weak. She sat cross-legged on the carpet and he stretched out next to her, bracing his body on one elbow.

"A man in another line of business might not understand your career," he said. "I do. We can be partners in everything. Raising kids, doing our research together."

"The Louis and Mary Leakey of the human sexual response?"

He rested his fingers on her thigh. "I do love your Rift Valley."

She batted his hand away. "Get serious."

"Seriously," he said. "We make a great team."

"Dr. Feelgood and the older woman. I'd be a laughingstock."

"No one would laugh at us."

She stared into the fire. "Really, Rick. You saw today what the world thinks of a woman my age with a man your age."

"Fuck 'em. I don't care."

"That's fine for strangers. How about our colleagues?"

He looked up at her, to her furrowed brow and the worry lines around her eyes. She really was concerned. Couldn't she see that none of it mattered as long as they loved each other? Let the world disapprove. Let her staff disapprove. Let the whole fucking research institute disapprove. They belonged together. End of story.

"They'll snicker about you too," she said. "They'll think you married me to get ahead. Sex research is a small community. Everyone will think that."

"So if we don't get married, they'll think I slept with you to get ahead," he said. "That really *is* sleazy."

She looked down at him. "They won't think anything because they won't know."

"What?"

"I'm not going to tell anyone about this." She gestured around, indicating everything was *this*. "And neither are you."

He sat up and stared at her. "You're going to deny we ever came here?"

"Neither confirm nor deny. I'm not going to mention it."

"But people will notice how things are between us. How we look at each other. How we touch."

"No looks. No touching. When we leave here at the end of three days, it's over," she said.

"No way. No fucking way."

"I agreed to this weekend with you, no more," she said.

"You agreed to a hell of a lot more. Just now. Right here. It's a different ballgame now."

"No, Rick." She rose. "Nothing's changed."

If she thought that, she was out of her mind. He loved her. She loved him too, the stubborn woman. That changed everything.

She didn't look at him but stared into the fire, her jaw set in a determined line. After a moment she straightened her shoulders. Even though she only wore a towel and he was still buck-naked, she assumed an air of detachment, as if she'd lowered a curtain between them.

"I'm going to get dressed now," she said. "My turn to make dinner."

She went to the staircase and climbed the steps without even glancing back at him. He sat and stared into the fire as if the flames might provide an answer to this idiotic woman.

Damn it all to hell. What was he going to do with her?

* * * * *

Sarah pushed the pieces of salmon around on her plate. The fish had tasted wonderful with the hollandaise she'd made for it but she hadn't had much of an appetite and now the sauce was a congealed and greasy mess on the plate. Rick hadn't eaten much more than she had. He hadn't even shown any interest in replenishing the fire and only a few coals glowed in the grate. The evening had started so splendidly and then gone downhill after she'd explained reality to him.

He set his napkin beside his half-full plate and picked up his wine. "Mozart tonight?"

"That sounds nice."

"Nice," he said. The word held a clang of disapproval.

"Mozart would be lovely. One of the piano concertos? *Marriage of Figaro*?"

"Or the *Requiem*."

"Oh for heaven's sake, stop it."

He raised an eyebrow and took a sip of his chardonnay.

"You accused me of sounding like a tragic opera," she said. "You're being ridiculous."

"Sorry. *Marriage of Figaro* it is. A little domestic comedy."

"I'll clear the table." She rose, picked up their plates and walked to the kitchen. After dumping the uneaten food into the trash, she went to the sink and rinsed the china.

What was wrong with him? Why couldn't he see reason? He claimed to love her and when he'd said it, it was probably true. Men would say anything after a really good fuck and what they'd shared went way beyond really good. It had scrambled his brain, that was all.

She set the dishes down, the silverware clattering against the china, and clutched the stainless steel rim of the sink. It had scrambled her brain too. For just a minute, she'd pictured herself living with him forever. Sleeping every night surrounded by the warmth of his body. Even though she'd known the moment he'd mentioned marriage that it was impossible. But then he'd really said the magic word—babies.

She straightened. He'd entered the room. Almost silently but that didn't matter. She could feel his presence now as if an invisible string connected them. Turning, she found him in the doorway, a wineglass in each hand.

"Are you going to keep running away from me?" he asked.

"More melodrama?" He wasn't being melodramatic though. He was right. Every time he got close to her, she wanted to creep into his arms. Beg him to make the fantasy true. Implore him to turn back her personal clock so that she could be the twenty-five-year-old he needed. The one who could give him children. His children, not someone else's.

"I'll take that wine," she said.

He walked to her, put the glass in her hand and clinked his own against it in a toast. They each took a sip, looking into each other's eyes, until she couldn't stand the cold look in his blue-green ones.

"Rick, about tonight—"

"No big deal," he said. "If you don't love me, you don't."

"Love," she repeated. Perhaps she did. Was it love when you couldn't remember a time when you didn't know what the other person's body felt like? When your fingers itched for contact with his skin? When his voice resonated through you like a deep note of music?

He set his glass beside the sink and rolled up his sleeves. "Let me help you."

"It's just a few things."

"I don't mind."

She handed him the silverware and plates and he loaded them into the washer. The double boiler she'd made the sauce in took no time. She found the plastic scrubber and scoured the sauté pan.

"What would you like to do tomorrow?" he asked.

"The drive through the redwoods sounded nice."

"Top down on the BMW."

"Of course." She finished with the pan and handed it to him. He loaded it and closed the dishwasher. Then he stood looking at her.

"Rick, I'm sorry," she said.

He didn't answer but stayed where he was, neither moving toward her or backing away. She'd hurt him. He'd given her his love and she'd handed it back to him. He'd hate her for that. Hell, she hated herself. But after a while, he'd get over it and find the woman he needed to make him happy.

"Oh Sarah." The words came out of him like a moan and his arms went around her, pulling her against his chest. She went to him, running her hands around his neck and turning her face up for a kiss.

He took her mouth with a gentleness they'd never shown each other before. His lips lingered, sweet on her own. This wasn't lust but love and this love she could return. Yes, she'd pour her heart into this kiss and at least give him that. The rest she'd keep a secret, something she'd take with her to her grave.

She did love him. Had loved him all these years. Would always love him, no matter what. Somewhere, in an alternate universe, her counterpart *would* marry him and live happily ever after. She'd have to settle for that.

* * * * *

He'd gotten to Sarah last night. Today he'd deliver the knockout punch. Rick kept his smile to himself as they drove through the redwoods. The BMW took the turns smoothly, the engine's purr muted by the silence of the forest. Cool shade surrounded them, the huge trees only allowing a pool of filtered sunlight here and there. The perfect setting for a seduction—this one emotional rather than sexual. Although it would be that too.

He glanced over at her and smiled. She must have been watching him from the corner of her eye, because she smiled back. Just an upturn of the corner of her full lips—but communication. She knew how he felt about her. For crissake, she felt the same way. He'd make her admit it today one way or another. Sybil and Tom's secret spot would help in his quest. By the end of the afternoon, Sarah would tell him that she loved him. Marriage would come later.

"You've been to the redwoods before, I guess," he said.

"Many times. You never get used to the beauty though."

"I never do."

"You said this is original growth," she said. "Some of these trees must be a thousand years old."

"Most likely." He reached over and took her hand, interlacing their fingers. He'd keep it that way until he had to downshift. She'd have to get used to intimacy with him because he wasn't going to stop at the end of their weekend. When they went home, the whole world would find out they'd become a couple. Hell, he'd invite half the world to their wedding.

They rounded a curve and he spotted their destination. After releasing her hand, he steered the car into the turn-off, shut down the engine and set the brake.

The hush of the forest settled in around them, only broken by the occasional cry of a jay and the murmur of a breeze. He got out of the car and went around to open her door. "Here we are."

She got out. "Where's here?"

"A special place Sybil and Tom showed me." He shut her door and grabbed the blanket and picnic basket from behind her seat. Then he gestured toward a trail and followed her away from the road.

Nothing but ferns could grow in the deep shade under the redwoods. Only an occasional patch of sunlight nurtured saplings and other native plants. He draped the blanket over his shoulder and placed his palm at the small of her back as they walked. Another gesture of possession she'd have to get used to. She accepted it well enough now and her pace fell in step with his.

At the top of a small rise, he led her off the path several yards and approached a thick line of ferns. Almost waist tall here, they formed a hedge of sorts. He pushed through them and held the fronds aside for Sarah to follow. When she did, they stood alone—isolated on all sides by a ring of trees interspersed with ferns.

"Oh my goodness," she said. "A second growth ring."

"Right. These trees would have come up around the trunk of the original redwood."

The fifteen-foot circle wasn't even medium size by redwood standards but it made for a perfect nook for two human beings.

"What do you suppose happened to the parent tree?" she asked.

"Could have been fire. It wasn't logged or we'd see some evidence of the trunk," he said. "I like to think of it as fate."

She quirked an eyebrow. "Fate?"

"I picture fate making this place just for you and me."

"You said Sybil and Tom showed it to you."

"Them too." He set the picnic basket down in the soft redwood duff and spread the blanket. "You know what's perfect about this place?"

She sat and looked up at him. "What?"

He sat next to her. "It's completely private."

"Ah-hah."

"The perfect place..." He took her chin between his thumb and forefinger and pulled her to him for a brief kiss. "To fuck."

"Well..." She kissed him back, her sweet mouth lingering against his. "We've done it in Sybil and Tom's guest room." Another kiss, this time a bit deeper. "We've done it in their hot tub."

He cupped the back of her head with his palm and slid his tongue over her lips. "We've done it in front of their fireplace."

She sighed, a soft note of pleasure. "We might as well do it in their secret spot."

"That's my girl." Before she could protest the "my girl" reference, he captured her lips and pressed her backward against the blanket.

Her mouth answered his, her lips parting to allow her tongue to graze his. All the while her fingers worked the buttons of his shirt. When she had them undone, she reached in and stroked her palms over his chest. Her fingers found the nipples and toyed with them, sending a shock through him all the way to his hardening cock. Her touch drove him wild, even more than he'd imagined when he lay on the table in her lab and imagined her sucking him into her mouth. He held himself above her on his elbows, in part to keep his weight off her but also to allow her room to touch him. She tugged his shirt from his jeans and smoothed her palms over his ribs. When she reached for his belt, he stopped her and sat up.

She rested back and watched him, a lazy smile on her face. Instead of reaching for him, frantically searching for more contact, she lay and looked at him out of eyes gone hazy with arousal.

"Do you have any idea how beautiful you are?" he said.

She sighed deeply, her breasts rising and falling. "I imagine you'll tell me."

"When we came here, sex was a desperate thing for you. You'd rush into it as if you had to grab it before it got away."

"You're a good therapist."

"It's love, Sarah. We're in love."

"We discussed this, Rick."

"No you discussed it," he said. "It's your turn to listen."

"All right. Talk."

He took a deep breath. He'd rehearsed this for hours the night before when he'd lain next to her, trying to sleep. Only a creep used guilt on someone he loved, so he'd have to be a creep. Obviously she'd felt some regret for rejecting the idea of marriage. She'd seemed unhappy to have hurt him. Fine. He'd make her really unhappy now. Besides he didn't plan to tell her anything that wasn't one hundred percent true.

"I had no idea how I felt about you when I came back," he said. "I only knew you had something I needed. I thought it was just sex."

"But it *is* sex."

"Wrong. It started out that way but all that changed yesterday."

"I don't see why."

He stroked the side of her face. "You made yourself open to me. You trusted me. We shared something I'll never have with anyone else."

She bit her lower lip and looked at him out of huge brown eyes. She understood. Deep down in her soul, she felt the same way.

"I need you, baby," he said. "You're breaking my heart."

She reached up and ran her fingers through his hair. "Make love to me."

"Say it first. Tell me you love me. I need the words."

"Why?"

No doubt she meant the word to express frustration but it held a note of fear too. She realized now that things had gotten out of her control. Now to hammer the point home.

"Love takes this to a new level," he said. "I need you on that level with me."

"Why do the words matter?"

"Once you've said them you can't take them back. Come on, baby. You know it's the truth."

She didn't answer but bit her lip.

"Sarah, you owe me the truth."

"I love you, Rick," she whispered.

Finally! He bent to her and kissed her again. She was everything beautiful in the world. She was the music, Beethoven and Verdi. She was the redwoods and the ferns beneath them. Summer sunshine and gentle rain. She was the woman he loved and she loved him back.

He pressed himself against her softness and gave every inch of her mouth the devotion it deserved. Taking her breath as his own, he sampled her lips. She moaned and leaned up into him, her arms clutching at his shoulders. Their tongues caressed each other as their bodies prepared to join. His cock grew hard and thick, pressing against his fly, eager to be inside her. Her hands moved over his shoulders and her hips began a sensuous dance against his pelvis.

Clothes separated them, the layers of fabric an intolerable barrier. He sat up and pulled her with him so that he could tug her blouse over her head. Her bra fastened in front and as soon as he had the clasp undone, he could cup her breasts. The nipples tightened and pressed against his palms. He could have touched them all day, feeling their weight and her soft skin. Right now he needed all of her naked.

After setting her bra aside, he laid her back and undid her belt, pulled down her zipper and tugged her slacks down her legs. Her sandals came off easily and the pants followed. Now she only wore panties—a scrap of lace and silky material. He removed those too and raised them to his face to inhale her scent.

"And to think I bought you perfume," he said. "Waste of money."

"Now you," she said. "Naked."

He set the panties on top of her slacks and shucked out of his shirt. Shoes and socks went next, followed by his jeans and shorts.

She watched the whole time, her eyes widening. "And you think *I'm* beautiful."

"I know you are."

"Let me love your cock with my mouth," she said.

"You bet." If giving him head would give her pleasure, who was he to deny her? He lay back against the blanket, signaling his willingness. With a huge smile, she sat, grasped his erect member and guided her mouth down to it.

She licked the tip of him, sliding her tongue around the rim of the head and into the pucker at the opening. Heaven. She caressed him, somehow sensing where every nerve ending lay under the surface and how to draw the maximum response from each one. His eyes wanted to drift closed but no way in hell was he going to miss the sight of her mouth on his turgid flesh.

Her fingers circled his shaft as she went lower and closed her lips around him. She sucked on the head while her fist moved in a slow stroking motion. Gentle and easy, enough to let his arousal build slowly.

She took more and more of him into her mouth. When her hair fell over her face, he pushed it back so that he could watch. Lower now she sucked him deeply and her cheeks worked with the effort. Each time she lifted her head she exposed moist flesh, glowing crimson with excitement. What a sight.

She stopped to admire what she'd done. "You're so big," she said. "I want all of this inside me."

"Any time."

"In a minute."

Then she was sucking again, driving him harder. Her fingers worked their way to the root of his cock and then to his balls. They tightened at her touch, so soft and yet so incendiary. He couldn't hold back a groan as she continued. Damn she was good. In another minute he'd lose control.

"You'd better stop now," he said.

She raised her head but continued the movements of her fingers against his shaft. "You're delicious."

"I want to taste you too."

"Nasty man." She released him and lay back against the blanket. He rolled onto his side and propped himself up on his elbow so that he could look at her. She gazed back, a soft smile on her face. His chest almost busted wide open with feeling. Love, joy, disbelief that this miraculous creature wanted him. He ran his fingertips over her cheek to her lips and she parted them to kiss each one in turn. Then past her chin along her throat and over the length of her collarbone. She closed her eyes and tipped her head back in what looked like bliss. When he cupped one breast, her breath caught and that pressed her flesh up into his hand. He squeezed gently until the nipple beaded to a hard peak and then he repeated the process on her other breast. By the time he finished, her breath was coming hard and fast and a blush covered her chest.

He took his fingers lower, along the furrow between the soft mounds and over her belly. Finally he reached the hair that covered her mound and her pussy lips.

They were swollen and moist. She'd already grown wet for him so he slipped a finger inside her.

Her back arched and a little "Oh!" escaped her. She needed a lot more than a finger and he was just the guy to give her everything her body craved.

He moved down to spread her legs and drape her thighs over his shoulders. When he separated the folds with his tongue and stroked her clit, she shuddered. Her scent invaded his brain—hot, ready woman—and his cock twitched in anticipation. It would have to wait.

She didn't clutch at him or beg for more. After her initial tremor, she lay relaxed and allowed him to give her pussy a slow but thorough eating. He slid his tongue along her lips from bottom to top and then flicked at her hard nubbin. Her nectar flowed freely, hot and sweet.

He continued, even sucking her clit into his mouth, until her breaths turned to gasps. Before she got even closer to orgasm, he stopped. They could have a long, slow fuck before they came together.

He rose above her and positioned the tip of his cock at her entrance. "Open your eyes, Sarah."

She did and looked at him, while her lips parted to take in ragged breaths.

"Look at me when I enter you," he said.

She nodded and he pressed forward slowly, burying himself deep inside her. Her eyes widened and she gave him a smile that busted his heart wide open.

He pulled back and thrust forward again and she watched him the whole time.

"I love you," he said.

"I love you too," she whispered back.

Another thrust, deeper and harder this time. "So much, baby."

"I know. I understand."

"Oh God." He squeezed his eyes shut and lowered his face alongside hers. Lovemaking had never made him cry before but tears threatened now. They clogged his throat until he could hardly breathe but he kept moving inside her. In and out while her muscles gripped him.

Her legs came up to circle him and she raised her body to meet his thrusts. They went on and on like this as the jays called overhead and a warm breeze fluttered through the ferns. They'd found perfection in this joining of hearts and bodies and souls. After all the searching and grasping, they'd mated so naturally, no boundaries existed between them. As her lust mounted, so did his need to fill her. The deeper he surged into her, the more she took of him. Together—as one being—they climbed higher.

"Rick!" she cried.

"Yes, baby."

"Don't stop!"

"Never," he answered.

"I don't believe it... Oh... I've never felt this way."

"Love me, Sarah. Love me."

"Yes oh yes!"

She came then. Her pussy gripped him like a fist then burst into spasms. Hard and fast, all along his length. She shouted and her hips bucked wildly beneath him.

Her body sent him past the brink. While he still pumped into her, the pressure built at the base of his spine. His balls tightened and then all hell broke loose inside him. He thrust savagely now as his orgasm claimed him and he shot hot lust into her.

Her pussy still clenched around him until she'd pulled every drop out of him and he fell, weak as a kitten, against her.

They lay together until their hearts started beating again. He clutched her, his cock going soft but still inside her.

Finally he had the strength for two words. "Marry me."

She didn't answer.

Chapter Six

✂

Sarah glanced up at her house and then at Rick. Normally he'd jump out of the car and go around to open her door. Now he seemed stuck in his seat, his hands gripping the steering while he stared out the windshield and over the hood. A muscle worked in his jaw.

"I had a wonderful time," she said. "Thanks."

"You didn't give me an answer."

She could pretend ignorance and ask what he meant but they both knew what he was talking about. "I can't marry you. It's very flattering but impossible."

He turned toward her. "Bullshit. We go to the courthouse, get a license, get blood tests, get married."

"Don't pretend you don't know what I'm talking about."

"Because you're older than I am?"

"Eleven years older," she said.

"More bullshit."

For heaven's sake, why couldn't the man see reason? "Bullshit" wasn't some sort of magic spell that could change reality. "You saw how people reacted to us in town."

"One old biddy."

"And the waitress," she said. "Who knows what the people at the other table were thinking?"

"I don't care what they think."

"I don't either but I care what my colleagues think." Especially in a field like theirs. They got enough strange looks from people in academia no matter how hard they tried for respectability. Throw in speculation about the senior

373

researcher and her boy toy and the dirty jokes would fly. "They'd probably assume we've been using our equipment on each other."

"You did used to use the equipment on me."

She put her hand to her forehead. "That was different. You were a subject."

"What do you imagine they'll think when they figure out we're having an affair?"

"They won't."

"Get real," he said. "I get a hard-on whenever I'm around you."

"Wear loose pants."

"You look at me as if you want to eat me alive," he said.

"I do not."

He crossed his arms over his chest.

"All right, I'll stop," she said.

"How are you going to manage that?"

"I don't know," she snapped. "I just will."

"I'm not going to make this easy on you. I'm going to be after you every chance I get."

Wonderful. What an image—Rick stalking her in the lab. He knew her too well. Even that night at the party, he'd suspected why she'd sneaked away from the others. Now he knew every intimate detail of how she responded to him. Just a touch in the right place set her motor to racing. Already her body wanted him again, even after three days of incredible sex.

"I swear, Sarah," he said. "If having someone discover us fucking in a broom closet will do me any good, I'll arrange that."

She stared at him. "You wouldn't."

"We love each other. We belong together until death do us part."

Lord, she'd created a monster. She wouldn't get any peace until she figured a way out of this mess. Only how?

"Think about it," he said. Then he opened the door and got out of the car.

She wasn't likely to think of anything else. Until she had a plan, she'd have to stay out of his way. Easier said than done.

* * * * *

Back in the lab and Rick felt like smashing things. Three whole fucking days and Sarah hadn't said more than good morning to him. He'd phoned her but she was screening her calls. He'd sat in the BMW outside her house for hours the night before but she hadn't even parted the curtains.

Fuck that.

He walked down the hallway to her office, didn't bother to knock and opened the door. Well shit. She wasn't in here. Where in hell could she have gone? She'd better hope he didn't find her with any of the others because the time for confrontation had come. Even if she agreed to talk to him privately, no one could imagine the conversation would be casual.

Earl emerged from his office. "Morning, Rick."

"Have you seen Sarah?"

Earl's eyes narrowed as he studied Rick. "She had an errand to run."

"Shit."

Earl stared at him for a moment. "You okay?"

"Fine. Just fucking wonderful."

"Sorry I asked." Earl raised his hands in surrender and backed away. Rick turned, went to his lab and let himself in.

What the hell? The equipment was going and a naked woman lay on the table. He turned his back. He wasn't running subjects today and he never went into the room during a session anyway.

"Sorry," he said. "I'll come back later."

"Don't go. We can have some fun."

Holy hell. Lynn?

"This machine is so good but you'd be even better."

He turned around. It *was* Lynn. She'd slipped her legs into the stirrups and pulled the equipment between her thighs. Now the mechanical phallus moved in and out of her pussy.

"Enjoy yourself," he said. "You know how to…um…clean the equipment when you're finished."

Instead of continuing, she switched off the thruster, pushed it away from her and sat up. "You don't have to pretend, Rick."

"Pretend what?"

"Sarah told me all about it."

Sarah. What in hell was the woman up to?

Lynn removed her legs from the stirrups, stood and walked to him. Smiling, she took his hand in both of hers. "It's sweet that you wanted to keep our relationship professional. But heck…we all fool around sometimes. At least the single people do. It kind of comes with the territory, you know?"

He removed his hand from hers. "What *exactly* did Sarah tell you?"

"Don't get mad at her. I had to worm it out of her."

He crossed his arms over his chest. "I'll bet you did."

"Rick?"

"Tell me what she told you."

"She let slip something about how you watch me." She shrugged. "I finally got her to confess that you'd been in her office asking for guidance."

"Go on."

"She said you had feelings for me but you were afraid that wasn't professional." She backed up a step. "She was telling the truth, right?"

"I'm sorry, Lynn. She wasn't."

"Why?" she gasped.

Because the little shit thought she could distract him with another woman but he wasn't telling Lynn that. "It's complicated."

"But she pretended she didn't want to tell me."

"That made the story more credible."

Pure horror entered her eyes and she covered her mouth with her hand. "Oh God, I'm so embarrassed."

"Don't be. She thought I'd enjoy you. Any sane man would. You're beautiful."

Her face crumbled and tears filled her eyes. "Oh God!"

Shit, piss, fuck. "I swear to God, she'll make it up to you. I will too."

Sobbing now, Lynn ran into the changing room and slammed the door behind her. He did smash something then. He turned and slammed his fist into the wall so hard his knuckles dented the plaster. Sarah Dalton was through fucking with people.

* * * * *

Sarah found Rick standing outside her office when she got back to the lab. He lounged against the wall but nothing else in his posture or his expression looked calm. She'd never seen him angry before but no one could mistake that scowl. Something had really set him off.

She averted her gaze and did the best she could to keep her hand from trembling as she reached to the knob of her door. "Hi, Rick."

"Forget 'hi'. We have to talk."

Damn. She'd known all along she'd have to confront him. They worked together, after all. She'd hoped that a few days without him in her life would let her clear her head. It hadn't worked.

She took a breath. "Not here. Come to my house tonight."

"We're going to talk *now*," he said.

She looked up at him. His features might have been carved out of granite but his eyes held a light of fury. They'd start shooting sparks in another minute. She'd better get him out of this hallway in the next couple of seconds or the entire staff would get an earful.

"Okay," she said. "Inside."

"Not in there either." He grabbed her elbow none too gently and tugged her down the hallway toward his lab. "Come on."

"What the hell do you think you're doing?" She looked down at his fingers. "What did you do to your hand?"

"Nothing."

"It's bleeding."

"Flesh wound," he gritted. "Keep walking."

"Let go of me."

He ignored her and continued propelling her toward his lab. When they got there, he pushed her inside, followed her in and closed the door.

Then he turned and glared at her. "You really fucked up this time, lady."

"May I remind you I'm your superior?" That probably wouldn't work with him but she had to try something. This looked like it was going to get messy.

"Lynn was in here earlier."

Oh Lynn. Her suggestion to Lynn had obviously worked, not that it had taken much to convince her to pursue Rick.

"I've been meaning to tell you that Lynn's quite taken with you," she said.

"I'll say. She was using the mechanical phallus. She thought I'd enjoy a threesome with my own damn equipment."

"She what?"

"I found her in here—naked—using the thruster. She seemed to think that would turn me on."

Good Lord. "Did it?"

The fury in his eyes ratcheted up a few notches. "You're really a piece of work, you know that?"

She shrugged. "Lynn's an attractive young woman."

"I had to tell her I wasn't interested. She left here in tears."

Oh God. Lynn must have been completely humiliated. Her heart sank to her stomach. She walked to the table and sat on the edge. What had she done? "I had no idea she'd do anything like that."

"You had no idea, period," he said. "You didn't think about anyone but yourself."

She rubbed her forehead. "Okay, I'll fix this. She's in her last year, only needs to write her dissertation. I'll get her a good tenure track job somewhere. I'll make it up to her."

"I told her that too. She wasn't convinced."

"All right." She threw her hands up in the air. "I made a mistake. I thought she'd come on to you. I thought you two would make a good fit."

"I think that pisses me off the most." He walked toward her and towered over her. "Do you really think I'm that shallow?"

God she'd misjudged everyone. She hadn't even considered how miserable she'd be if he had taken Lynn up on her offer. Just thinking of him with another woman made her heart sink deeper.

"I love you, Sarah," he said. "Although sometimes I wonder why."

"I'm sorry."

"I *thought* you loved me too."

"I do. It's just..." She hugged her ribs. "I'm confused."

Actually, frightened was more like it. She hadn't realized until this moment that she'd set Lynn up as a test for him. If he'd allowed himself to be seduced, it would have proven what she'd thought was the truth—that he wouldn't want her if he could have a younger woman. Damn it, he was right about her. She'd only thought about her own needs and she'd hurt a perfectly fine person as a result.

"I do love you," she said.

He rested his fists on the table on either side her and leaned in until she had to back away. "Then it's about fucking time you started showing it."

"I'm sorry. Lord, I'm so, so sorry."

"All right. You're going to start fixing things. First you need to apologize to Lynn."

"Of course. I'll explain everything and ask for her forgiveness. I'll give her time off with pay to write her dissertation."

"That's a start. Then you're going to start being honest with me...and yourself."

"I owe you that."

His anger seemed to drain away, leaving what looked like sadness. He straightened. "What am I going to do with you? I love you so much I can't see straight."

"I don't know why."

"When you open up, you're like a flower. Precious. Beautiful. Delicate. I want that all the time."

So did she, when she got right down to it. Those days with him by the coast had been the best of her life. She'd felt alive and not just when they made love. Cooking with him, listening to music. Staring out at the ocean for hours without saying a word. How could she have thought to throw something like that away?

"God help me, I ought to turn around and walk away from you," he said.

"You wouldn't do that, would you?"

"At some point, I'll have to if nothing changes," he said. "I see you every day but I can't touch you. I want you every night and end up driving by your house and sitting there."

That had been him. In the dark, she hadn't seen the car clearly. She'd hoped—and feared—Rick had been out there.

"I can't take any more." He ran his fingers through his hair in a gesture of desperation. "What would you do in my place?"

Put that way, the answer was simple. "I'd leave."

"God knows I don't want to but then you pull something like this with Lynn."

She reached up and put her hands on his chest. "So where does that leave us?"

He took her fingers in his. "Marry me."

"I really don't think I can give you children."

"We'll adopt. Foster care. We'll work it out."

"The age difference is too great. I'll get old before you do."

"When you're eighty, I'll be sixty-nine. Not exactly teen heartthrob material."

She looked at where their hands were joined. "I suppose—"

"Don't suppose. Do it."

She couldn't really marry him, could she? But if she didn't, he'd really leave. He'd get fed up trying to convince her and give up. She'd never see him again, never hear his voice, never feel his hands on her body. Life would feel so empty without him.

Things sure as hell couldn't go on the way they were. She couldn't avoid him and every time she saw him, she wanted to walk into his embrace. If she'd thought society would mock their marriage, imagine what society would say about an affair.

And who gave a flying fuck what society thought anyway? They could make each other happy. Nothing else mattered.

She looked up into his face. "All right. I will marry you."

He tipped his head up and stared at the ceiling. "About damn time."

"Don't start celebrating just yet. We have a wedding to plan."

* * * * *

Like an idiot, Sarah planned the ceremony in her own back yard. Even a simple gathering of friends was so much work. Rick helped her with the cooking and Earl and Jan took over the last-minute details so that they could get dressed. In the end, everything worked out just fine.

Rick held her hand through the whole service and reading of their vows but that didn't keep her knees from shaking. When his voice cracked on "death do us part", she almost melted into tears. But they got through that too. After their kiss the whole gang clustered around them. Including Lynn, bless her.

Earl clapped Rick on the back. "You two didn't have any of us fooled, you know."

"You suspected we were involved?" she said.

"The air between you sizzled," Lynn said.

Clever thing for Lynn to play along. Amazing what you could accomplish with the promise of a good job. Sarah slipped an arm around her and squeezed. "I can't fool you."

"And you disappeared together at the first party," Jan said.

Sarah groaned inwardly. They'd noticed that too. Lord help her if they figured out what all had happened in her closet.

Rick pulled her against his chest and smiled down at her. "You wouldn't believe what I had to go through to get her to marry me."

She punched him in the ribs. "No details."

The group laughed, but with them, not at them. This might work out.

"Let's eat before the ham and turkey get cold," Jan said.

"When my wife calls you to the table, you'd better go." Earl herded them all off toward the inside of the house where Jan had laid out the buffet.

Lynn hung back for a minute. "Congratulations you two."

"Thanks," Sarah answered.

Lynn moved to Rick, planted a kiss on his cheek and then turned to join the others.

The moment she'd left, he pulled Sarah's face up to his for a quick kiss. "Happy?"

"Delirious." She grinned until her face felt as if it would crack. "I suppose this makes me Mrs. Dr. Feelgood."

"You have a Ph.D. You're Dr. Feelgood too," he said. "You always have been to me."

She hugged him. "We can go into private practice together."

"Very private." Then he closed his eyes and kissed her for real.

Also by Samantha Kane

SO

Brothers In Arms 1: The Courage to Love
Brothers In Arms 2: Love Under Siege
Brothers In Arms 3: Love's Strategy
Brothers In Arms 4: At Love's Command
Brothers In Arms 5: Retreat From Love
Ellora's Cavemen: Jewels of the Nile II (*anthology*)
Hunters for Hire: Tomorrow
Islands

About the Author

SO

Samantha has a Master's Degree in History, and is a full-time writer and mother. She lives in North Carolina with her husband and three children.

Samantha welcomes comments from readers. You can find her website and email address on her author bio page at www.ellorascave.com.

Also by KyAnn Waters

છ્ર

All Lycan's Eve
Ellora's Cavemen: Jewels of the Nile II (*anthology*)
Eternal Rapture
Hard Ride Home
Rough Justice

About the Author

છ્ર

KyAnn Waters lives in Utah with her husband, two children and two dogs. She spends her days writing and her evenings with her family. She enjoys sporting events on the television, thrillers on the big screen, and hot scenes between the pages of her books.

KyAnn welcomes comments from readers. You can find her website and email address on her author bio page at www.ellorascave.com.

Also by Katie Blu

ဆ

Beloved Brother

Ellora's Cavemen: Jewels of the Nile I (*anthology*)

About the Author

ဆ

Katie doesn't let the fact that she has lived in the same small town her whole life keep her from experiencing all life has to offer. A hopeless flirt, Katie has had her share of embarrassing moments and red hot encounters. She believes in living life to the fullest, and standing in her way just gets you run over. Katie loves to hear comments from readers.

Katie welcomes comments from readers. You can find her website and email address on her author bio page at www.ellorascave.com.

Also by Regina Carlysle

80

Breath of Magic

Elven Magic *with Desiree Holt & Cindy Spencer Pape*

Feral Moon

Highland Beast

Killer Curves

Lone Star Lycan

Spanish Topaz

About the Author

80

Regina Carlysle is an award winning, multi-published author. She likes writing that is hot, edgy, and often humorous, and puts this trademark stamp on all of her stories. Regina lives in west Texas with her husband of 25 years and counting and is a doting, fawning, and over-indulgent mother to her two kids. When she's not penning steamy erotic tales or hot contemporary stories, she's indulging in long chats with friends who help her stay sane and keep her laughing.

Regina welcomes comments from readers. You can find her website and email address on her author bio page at www.ellorascave.com.

Also by Alice Gaines

ℛ

Sans Regret
Wedding Night Surprise

*Also check out the author's book at Cerridwen Press
(www.cerridwenpress.com).*

Can't Hide Love
Child of Balance

About the Author

ℛ

Award winning author, Alice Gaines has been published in other genres, including paranormal and historical romance. She's delighted to join the Cerridwen Press/Ellora's Cave family with her fantasy work.

Alice loves stories that stretch the imagination, either through exotic or superhuman characters. She has a Ph.D. in psychology from U.C. Berkeley and lives in Oakland, California, with her collection of orchids and two pet corn snakes, Casper and Sheikh Yerbouti.

Alice welcomes comments from readers. You can find her website and email address on her author bio page at www.ellorascave.com.

Tell Us What You Think

We appreciate hearing reader opinions about our books. You can email us at Comments@EllorasCave.com.

Why an electronic book?

We live in the Information Age—an exciting time in the history of human civilization, in which technology rules supreme and continues to progress in leaps and bounds every minute of every day. For a multitude of reasons, more and more avid literary fans are opting to purchase e-books instead of paper books. The question from those not yet initiated into the world of electronic reading is simply: *Why?*

1. *Price.* An electronic title at Ellora's Cave Publishing and Cerridwen Press runs anywhere from 40% to 75% less than the cover price of the exact same title in paperback format. Why? Basic mathematics and cost. It is less expensive to publish an e-book (no paper and printing, no warehousing and shipping) than it is to publish a paperback, so the savings are passed along to the consumer.

2. *Space.* Running out of room in your house for your books? That is one worry you will never have with electronic books. For a low one-time cost, you can purchase a handheld device specifically designed for e-reading. Many e-readers have large, convenient screens for viewing. Better yet, hundreds of titles can be stored within your new library—on a single microchip. There are a variety of e-readers from different manufacturers. You can also read e-books on your PC or laptop computer. (Please note that Ellora's Cave does not endorse any specific brands.

You can check our websites at www.ellorascave.com or www.cerridwenpress.com for information we make available to new consumers.)

3. *Mobility.* Because your new e-library consists of only a microchip within a small, easily transportable e-reader, your entire cache of books can be taken with you wherever you go.

4. *Personal Viewing Preferences.* Are the words you are currently reading too small? Too large? Too... ANNOYING? Paperback books cannot be modified according to personal preferences, but e-books can.

5. *Instant Gratification.* Is it the middle of the night and all the bookstores near you are closed? Are you tired of waiting days, sometimes weeks, for bookstores to ship the novels you bought? Ellora's Cave Publishing sells instantaneous downloads twenty-four hours a day, seven days a week, every day of the year. Our webstore is never closed. Our e-book delivery system is 100% automated, meaning your order is filled as soon as you pay for it.

Those are a few of the top reasons why electronic books are replacing paperbacks for many avid readers.

As always, Ellora's Cave and Cerridwen Press welcome your questions and comments. We invite you to email us at Comments@ellorascave.com or write to us directly at Ellora's Cave Publishing Inc., 1056 Home Avenue, Akron, OH 44310-3502.

COMING TO A BOOKSTORE NEAR YOU!

ELLORA'S CAVE

Bestselling Authors Tour

UPDATES AVAILABLE AT

WWW.ELLORASCAVE.COM